CALL

OF THE

BRAZOS

BY

ERMAL WALDEN

WILLIAMSON

Giant Shadow Publishing
An imprint of Seven Locks Press
Santa Ana, CA

Second Edition 2005

Library of Congress Cataloging-in-Publication Data is possible
From the publisher

Printed in the United States of America

ISBN: 1-931643-18-0

Call of the Brazos is published by:

Giant Shadow Publishing
www.ermal.com
An imprint of Seven Locks Press
P. O. Box 25689
Santa Ana, CA 92799
(800) 354-5348

Production Credits:
Edited by: Bud Sperry, Conan Tigard, Pat and Cheryl Pruett,
and Paul Press.

Design, Layout and Production by: Heather Buchman
Front Cover Photo by: FCB Productions, Chicago for Coors Light Beer
commercial "El Dorado" film by Steve Broadwolf and staff

Dedicated to

Today's Buffalo Soldiers 9th Cavalry

who are keeping the spirit of the

black soldier of the Civil War alive

to

Lou Baker

who is keeping the spirit of the

black cowboy alive

And to my wife, Betty

who always shares my dreams.

ACKNOWLEDGEMENTS

Being reared in the South with Black schoolmates and friends and, having served for a time in the U. S. Marines out of South Carolina, have given me insights on how both sides of the Civil War might have felt towards each other.

I want to give great appreciation to Sidney Bennett of Tennessee, and to Rhonda Stearns of Wyoming for their wonderful help in providing me with the much needed information for these parts of America. I also want to acknowledge my editors, Bud Sperry, Conan Tigard, and Pat and Cheryl Pruett, and Paul Press.

Years of research and study go into the making of a novel, keeping with historical accuracies, even of the minute kind. I want to acknowledge the following internet sites which have helped me in this endeavor:

"Causes of the Civil War"
http://members.aol.com/jfepperson/causes.html

"Americas Civil War"
http://www.thehistorynet.com/AmericasCivilWar/articles/1997/0997_text.htm

"Civil War Generals"
http://www.crt.state.la.us/crt/tourism/civilwar/generals.htm

"Ad for Runaway Slaves, Feb. 10, 1864"
http://jefferson.village.virginia.edu/vcdh/fellows/runaway.html

"Letter from Juliana Dorsey to General Cocke"
"Letter from Nelia W. of Edge Hill plantation"
http://jefferson.village.virginia.edu/vcdh/fellows/women1.html
http://www.ninetyone.canby.k12.or.us/Classrooms/wigowsky/civilwar/civilwar.htm
http://www.civilwarhome.com/ftsumter.htm

"Document of slave life"
http://www.campus.ccsd.k12.co.us/ss/SONY/psbeta2/slavpho2.htm

"A poster asking for the return of a runaway slave"
http://www.campus.ccsd.k12.co.us/ss/SONY/psbeta2/shriver.htm

"Cotton Gin" by a student in Mr. Munzel's 8th grade Social Studies class of '99
http://www.pausd.paloalto.ca.us/jls/virtualmuseum/ushistory/cotton/

"Gin Helped Expand Cotton Industry"
http://www.concentric.net/~Pgarber/gin.html

"The Online Archive of Terry's Texas Rangers Sharing & preserving the history of the 8th Texas Cavalry Regiment, 1861-1865"
http://www.terrystexasrangers.org/

"Notable Notes about the Terry's Texas Rangers"
http://www.tyler.net/stark/notable.htm

"Eighth Texas Cavalry"
http://www.tsha.utexas.edu/handbook/online/articles/view/EE/qke2.html

"Horse Artillery of Terry's Texas Rangers 8th Texas Cavalry"
http://home.flash.net/~porterjh/whitesbattery/

"AEC Cemetery #2 – Slave Cemetery"
http://www.roanetn.com/slave/part6.htm

"East Tennessee's Mountain War"
http://www.state.tn.s/environment/hist/PathDivided/east_tn.htm

et al.

And last, but certainly not the least, I want to thank the many Civil War re-enactors I have met and talked with at their events, too numerous to mention, and especially those from Terry's Rangers.

PROLOGUE

GHOSTS

"**C**hange" is a word not found in many a cowboy's vocabulary, especially one Matt Jorgensen, a cowboy from Montana. A cowboy's way of living can take many turns along life's trail before he finds his ultimate calling. One never knows from where the calling comes or, in most instances, how to best answer it. A cowboy only knows that he's got to trust what he's got to trust, and some of the time it's difficult to understand, especially when one is torn between right and wrong, place of birth, and color of skin, and then change becomes all important to get one's perspectives in order.

Matt Jorgensen's call was to a ranch in Texas, south of Waco, across the Brazos where he earned the nickname, "The Brazos Kid." The reverberating echo of his calling and the continuing plague of his southern culture against his northern heritage was his birthplace in Montana. Although many Montanans were sympathetic to the South, Matt had been reared twenty-one years without being prejudiced, mostly because he had never encountered a race or slavery situation. He left Montana clean of any racial biases and came back a different man. His life had again changed and taken on a different perspective when he met beautiful but rugged Ginny McBride, whom he lost soon after the mortar struck at Fort Sumter. He vowed to the wind that he would never fall in love again.

Twenty-one years and a Civil War later, he returned to Montana too late to attend his mother's funeral. He found himself about to make another major change in his life when he met Mary Beth Paterson, a refined attorney with many frills and laces, the complete opposite of Ginny. She preferred to be called by her middle name.

From an eagle's eye view, two figures silhouetted by the pale pink Montana sunset appeared on the Ruby River Ranch. It was late afternoon of Thanksgiving, 1882.

Matt's arm cradled Beth's back as they stood in the stillness of the evening. She was a lovely young woman, with long flowing brunette hair to match her sparkling brown eyes. She was thin, and to Matt's thinking, just a little too thin. She had come to Virginia City as an attorney from Richmond, Virginia, and in setting up her practice, took Matt's mother on as a client to put her property in order in her last will and testament.

The cowboys on her ranch had laid Mrs. Andersen in her grave before Matt made it back from Texas, a place he had called home for over twenty years. He was a cowboy in his forties who stood six-feet-four-inches tall with a rugged look and scars he had earned in the Civil War and various battles in Texas. At his mother's request, he had returned to his birthplace to see her before she died, but she succumbed before he could reach her. Being her only surviving heir, he was the new owner of the Ruby River Ranch.

The faint sound of a rifle echoed through the woods, causing the forest creatures to take shelter out of fright. Matt turned his face towards the sound, listened to the wind as it whistled through the treetops and, hearing nothing else, settled his eyes back on Beth.

"What was that?" Beth asked, quickly turning her head and looking into the tall timbers on the hillside.

Matt looked intently into the northern wind. "Monty cleanin' out his rifle, I s'pose." He knew different, but for the moment, he let it pass as he looked at Beth's curious face.

The first snow of the season fell softly around them. Matt had not seen snow for some time having lived in Texas for so many years.

Beth looked around, and seeing nothing unusual, said, "You're looking puzzled about something."

Matt felt something evil in the wind, but the quietness of the moment and the excitement he felt being with Beth left him with the task of assuring her that nothing was wrong. He rationalized to himself that Monty, the foreman of his ranch, or any of his cowboys riding the range could simply be shooting at something. But he thought, "Not likely, though, because they know that the noise will disturb the cattle." He sensed it, but as the herd remained undisturbed, he put it behind him, hoping that nothing was wrong.

He brushed the snow from Beth's coat and said, "There's white stuff all over us."

Beth laughed. "Snow, silly. Pure, unadulterated snow." She wiped the few flakes from his face and kissed him. "Like it?"

He shrugged his shoulders, feeling like a kid as he watched her face beam with happiness.

"Don't you remember what snow is?" she asked with a slight giggle as she pulled her woolen scarf tight around her neck, locking in her coat's collar.

"Sure. Just haven't seen it for awhile. Gotta get used to it again." He took his bandanna and wiped the snow from Beth's face. "You sure do look pretty."

She received his kiss with increased passion, sliding her arms through his jacket and around his back.

"Wanna go back inside?"

"Later. Let's enjoy our first snow alone together." Reflecting quietly, he added, "I'm glad Dan brought me back."

The Wrisleys were long-standing friends and neighbors of the Andersens for many years. It was their son, Danny, who had brought Matt back to Montana from Texas.

Beth looked at him lovingly, took her arms out of his coat and walked with him down the path to a clearing in the trees where they stood to watch the wind blow the snow around in gentle swirls. She knew she was in love and was waiting for him to give her the chance to show it.

The snow was wet and stuck to their faces and clothes until they soon became whitened with it. A Montana snow comes up suddenly and stays for a great while. The temperature, having dropped into the single digits, caused the first snow of the season.

A cow lay dead on the outlying slopes of the ranch from a bullet wound through its head.

"We got meat, boys!" a mean-looking cuss yelled out as he rode with his men down the slope to pick up their game, one of Matt's cattle.

They were six of the worst looking, worst smelling men anyone could ever come up against. Men of no morals. Each of them looked mean and ornery enough to strangle a rattler with his bare hands.

Biggun was their leader, a large grizzly of a man who appeared to have never gone without a meal. He stood about six-foot seven inches tall and looked meaner than sin. His beard had the look of a mop dragged through a pigsty, gray like his long dirty curls and moustache. His clothing, with food stains up and down his vest, had never been cleaned. His coat was long and shabby-looking, torn at the hem.

"Cut it up and cook it now," he barked at his men. "I don't aim to go a day without good food, and I'm hungry."

He let out a mountain yell that sent shivers down the gullets of the nearby coyotes and scared the hawks out of their tree nests. He pulled his Bowie out of his belt before the others, and slid it into the belly of the beast, carving it upwards.

Three of the men joined in with their knives while the other two started building a fire.

Matt watched the snow as it continued to fall, and tried to lick it as it stuck to his face. "Isn't this kinda early for snow, even in Montana?" he asked. "I mean, this is Thanksgiving."

"Look at how it's coming down! It's good that the Wrisleys and I will be leaving for home in the morning." Beth slipped her arm through his. "I'm happy you asked me to visit you here on the Double R. Having spent so much time with your mother before she passed on, it's almost like home to me."

Home to Beth was now a single-story dwelling behind her office in Virginia City, Montana, where she hung a shingle to advertise her services as an attorney-at-law.

"I'm glad you accepted my invitation. Out here with a bunch of rowdy boys is not my idea of a good Thanksgiving. Down in Texas, we had several ladies in the household who could cook up the finest dinner this side of heaven."

They turned back and walked in a slow rhythmic pace down the long trail leading to the main road and watched the sun become engulfed by a dark sky. The wind picked up and the temperature dropped a little. They made fresh tracks in the snow that painted the land and forest surrounding the Ruby River Ranch.

"The way the sky looks," Beth said, "it wouldn't surprise me any if an early blizzard might be moving in."

"You lookin' for a fight?"

"Huh?"

"*Bluster.* That means someone lookin' for a fight down in Texas."

"Oh, no. I said, *blizzard.* It's when the snow falls fast and furious like sand in a windstorm. We call that a *blizzard.*"

"Well, I've seen many of them up here when I was a kid. Never called them *blizzard*s, though, jest snowstorms. New lingo, I 'spose."

The sun slipped silently behind the ridge of trees and darkness quickly engulfed the land, and yet, it was still early in the evening. The wind howled through the treetops, and the full moon lit upon the new fallen snow, lighting the way as they walked down the gutted road. Clouds soon covered the moon, making visibility more difficult.

"Don't know if it's safe for you to go anytime soon with a blizzard comin'," said Matt.

"I've got a lot of catching up to do with some of my other clients in Virginia City," Beth replied.

"How many clients you 'spose you have?"

"I've got some. Enough to keep me busy anyway."

The cowboys' singing and guitar strumming drifted from the wranglers' quarters, but the lovers were oblivious of everything except each other.

When they reached the corral just past the bunkhouse, Matt climbed up to the orchestra seat and pulled Beth up alongside him. Through the shroud of darkness, they viewed the outline of the mountains surrounding them.

"I'll be all right. We'll stop at the Wrisleys' along the way before they take me to Virginia City. They'll see to it that I'm looked after." Matt was shivering. "Didn't Texas ever get this cold?"

"If it did, I wasn't there to feel it. I plumb forgot how cold it could get here in the mountains."

Through the halting moments of the wind, they caught the faint sound of the animals of the forest scattering through the brush.

"The animals running is a sign that a winter storm is heading our way," Beth said, looking into the hills.

As a hired gun from Texas, Matt knew the smell of death and sensed that their running was caused by something far more serious than merely a winter storm.

As they watched the windblown snow drop against the north side of the trees and fence posts, they continued to listen to the gentle music playing from the bunkhouse behind them. For a long time, neither said anything. Unaware of the gunshot that Matt and Beth had heard, the cowboys continued talking, singing, and playing cards within the close confines of the bunkhouse.

"I'm supposing you're thinking about Texas, aren't you, Matt?"

Matt said nothing but looked out into the hills.

"She must have been a real pretty girl," Beth continued.

Matt reflected, showing he was a little amused by her statement, then began reminiscing. "My pa and the others fought Injuns on that hill there as they'd come whoopin' down upon us. The fightin' didn't seem to last long. We'd shoot some, I remember that. Later, most of them were jest young bucks seeking some fun, scarin' us and stealin' one of our cows to take back with 'em. Pa'd let 'em, jest to keep the peace. He knew they needed food."

"Was she real pretty?"

He ignored her question, although not intentionally. He was just completely lost in thought about his youth. "Lukas and I came ridin' bareback down that slope yonder, chased by a couple of Sioux right about there." He pointed to a wide trail leading from the top of the hill to the bottom that, over the years, had become a natural trail leading to Bozeman. "We were ridin' bareback, jest like them. Never thought my horse could run so fast. I looked back at Lukas, who was right on my heels, when a stupid branch stood out and swatted me in the face. Knocked me off Skeeter and I tumbled all the way down. See? The tree is still a standin'. Busted my arm up. Had to write left-handed in school for awhile."

"You got away, naturally?"

"Wull, I'm here, ain't I?"

"How do you know it's the same tree?" She watched him for awhile as he stared out into the distance.

"Are you thinking of going back to Texas?"

Matt sat silent for the moment and then turned to look at her. "Looking at you just now reminds me of how little I really know about you."

"A lot about you I don't yet know either."

"You will, my darlin'," he answered. "It'll just take time."

He climbed down and stood for a moment, looking out to the hills as he closed his coat tighter.

"Lukas was wild, but I was a hell of a lot wilder. I could out drink him, out cuss him and out shoot him anytime. But he had a crazy way about him I couldn't tame. He was like a mustang. You know what I mean?"

"Well, mister," Beth said. "Are you going to give a lady a hand?"

He reached up and brought her gently down.

She clasped his hand in hers as they walked into the night, away from the bunk house and the singing of the cowboys. "For openers, I'm a graduate of William and Mary College, received my law degree there. I have a family of two brothers and a sister living in Virginia. Mom and Dad passed away. I left home and came to Virginia City to set up practice. I'm single, never been married. Not that I haven't had the opportunity. There have been plenty, I must tell you. Just never met a man I could love, or really liked, for that matter. Been here for almost a whole year, and then your mother came in one day and hired me. And, now . . ."

"Now?"

She let go of his hand and ran away a couple of steps, then stopped and bent down to roll a snowball and threw it at Matt. She laughed as it splattered in his face.

Wiping it away, he scooped up a handful of snow and ran after her. Their shadows moved in the moonlight as they ran toward the hill where his parents were buried.

Matt caught up with Beth and brought her down laughing in his arms.

He rose just as quickly and helped her up. Looking back at the hills he began to reminisce again.

"He's like a ghost up there, Beth."

"Your brother?" She followed his gaze. "Then let him be a ghost. You're not."

"I feel like I don't belong here."

Beth slipped her arms around Matt to console him. "Don't think about it."

He thought about the day his pa made him leave his ranch, the Double O. He never liked the name, so, when he inherited it, he renamed it the Ruby River Ranch, then shortened it to the Double R.

"Your father had that boy removed and buried somewhere else," Beth said. Matt looked at her. "I never thought about telling you until now."

Matt gazed into her eyes as if searching for something deep within his spirit. Looking at her made him search deeper.

"I spent the better part of my life in the South running from my past. Those ghosts made me fight a war against my own people." He said, referring to the part he had played in the Civil War when he served as a captain with Terry's Rangers.

Beth put her head on his chest.

"Just before that," he said, almost inaudibly, "I fell in love for the first time."

Beth looked up into his eyes and saw the pain.

"My people took her from me." A long pause stretched seemingly throughout the night while she waited for him to continue. "She was lovely."

Beth bit her lip, closed her eyes, and buried her face deep into Matt's coat. She wanted to hear, but was afraid to listen.

"My land here, these hills, this ranch, these people were taken from me." He pulled away and gazed off into the distance as if looking beyond the hills.

"I came back, and it's like I'm a stranger. The townsfolk remembered. They remembered that I was a murderer who killed their minister in a botched-up robbery."

"You proved you weren't involved. They believed you."

"But they were waiting, Beth. They were waiting. It was like the ghosts from twenty-four years ago were all waiting for me to come back."

"Are you going to let the ghosts beat you, now that you've won your freedom and proven yourself?"

"They 'spected who I was, Wil and Anne Andersen's surviving son, the one who ran away."

"You did not run away, Mr. Jorgensen." Beth stood firm before him, her fists clenched at her side. "You weren't going to run. Your father made you leave. The townsfolk would have lynched you had they known you were at the robbery. Instead, the law gunned down one Jeff Manning, mistaking him for you. You had to run to stay alive."

"And now I'm supposed to accept this ranch as if I had never left?"

"You're home." She caressed him again. The snow fell harder and the wind picked up.

"Want to talk about her?" she asked, pulling away and looking him straight on.

"Someday, maybe," Matt answered, grabbing her hands and holding them gently. "You've no cause to worry."

"Oh, hell, Mr. Jorgensen, I know that. I only want you to know that *you* don't have to worry."

He felt an aching disturbance, much like one feels without any apparent explanation for it. He couldn't put a finger on why he felt that way. It had nothing to do with his first love. He just knew something was gnawing at him, and that he had to get a grip on it.

When looking at the cemetery, the hills, the ranch house, the corral, and even in Beth's eyes. He could see only ghosts.

Matt turned, faced the cemetery, and pulled his coat tighter for warmth. He gripped her hand, and they walked toward the cemetery on the north side of the ranch. "There's no one in my grave?"

They stopped by the fence and stared at the crosses.

"It's just an empty grave." She looked at his face and saw a curled smile appear. "Feel better?"

Matt stared at the markers and affixed his eyes on one that read

Charlie Nightlinger
? – 1882
Trail Cook

"Charlie's a nigger, ain't he?" Matt asked without taking his eyes from the marker.

A couple of wranglers, Danny Wrisley and Cookie Benson, walked out of the bunkhouse after having watched the couple walk up to the gravesite. Danny was a young cowboy, barely twenty, lean, clean, and good-looking. Cookie was the oldest man on the ranch with a set of store-bought teeth and a baldhead that he kept covered with a well-seasoned Stetson. He looked underfed, in the face as well as his belly, and wore a rope around his pants to keep them up. His beard was long enough to catch snow and make it appear white, though most of it was still black. He had been with the ranch ever since Nightlinger passed away.

"Mr. Nightlinger?" Beth asked.

"Mr. Nightlinger," Matt answered, with his hands on his hips, almost defensively.

"He's a Negro," Beth answered. "You knew that from the moment you arrived on the ranch."

"Point I'm makin' is, shouldn't he be buried in another field somewhere?" Matt looked around at the men staring at him, and then at Beth. "Just askin', mind ya."

"Ordinarily, yes," Beth replied. "But your mother and the boys saw it fittin' to bury him here."

"That's what's been botherin' me all day yesterday and last night."

"Surely you aren't having second thoughts about Mr. Nightlinger? He was a kindly old man."

"Never gave it first thoughts, I guess." He rubbed his gloved hand under his chin, looked around, then pointed to the north. "What about the other side of the hill?"

"You mean to dig him up, boss?" Cookie asked, handing Matt a tin of coffee.

"And move him?" Danny looked sternly into Matt's face, then took his hat and brushed it on his pants.

"That don't make sense."

"It does if you're a Reb," Beth reminded him. "You can send four men to their graves and not bat an eye. Now you intend to dig up a dead man and inter him in a piece of ground away from his friends. What is it about you that makes you so callous?"

"Callous? Yeah, guess I am." Matt nodded to the hill behind the ranch. "Right about over there would do nicely."

Other wranglers gathered around them with their plates in their hands, enjoying leftovers from the dinner.

"We havin' a meetin' or sumpin'?" one of them asked, smiling broadly from ear to ear, thinking nothing was wrong.

"Gentlemen," Beth addressed them, holding back her anger. "Your boss wants Mr. Nightlinger dug up and interred behind the ranch house."

The men looked at one another and chattered amongst themselves.

"That's right," Matt assured them. "I've looked out back and saw a nice place where he would be all by himself. Cozy and warm, so to speak."

Danny spoke up, "You talk like he's still alive."

"No. No, just dead. But he needs a new home, away from my parents."

"Why?" Beth asked annoyingly.

"Jest because I said so, Miss Paterson."

The men sensed a little orneriness in Matt's tone.

"'Spose he's right," one of the older wranglers said, picking pieces of food out of his teeth. "His land and he's the boss."

"He's the boss?" Beth repeated. "Yes. Do what he says."

"Wait a minute," Matt interrupted. "You don't have to tell 'em again. I already told 'em."

"Yes, you did. I'm sorry," Beth replied and stomped away, packing the snow hard with her boots.

"You don't have to do it this very minute," Matt said.

Beth stopped, turned, and asked, "Just when do you want the men to do this?"

"They're my men. I'll tell 'em."

"Well, Mr. Jorgensen. Tell them!"

"He's a nigger," Matt yelled out to her. "He's no right to be by my parents in their restin' place."

"Oh!" Beth walked back and stopped within a few feet of Matt. With a stern look of seriousness about her, she said smartly, "He's a Negro. And just because you came from Texas and fought on the side of the South doesn't cut it with me, Mister."

"That's right," Matt came back angrily, swinging his fist into empty space. "I fought, and now I demand my rights--I want him removed!"

"I was born and raised in the South," Beth retorted.

The wranglers were enjoying this argument. Some sat down in the snow to watch, while others leaned up against a tree or sat on a nearby stump.

Beth noticed the group and gathered her senses about her. In a more calm fashion, she continued. "If anyone has a prejudicial right to hate the Negroes, it could be me, but I don't. I take pride in living here in Montana, and in helping you get back your ranch. But I don't take pride, Mr. Jorgensen, in watching a mean man take vengeance against someone who never did anything but good for your folks."

Matt also sensed the group watching them but went ahead and stuck his chin out. "You through?"

Beth turned and continued her trod to the house without looking back. Once in the house, she slammed the door hard enough to cause snow to fall from the roof.

Matt cringed and said, "What bee's up her bloomers?"

"She's got a good point," Danny said.

"But it's my land, and I'll damn well do as I please with it."

"When?" Danny asked, watching the house for Beth to return.

"Why not wait 'til spring, I'm thinkin'," Monty said with a smile. Monty was a man who always obeyed orders without putting much thought to it, but he pondered well this time. "The sod will have been thawed by then," he thought aloud to himself. He took out his makings and rolled himself a cigarette.

"Damn if she don't remind me of someone," Matt said, gritting his teeth.

Monty smiled and said, "Yeah. You."

Matt looked at Monty, took the rolled cigarette from him, and said, "Thanks."

"No bother," Monty said, throwing an empty tobacco sac away and licking his lips. "Want a match?"

"Yeah," Matt answered. He lit his cigarette, and stared at the house. He took a drag and then, as Monty watched in consternation, threw the cigarette to the wind. "You ever want something so bad you hurt deep down inside?" he asked, his eyes fixed on the warm-lit ranch house. Monty reached down for the cigarette and said, "Yep. Know jest whatcha mean."

CHAPTER 1

THE TERROR OF BOZEMAN

T he smoke from the Biggun gang's fire and the rifle shot had alerted Russ, a lone line rider on the slopes of the Ruby River. He was out keeping the cattle from drifting too far off the range of the Double R. He rode slow and easy towards the sound of the rifle to investigate what was happening. He was a Norwegian with plenty of muscles who had met and brought Matt and Danny from the train to the ranch when they came up from Texas. He was one man that Matt sized up real quick, and decided that he wouldn't want to pick a fight with him. On the other hand, Russ was also a tame man of a gentle nature, with blue eyes and blond hair.

At the top of the ridge, he saw the men spearing chunks of beef onto the fire with their knives. They saw no need to take the time to build a proper campfire with a skewer to cook their food.

While the whinny of his horse let the men know he was approaching, his gentle nature proved to be a detriment, as one of the men drew and fired in his direction without warning, bringing him down. He lay still once he hit the ground.

"Why'd you go and do a thing like that fer, One Eye?" Biggun screamed in anger.

"Jest thought he might be the law," One Eye returned with a big yellow grin, throwing his smoking Winchester rifle over his shoulder. He was a short stocky person with red hair, and a patch over the socket where his right eye had been knocked out in a saloon fight with a whiskey bottle.

"Take what you find and toss him down the slope, saddle's mine." Biggun walked over to the horse standing by its master and stripped it of its saddle and tack. "Want the hoss, anyone?"

"Naw!" said one of the men who seemed to answer for the rest of the gang. He was lanky and as ugly as mud in a pigsty. "Jest got mine broke in where I can ride 'em real good."

"Haw!" Biggun slapped the rump of the saddle-less horse to make him run.

"Hell with that, Biggun," a short-fat ruffian shot back at him. "One Eye just done kilt a man. And now you set his horse free. Someone's gonna see it and come after us. Let's git the hell outta here."

Biggun unsaddled his horse and threw the saddle by the man stretched face down on the ground. He took his newly acquired saddle, threw it on his horse, cinched it tight, then joined the rest of the men as they headed in the direction of the Bozeman Trail.

"Trouble with you is," One Eye said with a graveled voice, "you scairt. Hell. Look 'round you boy, there's nothin' out here to be scairt bout."

"Rider comin', Biggun," one of the gang members warned only loud enough for him to hear.

"What'd I tell ya," the ruffian screamed out in fear.

At the sound of the second gunshot, the door of the bunkhouse flew open and the rest of the wranglers spilled out into the snow, dressing as they ran.

"You men thinking somethin's wrong?" Matt asked, listening to the wind as if waiting for another shot. None came.

"Wanna be ready," Danny explained, buckling his gun belt.

"I don't want my men going out after every gunshot. Don't make sense."

"On a quiet night, boss, we don't expect gunshots unless something's wrong," Danny countered. "Could spook the cattle. Let me ride out and see."

"We heard the gunshot," a cowboy shouted to Matt as he cinched up his girth.

"Well, there were two." Matt looked at the cowboy who stepped into his stirrups. "You, go ahead with Danny. The rest of you men stand easy."

"Might not be anythin'", Danny said, throwing his spurs into his horse's side, "but let's go see." The two wranglers rode out and disappeared into the darkness.

Matt looked out into the empty cold and waited with the rest of the men, hoping for the best. It seemed to be a long wait.

Suddenly, the two cowboys rode back at breakneck speed with a saddle-less horse.

By the time Russ' horse galloped past them to the barn, the men were in their saddles and ready to ride.

"Russ' horse, boss," Danny said, following Matt to the barn.

"I'll get Skeeter saddled and be right with you," Matt yelled back at Danny.

With the expertise from his days in the cavalry, Matt threw his tack on Skeeter and tightened down the cinch with lightning speed. He threw his foot into the stirrup, turned Skeeter's head to the north and barked at the men, "Let's ride!"

Monty, the foreman for the Double R Ranch, a tall thin cowboy in his late twenties with sandy hair covered with a dirty Stetson, was riding up the riverbed on his way to meet Russ when he heard the two gunshots. He rode out from the riverbed in search of Russ until he came across the smoldering campfire and burnt animal carcass. He saw the killers in the distance, and watched them ride away, not knowing but suspecting something had happened.

The gang rode fast and hard at first out of fear, tiring their horses early in their ride. With their mounts cold and the sweaty, they slowed down to a walk, believing they were out of harm's way.

Monty walked his horse around the fire they had left smoldering. Farther down the hill, he came across his partner of the range strewn on the ground. He knew by the way he lay face down that he must be dead. He knelt down and turned Russ' cold body over and then saw a muscle twitch in his eyelid. Even though he was bleeding from a wound in the side of his head, the Norwegian cowboy was still alive.

"Take it easy, Russ," Monty said as he saw Russ' eyelids flutter and open a slit. "We'll get you fixed up and back to the ranch." Without wasting time, Monty cleaned the wound with snow, wrapped a bandanna around his head and propped him up on his saddle. He got Russ into the saddle then climbed on behind and whipped himself up on his horse behind Russ and cut across the range towards the ranch house.

He prayed for a safe ride across the snow-covered, rocky field to get Russ back to the ranch and get help before the snow covered the gang's trail. He gave a shrill whistle for two other cowboys tending the herd to follow him. Together, they rode hard and fast to the ranch.

Monty held Russ tightly, reining to a stop in the road when he met up with Matt and the other cowboys on their way out.

"Six men just gunned down Russ, Matt." Monty yelled against the wind.

"How is he?" Matt asked with gritted teeth.

"Alive," Monty answered exhaustedly, wiping the snow from his face. "They lit out in the direction of the Bozeman Trail."

"Get 'im to the ranch. Two of you boys go back and help him."

"They headed towards the Bozeman Trail," Monty repeated, kicking his horse into a gallop to the ranch.

"Best we go back and regroup," Matt said grimly, looking at the other cowboys. He remembered how he had made the same type decision as a captain in the cavalry. He knew that going out into nowhere, unprepared, was a sure way of getting killed.

He and his men followed Monty back to the ranch house. The two cowboys with Monty gave him a hand with Russ and took him into the bunkhouse. Beth came in the bunkhouse and prepared to care for Russ.

A well-groomed couple came out of the ranch house. They were Danny's parents, Reeves and Jean Wrisley. "What is it, Matt?" Reeves shouted out, trying to be heard over the noise of the wind as it whipped the snow around in swirls.

"One of my men got shot, Reeves," Matt yelled back. "We're goin' after 'em. I'd appreciate it if you'd watch over Beth. She's in the bunkhouse tending to him."

"Will do," Reeves yelled back walking over to the bunkhouse with Jean picking up her long-hemmed dress and following. "How is he?"

"You find out and let me know, will ya?"

Cookie stepped out of the bunkhouse and held the door open for the Wrisleys. "Mister Russ is all right, Mr. Jorgensen," he yelled out. "He's comin' to."

"Good," Matt yelled back. "Check your ammunition. Make sure you've got plenty. If ya ain't got a rifle or shotgun, get one."

Most of the cowboys always fitted their tack with their rifle tied to it. Some didn't out of plain laziness. Matt knew he had a group of men who needed training, so this was one moment he would use to exert his authority.

"Get enough clothing for you. Double your socks and wear your chaps. Every man take a slicker whether you like it or not."

Matt and the men hurried to get their gear together. Matt reined Skeeter towards the road and walked him out. He stopped, and almost fell off his horse when he saw Cookie climb up on his horse.

"You're not goin', Cookie," Matt said sitting high in his saddle. "Your place is in the kitchen."

"It were my turn out there. Were it not for him takin' my turn tonight, it would've been me and I would have been dead," Cookie replied spurring his horse. "Now, I done said too many words. We can overtake 'em if we go up and over." He rode up a rocky trail leading into the mountain. He had proven before that he was as much cowboy as he was a chef.

"He's gotta coupla sacks of food to fill all of us, boss," Danny said putting more .45 shells in his jacket pocket. "We'll need him out there for sure."

Beth stepped out of the bunkhouse and watched Matt. He had changed and become a man filled with a pent-up cause that seemed to consume him.

"You're going to ride as a posse?" she briskly asked Matt, folding her arms and standing stiff spined, as if in complete defiance to his action. "You can't take the law into your own hands. Fetch Sheriff Saunders and let him get the men who shot Russ."

As sheriff of Bozeman, it had been Bill Saunders who had saved Matt from a mob lynching when the townsfolk suspected him of being the prodigal son who had returned to town after twenty-four years. Matt was to have been killed in the shoot out, but rumor had it that the man who murdered the town minister was still alive. His brother and another were caught and killed. With the face of his brother's accomplice blown away the other man was mistaken for him, so Matt fled to Texas.

"By the time we got the law, they'd be gone."

"Then let them!" she shouted out in anger. "You're killing them makes you just like one of them. A killer!" Her face grimaced in anger, giving Matt a different view of her—one that he had hoped to never see.

Matt looked down at her from his horse, pushed his Stetson back on his head, and frowned, creating a row of furrows across his brow. "There's a difference. Being an attorney, you should understand that."

"You're set on killing. What makes you any better than them?" Her anger softened for a moment when she realized the man she loved might not come back. "And, and what if you get killed? You ever think of that? And your getting killed isn't going to help that man inside there." She pointed her long fingers at the bunkhouse where Russ was laying.

"Who said anything about me gettin' killed?"

"You can. Oh, I know you're a fast gun, but . . ."

"You've known that from day one. Besides, there are more of us than there are of them."

"And one bullet is all it'd take to kill you."

"Seems like someone is real serious about you boss," Danny chided, shifting in his saddle and checking the cylinder of his .45 to make sure it was loaded. "Like you said, we're more than they are. We can go after them, if you want."

"And they're killers. You're not, Danny." Matt pulled the brim of his hat down over his forehead and spurred Skeeter towards the hills. "Let's go, men!"

"I won't be here when you get back," Beth yelled out in hope of stopping Matt. "We're leaving first thing in the morning."

"I know," he yelled back. "You done told me. We'll catch up again soon."

"Maybe. Get Bill, Matt," Beth yelled. "It's his job." The wind blew harder, drowning out her words. He thanked the wind for drowning some of it out so he could ride as if he hadn't heard her.

Matt felt a warm reaction when he heard the caring tone of her voice, even though it was also loud with anger. He thanked the wind for drowning out some of her voice so he could ride as if he hadn't heard her.

The men followed Matt and Cookie up the mountain to the Bozeman Trail. Matt was familiar with the mountainous terrain from his childhood and knew Cookie was right, that the would-be killers would take the Trail. He knew, too, that his men could cut them off, if the snow didn't hinder them on the high ground.

The trail across the mountain was treacherous enough in good weather, but at nightfall, with the first snow and the wind blowing, staying on it depended on good horses and horsemanship. Matt and his men had both, and they rode as fast as their horses' hoofs could travel.

Matt and his men rode the high country. They spent the whole night in the saddle, counting on the outlaw gang resting, thinking no one would follow them.

In early morning, they spotted the six men breaking camp below and climbing into their saddles.

The Biggun gang rode slow, unsuspecting that anyone was following them. Matt had brought his men around and in front of them and counted on the bright morning rays of the sun to keep anyone from spotting their imminent arrival. They rode their mounts down to the road just around the bend, out of their sight, where they prepared to apprehend them.

"Monty, take three men and cover the other side of the road," Matt commanded, keeping an eye out for the six men coming around the bend. "We'll stay here. I don't aim to waste words."

Cookie joined Monty and his men and rode across the road into cover. Danny rode with Matt and stayed on his side.

The early rays of the sun blazed her winter beams hard against the unsuspecting gang, blocking their view of what lay ahead. They held their reins loosely and allowed their horses to fend for themselves on the snow-slicked trail.

When the gang was within a few feet of them, Matt spurred Skeeter and met them head on with his shotgun cocked and aimed. "Stop right there and throw down your guns."

Startled by Matt's sudden appearance, the men reined up tightly, causing a couple of their horses to rear up and almost dump them.

"Who's talkin'?" a heavy man with a dirty gray beard spoke up.

"You go for that .45 and I'll show ya who's talkin'," Matt warned.

"What d'ya want?" another member of the gang yelled out. He was high on the saddle because of his short stature, and wore a face that could scare a preacher.

"You tried to kill one of my men."

"The hell you say?" One Eye yelled out from the back.

"That fella in the back is ridin' Russ' saddle, Matt," Monty called out as he and his men rode up a gully from across the road.

The gang drew their weapons but before they could fire, Matt's shotgun broke the stillness of winter and echoed through the woods. His men joined him in firing at the ruthless gang.

Bullets carved their path through the snowy morning like firecrackers on the Fourth of July, hitting the gang, whose own guns fired lazily into the thick woods, missing their intended targets. Four would-be killers fell dead from their mounts and plunged into the freshly fallen snow. But Biggun and One Eye split fast and furiously, riding like the devil was behind them down the slope and into the thickets. They were more concerned with getting away from Matt's men than of the terrain that lay in front of them. The snow of the morning enveloped their shadows and they were soon out of sight of Matt and his men.

"Did we get 'em all?" Matt asked, lighting from his horse. He examined the bodies that lay bleeding on the ground.

"There were six," Monty shouted.

"Well, then two of them escaped. Damn!"

"They went down this slope." Danny dismounted and examined the broken bushes that showed where the two fleeing badmen had ridden.

Matt stood up straight and looked down at the broken trail made by Biggun and One Eye. In the stillness of the morning, he could hear the faint rustle of bramble and bushes from the escaping men. Soon the quietness overcame the faint noise, and he knew they had gotten away.

"Well let's ride after 'em!" Cookie shouted raring to ride down the slope.

"No need in getting yourselves killed. If the snowy slopes didn't getcha, and they survived, they'd ambush ya, sure as you're sittin' that horse." He looked over and saw Cookie's face fall. "We'll get 'em, Cookie, sooner or later. I promise ya."

Cookie shook his head, took off his hat, and shook the snow from it. "Jest can't figure it out."

"What?" Matt asked in bewilderment.

"How they missed us with all that shootin' goin' on."

Matt smiled, almost laughing aloud. "They had their eyes closed." Then he looked down at the dead men on the trail and barked out. "Pack 'em on their horses and we'll take 'em back to the ranch. I'll take 'em into Bozeman to the sheriff later."

"And if the other two make it into town?" Monty asked, dismounting.

"Then we'll have caught 'em all."

"They'll shootcha," Cookie came back, leaning on his saddle horn.

"They'll try."

"Did you get a good look at the other two men?" Danny asked.

"Nope. From a distance, they simply looked like two saddle tramps."

"Why don't you let us come in with you?" one of the cowboys asked, pulling a body up on the dead man's horse.

"Danny, you come with me." Light clouds had filled the sky and brought about a sudden chill. "Look at the sky, gentlemen," Matt said with tight lips as he tried to keep from shivering. "It looks like we might be in for one of them blizzards," he said, remembering the new word he had learned earlier from Beth, " . . . and soon. "We got cattle to tend to. Need you men back at the ranch. Danny and I can handle things."

"Danny and you and me," Cookie said, grinning. "'Member, it were because of me Russ was almost killed. I owe him."

Matt looked at Cookie, then turned and mounted Skeeter. "We'll think on it."

The snow had quit the next morning and left its white blanket on the earth. The Wrisleys sat in their buggy ready to leave the Double R, Reeves in front and Jean in back. Beth stepped out from the ranch house with her satchel in hand.

"Gonna miss ya, Miss Paterson," the chubby wrangler said with hat in hand.

"Thank you, Sammy," Beth replied. She stepped off the porch and walked up to the buggy.

Sammy bounced around in back with the luggage and tucked the satchel in and tied it down. "Sky's clear. No more snow 'spect for a few days. Should give you a nice ride all the way."

"We're countin' on it," Reeves said, holding the reins firmly.. Beth stepped up into the leather-seated buggy and took her place in back with Jean.

Once everyone was settled, Reeves looked around, then gave a whistle to the team of horses and headed out.

Some of the ranch hands were milling around as the buggy proceeded on to the main road. "Sure did love your cookin', Mrs. Wrisley," one of the wranglers called out.

"Yours, too, Miss Paterson," another wrangler quickly added.

"Beats Cookie's any day," another quipped. "You people come back real soon."

Reeves snapped his whip in the air above the horses. The sound, much like a small gunshot, moved them into a trot. Within moments, they were down the road and out of sight of the Double R Ranch.

Danny rode alone back to the ranch and then out onto the main road to catch up with their buggy.

"Pa," he yelled as he broke his long ride and reined up to them. "Ma," he addressed Mrs. Wrisley. "Miss Paterson," he nodded.

Reeves pulled his team to a halt.

"What happened?" Beth asked with excitement.

"We done caught 'em," Danny came back with a halfway grin on his face.

Although he and Jean were elated to note that their son was safe and unharmed, knowing that Beth was anxious about Matt, Reeves asked, "What happened, Danny?"

"We caught up with 'em. They gave us a fierce fight, but Matt's guns lit into them like fire from hell. They fired back and we fired, and afore ya knew it, there were four of 'em on the ground."

"Did any of our boys get hurt?" Reeves asked, looking Danny over, seeing that he was alright.

"Not a one, Pa," Danny replied, removing his Stetson and wiping his forehead with the back of his glove. "Two of theirs escaped though."

"And Matt?" Beth asked, wanting to hear more but trying to contain her concern.

"He's alright. They're on their way back. I just wanted to get back to tell ya." He looked at his ma and pa, dismounted, and went to their side. "You headed home?"

"We'll stop by the house, son," Mrs. Wrisley assured him with a smile. "We're taking Miss Paterson into Virginia City. After that, we'll pick up some provisions."

"Tell your boss we said goodbye," Beth said, straightening the blanket across her legs. "And take good care of him."

"I'll be sure to do that. Want me to ride with you a spell?"

"We'll manage." Reeves said as he snapped the whip, making the team start off again in a gentle walk. "Tell Matt we're glad he's safe."

Matt and his men finally rode up to the Double R that evening with four dead men draped over their saddles. The ride had been slow and tedius. Sammy and a couple of wranglers met them at the ranch house.

"Take Skeeter into the barn for the night, Sammy," Matt growled as he reined up and lit from his saddle. "You men throw them on the ground and blanket 'em." He motioned to the rest of the wranglers in the direction of the dead, then headed to the ranch house.

The night passed swiftly for Matt as he and his riders met sleep instantly upon hitting their bunks.

Just after sunrise the next day, Cookie saw Matt standing at his family plot on the hill. He put the pot of coffee on to brew. Looking out the window again, he saw Matt had not moved. Cookie figured the aroma of bacon and eggs frying would bring him about, but it didn't.

Strapping on his galluses, Danny joined Cookie. The two watched Matt standing as though frozen.. They grabbed some coffee and grub and walked up to him.

"Hungry, boss?" Danny asked.

"We brought you some vittles," Cookie added.

"Coffee sounds good, Danny." Matt took the cup and took a swig. It did the trick. It warmed him up and made him move a little. "Been wonderin'."

"Still thinkin' about Charlie, Mr. Matt?" Cookie asked.

"You call me 'mister' again, and you'll be wishin' ya hadn't." He let a smile creep across his face for a moment, turned his head to the crosses, and then turned serious again. "About

Charlie? Yup! But, let's talk about it when we get back." Handing Cookie the tin cup, Matt strutted his long legs to the barn.

"You got the wagon hitched and ready, Danny? We've got four dead men to deliver in town."

"Had the wagon and mules ready and waitin' behind the barn." Danny walked at a fast pace to fetch and bring them around.

Matt stopped and waited for him, smiling as he heard Danny muttering to himself.

"Well, it jest don't seem right," Danny murmured to himself. "I mean, movin' Mr. Nightlinger like that."

"You sayin' somethin'?" Matt asked as Danny brought the wagon around.

"He's family. Been with us when your pa got killed and helped us get them that done it."

"I'm grateful for that, Danny. Real grateful." Matt climbed aboard and took the reins from Danny. "I never met the man, yet I like him. It's jest that he's a nigger, and niggers got no right to my parents' grave." Matt saw Monty out the side of his eye walk up to the wagon. "Now, I'm done talkin'."

"Good mules, Matt," Monty remarked, rubbing the shank of one of the mules.

"Yep." Matt knew Monty heard the argument but said nothing about it.

"Sure you don't need us?"

"Jest take care of the ranch while we're gone."

"Ridin' out as we speak." Monty threw his lanky body into his saddle. "Let's tend to the beef, men," Monty ordered as he rode out with the men towards the range.

"We're gonna take some of them down to the creek by the spruces," he said as he rode past Matt. "That way they'll be sheltered from the wind and cold and on land where they can forage for food."

There was little a cowboy could do to protect cattle from freezing except keep them in the pastures where there were big, deep, rough draws, perhaps trees along a creek or hills to provide a lot of shelter from the wind. The wind was always the enemy. The cattle could stand the stillness of the cold, but it was the severe cold, with wind, that was almost unbearable. They counted on trees like the spruce and the cottonwood, which were prevalent in this region and willows that lined the creeks and grew very thick to provide some shelter. Old trees that had fallen would also provide some windbreak.

"Think we're in for a heavy snow, Monty?" Matt asked, looking into the clear blue sky.

"Can't let the sky fool ya, boss," Monty said, shifting in his saddle and reining up in front of Matt's wagon. "The winds up here can change the sky in a blink of an eye. If it does start a heavy snow, the winds would pile it up. We'll get the cattle settled in where they can forage in the open places." He took makings from his coat and rolled himself a cigarette.

"Cattle could fill up there and use the existing pasture if the temperature got below freezing after a snow."

Matt pushed his Stetson back and listened to a seasoned cowboy explain to him something he had learned as a boy growing up in these wilds. He knew cattle could graze through several inches of fresh snow as long as a good supply of ungrazed forage was under the snow. But he also knew that cattle don't paw snow to open up grass like horses and elk and other animals. They simply nose right down to it, and if the snow thaws and freezes and becomes hard and crusted it's really rough on them. That's where they would injure and cut their noses.

"You do what you have ta. We'll be back afore the heavy snows." Matt joined him in rolling his own. "I remember the winters."

Monty moved on with his men. It was hard work for a cowboy riding the winter Montana ranges, tending cattle as if they were children.

"Good man," Matt remarked to Danny as he drew on his cigarette. He made it a point not to tell Monty his business, as he never wanted to follow in his pa's tracks as a cattleman, especially in the cold winter. His trait was the fast gun.

Cookie hopped into the back of the wagon and let his legs dangle. He had a large grin on his face like a dog going for a ride.

Matt looked back at Cookie and grunted, "Where d'ya think you're goin'?"

"With you."

"The hell you are. You've got grub to fix for my men. Stay here. Danny and I'll take these dead men to Bozeman."

Cookie slid out of the wagon and walked back to the ranch house, complaining as he waddled. "Can't go 'cause I'm a cook. Think I'll turn in my apron."

"Can't afford to lose you on the trail," Matt said whipping the team of horses. "You're too good a cook."

"Oh, sure," Cookie grumbled some more, "too old and got no teeth you mean." Cookie bit back at him angered that he wasn't going, but loyal all the same.

The two men moved out with a wagon drawn by a team of strong mules on their way to Bozeman.

"We'll be back inside of a few days," Matt yelled out at some ranch hands meandering by the side of the road. "Gonna get some supplies while there."

"She's mad at me," Matt thought as he whipped his team of mules into a trot towards Bozeman. "But she's gotta know I'm a Texican first now. No matter me being born in Montana, I'm still a Texican first." He smiled a little, "I'm who I am, and there's no changin' me." He snapped his whip and the mules started out with a jolt and kept at a fast gait. "Hell, I'll bring her somethin' from town and visit her someday with it," he said aloud.

"You can slow down a little, boss," Danny shouted, gripping the rail of the buggy.

"What? Oh, yeah. Sorry." Matt pulled up on the reins, bringing the mules back to a trot.

Danny watched his face and knew by the smile that he had been thinking of Beth. He gave out a chuckle and softly said, "And no woman is gonna change the Brazo's Kid?"

"What?" Matt asked with a quizzical look on his face. "What are you talkin' about this time?"

"Nothin', boss," Danny replied, turning his chin towards Bozeman.

CHAPTER 2

THE TRIP TO VIRGINIA CITY

"Tell me it's none of my business and I'll butt out," Jean Wrisley said as their buggy wended its way to Virginia City."

"The hell she will," Reeves whispered, chewing on a cigar he'd had in his mouth since they left the Double R.

"What is it you'd like to know? Do you want to know about my relationship with Matt?"

"Yes. You know that. Why? Why are you paying so much attention to *that* man when you can have your pick of any man in Virginia City?"

"You flatter me, Jean. Thank you."

"You're embarrassing Beth," Reeves interrupted. "Your ma said the same about you."

"I think you just saved yourself," Beth whispered over at Reeves, hoping Jean wouldn't hear, but she did.

Jean smiled back. "I've got a twenty-two year old son who's looking for a girl."

"Danny is a handsome man," Beth agreed. "He'll not have any problems finding one." She looked at the scenery covered with snow, catching sight of various animals running through the woods. "Now, to answer your question concerning Matt, I'm not quite sure how I feel about him. He excites me when I'm with him. Yet, when I look into the man's eyes, I admit I don't really know him."

"He's a fast gun," Jean was quick to interject.

"Yes, but I thank God that he is, I suppose. Were he not, I might never have met him. You see, he's been rather an adventurous man, a soldier of fortune if you may."

"A Don Juan?" Jean asked.

Reeves sat quietly with his chewed-up cigar, somewhat amused and enjoying being able to listen to such a conversation about another man. He finally gave up and threw the cigar away.

"I certainly hope not," Beth answered wide-eyed. "If I thought that of Matt, I'd never have given him a second look."

"Oh, certainly he's had other women. You can't be the first."

"If you're insinuating that he's *had* me, you're quite mistaken. Our relationship is purely platonic. His mother was my client, and since he's the heir to the ranch, I must deal with him, too."

"Will you see him again?"

"Perhaps. I really don't know."

Reeves rolled his eyes after looking over at Jean as if to say, "Stay out of it, woman."

"Do you want to see him again?" Jean asked, giving a dagger look back at Reeves.

"I suppose so." She leaned into Jean's side and began to giggle. "We did leave in a hurry without saying our goodbyes."

"Yes, we did," Jean agreed, knowing how little of the truth she was getting from Beth. "I wouldn't blame him if he never wished to see you again."

Reeves looked angrily at Jean for a moment and then said, "You talk about him like he was incapable of loving a woman. I think of him as a very sensible and caring man. After all, he came all the way from Texas at your request, Beth."

"At his mother's request, darling," Jean interjected for Beth.

"You're right," Beth said glancing at the countryside. Without looking back at either of them, she continued, "He is a caring person. He put his life at stake just to see his mother again.

A fast gun, a man without scruples, would not have been so concerned after twenty-four years away from home."

"Especially when his return could have caused his demise," Jean added.

"Precisely," Beth agreed, turning to face Jean. She smiled and said, "And, yes, I think I do love him. But, you didn't hear that from me."

"I knew it but still can't see why. When you could have any man of your choice, why you'd jump at a guy like Matt is beyond me."

"Oh, pooh!" Beth returned.

"Pooh?" Reeves asked with a laugh in his voice.

"I couldn't think of another word to utter and still be a lady."

Before the sun set, they came to the Armstrongs' house and pulled alongside the barn. Jack and Phyllis Armstrong, an elderly couple, came out to meet them.

"Got a couple spare beds, Phyllis?" Jean asked, taking Jack's hand as he offered to help her out of the buggy.

"You know we do," Phyllis answered, holding the bridle of the lead horse. "Now that the boys are grown and gone, we've always got a couple spare beds. Come on Pa and put the horses in a stall while I help the ladies."

Jack watched as Phyllis served the fine dinner she had prepared for Beth and the Wrisleys. Their house was quaint, a little large for only them, but it had been their home for many years.

"Certainly you've thought of marriage before now?" Jean asked Beth, sipping her coffee after finishing her meal.

"Most definitely, but my law career had to come first. Now that I've set up office, I think I shall have time to pick out my man."

"Pick?" Reeves asked, almost spewing his coffee before he had a chance to swallow it.

"Maybe I should use a better choice of words, Reeves," Beth answered with a giggle. "Select. Choose. No, I like the word, 'pick'. I picked Matt."

Phyllis replenished their cups with fresh coffee from the stove.

"This Matt fella sounds real excitin'," Phyllis said, filling Beth's cup.

"Thank you, Mrs. Armstrong," Beth replied with a smile.

"How does Matt feel about you?" Reeves asked.

"Yes," Jean was quick to join in. "How does Matt feel about you?"

"Well, I think he likes me." She pondered, then added, "Yes, he likes me. I think. No, I'm certain."

"Enough to marry you?" Jean asked with a twinkle in her eye, dying to find out more about the loving couple.

"To be honest with you, I don't know." Beth took her napkin and dabbed at her lips a little to wipe some drops of coffee. "We never got that far."

Breakfast consisted of eggs, sausage, gravy, and biscuits with buttermilk. What Beth and the Wrisleys didn't eat, Phyllis packed in a bag, telling them to take it with them.

"It's still a piece to Virginia City," she reminded them. "I've got plenty of biscuits with pear preserves on them, and some egg sandwiches."

"We've got a clear day for driving, and I'm taking advantage of it," Reeves replied, climbing into the buggy.

With the two ladies aboard, Reeves gave a whistle to his team of horses and headed them out. The sun had been up for almost an hour.

Jack and Phyllis stood in the road and waved incessantly until the buggy was out of sight. They enjoyed visitors, whether from friends or passersby.

"They're a great couple," Beth said as sher saw them return to the house.

CHAPTER 3

A NEW SHERIFF IN BOZEMAN

heriff Bill Saunders, tall and good looking, stood and observed the four bodies stacked in the back of Matt's wagon.

"How's the new job comin' along, Sheriff?" Matt asked, tying the lines to the hitching post in front of the sheriff's office. "You been sheriff now, what, two months?"

Bill had replaced Sheriff Whitey, who was killed looking for Matt on the trail drive to Belle Fouche, South Dakota, to deliver a letter from his mother clearing him of the murder and bank robbery committed twenty-two years earlier by Matt's brother, Lukas, and another man. To collect the reward on Matt, a trio of outlaws killed the sheriff and took the letter so they could destroy it and the reward would still stand. Then a deputy, Bill Saunders soon became sheriff. Later, in a fair fight in the middle of town, he witnessed Matt's fast draw when he killed the leader of the outlaws. Since then, Matt had been exonerated of the crime he was wanted for and took rightful possession of the Double R Ranch.

Though he admired him as a man, Bill had a reason for disliking Matt at the time. He had a crush on Beth Paterson who, as a lawyer, had helped get Matt's freedom. Since no marriage vows had ever taken place between Matt and Beth, Bill hoped that he just might still have a chance with her.

"Two of these are the Parrish boys," he said. "Where's the third one?"

"Which one would that be?" Matt asked climbing down from the wagon.

"A mean cuss. Name's Biggun."

"Biggun? There was one big fella. He and another got away."

"Shame."

"How so?" Danny asked, walking up to the sheriff.

"They're all wanted for murder and robbery. Got a notice from Helena a few weeks ago about them robbin' a bank and killin' some people inside. Mean ones. Did it with shotguns. One was a woman. No reason for it, from what I heard. Jest had to shoot someone."

"Well, Sheriff, if you'll see to it that they're takin' off our hands, we'd like to get some grub in our gullets and visit the general store."

"Leave your wagon here, Matt, and I'll see that they're taken care of. Where ya be stayin'?"

"Down at the hotel, reckon. We'll leave at daybreak."

"I'll have one of the boys drive it over to the general once we're done with 'em."

"Fair nuff."

"By the way, there's a reward comin' to ya. Seems ya always have a reward comin'." He said sarcastically, and not in a friendly manner.

"Reward?" Danny asked shifting his Stetson back on his head, and turning abruptly to look back at the sheriff. "What kind of reward?"

"Five hundred dollars for the lot. I reckon you've got some of it comin', maybe three hundred, seein' how you got four of 'em."

"I'll see that my men get it all evened out." Matt grinned a little, hoping to wipe Bill's sarcasm off his face. He grabbed Danny by the arm and headed to the Red Garter Saloon. "Calls for a drink, Danny boy."

"Course, I'd be on my guard at all times, seein' as how the big brother might want to take revenge." Bill threw it back at Matt, hoping to shake him up a bit.

Matt stopped and turned and faced the sheriff. "Hope he tries." He slipped his .45 out of its holster lightning fast, twirled it, cocked it, uncocked it, and then put it back. "I'd kinda like to have the whole five hundred."

Danny gulped a little and smiled at the sheriff. "Yeah. Me, too."

CHAPTER 4

THE BENNETT HOUSE

T he Wrisleys pulled up in front of Beth's place on Wallace, the main street in Virginia City. Reeves hopped off the leathered-seat and tied his rig to the post as the ladies awaited his escort from the buggy.

"Could've got ya here sooner," Reeves said, helping Beth down from the buggy, "had we not stopped at the McDonalds."

"Oh, pshaw," Jean said sitting high in the back seat looking at Beth's place of business from the street side. "They would have been miffed had we simply passed on by."

"Like I said before, Reeves, I was in no rush to get back." Beth took his hand and stepped out of the buggy.

"So this is where you live?" Jean asked, following Beth's lead from the buggy.

"In back. Not much to look at. My office is in front, small as it is."

"I'll take your bag for you," Reeves said, picking up her satchel and toting it as he and Jean followed.

Her residence consisted of the front room, an adjacent kitchen with a wood-burning stove, and a bedroom in the back closed in by a curtain.

Leaving her bags in the front room, Reeves looked around, noticing that her place was filled meagerly, yet expensively, with newly purchased items mixed with furnishings she had brought from Virginia.

"You sure do have a nice place, Beth," Jean said as she stepped into the front room.

"Thank you, Jean." Beth replied. "Are you going to stay in town before you return home?"

"Yep," Jean answered, "we have some things to buy so we'll be stayin' over."

"In that case, dinner's on me. Where will you be staying?"

"The Bennett House up the street looks good," Reeves answered. "Now you don't have to go buyin' us no dinner. But," he added, "if you insist, I'm not one to turn down a free meal."

"I insist," Beth returned, standing menacingly with her hands on her hips. "You want to make somethin' of it, pardner?" she jested, giggling a little. "I'll meet the two of you there later."

Jean gave Beth a casual hug and kiss on the cheek. "It'll give us some time to catch up on our conversation. Not easy talking in a buggy."

Reeves and Jean left and drove down to the Bennett House, a hotel of Victorian architecture, complete with kitchen.

Beth enjoyed settling into a tub of hot water for awhile, which helped take away the soreness and stiffness of the buggy ride. Her thoughts were on getting her body back in shape and enjoying a good dinner with her friends.

She casually donned some of her best clothes, primped her hair, and made sure she looked the part of a lady before she entertained the thought of leaving for the hotel. She walked down the boardwalk to the sheriff's office.

As she turned into his office, Sheriff Charles Mallory walked out and almost knocked her over. He was a short stocky man with long dark sideburns. When he smiled, he showed a vacant space in front where two teeth were once present. He lost them in a fight trying to subdue a man much taller than he and just about as wide. He never did subdue him.

"Oh, excuse me, miss," he said as he doffed his hat to Beth.

Beth straightened herself, leveled her parasol to a closed position, and smiled back at him. "Are you the sheriff?"

"Yes, miss. Sorry. I'm not usually this clumsy. Can I help you?"

"I'm looking for some information about a certain person. How would I go about finding it?"

Impressed that a beautiful lady had stopped to chat with him made him feel good. "Come on in and let's see how I can be of service."

The jail contained a small office in front with two cells in the back. A drunk was sleeping it off in the last cell and another man stood eyeing them from the first cell as Beth and the sheriff entered.

"Hey, sheriff," the rough, dirty looking cowpoke yelled out with a toothless grin. "She can bunk in here with me."

"That's Dirty Pete," Sheriff Mallory informed Beth as he pulled out a chair by the desk. "Pay no mind to him. Have a seat."

"What's he in for?" Beth asked sitting down and standing her parasol against the desk.

Mallory went in short steps behind his desk and sat, unmindful that he was still wearing his hat. "Killing a man. He'll hang come mornin'."

"Oh." Beth eyed the prisoner contemptuously, looked at the sheriff's Stetson, and said nothing.

The sheriff looked up and removed his hat, then placing it on the desk, said, "Sorry."

He picked up a pile of wanted posters and fanned through them slowly. "Now just who is this person you're lookin' for?"

"He's a Negro."

"Well, that certainly narrows it down. What's he wanted for?"

"He's dead."

Mallory looked up from the pile of posters and frowned. "Then, why are we looking for him?"

"*We're* not. *I'm* looking for information about him."

"I see." Mallory stacked up the pile of posters and neatly shoved them back into a corner on his desk. "Who is he? This person *we're* looking for information on?"

"His name is Charlie Nightlinger, and he died within the last year or two. He was a trail cook on the Double O Ranch in Bozeman."

"Well, it seems you have a lot of information on him already. What else do you want to know about him?"

"I want to know if he's been married, and if so, if he had a family."

"Well," Mallory said in deep thought.

"Well?"

"How'd he die?" Mallory asked, seemingly groping for time as he admired her beauty. He had not seen such beauty grace his office since he took over as sheriff.

"Old age, I suppose."

"Oh, then he was an old man. Did he have any kin?"

Beth became a little annoyed at his question and looked straight away from him. "I told you, I am looking for information about whether or not he had a family."

"Why?"

"I am an attorney at law, and my client needs to know."

"Oh. You're a lawyer? My, my. And a pretty one, too." With sin in his heart, he eyed her carefully.

"How can we find out about this person, sheriff?"

"Well, for openers, why don't you ask your client?"

"I have. There was never any mention of a family."

"Then we don't have much to go on."

"It's worth a double eagle to my client."

"Well," he hemmed and hawed. "Eh, I know." He stood up and put his Stetson back on. "The marshal in Billings might be able to help. They have a courthouse and coupla newspapers. He can check with the census taken recently and see. What's his name again?"

"Charlie Nightlinger. About fifty or sixty years old."

"I'll wire him and get back to you."

Beth stood up, picked up her parasol, and walked to the door. "Thank you, sheriff. I'm depending on you."

"Come again, kind lady," the prisoner yelled with a smile from his cell.

"Where can I find you, Miss . . .?"

"Beth Paterson. My office is up the street. There's a shingle out in front, so you can't miss it."

At the livery stable, she hired a buggy and driver to drop her off at the Bennett House to have dinner with the Wrisleys.

She was seemingly oblivious to the attention her entrance caused as she sashayed into the room, her light blue dress sweeping gracefully across the floor. She wore a small waist jacket inlaid with flowers, and a strand of pearls hung loosely above her bust, adding to her elegance. Her hair was combed upwards, held in place by a comb of inlaid pearl. She wore a tall plumbed hat that accentuated her slender frame.

Spotting Reeves and Jean, she walked over to their table. "Good evening, you two," she said as Reeves and the waiter both scrambled to assist her with her chair. As though unaware, she then looked at Jean and said, "That's a darling outfit you're wearing, Jean. It becomes you quite nicely."

"Thank you, Beth," Jean replied, "but it's nothing compared to what you're wearing, or for that matter, how you're wearing it. You look adorable. On you, anything would look great, don't you think so, Reeves?"

"Yes. Yes, indeed." All of a sudden, Reeves was self-conscious of his still standing behind Beth's chair. He took his chair and sat down, placing his napkin across his lap. His eyes stayed on Beth.

"You're staring, Reeves," Jean said quietly so that the diners at the next table would not hear.

"I'm sorry. Please forgive me, Beth, but I have never seen you look so beautiful. I mean, I know it's a clumsy choice of words."

"Thank you very much for the compliment. Please sit down. I understand fully." Beth smiled and winked at Jean.

"You're leaving tomorrow?" Beth asked. She saw the headwaiter motion for the waiter to take their drink order and smiled as she said, "Just wine for me, Reeves, thank you."

"We'll pick up what we need and head back before noon," Jean said. "If you don't mind my saying, Beth, you are attracting quite a lot of attention here." She looked around at the gawkers and then back at her friend. "And now, let's order so we can talk about you for a few minutes before our food arrives."

"We said a lot already," Beth said slyly, her way of indicating that she was fully aware of what Jean really wanted to discuss.

The three enjoyed their wine and dinner to its fullest, complete with talk about little things, but not to the core. When they had finished their meal and the waiter had removed the dishes from the table, they sat quietly, continuing their conversation over coffee.

Taking a cigar from his coat pocket and lighting it, Reeves asked impetuously, "Are you going to wait for Matt to visit you here?"

"Oh, there is one little bit of business he was about to do before I left, which just might involve me, if I let it."

"What's that?" Jean asked, sipping her coffee.

Without preamble, Beth blurted, "He wants to take Charlie's body from the family plot and inter it in the field on the other side of the gully, behind the ranch."

Reeves gasped and Jean almost dropped her cup.

"What?" Reeves asked exhaling a stream of cigar smoke. "What in heaven's name would make him want to do that?"

"*Our* Charlie Nightlinger, the trail cook?" Jean asked, noticing other diners were now listening to their conversation.

"Keep your voices down." Beth motioned with her hands for them to keep quiet. "He has this thing about Charlie being a Negro and buried in his family plot."

"Well, he does have a point," Reeves responded, puffing on his cigar.

"No, he doesn't!" Jean kept her voice low so others wouldn't hear. "Charlie's family. It's high time Matt knew that."

"Matt's talk is coming from the war," Beth pointed out.

"The war's been over for almost twenty years," Jean countered.

"Not for him. He's still got a lot of the South in him, and we're trying to make him think North. Like the old saying goes, 'you can take the boy out of the South but you can't take the South out of the boy.'"

"You've got a point there," Reeves said, blowing rings of smoke into the air.

"He was born and bred a Yankee. I'll have Danny tell him a thing or two. He knows how to handle him. After all, he fetched him from Texas to begin with."

"Seems to me that you've got a big problem right there," Reeves suggested, rolling his cigar between his fingers. "How do you feel about Negroes?"

"I'm from Virginia. Does that tell you something? I'm also a Southerner. I know how Matt thinks. I left those thoughts behind me when I chose to live in Montana. I am not prejudiced. Never have been."

"Are you going to let him get away with it?"

Beth stared at Reeves before answering haltingly, "Get away with what?"

"I kind of think our conversation has ended, Reeves," Jean said looking at Beth's frozen expression. "Let's take her home."

Between the cold air and the ride home, Beth's senses were awakened, enabling her to sit erect behind Jean as the buggy neared her apartment.

"In answer to your question, Reeves," Beth said sitting up straight. "I don't know what I'm going to do. I don't have a definite plan. I know no law that will prevent him from doing what he intends doing. I hope Circuit Judge Leonard W. Stanford can give me some ideas. I had some ideas of my own, which passed through my mind on the drive up. You see, the judge presided over Matt's estate hearing last month and had the deed to his inheritance, the ranch, turned over to him."

"He's here in town?" Jean asked.

"His office is. I don't know if he is or not.

"And exactly what can he do?" Reeves asked, turning slightly to get another glimpse of the beautiful woman seated beside his wife. "Damn," he thought to himself, "she is one hell of a beautiful lady."

"If there is an heir or heirs, they can take the body and have it buried wherever they so choose, and it would end a conflict Matt is having with me and his men. Simple. See?" She smiled and threw her arms into the air, settled back in her seat, and closed her eyes.

"We've arrived, Sleeping Beauty," Jean said, jostling Beth's knees.

Reeves reined up the team of horses and then escorted Beth to her door. Jean remained seated in the buggy and watched.

"Thanks, the both of you," Beth said as she walked through the door Reeves held open for her.

"We'll be back home by nightfall tomorrow," Jean reminded her. "In the meantime, if you need anything, you know where we'll be tonight."

"I know. Again, thanks. My work's cut out for me for the next few days. Good night."

When Reeves climbed back into the buggy, Jean was quick to say, "You've got fifteen years on her."

"A man can still admire beauty, can't he. After all, I've got the prettiest filly in the whole, wide world sittin' right next to me."

"Wipe that silly grin off your face. You can prove it to me later."

Reeves winked at her, whistled at his team, and headed them back to the hotel.

CHAPTER 5

A SHOPPE FULL OF LADIES

Beth slept in the next day until noon. She dressed in another long, frilly dress that skirted the floor, and a wide brim hat with a small feather. She was in Virginia City, and she definitely wanted to keep an air of pretense about her that would make the town believe she was someone important, whether they knew anything about her or not. She strolled to the east end of town to visit her good friend, Mrs. Dorothy Phillips.

The walk was not too long, and she rather enjoyed it because the weather had warmed up a bit.

Dorothy was a woman in her fifties who could wear fine clothes well. Her husband, Roger, a retired gentleman in his sixties, worked in the assayer's office in Virginia City. He did this for pleasure and to stay active more than to earn extra income, although he did this rather nicely, too. He was a middle-size Scotsman with balding features and long sideburns. He wore spectacles of a kind, which revealed him as being a man of wealth. Dorothy had first made friends with Beth while she was shopping in the general store, shortly after she had arrived in town.

A lovely, young black woman answered Beth's knock and opened the huge door to the Phillips' stately mansion.

"Mrs. Phillips, please," Beth requested.

The young woman recognized Beth and motioned for her to enter as Dorothy entered from a room adjacent to the foyer with arms outspread in welcome. "Well, well, well, Beth Paterson," she exclaimed, "how wonderful to have you here again."

"With too many things on my mind, I gave up trying to work with my clients, and thought I'd visit with you awhile."

"Where's your buggy?" Dorothy pulled back the chenille curtains and looked out her front window in all directions. "I don't see a buggy anywhere."

"It is such a beautiful day, I decided I needed the walk and fresh air."

"Most certainly, darling. Please sit. I'll have Ellie get us some tea, if that's all right with you."

"Certainly could use something hot."

"Ellie, would you bring the tea cart out, please?"

The afternoon passed quickly as the two women chatted about what was, what is, and what was to come with the townsfolk of Virginia City.

"You are planning to spend the evening?" Dorothy asked rather rhetorically. "I won't let you out of this house."

Since Dorothy was a wealthy woman, greatly admired by the citizens of Virginia City, she welcomed many an overnight visitor to her home, using the extra bedroom for such purposes. So it was then, on this night, that Beth was no exception.

Beth felt their time together was too short as they enjoyed each other's company. Dorothy was the sister of Sheriff Wiseman who was killed trying to help Matt prove his innocence. It was during the trial where Beth was defending Matt that Dorothy traveled to Bozeman and stepped forward with a letter she found in the pocket of her brother's jacket, which exonerated Matt from the charge of murder and bank robbery, and helped Beth win the case. Since the trial, Beth and Dorothy had become good friends, being about the same age, and both living in Virginia City. They shared dinner and caught up on all the news in their first evening together.

"Tomorrow, honey, we are going shopping," Dorothy said as she finished her tea for the evening.

The wind was a chilling cold outside for a bright new morning, so Beth dressed well for the occasion with woolen clothes, another fancy hat with a feather, laced boots, and a long coat. She walked out of the house that morning and into the cold where she met a black man standing in front of a beautiful carriage. It was Dorothy's private carriage. Dorothy spared no expense in her taste for it was a six passenger, natural oak wagonette, with spindle seats, cord cushions, leather top and was drawn by a matched pair of bay quarter horses.

"This is Willie, my driver," Dorothy said as she followed Beth to the carriage.

Willie was a black man in his forties with graying hair and a smile that befitted his pleasant personality.

Beth accepted Willie's hand and stepped up into the carriage. She and Dorothy rode proudly down the street with Willie, dressed in his tall black hat and burgundy coat, driving them through town. Because the snow had made traveling difficult for some carriages, a few sleighs appeared down on Wallace. but Dorothy's high and narrow wheeled carriage rode the ruts as smooth as any sleigh.

The couple spent the day in town and Beth did some extra shopping for apparel for herself as Dorothy tagged along for support. She admired Dorothy as she was a woman of great taste.

"You'll not be wanting to dress like a lawyer all the time, Beth," Dorothy said, "but, very smart looking, elegant still the same."

Beth returned, "Dorothy, I'm thanking you for your assistance, but I kind of know what I'm looking for."

"And I'm thinking that you might be looking for a husband. Am I right?"

"And if I were, what would you suggest I wear?" Beth asked laughingly.

They stopped at Molly's Dress Shoppe and went inside. Mulling over some dresses in the store's catalogue, they giggled and talked like two young girls about what to wear.

"As an attorney *and* as a woman out for a husband, I would suggest this green skirt, with the white frills, and the bustle in the back, *and* the low cut bosom." Dorothy held her finger on the page to point out the skirt to Beth.

"I'm thinking you're right," Beth replied. "It does look rather darling."

Dorothy saw the shop owner coming over to them and asked, "What do you think, Molly?"

"It's lovely," Molly responded. Then, putting her finger on her chin reflectively, she turned and went to the other side of the store, returning with a skirt much like that in the catalogue. "Here. I have one as an example that we made just this week from that pattern. Try it on. It might be a little big here or there, as you are rather a thin woman, but we can take care of that," she suggested. "My lady here does some alterations." She pointed to a Negro woman sweeping the store.

"Yes, Dorothy," Molly continued as she pressed the skirt against Beth's body. "I certainly agree." She looked at Beth, and said, "Tsk, tsk. You are rather a frail sort. Don't you eat regularly?"

"Well, I must say I eat more than my share here with Dorothy, than I did in Bozeman. I stayed here for awhile back before I took on the Andersen case. Thereafter, I ate when I could, and meagerly at that, I must confess."

"The Andersen case?" Molly asked. "Is that where Annie Andersen died and left an estate to a stranger?" Getting a nod from Beth, she continued. "I heard about it. Absurd, if you ask me. Giving an entire ranch to someone she didn't know, nor ever even saw, I imagine."

As if in defense of Annie, Beth responded quickly, "Oh, she knew him. It was only that she hadn't seen him in many years, and she wanted him to be well taken care of."

"I see," said Molly, hinting with her eyes to Dorothy that she had not yet been introduced to Beth.

"Oh, my goodness! Please forgive me, ladies," Dorothy interrupted. "My manners. Beth, this is my good friend, Molly Jefferson. And, Molly, this is Mary Elizabeth Paterson. She's an attorney. But, of course, you know that already."

"Hello, Molly. Please call me, Beth."

"Hello, Beth," Molly responded warmly. "I've been in Virginia City for fifteen years and know just about any type of gossip that could go on. What case are you working on now, if I'm not being too nosy?"

"Not at all," Beth answered. "I'm visiting Judge Stanford on a legal matter."

"About what?"

Dorothy stepped in, saying, "Could Beth try this skirt on, Molly?"

"Well, certainly," Molly replied, a little embarrassed that they were just standing there talking. She took Beth to the back to try on the skirt. When Beth came out looking like a princess going to a ball, she allowed Molly to fit her for her measurements.

"Wish I had a figure like yours," Molly said.

"Oh. I thought I was rather too thin," Beth remarked honestly.

"I can do with thin. I've got more blubber on me to share with both you girls, and believe me, no corset can hide it. You'd think the good Lord would give me a figure to die for." She began folding a bit here and sticking pins there.

"By the way, Mrs. Andersen's estate," Beth said to Molly. "You asked me what case I was working on. I'm still working for her."

"With the new owner, no doubt?" Molly asked, sticking more pins into the hem of Beth's new skirt. "What's happening?"

"Oh, I've got the new owner riled up because he wants to remove Charlie Nightlinger's body from the family plot. He was their trail cook at one time. The new owner wants to remove it and inter it somewhere else."

"Now, why on earth would he want to do that?" Molly asked, through a mouthful of pins.

"Because he's a Negro," Beth answered politely, yet curtly.

Dorothy heard Beth answer while thumbing through some of the raw materials laid out on display on the counters. She walked over to the couple. She and Beth had already talked about the situation the evening before.

"A Negro, did you say?" Molly asked.

"Not the word he actually used, but yes, a Negro."

Molly looked up and smiled, the pins between her lips making her look like a Halloween mask. She took the pins out and placed them in her apron. "We'll have to make you a blouse to go with this."

Then she motioned to the black woman who was still sweeping. "Come over here a second, honey," she ordered her. "Take over for me, honey. She wants this skirt, and of course, we'll have to make her a blouse and waist jacket to match."

The black woman laid her broom against a backboard and sauntered over to the ladies.

Molly introduced her. "This here is, Haciola. She's been with me for quite awhile now, and let me tell you something, she knows how to make clothes."

Haciola looked at Beth up and down and sideways and then began fitting her into her skirt. She turned her this way and that, then began removing some pins Molly had already put in, and putting some in where they were needed. She pulled and she tugged where she felt Beth would need more fitting.

"For lands sake, this woman is sho' skinny," she said as she tucked and stuck in more pins.

"Gonna have to charge her half price," she jested without smiling. "Youse gotta eat some, woman," she continued. "Ain't healthy to go skinny like youse is." Turning Beth around again to get a good look at her, she said, "Wants soma my fats?"

"She was not always this big," Molly said, indicating her size with her hands on Haciola's hips as she watched her work on the skirt. "Only until after she came to work for me. She was as thin as you when she arrived in Virginia City one fall afternoon. I had just started my dress shop when she came by way of the back of a covered wagon with her son, Banjo."

"Banjo helped drive the wagon," Haciola added, "and both us did chores for the owner."

"Haciola is a runaway house slave who left the South with her son in search of her runaway husband," Molly continued throwing a smile Haciola's way.

"You are very pretty, Haciola," Beth said, watching her as she carefully worked on her hem. "Did I pronounce your name correctly?"

Haciola looked up, took the pins out of her mouth and smiled. "Yes, ma'am, and thank you, ma'am."

She was more on the beautiful side, Beth thought. She had a round face, small nose, and pretty brown eyes. She wore her hair long and neatly tied with a bow. Her skin was light bronze and smooth as silk, indicating that she had seen little work in the sun. Her manners were impeccable, for she had worked for some of the finest slave owners in the south.

"How'd you wind up here in Montana?"

"I followed tips about Charlie from one slave master t'other."

"She became quite adept at sewing, which she loved and was so good at it," Molly added. "Each master knew he would lose her because of her constant trek to find her husband, so, they offered her more than her worth to assure that she'd stay on."

"I kept on movin' whenever I heard about my Charlie jest bein' a short distance away." Haciola emphasized the word "jest" with her first two fingers slightly touching each other.

"You have a son?" Beth inquired.

"Banjo," Molly answered. "He was immediately hired on as an apprentice at the smithy, while Haciola continued to stroll down the boardwalk in search of work. When she saw me sweeping out my shop one day, she knew she had found her place.

"Haciola stood there that day and watched me sweeping out my store, then said, 'My, my, my, my, my. You do needs some help, don'tcha, ma'am?'

"Well, I stopped, straightened my hair a bit, leaned up against my broom, and looked at her. For the first time in a long month of Sundays, I saw someone I admired as a first class woman, even if she was a Negro.

"Looking for a job? I asked her."

"How coulds ya tell, ma'am? I says," Haciola answered from where she was kneeling at the bottom of Beth's skirt.

"She had the biggest smile I had seen in all my life. I told her, 'You got luggage all around you, and none of it is fit for travelin'. So, figured ya best for a woman out of work that just got here. That wagon train brought you?' I asked her, pointing to a pair of covered wagons parked at the other end of town.

"She sat her bags down next to a big bag she had already set on the walk next to her, and gently took the broom away from me. 'Ma'am,' she said, taking her hat off and placing it on her bag. 'You jest gotcherself a helper.' She picked up her small bags, walked into the shop, and made herself at home. She came back out and brought her big bag in and placed it in the corner with the other bags. Rolling up the sleeves of her jacket, she began sweeping.

"I told her I couldn't pay her much. Next thing I knew, I just stood there watching Haciola take charge of my store."

"And she's been here ever since?" Dorothy asked, looking at other material as if not too interested in what Molly was saying.

"I asked her if she had an extra cot someplace for these weary bones of mine," Haciola said still pinning. "Price of some vittles and a cot, alls I need, ma'am. What does I call ya, ma'am, I says? Sign above say Molly, sos I figure that be you?"

"I told her to call me Molly and said I had an extra room in the loft, you can put a bed up there.

"She became a seamstress for me when I discovered her talents later quite by accident. A friend, who had invited me and my husband for dinner one day, also extended the invite to Haciola. During the evening, Haciola demonstrated her handiwork when she sewed a rip in my friend's coat that showed little repair afterwards. I saw real talent and began to give work to Haciola on occasion and increased her wages. And that's how it's been ever since. It started on a Monday morning in 1869."

Dorothy smiled. "All alone in a strange new world. At the very least, she must have been terrified some."

"As for Banjo," Molly continued. "He got hisself work as an apprentice with the smithy. Turned out to be a dang good man. Better'n the smithy himself, I'd say. He bunks there and causes no one no trouble."

Dorothy left the material on the counter and joined in with more serious talk. "From there, Haciola's skill with needle and thread became her trademark, and with Molly's coaching in designs, Haciola became a very good seamstress. Her work here was demanded throughout the town. Everyone who came in would ask for Molly's expertise, which of course is Haciola's."

"I'm right proud that she had the opportunity to help me get started in town," Molly said, watching Haciola do her work. "She finally moved in with us, has her own quarters in back of our house. And whenever company came over, she would cook up the finest supper in all of Virginia City and, of course, we always asked her to join us at the table. Most had no problem with that."

"What about your son, Haciola?" Beth asked.

Haciola stood up and turned Beth around so she could see her handiwork. "Banjo earned a good reputation in town for being a smithy. His muscles done give the owner, Mr. Swenson, a business worthy of the envy of all others in town."

"I take it you like living here?" Beth asked, looking down at her new skirt being made into her size.

"Ma'am, in Virginia City, there ain't no masters and ain't no slaves." Haciola smiled and then asked, "How you likes it now?"

"You thinkin' she might be, Beth?" Dorothy whispered so only Beth and Molly could hear.

"I like it fine, Haciola." Beth turned and whispered back, "I'm thinking it could be so. What do you think, Molly?"

"Her?" Molly thought for awhile and then said, "Wouldn't be Haciola's ubiquitous husband you'd be thinking about who would be lying in that grave, now would it, Dorothy?" she asked. "You're thinking about that?"

Haciola heard her name mentioned but kept on pinning.

"Haciola talked about Banjo's father, but never told me what happened to him. I figured he ran away or got killed, or something." Molly stepped closer to Haciola, then took her hand and patted it. "Haciola. This here is Miss Mary Elizabeth Paterson. She is looking for someone."

"Yes, ma'am," Haciola said. "I figured that out by how you all been talkin'. Pleased to meet cha, Miss Mary Elizabeth Paterson."

"You said you were married, once?" Molly asked.

Hacioloa looked somewhat bewildered at the three women who were standing next to her asking questions that were rather personal and private while she was trying to work.

"Yes, ma'am," she replied. "Once, only once. Youse knows that, Miss Molly."

"You said your last name is Morgan?" Molly asked.

"What's this all about, Miss Jefferson?" Haciola asked. She used Molly's last name when she was trying to be formal, as when someone was asking questions, like they were now.

Molly took Haciola by the hand and led her to a chair by a round table in the middle of the store where the ladies could sit to admire themselves in the vanity mirror.

"Your last name's Morgan. That's you, isn't it, Haciola?" Molly spoke softly to Haciola, hoping not to upset her. "I have known you for at least thirteen years, and I know you've been searching for your husband. Oh, I know you kept telling me you'd find him some day soon. But the fact is, you haven't found him yet."

"No, Miss Jefferson. Mr. Morgan, he not be here," Haciola replied, half smiling and half crying.

Dorothy spoke to Haciola gently, hoping to ease her mind about what they were talking with her about. "You say, he's not here, like not home? Gone to another city? What, Haciola?"

"You see this lady here?" Molly brought Beth closer for Haciola to see. "She's a lawyer. She's looking for a man named Charlie. What's his last name, Beth?"

"Nightlinger," Beth answered.

Haciola stopped smiling and began to cry. "This mean my job, Miss Jefferson?"

"No, Haciola," Molly answered. "It has nothing to do with your job. Could his name be Nightlinger, Haciola," Molly repeated the name. "Charlie Nightlinger?"

Haciola's eyes popped open and she cried harder. She sensed it might be her Charlie they were talking about. Other than mentioning that her last name was Morgan, she never mentioned his.

"His name is Charlie Nightlinger," Beth repeated. "Do you know a Charlie Nightlinger, Haciola?"

Haciola looked around, still in fear that she was about to lose her job with the only friend she had. Her mind reeled as to why they were now asking, after all these years, about her Charlie.

Yes, this was her Charlie, but he was only a mere acquaintance, not a husband.

"I was older than my Charlie when we got married. But we were in love, and nothin' was gonna separate us."

She liked her job and was proud at having raised Banjo by herself. To save her job, she thought she'd have to continue to lie.

"A woman without a husband has a hard time gettin' along in this world," she sobbed. "And to be a Negro makes it even more difficult." She wondered on how she could avoid trouble by lying on one hand, and she thought as to how deep into trouble she could get without revealing any of the truth on the other.

"Ma'am," Haciola continued, straightening her shoulders. "My name's Morgan. I don't know no Nightlinger." She wasn't willing to admit to anyone that it might be her Charlie, out of fear of getting him into any trouble, but more importantly, not getting herself and her son into trouble. She had no idea what this female vigilante wanted with Charlie.

"He might have changed his name, Haciola," Beth suggested.

"Yes, ma'am," Haciola replied. "Reckon he could. Don't know why he would though."

"Where is Charlie?" Molly asked gently.

"You saw my man, Charlie? How he be?"

"You answer her, Beth," Molly suggested.

"Haciola. Would your Charlie be in his late fifties, say, and good at cooking?" She said this, aware that Charlie had been well known on the trail as being an excellent cook.

"Yes, ma'am," Haciola answered, frittering with her apron. "That could be him, alright. But his name be Morgan." Then out of curiosity, she again asked, "Where he be?"

"Haciola," Beth asked again, "how long since you saw Charlie?"

"Long time. I don't know," she answered wiping her runny nose with a dainty handkerchief she kept in her waistband. "He be a good man. He said he would return when he got money. Ain't never returned, yet. But, he will. Cause he said he will."

"How long?" Beth asked again. "Haciola, how long has it been since you've seen Charlie?"

Haciola began to cry, her tears quickly filling up her handkerchief. Then she tilted her head up and looked proudly at each of them, one at a time. Then, almost inaudibly, she said, "Many years."

"Wait a minute." Molly went down on her knees to confront Haciola eye to eye. "You said you got your name from one of your masters. That doesn't mean your Charlie's name is Morgan."

She rose and looked at the women. "I'll bet she really doesn't know what his name is."

"And it could be 'Nightlinger'," Dorothy exclaimed with a surprised look on her face.

They walked to the back room to continue their conversation.

"Well, ladies," Beth said, "we've got ourselves a lulu."

"What are you going to do now, Beth?" Dorothy asked.

"We're not sure her Charlie and my Charlie are one and the same," Beth answered, as she started unbuttoning her skirt. "I'll see Judge Stanford when he gets into town and hope he gives me an injunction. That will at least give me some time to work this whole thing out."

"Then what?" Dorothy asked.

"I'm not at all sure right now. Just stick with me."

Molly was not one who would let an issue die simply because someone said so. "Beth," Molly said, slipping beside her conspiratorially. "Come on. You can tell your friend. I just got to know."

"Well, for starters, I want to see if any of the cowboys at the ranch who knew Charlie Nightlinger can see any resemblance between that Charlie and Haciola's son, Banjo. That, in my eyes, should clinch it. Right now, I need to see Judge Stanford for that injunction."

"Then what?" Molly asked in a mocking voice, placing her hands on her hips.

"Then present it to Matt. He's the new owner of the estate. We'll see what he plans on doing. If we find that Haciola is our link to Charlie Nightlinger, we can bring her in, too. After all, she's his rightful heir."

Dorothy excused herself and went back to the counter.

Molly continued to help Beth finish unbuttoning her clothes. "A lot of work," she said. "Then what?"

"Molly," Beth said, stepping out of the skirt, "the rest is confidential at this point. For Haciola's sake, I'll have to keep it on a lawyer-client basis."

"Do you really think she could be Mrs. Nightlinger?" Molly asked.

"Time will tell, Molly," Beth said, slipping back into her own clothes, "time will tell. Meanwhile, with your permission, I'd like to spend some time with her. I'll pay her wages."

"By all means," Molly agreed, buttoning up the back of Beth's skirt. "No need to pay for her. She deserves some time off."

The two returned to the counter where Dorothy had kept Haciola in conversation. Molly placed the skirt across the counter and took Haciola's hand. "Haciola, I'm giving you the rest of the day off to go with Miss Beth. She wants to talk with you. Would that be all right with you?"

"Sure, Miss Molly," Haciola answered. "What we gonna do?"

"Well, first, how about a cup of tea?" Beth asked.

"No, ma'am," Haciola remarked.

Beth stood for a moment thinking she was going to run up against some resistance from Haciola that would result in her inability to solve this dilemma.

Then, with a quirk in her smile, Haciola returned with, "I'm a coffee woman, pure and simple. Loves my coffee. Hates tea, but loves my coffee."

Beth breathed a sigh of relief and smiled at Haciola. "Then, let's have a cup of coffee."

"Got some in the back room, Miss Beth," Haciola remarked, heading in that direction.

Beth stopped her and said, "No, Haciola. Let's be fancy and go to the Bennett House down the street."

Haciola turned and looked puzzled for a moment. "Me? Why, they don't let me in there."

"They will today, Haciola," Beth returned. "You're my client."

"Wowee! Lordy, lordy! I gots myself a big ol'- fashioned lawyer, and we all is gonna have coffee together in the Bennett House," Haciola said, with a smile that filled the room from wall to wall. "My, my, my, my, my. What gonna happen next, I'm a thinkin?"

Beth returned her smile but only briefly because Haciola's quickly turned to a serious frown.

"What I gonna do with a lawyer, Miss Beth?" she asked.

Beth was almost at a loss for words. "Well, let's just pretend you're my client, because I'm really working for a rancher, and he's the one that pays for the coffee," she stuttered.

"That's good," Haciola agreed. "That's real good. People gonna think I'm up to somthin', and I'm gonna have fun foolin' 'em."

"And Molly, Dorothy," Beth continued, putting her finger up to her lips, "please don't either of you mention any of this to anyone."

"Oh, I'm not one to blab it all over town," Molly quipped. Dorothy shrugged her shoulders as if in agreement. Of course, that promise would only last until Beth was fully out of town and away from earshot—something they didn't know she was counting on, especially if it reached the ears of Judge Stanford to reinforce her reasoning for the injunction.

"Not a word," was all Beth had to say about that. Then she asked in a whisper, "When will the skirt be ready?"

"When you return with Haciola, she'll get right on it," Molly answered. "I do the preliminaries, and she finishes up."

The ladies giggled as their whispering continued. It was more than apparent then that Haciola was more than a cleaning woman for the store, she was also a seamstress, the finest in Virginia City. Beth had an idea that it was Haciola's skill that had moved Molly's business into a successful venture.

CHAPTER 6

A CUP OF COFFEE FOR HACIOLA
IN A BIG HOTEL

Willie met the ladies as they left the store and escorted them into the carriage.

"I'll let Willie drop me off at the house," Dorothy told Beth, "and you and Haciola can have your tete-a-tete."

"What's that you be sayin', Miss Dorothy?" Haciola asked.

"Our coffee together," Beth explained.

Willie pulled the carriage up to Dorothy's house and helped her out.

"Ellie will have dinner at five," she said. "You'll have plenty of time until then." She walked into the house, and Willie climbed back up on the seat.

"Thank you, Dorothy," Beth replied, waving her handkerchief gently in the breeze.

Willie snapped the whip, turned the team around, and headed them in the direction of the hotel.

Haciola had never before been given so much attention, and Beth was enjoying watching the glow on her face.

Once at the hotel, Beth left the carriage with Willie.

"We'll be a few moments, Willie," Beth said.

Willie nodded and tipped his hat and made himself comfortable again in the driver's seat.

The two women were met by the gentleman from last night who showed he had remembered her. They went into the restaurant and were properly seated, although Beth could feel eyes staring at them.

Virginia City had been a Confederate city during the Civil War. Her townsfolk had accepted Haciola as Molly's helper and as a right expert seamstress under Molly at Molly's Dress Shoppe. Her social life was shallow because there weren't many Negroes living in Virginia City.

Molly's customers envied Haciola's work, and gracefully waited for her to perform tailoring for their clothes. Being with Beth in a public restaurant, however, raised many eyebrows, even among the gentlemen. To ease the tension, Beth set her briefcase on the floor, opened it, and removed some papers she had prepared for an injunction. None of it pertained to Haciola, but Beth pretended that it did to let on to those around her that she had a client. The pretense worked, for eyes began to fall back into their sockets and duties and activities resumed as normal.

Haciola felt quite uncomfortable about the situation. "What we doin' here, Miss Beth?" she asked. "I know what them people are thinkin'." Standing, she said, "They thinkin' I not good enough to sit in here with them. We better leave, Miss Beth, before I gets kilt."

Grabbing Haciola by the arm, Beth said quietly, "Sit down, Haciola. They know I'm an attorney. Now sit easy and let's have something to eat. You hungry?"

"No, ma'am," Haciola said, sitting down and eyeing everyone suspiciously. "Not since I came through that door."

When the waitress came to their table, Beth asked her to bring them two cups of coffee. "You're not going to let anyone make you feel uncomfortable, are you, Haciola?"

"Yes, ma'am," she answered. "I be normal jest like the rest of you."

"I'm sorry, Haciola," Beth apologized, "I don't mean to embarrass you. It's just that I've never had to talk with a . . ." Her sentence trailed off.

"A Negro, Miss Beth?" Haciola asked.

"Yes, Haciola. A Negro. A black woman. I didn't know what to call you."

"Yes, ma'am," Haciola nodded. "Same with you. We calls you whities, 'cause youse white. So, you calls us Negroes, or black people."

"Do you still take offense at being different, Haciola?" Beth asked, knowing immediately that she had asked the wrong thing in the wrong way.

"Different, Miss Beth?" Haciola asked, glancing around at the people still looking at them covertly. "We black people don't see no difference between you white people anymore than you white people claims to see any different in us black people. Only you calls us by different names."

"Oh," Beth queried. "What names?"

"Names."

"I'm not sure I know what you're talking about, Haciola." Beth paused for a moment and thought about what she had just said.

"Names, Miss Beth," Haciola continued. "Like niggers, nigs, or Negroes, names like that." Beth's eyes opened wide, now knowing full well she was offending Haciola with her questioning. She groped for words, but came up empty. Then she asked, "Haciola?

"Yes, ma'am?"

"May I call you, Haci?"

"No, ma'am."

"You may call me, Miss Beth."

"Where I come from, we calls you Missis if youse our boss. It's all to your likin', I 'spose."

"Where do you come from, Haci" Beth asked.

"Haciola," Haciola returned quickly with half a cocked-smile, still eyeing the people around them. "It's Haciola!" She was proud of her name and did not want to patronize others by letting them shorten it. It was the family name she had inherited from her paternal grandmother, perhaps from an Indian or Indian tribe from a region in Alabama.

"Haciola, then," Beth agreed. "Where do you come from?"

"Alabama."

"And your folks?"

"Don't have no folks."

"You came by yourself?"

"No, ma'am," Haciola answered shyly. "I had a husband."

Beth discovered that she was finally getting the answers she was seeking.

The waitress returned and served the two cups of coffee. She was anxious to walk away, but not before she gave Haciola a good looking over.

"That will be all, Miss," Beth said, giving her some coins from her purse.

Beth sat quietly, watching Haciola fill her coffee with plenty of sugar and cream. Then she asked, "How did you meet your husband?"

"On a farm," she said, sipping at her coffee and feeling a little more comfortable with the situation. Then a frown crossed her face. "The war. It ended, and he left."

"Charlie left?" Beth asked. "I thought he brought you to Montana."

"No, ma'am," Haciola answered. "I say that to get a job fer me. Ain't no one gonna give a slave girl a job without her havin' a man to protect her. You write that down in your fancy book."

"Then what?" Beth asked.

"I was with child," she responded quietly. "Do I have to tell ya this, Miss Beth? I gonna lose my job for sure."

"I want to help you, Haciola," Beth responded sliding her hand along Haciola's arm to help her feel less uncomfortable about the situation. "And I think I can. I'll make sure you don't lose your job." Then with a smile, she added, "I'm a lawyer, remember?"

"You think you can find my Charlie?" Haciola asked as tears rolled down her cheeks.

Beth removed a handkerchief from her purse and wiped Haciola's eyes. Then looking at her carefully, she said, "I don't know, Haciola. I only have a hunch."

Haciola sniffed, wiped her eyes clean, and returned the handkerchief to Beth. "What you mean, hunch, Miss Beth?"

"Well, Haciola," Beth explained, "this being Virginia City, Montana, well, we just don't have too many black people here."

"Y'all notice that, too?" Haciola asked with a big grin on her face.

Beth returned the smile. She saw that they were finally connecting. "You got me that time, Haciola."

Haciola smiled, then became serious. "This here Charlie. What's he like?"

"Well," Beth began, "like we said, he's in his fifties, tall, and gray haired."

"That could fit him," Haciola said. Then after taking a drink from her cup, she added, "Course it could be any man. He didn't have gray hair when I knowed him."

"But back at Molly's, you felt like it could be your Charlie?" Beth asked.

"Yes, ma'am."

"What made you think that?"

Haciola looked up from her coffee cup and smiled again. "Jest 'cause his name be Charlie."

Beth sat back in her chair and sighed. After looking into Haciola's eyes for a long time, she felt she could ask the one, all-important question that had been plaguing her. "You said Banjo works for the smitty. Can we go see him?"

Haciola nodded her head, and then the two of them rose from their table and left for the smithy at the end of the street. Some how, Beth just knew she had found Charlie's widow.

Banjo Morgan was thirty-eight years old, and tall and stout like Charlie Nightlinger. For all his years, he had never known his father. With his mother following his dad's trail, they wound up in Montana where the search had stopped. Through several years of stability, full-time work, and a place to call home, his interest in finding his dad had dissipated.

Haciola also gave up for the same reasons, when she found a home and employment for both herself and Banjo. Nightlinger might have had his horse shod here in Montana by Banjo without ever having known it. Banjo would not have recognized Charlie either.

They never realized how close they were to finding Charlie roaming the Montana territory as a trail cook. The revelation was about to become fact for Haciola, who watched, as Beth was about to talk with her son.

As they entered the blacksmith shop, a heavy Swede greeted them. He was a friendly man in his fifties and built like an ox. In the chill of the day, he wore no shirt, showing off his muscles, which bulged from the ironwork he did daily.

"Ma,am," he said "may I be of service to ya?"

"Yes," Beth replied. "We came to see your helper."

"Young Banjo?" the Swede asked. "What ye be wantin' with him, may I ask?"

"This is his mother."

"Yes, ma'am. I know Haciola," he countered. Then he said quite abruptly, "Banjo's real busy right now."

Looking around at the work, Beth could readily see that Banjo had work that had to be done. Apologetically, she said, "It will only take a moment."

"A moment he ain't got," came the Swede's reply.

Beth took a silver dollar from her purse and handed it to him. "Ten minutes at the most."

Taking the coin, he backed away, allowing Haciola to enter.

"Miss Beth," Haciola said proudly, "this be my son, Banjo."

Beth's eyes took their time to focus on Banjo's build and good looks. She didn't know that Nightlinger even had a son, let alone that this could possibly be his only heir, seeing he never married Haciola.

"I'm pleased to meet you, Banjo," Beth said, keeping her gloved hand to herself as it wasn't customary for a white lady to shake hands with a Negro.

"Yes, ma'am, Miss Beth," Banjo replied, realizing that he was the center of attention. "This here's my boss, Mr. Swenson."

"Mr. Swenson," Beth said. They both eyed the other cautiously.

Then she asked, "Banjo, what do you know about your father?"

"I have no pa," Banjo quickly replied without giving it a second thought.

"I know how you must feel, but we all have fathers, like it or not," Beth replied. "I think we might have found yours."

"Why?" was his only response as he began to return to his work.

Beth stopped him and eyed the Swede again. "I've got you for another nine minutes, Banjo. Can we talk now, here, or after work?"

"I have no time to talk," Banjo said.

"Then we talk here," Beth suggested and sat down on a wooden bench nearby.

After looking for another place to sit and not finding it, Haciola motioned that she would stand. It was apparent that smithies had little to sit on.

"Tell me what you know about your pa, Banjo," Beth repeated.

Banjo turned his back to Beth and walked to the opening in the doorway where the snow had begun drifting in. Although it was cold, the heat from the fire kept his body warm.

A bead of sweat rolled down his forehead, not from the heat, but from being made to feel uncomfortable by Beth's questions.

"I know he left me and Ma when I wasn't eben been born yet. He went north, and Ma followed a carryin' me. With the help of some friends, she run away."

"That must have been pretty rough," Beth said, watching Banjo as he shrugged his shoulders and turned his head away.

"What did your pa do for a living?" she asked.

"Ma knows."

"He was a cook," Haciola answered. "He loved to cook. He cooked on the farm. Showed me how to bake ham and pies and all kinds a good stuff. I told him I didn't like cookin'. He said he liked me anyhow. He'd cook and I'd sew. That's how we got along with the white folks. We was house Negroes." Then her face blanched.

"Haciola?" Beth asked. "What's the matter?"

"They turned on me when they found out my Charlie left. I told them we were not married. They didn't believe me. And then when they found out I was carrying Banjo, they beat me for lyin'. That be why I run away, Miss Beth."

"How awful," Beth shuttered. "They beat you for being pregnant?" Beth knew full well what Haciola was talking about, because she saw slavery in the raw in Virginia and witnessed the same type of punishments meted out by slave owners. She had to grit her teeth to keep from letting on as she continued to listen to Haciola's story.

"They wouldn't allow us to marry, Miss Beth," Haciola responded sadly. "They didn't want no mothers a carryin' childrun, even tho' I was a house nigger. Afraid I'd run away with him and they'd be out two Niggers."

"What makes ya'll think you found him?" Banjo asked. "Where he be at right now?"

"First, we've got to make sure it's your pa, Banjo," Beth cautioned. She looked at Haciola and then back at Banjo, knowing the answer she wanted might not be the right one. She asked it anyway.

"Is your real name Banjo Nightlinger?"

Banjo turned and looked at his mother. Her face showed no reaction to the question. He knew he had to answer it on his own.

"No, ma'am," he said, biting his lips and sticking his long hard fingers into the pockets of his overalls. "I be Banjo Morgan."

Beth looked over at Haciola whose face again showed no reaction.

Beth stood there looking at the two of them, and finally gave up hope. She watched Banjo resume his task of firing the coals. Then as she turned to Haciola and motioned to leave, Banjo yelled out, "I be a bastard!"

Beth stopped and looked back. Quickly she looked into Haciola's face that began to wrinkle up as tears came to her eyes. Beth knew she was close to the answer for which she was diligently searching. Banjo Morgan could very well be Charlie Nightlinger's son. She was sure of it, but she still had to have evidence to prove it.

The two women climbed into the carriage and drove away to Dorothy's house. Haciola said nothing, but the tears in her eyes and the frown on her forehead bore out the truth.

Early the next day, Sheriff Mallory came to her office and knocked on the door. Beth had just gotten up and wrapped her housecoat around her. When she saw who it was through the window, she yelled out, "Just a minute, Sheriff."

She went back to her bedroom and slipped into a day dress lined with lace around her cuffs. She walked back through her office to receive her visitor while brushing her hair.

"Come on in, Sheriff."

"Mornin', Miss Paterson," he said taking off his Stetson as he entered. "Thank you."

"I suppose you've found something for me," Beth said as she turned up the lantern on her desk to brighten up the dimly lit room.

"I received a wire from the marshal's office in Helena about Nightlinger."

"And?"

"Seems he never claimed a wife or any children."

"That's it?"

"Yes'm."

"Very well, Sheriff." She walked over to the door and showed him out. "Thank you."

"Sorry, miss." As he walked out backwards, he almost tripped over the tramway because his eyes were staring on Beth's beauty as the morning sun shown through her hair.

She closed the door and sat down in her leather chair behind her desk. "If only I had a photo of Charlie Nightlinger to see any likeness," she pondered. Then the thought hit her, and she said aloud, "Some of the cowboys on the ranch who knew Nightlinger would know whether or not Banjo looked like him."

CHAPTER 7

BACK TO THE DOUBLE R

On the third day of her return to Virginia City, Beth met with Judge Leonard W. Stanford, who found just cause to issue an injunction against Matt. He had already heard about the incident through the town gossip, so was pretty much prepared for Beth. It was an interesting story, and one that he wanted Beth to pursue to see what the outcome would be.

Beth picked up her evening clothes that she had left at Dorothy's house and shared morning tea with her friend.

"I am so pleased that you're making such wonderful progress with your, shall we call them, clients?" Dorothy finished her tea. Before she could pour a second cup for Beth or herself, Haciola and Banjo walked up to the porch with their sacks and waited outside.

"Your passengers seem to be ready," Dorothy said with a smile, putting her tea down on the table. "Roger has our covered carriage ready for you to take back to wherever."

"The Double R," Beth answered politely. "Dorothy, how can I say 'thank you' for all the wonderful help you've been to me?"

"Take it and enjoy the ride, and say no more about it."

She stepped to the porch where Roger met her. Willie had brought the carriage around pulled by the same fine quarter horses as before, now tacked and ready to take them to the ranch.

"M'lady, your carriage awaits," Roger said with a Gaelic tone in his voice. "I've had them clean it up so it doesn't smell any."

"Thank you, Roger," Beth replied stepping up into the carriage.

Banjo met his mother and helped her into the carriage as well. She joined Beth in the back seat.

Beth watched as Banjo picked up some steel runners and packed them in the back with their baggage. "What are those?"

"Runners, Miss Beth." Banjo walked back and ran his fingers across the steel. "In case we run into too much snow on the way, we can take the wheels off and make this into a sleigh."

"Oh," was all Beth could reply.

"It's a pair, front and back. Makes for easy steerin' that way, ma'am."

"You've got yourself a good man in Banjo," Roger said, untying the lines and handing them to Banjo. "Being a smitty has its virtues."

After saying her goodbyes, Beth gave the nod for Banjo to whip the horses in the direction of the Double R spread. And so they were, Beth and Haciola, settling in the back seat with their blankets across their laps, and Banjo, clothed in a jacket, which he kept open, and wearing an old wide-brim hat that had seen better days.

It was early evening on the third day's journey when Banjo brought the buggy around the bend approaching the ranch. The buggy had an appearance of a lower buggy, as it was low to the ground. The wooden wheels were propped and sticking up in the back, because, sure enough, he had replaced them with the runners.

The skies had blanketed the land with another two inches of snow, and the horses showed some weariness from pulling the sleigh through it.

Danny was on his horse on a nearby hill when he caught a glimpse of the odd looking sleigh with spoked wheels sticking out the back. Curious as to taking a better look at the sleigh, he rode up to them and escorted them to the ranch.

"Evenin', ma'am. Horses look like they could stand a rubdown."

"Evening, Danny," Beth returned. "It's been a long ride."

"That sure is a fancy sleigh, if I might say so, ma'am. Ain't seen one like that in these here parts."

"Made it m'self," Banjo said with a half smile, holding lightly to the lines to bring the horses to a steady walk.

All of a sudden Danny's jaw dropped as he looked and then stared at Banjo. "Old Lady!"

His sudden calling out startled Beth for a moment, and then she realized Danny had recognized something familiar about Banjo.. "Does he resemble Charlie Nightlinger, Danny?"

"Yes, ma'am," Danny replied. "Younger. But, yes, ma'am. He sure do look like him."

Although Haciola's eyes widened at the news, she kept a calm countenance about her. She had not seen nor heard from Nightlinger since he left her. Now she was coming close to his presence again, buried in the cold, snow-covered ground. Banjo moved his jaw in anticipation of saying something, but remained silent. Instead, he felt a sense of loss about him never having known or seen his father, and soon he would be standing over his grave.

"Will you show Banjo where to put the sleigh and horses?"

"Yes, ma'am." Danny rode ahead of the sleigh as he led Banjo to the barn then slid down from his saddle. He took ahold of the halter, guided the sleigh to a slow stop, and tied the lines to the hitching post.

"Please allow me." He took Beth's hand and helped her from the buggy, while Haciola helped herself down.

Banjo alit from the sleigh and, with Danny's help, led the team into the barn.

"Quick, Danny," Beth said excitedly, "get the sleigh inside the barn."

Once inside the barn, Danny shut the door quickly while Banjo removed the harness from the horses.

"This is Haciola Morgan, Danny, and her son, Banjo." Beth introduced the pair to Danny and stood still, waiting for a reaction from Danny as he saw that they were Negroes. He looked surprised, but showed more interest in the sleigh.

"Mrs. Morgan. Banjo. Right pleased to meet you both."

"Pleased to meet you, too, Mr. Danny," Haciola said.

"I'll explain later," Beth said.

"Matt's inside," Danny continued, "if that's who you have a mind to see."

"That's who I have a mind to see."

Beth cracked the door a bit and looked over at the cemetery plot. Although lit up by the moon, she still couldn't make out any of its details.

"Nightlinger's still there," Danny replied with a half-smile.

"How'd you do it?"

"Wasn't easy. Got Matt liquored up and convinced him that it wasn't easy digging hard, cold ground, and that we should wait 'til the spring thaw. He agreed, and that's all there was to it."

"Well, I'm back. Do me a big favor, Danny, and take Haciola and Banjo and hide them until I have time to introduce them to our boss."

"Hide them where?" Danny whispered loudly, walking one of the horses into an empty stall.

"Clear some men out of the end bunk house. That should do it. Tell them to sleep in the barn."

Beth slipped through the crack in the door, walked over to the house, stepped onto the porch and walked in, hoping that Matt hadn't seen anything.

The wranglers had just finished their chores for the day and were getting ready for dinner when they had paused to watch her arrive. Danny caught a couple of the wranglers outside watching what was going on. It wasn't easy, but once a couple of them understood, the word spread around the bunkhouse what had happened. It seemed they were quite interested in the sleigh and the fact that they were Negroes didn't seem to play on their mind.

However, the noise that they made did stir up Matt in the ranch house.

Beth stepped inside the front room of the ranch house expecting to meet Matt head on. Instead, the room was empty. She removed her heavy coat and Stetson, and walked slowly and cautiously into the kitchen where she caught Matt in his union suit and jacket, sipping a cup of coffee from his tin cup and staring out the window.

Seeing her, he slipped behind the potbelly stove and yelled out, "The least ya coulda done was announce yourself. Any decent lady woulda done that."

"Why, Matt Jorgensen, you're blushing."

"Nah. Hot from this here stove," he growled making certain that he was well hidden. "Whatcha come back for this time a night? And where ya been?"

"Virginia City."

"What for?"

"To see my old friend Leonard."

"Leonard? You know somebody named Leonard?" he asked.

"Why don't you go put some pants on while I fix myself a cup of coffee? I'll hide my eyes."

Matt slid out from behind the stove and walked backwards into his bedroom a few feet away. From inside he said, "You still didn't answer my question. Leonard who?"

Pouring herself a cup of coffee from the big tin coffee pot, she answered, "Leonard W. Stanford. You remember?"

Pulling up his galluses, he returned to the kitchen, absent his jacket, and blatantly remarked, "Judge Stanford? That old coot?"

"That old coot."

"Whatcha go see him fer, Beth?"

Removing a piece of paper from her jacket pocket, she held it out for him to see. "Oh, just for a piece of paper."

"Give it here, Beth," he told her, grabbing the paper from her hand. Glancing at it quickly, he was able to make out the word

Injunction, printed in bold letters, and then noticed his name further down. "An injunction? For what?"

"As the attorney for the estate of one Mrs. Annie Andersen, I have an injunction against you, one Mr. Matt Jorgensen."

"Attorney for the estate? May I remind you, Miss Paterson, that I am the owner of this ranch, this *estate,* as you call it? Have you forgotten that?"

"Mr. Jorgensen, if you will read the fine print in your inheritance deed written by one Mrs. Annie Andersen, you will see that I am to remain with the estate, if necessary, having the power of attorney for said estate until all legal matters are settled and cleared of any taint for a period of one year from the date that you received it, and sir, your changing of property on that hillside will have tainted your inheritance." She untied the stampede strings and removed her hat, placing it on the counter. Then she whipped around and stared Matt down. "And, sir, you are to stay away from the grave of one Mr. Charlie Nightlinger until the court says you have a legal right to do so." Beth threw her coffee into the sink then turned to walk out. Stopping at the doorway, she added, "If that ever happens."

"And when is that, Miss Attorney?" Matt clamored, throwing the writ of injunction on the table.

"When the judge deems you capable, Mr. Jorgensen. You have a meeting with him when he goes into Bozeman in a week or you may visit him at his office in Virginia City. Seeing as how the snow is piling up between here and Virginia City, I would suggest waiting until he arrives in Bozeman." She walked out the door, but before slamming it, said, "Good night, Mr. Jorgensen."

"I'll be damned," Matt remarked to himself. He walked over to the door, opened it and began to yell, only to find Beth standing just outside the door. "And where do . . ." He stopped himself from yelling, softened his voice and finished, asking, "And where do you intend to sleep tonight?"

Seeing it was too late to visit with her friend, Jean Wrisley, Beth realized she would be spending the night there. Quickly, she suggested, "You can sleep in the bunkhouse, and I'll take my old bedroom here. Good night, Mr. Jorgensen." She returned to the ranch house again, and, as she began to shut the door, turned and asked, "Want your jacket and boots?"

Matt stood there shirtless and bootless and answered her in a dumbfounded manner, looking straight at her, "No, Attorney Paterson. No, ma'am."

She picked them up, laid them on the porch and shut the door. Matt came back, picked them up and hobbled over the cold and snow-covered stones to the guesthouse. The wranglers stood outside and looked with glee at their boss who had been broken once more by the lady attorney from Virginia.

CHAPTER 8

MATT RIDES TOWARD TOWN

T he snow fell lightly for the next few days, and Matt shied away from Beth as much as possible. His work with the wranglers was steady, and he began to build up his strength, which he had lacked since he visited Bozeman for a drunk.

Early morning, Matt rounded up the wranglers for a meeting of minds. Nothing had been spoken about Charlie Nightlinger all that week. Matt made sure the wranglers had their plates in-hand and were chowing down real good before he began talking to them, and then he let them have it, full barrel.

"The snow's come. Russ and Danny will be riding herd on you men pretty good now to keep our cows and horses alive. Plenty of hay and barley. Pick out the dogies and bring them to the corral along with their mothers."

Russ brought out Skeeter, saddled and ready for a ride.

"I've gotta go to town," Matt continued. "Be gone two, three days at the most. When I get back, I 'spect we'll be doin' some serious diggin'. Not that I like it much, but I figger it has to be done. If any of you has any apprehensions about this, speak up now, 'cause I ain't one to make apologies later."

As Matt figured, one of the wranglers spoke up. "What do you have agin' Negroes, Matt?"

"Niggers!" he corrected the man in his southern discomfort. "Don't like 'em." Standing with his hands in his hip pockets, he asked, "Anyone else?"

Another spoke up, "How come?"

"Yeah, how come?" another one echoed. "You're in the North, now, Reb. War's over."

That was all that had to be said that morning. Matt walked over to the wrangler who called him a reb. Never one for many words, he drew his fist back and let it fly. The wrangler never saw the earth coming up to meet him. When he got up, Matt told him, "Draw your pay from Russ, and get out."

The wrangler, who had questioned Matt first, stepped forward and said, "I asked the question, Matt. It's not fair to fire him because of me."

"You're right," Matt responded. "You're fired, too. Get out!"

Danny stepped up to Matt in their defense. "Matt, these are good men. You're not thinking straight."

"I don't need a lecture from you, Danny. As I said before, anyone here doesn't like what I'm doing, has the right to move on."

"That include me, Matt?" Danny asked. His face quivered, but he stood firm, waiting for Matt's answer. He also watched Russ' look from the corner of his eye—something he had trained himself to do in a gunfight—and he could tell Russ wasn't having any of this either.

Russ took Skeeter to the corral post and tied him up, then began to walk away with the other men.

"Do what you have to do, Danny," Matt suggested. "Goes for you, too, Russ."

"Glad you put it that way, boss," Russ said, stopping to see what was going to happen next. "Makes it easier."

Matt stood still, waiting for Danny to move, but Danny stood ground, waiting for Matt's answer. Matt began to feel his father's presence because Wil had thrown this type of attitude at him ever since he was born. "You don't like it, son, get out!" he remembered his dad saying time after time. "You think I'm too tough on ya, try workin' fer someone else. They'll damn sure make a man outta ya. But as long as you stay on my ranch, you'll do what I want, when I want, and how I want! Unnerstand?"

Still, he knew he had to stand firm just like his dad would have done. He looked steadily at Danny, hesitated only slightly, then finally said, "You, too, Danny."

Danny pivoted, doubled his fist and plunged it into Matt's stomach.

Matt had preconditioned his stomach muscles to receive the punch, but he still fell backwards. He caught himself from falling by placing his hand on the ground, twisted his body, stood up, and returned his clinched fist hard to Danny's jaw. Danny went crashing into Russ, who quickly turned to assist him.

Russ eased Danny's body to the ground, then came back up, bringing his left fist across Matt's face, sending him sprawling backwards.

Matt clumsily regained his balance, stood erect, but saw the power of Russ' right fist as it followed suit and slammed into his face again. This time, Matt went down for the count.

A rifle shot filled the air and caused the men to pay attention. They looked over and saw Beth standing on the porch with the smoking rifle.

"He hasn't eaten for two or three days," Danny yelled out. "Been drinkin' most of the time you were gone. Else he could have taken all of us. I guess I took advantage of that, Miss Paterson. But I can't see him destroy himself and this ranch all because of Nightlinger."

"Why, Danny?" Beth asked, walking over to the men.

"The war. The South," Danny said, sitting-up and rubbing his jaw. "All of that, I suppose. It's a different world in Texas than it is here, Beth. I saw it when I went after him. The Negroes are still treated poorly."

"No worse than here," Beth replied.

"Much worse, Beth!" Danny said as he stumbled to his feet. "What's gonna happen? I mean, Matt actin' like this. Crazy like."

"Get back to work, gentlemen. None of you are fired. I'll take care of him."

Out of respect for Beth in her official capacity as an attorney, the men obeyed her by returning to their chores.

Seeing the snow coming down from the mountains, Russ knew what had to be done and began riding ramrod on them.

Danny walked over to his horse and climbed aboard. He, Russ, and rest of the men rode into the mountains after the cattle and horses.

When Matt regained consciousness, he raised himself up and looked at Beth. "I don't know law, Miss Lawyer, but I know you're pushin' your authority around a little too much. Injunction or whatever, I'm still boss around here, and I will *not* have that nigger in my family plot."

Beth walked over and stood beside him, wanting to share some compassion. She sensed a young Matt trying to climb out of his pa's boots. She surmised the trauma that was happening inside Matt, and she succumbed to his moody side.

"So, Mister Jorgensen," she said, "you didn't eat all the time I was gone because you missed me?"

"I ate," Matt replied. Then he looked pitifully at her and said, "Some."

She moved behind him and put her arms around him to help him up.

"Powerful punch that kid had. Knocked the hell out of me."

"Lucky punch, you mean. You were too weak to defend yourself."

"Hell," Matt rebutted, "I got my strength back, and then some." He rubbed his jaw and looked in the direction Danny and Russ were riding. "Didn't expect it from Danny, though. Good man."

She looked into his beaten-up face and said, "They're all good men, Matt. Every mother-loving one of them. They know you're upset."

Matt wrinkled up his nose and wiped some dirt off his chin with his leather glove. He looked cockeyed at Beth and said, "I know it."

"Are you going to apologize to them?"

"Me? Hell, no!" He walked over to Skeeter.

She followed and stood beside him with her hands on her hips. "Matt Jorgensen, you are one stubborn son-of-a-buck!"

He brought her into his arms and said, "Why, Mary Beth. I've never heard you swear before."

"I'll say it again. You're a rotten son-of-a-buck!"

He drew her against him and kissed her lips, then winced from the pain he felt in his jaw from Russ' punch.

After rubbing Beth's hair into a mess, he climbed aboard Skeeter. "But I'm *your* rotten son-of-a-buck! I'll do better than that when I get back."

"Where are you going?"

"Tell 'em what you have to tell 'em to keep 'em here," he continued. "I'm goin' to pay a visit on our ol' friend Leonard." With a nod of his head, he pulled the brim of his Stetson down and turned to ride towards Bozeman.

"What do you mean, Mr. Jorgensen?" Beth yelled at him. "I have an injunction against you."

"Well, it's a piece of paper, and you know what you can do with that, Lawyer Paterson," Matt yelled back.

"But, Matt," she said, trying to pierce the wind with her voice.

She stood watching Matt ride down the road, knowing in her heart that he was the only man who could make her feel the way she felt at that moment, confused, and full of love.

From a hillside, Russ and Danny watched the two and smiled. Somehow, things would work out all right. They just knew it. And, with that, the snow began to fall again.

CHAPTER 9

TWO BAD MEN AGAINST
ONE DRUNKEN COWBOY

T he thirty-four mile trip to town seemed longer than usual. Even though the moon was full, the weather conditions and the darkness of the night didn't make it any easier.

Matt made the trip without incident, only to find that the town was closed. He chose a hotel and bedded down for the night.

Having a good sleep would seem to some to clear a man's head of bad thoughts, but with Matt, it seemed to make matters worse. The Red Garter was open by mid-day and Matt found it to his liking. One drink loosened him up to wanting to talk to someone, and the only person in the saloon at this time of day was the bartender, so Matt elected him to hear what he had on his mind.

"Your name Joe?" Matt asked politely, wanting company.

"No, it's Ernie," the bartender answered, pouring Matt his second drink. "Ernest to some, but this early in the morning, just call me, Ernie."

Matt introduced himself as the new owner of the Double R Ranch.

"I know you, Matt," Ernie remarked politely. "Hell, ever'one knows who you are. Why, you're the one who almost got himself hung last month 'cause of that bank robbery back twenty-some years ago."

"Yeah. That's me, Ernie."

"You got that fella, Poker Face, with three, maybe four shots from your Colt, right together between the eyes. That was mighty good shootin', Matt. Never seen nothin' like it. Probably never will agin, I reckon."

"One between the eyes," Matt said, wanting desperately to talk to Ernie. But the more he tried, the harder it was to get a word in edgewise because Ernie could sure talk fast.

"No need to go making it any bigger than it was." Matt was finally able to say.

"Yes sir, I seed the whole damn thing. Tell me somethin', Matt. You are the Andersen boy, ain't cha? I know. I know. It's none of my business. But, if I were willin' to wager on it with anyone in town, I'd say you were. Am I right?"

"Ernie, my name is Matt Jorgensen, and I come from Waco, Texas. I was just a good friend to Annie, and let's leave it at that. Okay?"

"I know who you are, Matt," Ernie quipped real fast leaning on the bar. "Sure, sure. Anything you say. 'Nother drink?"

"Ernie, could I ask you a question?"

Ernie walked over to the table and poured a third shot of whiskey for Matt. "Shoot. Whatcha wanna know?"

"How do you stand on niggers?"

Ernie was taken aback a little and then straightened up and answered Matt as if he wanted to keep him for an all-day customer. "Niggers? Ain't got nothin' agin' 'em. But they're niggers, and they ought to be kept in their place. Why?"

"You call them niggers, too?"

"Sure. Didn't you? Don't ever'body?"

"Nope. A lawyer friend of mine calls 'em Negroes."

"Well, Matt, I suppose they are called that. They're black people, but black people here in my saloon are still called niggers."

Matt took his fourth drink and when he was through, reached over and pulled on Ernie's shirt to bring him closer to him, "I don't like people callin' 'em niggers. I don't like you callin' 'em niggers. And I sure as hell don't like me callin' 'em niggers." He let go of his shirt. "What's wrong with me, Ernie?"

Ernie felt more at ease when Matt released his grip on his shirt. He stepped back and began to walk away.

"I'm sorry, Ernie," Matt apologized. He grabbed the bottle of whiskey Ernie had been pouring from and took it to another table.

It wasn't long before two cowboys walked in and stood at the bar. After ordering their drinks, they sashayed over to Matt's table and one of them asked, "Want company, cowboy?"

"Sit down," Matt answered. He looked up and saw a red-bearded cowboy somewhere in his late twenties, tall and lanky and real ugly. The other one looked about ten years older, medium build with a patch over one eye, fat, with his shirt opened at the belly. They were Biggun and One Eye. Matt didn't know they were the two men who escaped his wrath on the ridge in the shootout. Neither did anyone else in town.

"Join me," Matt said, offering the bottle.

Biggun said in a kind gesture, "Looks like you've got a good start for a binge. Got troubles?"

"Why? Am I givin' an impression like that?" Matt answered, pouring himself another drink.

"It takes one to know one," Biggun said. "I've been there, and it looks like you're headed there mighty early."

"Name's One Eye, from Oregon way," the short man said by way of introduction.

"Just call me Biggun, cause of my size," the other one offered.

"I'm Matt Jorgensen. Double R Ranch."

The cowboys' stood frozen with their eyes opened wide as they stared down at Matt. They looked at one another, then sat down. Biggun pushed back his hat and asked, "Not the cowpoke who ambushed those men on the Bozeman Trail t'other day?"

"Weren't no ambush."

"Heard about it. Wondered whether it was true or not."

"Heard you were real fast with a gun," One Eye ventured. "Faster'n Wyatt Earp?"

"Wouldn't know. Never met him."

"I saw him in Tombstone. Saw Wild Bill onest, too. They were awfully fast."

"That why you're drinkin' alone,?" Biggun asked, swigging his first drink down. "No friends. No one to drink with?" He looked around the empty saloon and only saw a nervous bartender eyeing the shotgun he kept under the counter.

"I think you're a liar!" Biggun challenged Matt with his hand shaking over his gun grip. "You killed my only brothers in cold blood."

"You're the two that escaped?"

One Eye took a swig of whiskey and asked, "Think you can beat Biggun here?"

"Nope," Matt replied.

"Now, he's a sensible man, Biggun," One Eye said, leaning over the table and pouring Matt a drink, and then one for himself, too.

"Gettin' me liquored up ain't gonna prove it either, One Eye," Matt said menacingly.

"Stop it, One Eye," Biggun interrupted. "Can'tcha see he's drunk, and too yeller to draw." His hand went lazily to his gun grip. "Hell, I could shoot him right now before he'd clear his holster. Nice and easy like." His hand pulled out his .44 and just cleared leather as Matt stood up, slammed his chair away from the table, and whipped his .45 from its holster. Before Biggun could cock the trigger, Matt brought the barrel of his .45 across Biggun's face. While Biggun fell to the table, Matt turned and laid the butt of his gun hard against One Eye's head, slamming him to the floor.

Looking at the men as they fell, Matt answered One Eye's question with his Colt still pointed at them. "I know I can." That said, he picked up their pistols, and with his bottle in hand, went to another table.

Ernie watched but, out of fear, remained silent.

Slowly the men regained their senses and slid back into their chairs, still rubbing their wounds.

"You men all right?" Ernie asked.

"Hell no!" One Eye answered, wiping the blood from the top of his head with his dirty bandanna. "You jest gonna stand there? Where the hell's the sheriff?"

"What for?" Ernie asked. "You men started it. And if you're who he says you are, I wouldn't be callin' for any sheriff right about now."

Biggun spit a tooth out, swished some whiskey in his mouth to deaden the pain, then swallowed it. His jaw had swollen up like a honeydew melon.

"That wasn't fair, mister." Biggun had a hard time speaking while rubbing his jaw. "Hittin' with the gun like that."

"I don't have time to play fair," Matt answered, his hand gripped tight around the bottle as he poured himself another drink. "You want a fight, fight! Don't jest stand there talkin' about it."

Sheriff Saunders cautiously walked in with his two .45s drawn. He saw the beaten men and asked Ernie what happened.

"Two ugly cayutes started a fight with Matt and got beat up. 'At's all."

"Mornin', Bill," Matt greeted him from his table without getting up.

"Mornin', Matt." He sauntered over to the table, pulled out a chair and placed his boot on it while looking across at the seemingly depressed cowboy.

"Arrest him, sheriff," Biggun yelled, holding his bandanna to his injured face. "He murdered my brothers."

"Your name Biggun?"

Biggun sensed he was talking to the wrong person and looked away. "You gonna arrest him or not?"

"Stay where you are, Biggun. You, too, Fats." Sheriff Bill held his .45s on the two ugly killers as his young deputy rushed into the saloon. He was a young man in his early twenties, tall and slim with straight black hair. He had a shotgun in one hand and a .45 in the other.

"What's goin' on, sheriff?" the deputy asked as he quickly sized up the situation.

"Help me take 'em over to the jail, Norm," Bill ordered. "If they make any funny moves, shoot 'em. They're the killers who've been terrorizing the territory."

He then turned back to Matt and said, "Looks to me like you got yourself a full-house. Be right back. Don't go anywhere."

Matt smiled and took another drink as the sheriff and his deputy escorted the two men down the street to the jail. He sat in the silence of the saloon, gazing into his glass. Then he heard Biggun grunt loudly, and the sound of bodies falling, followed by two quick blasts from a .45. Matt got up from his table and tore through the saloon doors with his Colt drawn.

When he cleared the doors, he looked down the street and saw Biggun on top of Norm. Bill was on his knees with his .45 smoking.

"Make a move, and you're dead!" Matt yelled, his .45 aimed at Biggun. "What happened, Bill?"

"He shoved me into Norm." Bill rose to his feet. "The other one got away."

Norm pushed his shotgun into Biggun's midsection. "Git up, mister!"

"I'll walk with you to the jail," Matt said, his pistol aimed at Biggun's back. "This guy's like a rhino."

It took the three men to get Biggun into the cell, which he dwarfed with his huge body. Grunting, he paced back and forth. "I'm gonna kill ya, mistah," he said vehemently, shaking the dirt off his face and hair.

"Quit dirtying up the place," Norm ordered him, throwing the keys into a desk drawer.

The cell was a distance removed from the front office, separated by a set of locked barred doors. He could be heard, but not seen. A back door was also barred and locked. Two empty cells adjoined his.

"Like I said, looks to me like you got yourself a full house." Bill sat down behind his desk. "Almost. The other fella got away. When we catch up with him, and we will, I'll see you get the rest of the reward money."

"Too early for a drink?" Matt asked, motioning towards the saloon.

"You come to talk or you got business?"

"I'm in town to get drunk, Bill. Those two yahoos thought they'd have fun with me in that condition." Then he winked at Bill. "That's when I'm at my best. Just enough drink to settle the nerves and clear the head. Had they waited around for a coupla more drinks, they mighta had me."

Norm looked around the office before hanging up the shotgun, then excused himself. "I'll take a walk around town and see if I can find One Eye." He looked at Biggun once more, then at Matt. He nodded his head at the sheriff, then walked out into the street.

"You all right, Matt?" Bill asked.

"Madder'n hell, Bill," Matt answered.

"At me?"

"I'm not mad at you anymore, if you're talking about Beth."

"I'll take her any way I can, Matt," Bill remarked. "You know that."

"Hell, you can have her."

Bill's eyes widened at the thought. "Why?"

"She's tryin' to play lawyer with me."

"About what?"

"Well, I've got no hooks on her. Not now, leastwise."

Bill pulled out a drawer and came up with a bottle of whiskey and two glasses. He poured a glass for Matt and set it down in front of him, and then poured himself a glass.

Matt looked at Bill, then said with a smile, "I thought it was too early to drink."

He watched Bill take the glass, glare back at him, and then swallow it down. "After gettin' Biggun in jail, and now hearin' the good news about Beth, I figure it's time to have a drink." He watched Matt gulp his drink down before he poured him another. "So, what's up?"

"Jest tryin' to find out how one should feel about niggers. That's all."

"Niggers!" Bill exclaimed almost laughingly. "Is that what that ruckus is all about?"

"Nope," Matt answered, rubbing his knuckles. "Jest a down and dirty fight."

"Then, what's your beef about niggers?" Bill asked.

"You know as well as me, Bill," Matt said drunkenly. "I got a nigger buried on my lot next to my ma and I aims to do somethin' about it."

"You mean Charlie Nightlinger?" Bill asked. "Well, seems to me, you do have a problem. Whacha aimin' to do about it?"

"I'm aimin' to have him dug up and buried somewhere else."

"Why?"

"Cause he's a damn nigger!"

"Well, legally, that's your choice. Frankly, if it was me, I'd leave him be. He was a nice man."

"Well, I ain't you," Matt said belligerently, pouring Bill another glass of whiskey. "It's my problem. Drink up." Realizing he was getting tipsier with each passing drink, he asked matter-of-factly, "So, why shouldn't I have the right to get him off my property? It's my damn property. Right?" he muttered to himself. Then, "Injunction!" He blurted, swallowing more whiskey.

"What, Matt?" Bill asked.

"Injunction. Said she's got an injunction."

"Well, then you'll have to leave him rest," Bill said, removing his hat off and slapping it on the side of the empty chair beside him.

"Bill. What do the word 'taint' mean?"

"Taint?" Bill repeated. "Like, tainted evidence?"

"Yeah," Matt answered. "Tainted evidence. Means someone tampered with it, huh?"

"That's my guess." Bill said. "Why?"

"That's her reason behind gettin' an injunction. She said that Annie Andersen gave her the power of attorney over the estate if I tainted it. Then she said that I tainted it by wanting to remove that nigger's body from my property."

"Well, Matt," Bill reflected, "like I was sayin', it kinda looks like she's right. That could be reason enough, I reckon." Then he smiled and said, "So, she's got an injunction agin' ya."

Bill took a swig of whiskey and smirked a little behind his glass. He felt this was the most opportune time for him to get Beth away from Matt. He rose, picked up his hat, turned, and said, "Well, then it becomes my job to keep you from doin' anythin'

86

with Nightlinger. Want me to ride out and have a talk with her? Not that it'll do any good." Bill said, trying to hide his excitement.

"Not on your best day, Bill." Matt rose and walked to the door with him. "Not that she's my girl or anythin', but jest to keep things straight between you and me. Know what I mean?"

"Hell, Matt," Bill remarked, throwing his hat on his head, "nobody knows what you mean half the time," then walked out.

He strutted over to his mare, which was hitched to the rail, mounted her and, giving Matt a smile, rode out. He knew he had an opportunity with Beth, and he was not about to throw it away. Of course, he was hoping his knowing about the injunction would be reason enough for Beth to let him visit with her, officially.

Matt stood on the boardwalk and pondered his next move of the day. It was past noon, and he had already been in a fight and in an argument with the sheriff. Now it was time for him to find and meet with Judge Leonard W. Stanford.

CHAPTER 10

MATT MEETS THE JUDGE

Matt looked through the window of the Baltimore Hotel and then walked on by. He looked at the Baxter across the street, shook his head, and then continued to the Bozeman Hotel at the end of the street. From the boardwalk, he saw the judge sitting at a table in the hotel's restaurant enjoying a meal. He walked in and sashayed up to his table. "May I join you?" he asked.

"Free country, mister," the judge replied. "Sit down, please."

Matt motioned for the waiter to bring him a cup of coffee.

"Not drinking today?" the judge asked Matt while cutting his steak.

"Just got through drinking for the day," Matt replied. "Want a clear mind when talkin' to you. You know what I mean, sir," Matt said in a somewhat slurred manner. "Coffee will do it."

The waiter brought a cup, received his money from Matt, and returned to the bar.

Matt began to drink his coffee without adding anything in it.

"I like sugar and plenty of milk in mine," the judge remarked, as though making small talk might put Matt at ease.

"Yes, sir," Matt replied, placing his hands around the coffee cup to steady himself. "My attorney said she filed an injunction with you agin me."

"Oh, Miss Paterson?" he asked.

"Yes, sir."

"Your attorney?"

"Yes, sir."

"Now, son, seems to me that one's attorney should not need to file an injunction against his, or in this case, her client," the judge said, while wiping his mouth with a calico napkin from time to time to remove the grease from his steak. "That is, unless there is just cause for an action such as this, which would be contrary to one's best interest." Then looking at Matt sternly, without blinking, he asked, "What would that be, son?"

Not quite understanding the judge as he talked in judicial jargon as if intentionally trying to confuse him, Matt asked, "What?"

"Good grief, son! What have you done to deserve your own attorney filing an injunction with a court of law to keep you from doing it any further?"

Matt straightened up and sat erect. After taking another swig of coffee, he said, "I want a person ejected from my property."

"Oh, is that all?" the judge asked, while he resumed eating. "Then, my son, the property being yours . . . It is yours, is it not?"

"Yes, sir," Matt replied. "You remember, just a month ago, you declared me to be the rightful heir . . ."

The judge cut Matt off, saying, "Yes, I remember. You are that flamboyant hero of the hour who came bursting into town with two guns blazing, and defied the rope of a hanging party, saved the marshal's life, and got a female lawyer to defend you, finally ending up with me deeding a sizable piece of property over to you. Am I correct?"

Matt tried his best to understand how such a learned man as the judge could take time to memorize all the cases that came before him in a courtroom and then spit out the best of them while eating. He nodded his head and then leaned forward to listen carefully to the judge as he drank his coffee down without stopping.

"Then, son, you have the right to evict anyone from your ranch as you see fit."

The waiter, a young Negro lad, seeing the judge's wine glass to be slightly full, accompanied him by filling it almost to the brim, slightly pouring it to flow down the inside of the glass without splashing, so as to retain its delicate flavor. He showed that he had proper learning and a gentleman's demeanor, even though he was a Negro. He left and then returned immediately with a pot of coffee and poured Matt a fresh cup.

Nodding approval to the waiter, the judge continued. "Is there anything else, son?"

Matt curiously watched the waiter for the longest while, puzzled by his mannerisms and politeness, then turned and eyed the judge slightly with a disapproving dissent to suggest that he did not like the term, son. Then he said, "Eject."

"Pardon, son?"

"Eject, sir," Matt said again, hoping to get the judge to understand the situation more correctly. "I want to eject him."

The judge kept eating, cutting his meat ever so slightly as if to be sure that he did not damage the taste. He waited for Matt to continue.

"Well, sir, am I to assume that I may take your answer to mean that I can eject this person from my property in the most discrete manner possible, and that this injunction would not prevent me from doing so?"

The judge kept eating. "Is he dead?"

Matt's eyes widened when he heard the judge ask this.

"Son, your attorney filed for the injunction in my office in Virginia City just a week ago. I know all about your wanting to excavate a body and haul it out of your family's burial grounds."

Matt looked relieved, yet at the same time perplexed, as he wondered whose side the judge was on. "Well, dammit, sir. I mean. If you knew, why did you play this cat-and-mouse game with me?"

"Kind of an interesting injunction," the judge answered. "Don't get too many of this kind. A judge's got to have some fun out of life." He kept eating and cutting, and cutting and eating, little bites at a time.

"Gets dull sitting alone, having little company. Besides, your case interests me."

"Yes, sir," Matt said. "Then is it all right?"

"Mr. Jorgensen," the judge said defiantly, "this is a matter for the court to decide. I merely issued a writ of injunction disallowing you to continue with your so called excavation, if you understand what I mean."

"Sir?" Matt pressed.

"You, sir, cannot dig up a body and discard it to the winds, or dump it in the river, or whatever you intend doing with it just because you want to, or because it's on your property. I don't care where you found it. That body is, or was, a person. He has rights, which you may or may not realize are viable. Those rights are passed on to his relatives, and they, not you, will decide what to do with Mr. Nightlinger. Acting in response to your attorney's request, I issued an injunction to stop you from proceeding any further without bringing it to my court's attention."

Matt again nodded his head. Then he said, "Even if the body is a nig- . . ."

The people sitting around them and especially the waiter stopped what they were doing and turned towards the pair, listening intently to their conversation.

"A Negro, Mr. Jorgensen?" the judge corrected him. Then turning to the eavesdroppers, he said, "This is a private matter. Go on with your business, and we'll continue with ours."

After he was certain the people heard and complied with his request, he continued. "Yes. Now, if it pleases you, I will set a court date in Virginia City for a month from now and we can settle this issue then."

Matt stood up and shouted, "A month from now?"

"Son, if you want me to help you, you've got to learn to control your temper. My calendar is full. I'll get to it when I get to it." He harrumphed and chewed his food slowly before adding, "I'll see if I can get it done earlier. But, don't count on it, son."

As a number of the other diners turned their heads to listen again to their conversation, Matt sat down and politely acquiesced to the judge's advice. After gaining his composure, he asked, "When, sir?"

"I need time to look into the matter, do some research in my law journals, and such. Talk with a colleague or two. I'll have my clerk mail you an invitation. Now, please, allow me to eat in peace."

Matt rose from the table and slapped his hat against his leg in obvious anger, put it back on his head, turned, left the hotel, and returned to the saloon.

The judge motioned for the waiter. When he came over, he gave him a silver dollar. "That's for the rude gentleman. You must'n mind him."

The waiter nodded approvingly, smiled, and pocketed the coin. "Thank, youse, sir," he said, and backed away almost coming in contact with an older couple, sitting at a nearby table, eavesdropping on the judge.

The judge downed his wine slowly without the slightest hint of being disturbed by Matt's angry departure or by the people talking about them. He was as indifferent to his surroundings as a pair of lovers in a haystack with the animals looking on.

CHAPTER 11

A SHORTCUT ALMOST BECOMES FATAL

That evening, after spending the balance of the day in the saloon, drinking, Matt left Bozeman, mounted his sorrel, Skeeter, and headed back towards his ranch taking the usual shortcut through the woods. The snow had built up heavily on the ground, and was still falling. He was in no shape to ride, but he knew Skeeter would not let him down. Matt left the reins loose in his hand, knowing Skeeter would find his way easier that way. He called all his horses, 'Skeeter'. He felt it was easier to remember their names that way in case one of them died or someone took one, or if he just happened to give one away like he did during the Civil War.

Skeeter knew the trail to the ranch like any smart steed, but the snow had covered the hair over his eyes, which began to blind him. Matt' thoughts were far and away from the trail and Skeeter's paying attention to it. He thought only about Charlie Nightlinger's body in his family's burial ground. Charlie had been the trail cook for Matt's father, Wil Andersen. Wil was murdered while on a trail drive to Belle Fourche. Charlie lasted only a year more and was buried on Wil's ranch. After Matt's mother passed away, he returned to claim inheritance to the ranch through Miss Paterson.

A long time lapsed before Skeeter felt his way along the deep-rutted trail, blinded by the snow. At times he slipped in the snow and found it difficult to keep his balance. He tried awfully hard, though. Skeeter was a good horse and faithful to his owner. But he tripped and this awakened Matt to the urgency of the matter. Before Matt could regain control, Skeeter fell and tumbled down a hill side throwing his master into a ravine.

Skeeter landed in the icy stream a distance from Matt but was safe from injury. He raised himself up on all fours and climbed back up the bank and waited for his master's voice. It never came. Matt missed the stream and rolled into the gully where his head hit a fallen tree branch and he gave way to unconsciousness.

Matt, hurt and weakened by the fall, woke and found the snow had covered him, making him look like part of the scenery. The cold began to settle in and he was aware of his predicament. He saw the low-lying branches of an old spruce nestled by a willow tree within easy reach. He rolled into it and covered himself with a clump of leaves and twigs sensing that the night cold and snow could freeze him to death. He lay still and heard the faint sound of Skeeter's hoofbeats as he trotted across the snowy trail and headed for his warm barn.

Matt looked at a small pool of blood in the snow and realized that he had been cut. The only place without protection, he thought, was his face or his head. He picked up his Stetson and found blood on the inside brim. Taking his bandana, he gently wiped around his forehead to find the cut. He found it, a lump that had stopped bleeding but caused him pain to touch it. He quickly cleaned it and packed it with snow.

Matt' thoughts now were about keeping warm. His thoughtful preparation of wearing two wool union suits under his California pants and shirt paid off. They were of thick wool and he wore wool-lined horsehide mittens because they bunched his fingers and kept them warmer. He sensed a feeling of relief to know that he had planned properly for any sudden turn in the weather as he pulled his wool scarf up around his throat and coat collar. He also knew that by covering the opening of the tree branches with other broken twigs, branches and the powder snow and leaves he could help preserve the heat in his body. His faith in Skeeter to bring help back kept him alive and alert. He tried desperately to stay awake, but his tired and weary body simply gave way to the darkness of unconsciousness once more.

The cold hand of death swept across the snow-covered ravine where Matt lay barely conscious, his eyes heavily coated from the freshly fallen snow. Even though, he could see the ghostly image of a young person looking down upon him. The image appeared to be that of a lovely lady in her twenties dressed in black clothing and a Stetson pulled down over her forehead. Matt sensed that everything about her was clean. She carried a whip strapped to her hip and she wore her leggings inside her boots.

Matt strained to look at her face but her Stetson overshadowed it and her long straight hair flowed around her ears and down her neck making in difficult for him to view her clearly. He could barely make out her sincerity and he seemed to know her but he could not recognize her.

"Stay awake, Matt," the young lady whispered in a soft and beautiful voice. "Stay awake."

Matt shook his head, wiped the snow from his squinting eyes and looked hard towards the woman's face. "Who are you?"

She said nothing.

"I need help," Matt managed to cough out as he raised up and fell backwards into the snow. He looked up and saw her bending over him. He moved his legs and managed to get into a kneeling position. Her strength startled him as he felt her thin fingers lift him under his armpits.

"Stay awake," she repeated as she braced Matt against the tree. "Stay awake. You hear me?"

Matt murmured, "I . . . can . . . hear you." He tried to reach out and touch her but his hands felt like lead and he couldn't lift them.

The young lady stacked branches around Matt to help keep him upright. She took some snow, saturated her bandana with its moisture and wiped Matt's wound and cleaned around his eyes.

She then took her bandana and packed it with snow and placed it back on the wound.

"The swelling will go down, darling," she said as she pulled Matt' collar up tight around his throat and pulled his Stetson down over his eyes. 'Stay warm and stay awake."

"Don't leave me," Matt whispered almost too soft to be heard, but the young lady heard him.

"I'll not leave you," she said and the wind blew through the tree tops. It was darker now and the cold wind began to find its way around his beaten body.

The warmth of his body quickly dissipated when full night set in, wrapped her icy fingers around the tree and blew her winter wind through its branches. Matt fell into unconsciousness and he felt neither cold nor pain, but his body was giving into the fiendish call for his soul. His feeble voice whispered, "Ginny." With his eyes half shut, he repeated it over and over again, "Ginny."

Morning came slow, but come it did, and with it an icy mist crept across the ground and seeped into the hollow of the tree branches. Matt moved his body in various positions as he tried to fight the dampness of the cold. His forehead perspired into beads of sweat from fever and his body grew weaker.

His heavy eyes looked up and around for the young lady who had helped him through the night. He could not find her. He whispered, "Ginny?" The air was ghastly silent, not even the sound of a crackling snow-ladened twig was heard. His eyes searched through his closed eyelids for the beautiful young lass and his ears yearned for her gentle voice. She was gone.

CHAPTER 12

GINNY

August 1860

A moment of sunshine filtered into Matt's eyes and he found himself as a young twenty-five year old cowboy by the name of Matt Jorgensen, riding another Skeeter south through the green hills of Tennessee. His mind, as he lay inside the shelter of the willow spruce tree limbs, was reliving his pre-Civil War experience of his journey towards Texas. It was a hot and sticky summer day.

He came across a plantation with rows of corn on one side of the road and cotton fields on the other side that seemingly covered a thousand acres of land. The sound of a whipping and the wailing of a human's cries caused Matt's head to turn in its direction. He saw a large man with a whip carving wounds into the bared back of a black slave who had all fours on the ground between rows of cotton. He saw the expression of the man as he brought his whip hard across the slave's back again and again.

The man with the whip was larger than Matt would want to tangle with, but, under the circumstances, young Matt was not one to keep riding and let a man be beaten, no matter the color of his skin.

"Mister, I wouldn't bring the whip down again, if I were you," Matt said in a distinct voice, unsure that he was going to be able to help the slave, eyeing the size of his opponent.

The man stopped for a moment, looked up at Matt and asked, "What business is it of yours?"

"Well, none if you let the man be. If you don't, I'm making it my business. Drop it, friend."

In defiance of Matt, he brought the whip down hard once more, and when he brought it up, Matt's .45 was out of its leather and aimed at the man.

"I said, drop it."

The man again ignored Matt and proceeded to bring the whip down when Matt fired his .45 at the man's hand.

The man fell backwards with pain as the whip flew from his hand.

The slave crawled away as fast as he could, until he got some distance away, then stood up and ran fast for the plantation house.

"My hand's busted!" cried the man as he held his hand close to his chest.

Matt looked down upon the big man in disgust and aimed his .45 in his direction again and said, "Be thankful it wasn't your head. What the hell was you doin' to that man?"

The man rose to his feet, and began wrapping his hand with his bandanna. "Mister, you're gonna git yours."

"Now, if'n I was you, looking at the insides of the barrel of my pistol, I'd think twice about saying anythin' bad about me," Matt reminded the man. "Get my drift?"

"I get it," the man said and started running towards the house following after the slave.

There were other slaves in the field who had been watching the incident without saying anything. They turned their eyes back toward their crops and kept working.

Matt holstered his pistol and rode the trail over to a couple of slaves working together who pretended not to notice him. "Your friend," Matt referred to the slave who was beaten, "will he be okay?"

The slaves continued working without looking up. Matt removed his Stetson and wiped the sweat from his brow.

The sun was straight up, the day was hot and the humidity tore into his clothes causing him to perspire more than usual.

He rode off, and after several minutes, seeing an apple tree in the distance offering fruit and shade, he rode Skeeter towards it in a walk. Letting Skeeter do the guiding, he dropped the reins around his saddle horn and reloaded his Colt.

Once at the tree, he plucked a couple apples while in the saddle, and then dismounted, ground-reining Skeeter. His body felt like he had been on a long ride and now deserved a rest. He dusted off the apples and ate them, and then stretched out on the ground for a nap, being completely unconcerned about the man whose hand he had broken with a round from his Colt.

After all, the man was in the wrong and should have sense enough not to come after more trouble.

Matt was not thinking right, for within a short time the sound of hoof beats awoke him from his short nap.

The horses reined up at his feet, and then he heard the crack of a whip about an inch over his head, which snapped away his hat.

Matt remained stretched out on the ground, but his eyes opened wide and he saw the person cracking the whip was a woman in her twenties, as young as he was himself. Her blonde hair hung down around her shoulders while her Stetson sat on her shoulders with a stampede strap. She wore a tight-fitting blouse the top three buttons unbuttoned, allowing her breasts to accentuate themselves quite naturally. She sported a good figure sitting on a horse for Matt to enjoy, had he had the time to do so. Three other male riders accompanied her with their guns drawn and pointed at Matt, but they let her do the talking.

"You, Mister," she said as she reeled in her whip readying it for her to swing it out again, "you shot one of my workers."

Matt reached out for his hat, but before he could retrieve it, the whip snatched it away again, causing it to land further down the road.

"That's my hat," Matt gestured rubbing his head. "It cost good money."

"You busted up my worker's hand," the woman replied. "He cost good money. You willing to take his place?"

"He'll be all right," Matt replied, rising to greet his newly-found friends. Looking at the man with the busted hand, he said, "You should be tendin' to your hand."

The man tightened his jaw and looked mean at Matt while he held a cocked rifle in Matt's direction keeping him from reaching for his .45.

The other two men holstered their guns, dismounted and grabbed hold of Matt's arms, pinning him to the tree. One of the men held out Matt's right hand. "Your turn, Mister. We don't like men shooting up any of our friends."

Matt realized the danger he was in, and fearing the loss of his good hand, asked, "What d'ya intend to do?"

The woman coiled her whip behind her and said, "I'm better with a whip than most men are with guns. I asked you a question. You willin' to take his place?"

Matt looked at her eyes and asked himself, "How could a God-created beauty such as this be so devastingly cruel?" He answered her, "Lady, you as much as touch me with that whip, and I'll break you in two. You and these three ugly baboons you brought with you."

He didn't have to hear the crack of the whip this time, for he felt the pain shoot across his hand and up his arm. Blood squirted from the back of his right hand. As much as he wrestled to get out of their hold, he could not loosen the grip of the two arresting men. Yet, he did not yell or whimper.

"Don't threaten me, Mister!" she commanded him. "I own this land as far as you can see, and as far as I'm concerned, you're trespassing on it." She coiled the whip and laid it behind her in position to bring it forward once more, then asked, "I'm only askin' one more time, Mister."

Matt looked steely into her blue eyes and tightened his teeth. "This is a private road." The whip lay across his shoulders and opened his shirt. The sting again brought blood.

"Face him to the tree!" she commanded her two hired men.

Holding firm in his place, Matt kept the two men from turning him around. "I'll watch it comin', if you don't mind."

She brought the whip again across his shoulders.

Matt winced in pain, but held back any verbal noises, as his pa also taught him that big men do not cry. It was one promise to himself he would keep.

As she brought the whip up and aimed it for his body a fourth time, Matt grimaced, but kept his eyes on her, waiting again for the lash of the whip. It never came.

She saw a look in his eyes that demanded her respect for him. For once in her life, she met a man whom she could like. Recoiling the whip, she gave the nod to her men to release him.

Before they did, the taller man punched Matt with full force in his stomach while the other one held him. As Matt went limp, the man surreptitiously removed Matt's Colt from his holster and stuck it inside his belt. Then they let go of their hold on him.

Matt stood still for a moment, letting the blood drip from his wounds while he eyed his new friends.

"You didn't have to do that, Sin," she said. "Get on back to the house. All of you." She did not see the fast action of Sin taking Matt's .45.

"You just gonna turn him loose?" the man with the wounded hand questioned her, while the others climbed upon their horses. "He said he would break you, Miss Ginny."

"I know what he said," she reminded him. Looking back at Matt, she yelled to the men, "Get!"

All three men now mounted, rode away, while the woman sat her horse and stayed, looking at Matt. She was feeling something, which she had lacked for a long time in her life, and she didn't know how to deal with it.

Matt reached for his Colt, and finding his holster was empty, said, "Your man took my pistol."

"I'll get it back for you," she said. She continued to watch Matt like a cat pawing at its toy while she played with her whip in her hand.

"Can I get my hat, or you gonna whip it to death?"

Motioning for him that it was okay, she said, "Name's Ginny McBride. What's yours?"

Picking his Stetson up with his left hand, he answered her, "Lefty!"

She smiled a bit, and dismounted her steed. Taking her bandanna off from around her neck, she walked over to Matt and cautiously gave it to him. "You're bleeding."

Placing his Stetson back on his head, he took his own bandanna off and, soaking it with water from his canteen, applied it to his wound. He tied it tightly around his hand and successfully stopped the bleeding. "Foolish of me to stop and rest a bit."

"A scared man would have kept riding," she said. Looking at him washing his wounds, she apologized and said, "I'm sorry for that other fella hitting you. He has a temper."

"What about you?" he asked.

She skirted the question by saying, "The one you shot was just taking orders from the tall guy. He's really a gentle man, once you get to know him."

"I asked about you," he said again.

"Evidently you know quite a bit about tending wounds," Ginny responded as she took his canteen from him and soaked her bandanna. She began to wash the blood from his chest.

"Should," was his reply. "Been beaten enough times."

"I asked you your name, and I know it's not Lefty."

Seizing the moment, he grabbed her shirt by the neck collar with his left hand and brought her close to his lips, and said, "Listen, lady. I said I'd break you if you touched me with that whip, and I meant it."

At the same instant he felt the barrel of her .44 in his ribs. "I said I was better with the whip. Didn't mean I wasn't good with a .44."

Matt remained holding her and looked into her softened blue eyes. He saw a a lovely amorous woman, and a woman he could so easily love.

The riders had reined their steeds on a rise in the road and watched the couple until they were sure Ginny was safe. When they saw her back in her saddle and holding her .44 at Matt, they straightened themselves in their saddles and rode towards the farmhouse. Sin showed strong jealousy in his eyes, for to him, Ginny was his girl.

Once Matt was in the saddle, he waited for Ginny's next move.

"Follow me to the river," she said, leading out with her horse. "It's a hoot-and-a-holler over this way. We'll get you cleaned up, and you can be on your way."

Matt followed, for the pain increased, and his thought was that he wanted to ride out far from this country. The Tennessee River wound shallow onto the Tennessee land from Knoxville through Chattanooga, whereas flatboats had to be used for travel. It was murky in the middle, but clear up around the shore. Matt plucked some moss off a nearby tree and carried it with him.

Once at the river, both Matt and Ginny dismounted and dropped down to its edge. Matt took off his shirt, and with his bandanna, he applied the cold water to his wounds. It was much more soothing than the warm water from his canteen.

Ginny wet her bandanna and applied it to Matt's' shoulders.

"What do you do, cowboy?" she asked.

"Just that," he answered. "Being a cowboy."

The moment was quiet, and then he continued. "I herded cattle in Wyoming. Worked on a few ranches down this way, driving cattle. When we'd sell them, I'd get my pay, and move further south."

"How long you been away from home?"

"Home?" he pondered. "Two years, more or less, I reckon."

"Where you headed?"

"Don't recken I really know," Matt answered, looking around at the beautiful rolling scenery of Tennessee.

Matt stopped her from continuing with the wet bandanna, and picked up some of the moss he had picked off the tree. "Here," he said. "Put this on my cuts. It'll heal 'em real good." Looking into her eyes as she responded to his suggestion, he added, "Of course, had someone been more patient with the whip, we wouldn't be here now."

While Matt did the same to the back of his hand, Ginny started packing the moss lightly into his wounds, and gave him a slight smile. Matt winced a little at the sting as she applied it across his shoulders and slightly down his chest. He re-tied his bandanna around his hand to keep the moss in place.

After they finished with the moss, he stood up. Taking his shirt, he slipped it back on, feeling the pain but not showing any outward signs of it. He left the front unbuttoned.

Lying down, he rolled over on the grass and leaned up against the nearby tree trunk. Ginny moved over in front of him and put her bandanna back around her neck.

"I'm sorry I whipped you," she said rubbing the front of his boots with her hand.

"No man has ever whipped me, and certainly no lady."

"Thank you."

"For what?" he asked, looking puzzled at her remark.

"For calling me a lady."

Matt leaned forward and grabbed her hand gently. "You are a lady. Oh, that whip don't take that out of ya. It's the way that you handle yourself. Your dress. Your hair." Matt's eyes surveyed her whole body, resting once in awhile on her breasts.

"You like what you see?"

Matt let go of her hand and leaned back again, slightly embarrassed. Looking at her more intently, he said, "Your hair reminds me of spun gold. Your eyes like sapphires, sparkling."

This elicited a laugh from Ginny. "You're a poet. Who'd a thought?"

"Nope," he replied, "just read it somewhere."

Ginny laughed a little, and looked more into Matt's eyes, wondering what kind a man he really was. Certainly a well-built man, six-foot four inches, solid muscle from working with cattle. A well-tanned man from having worked in the sun. And a gentle man, with blue eyes and wavy hair.

"Your real name is Lefty?" she asked.

"Could be, now," he said, motioning to his injured hand. "No, it's Matt. Matthew. I was named after the first book of the New Testament," Matt said, watching the ripples in the river play with one another from the fish jumping near by.

"See that?" he said enthusiastically as he saw a fish jump, and another one and another. Then he settled back a little against the tree again.

"I know the Bible," she said. "He was a tax collector."

"See. I knowed you were a lady, right off," Matt answered. "You probably went to Sunday School every Sunday.

"Yes," she agreed. "Every Sunday."

"Prim and prissy. You had to be."

"And you never did?"

"Oh, Ma would read the Good Book to us. She'd explain all about our names, and how we got 'em."

"Wasn't a tax collector kind of a sissy?" she asked Matt.

"That's where you're wrong, Miss Prissy," Matt interjected. "He had to be tough. Tough as nails. You see, a lot of people didn't like paying taxes back then." They both laughed. "You don't think Pa would let Ma get away with naming me after some sissy, now do ya?"

He returned to watching the fish play in the river and listened to the quietness of the air.

She let him listen, wondering what he would talk about next.

"My brother's name is Lukas. Second book." Matt continued. "He's dead. Measles, or somethin' got him."

Actually, Lukas was killed in a fouled-up bank robbery he attempted with another idiot companion in Montana, whom Matt was mistaken to be. Now, to stay alive, Matt was on the run and had an alias. He was safe, as long as it was believed that he was killed along with his brother, Lukas.

Matt leaned back against the tree again and looked straight into Ginny's blue eyes. "You named after someone?"

"Virginia," she quickly answered.

"The state?"

"And what's wrong with being named after a state?" she asked, sitting straight up with her hands on her hips.

"Nothin', I suppose," Matt replied. "Kinda like it." Then after a moment of silence between the two, he asked, "Are you?"

"That, Sir, is something you will never find out." She stood up and looked away from his presence. "What a thing to be asking a lady, and our first meeting."

"I've never taken advantage of a lady." Matt rose to his feet and stood beside Ginny. "Many times with a woman, but never with a lady, and you . . . are a lady." He stooped to pick up a stone, and skipped it across the river.

A broad smile came across Ginny's face but Matt did not see it.

Then the subject came up about shooting her hired man.

"Why was your man beating that black man?" Matt asked.

Ginny's smile turned to a frown, and she turned to face Matt. "He ran away."

"Why didn't your man say something?"

"Apparently you were too much in a hurry to help someone, and never gave him a chance."

"Oh, hell. I told him to drop the whip twice. When he didn't, I shot at it. Knowed I hit it, cause I saw it splintered."

"From what Al said, that man you shot, you busted his hand. He claimed he can't use it any."

"I saw my aim, and I hit what I aim at. If anything, he's got splinters in his hand." Matt returned to look at the bank across the river.

"Then you say that it was okay for Al to beat him?" she asked as she looked at Matt's' profile.

"It's your plantation. That's what it is, isn't it? I've seen enough of them now and then."

"Yes," she answered, putting her fingers along side his face to bring it back into focus with hers. "And Hezekiah's my slave. Worth two thousand dollars."

"That's what really bothers me."

"That he's worth so much?"

"We don't have slaves in Mon . . ., Wyoming," Matt said, trying to keep secret his home state for fear of being traced, but almost giving it away.

"What do you have in Wyoming, Matt?" Ginny asked.

"Cowboys. Men who can ride and rope and herd cattle to market. Real men."

Ginny bent over and picked up a rock, and, like Matt, skipped it along the river. "Almost a third of Tennessee is comprised of niggers, Matt," she said. "Our people brought them here years ago, and we've been using them ever since as workers. We buy them as property, and they belong to us"

"Why?"

"Look around, Matt, and you can see why. We have lots of land, and lots of crops such as corn and cotton. And cotton is a high commodity today, bringing in big dollars. We just don't have enough manpower to capture this market, unless we do it through slaves. You can understand that, can't you, Matt?"

"And that's another thing. You call them 'niggers'. I ain't never heard these terms exceptin' down here."

"What do you call them in Wyoming, Matt?" Ginny asked, picking a leaf off the tree and playing with it with her hands as if to tease Matt to want to talk about something else besides slaves. "I'm curious, that's all."

"Negroes," Matt answered. "Colored people, maybe. But, not niggers."

"It's short for 'Negroes', Matt," she answered. "And if we want to bring them to attention when we're talking to them, the term 'nigger' hits them right between the eyes. It's like calling someone you hate, a 'son-of-a-bitch' or 'bastard'."

Matt's eyes widened when he heard her say that, causing him to laugh a little. "I'll be damned," he said, grabbing her by the wrist again. "You swore."

"I did, and I often do," she replied, releasing his grip on her wrist. "We're not in Virginia where the ladies are ladies and the men look after them. We're in the midst of a plantation where we have to be tough."

Matt watched her fume without trying to abate her moment of anger.

She walked over to her horse and put her hand on the saddle, but left the reins tied to a branch she had done when they first arrived at the river. She pulled her .44 out from a holster attached to her saddle. She walked to the edge of the river, turned downstream and fired it at a branch sticking out of the water several feet from shore. Clipping it, she said, "And I hit what I aim at, too."

Matt got up, buttoned his shirt, and tucked it in. Then, he walked over to where she stood. He grabbed her arms and turned her around, and bringing her lips to his, kissed her passionately.

Ginny responded by dropping her pistol into the dirt, and placing her freed hands around the back of Matt's neck, bringing him tighter into her lips. He felt pain from his wounds, but ignored it for the pleasure of the moment.

Without warning, he picked her up and placed her upon her horse. "I like you tough," he said. "But I want to get to know your gentle side before we get to know each other better."

Ginny sat her horse sidesaddle, and held her quirt lady- like in her right hand. She wanted to start showing Matt this side of her. She grabbed the reins with her left hand, and looking down at Matt asked, "Does that mean you'll be staying awhile with us?"

Matt bent down and retrieved her .44, wiped it off with his shirt, and placed it back into her holster. "You asked me if I could take his place," Matt replied. "I was always taught, 'an eye for an eye, and a tooth for a tooth.' I'll ride back with you and, for the moment, let's say, I'll consider it. After all, work is work, and right now, I'm unemployed."

"Then follow me," Ginny commanded, and waited for him to saddle up.

CHAPTER 13

THE MCBRIDE PLANTATION

It was awhile after the other three men had left before Matt and Ginny rode back to the main house, but time only seemed short for the pair of amorous riders.

Two of Matt's newly acquired "friends" were waiting for Ginny on the porch as they rode up to the house. Al was in back having his hand tended to by a black woman. Matt dismounted and then helped Ginny from her horse.

Eyeing the plantation, he saw it was a lot bigger up close. The house now seemed to be ten times the size, though it was not. It was a two-storied house built of pine boards, with two brick fireplaces, one on each end of the house, and a portico in front.

After tying the two horses up at the hitching rail, Matt walked up to the man with Matt's Colt still stuck in his pants. Matt reached for it and pulled it out quickly. "I didn't hear anyone say you could take my gun. Thanks for keeping it for me." He rolled the cylinder and checked to see that all six bullets were still there. He never kept an empty sixth chamber, as many did, for fear of shooting off their foot. He felt this extra bullet would give him an edge in any gunfight.

"We did what we were told to do, mister," the man called Sin said. He was tall and muscular, but not Matt's height. He appeared to be ten years Matt's senior. He carried a mean scar across his forehead, apparently from being hit with a heavy object, ostensibly a gun. He was not at all handsome.

Matt held himself in reserve waiting to see what their next move would be.

The second man was a short, stocky man, and one who appeared to be muscle bound, but was mostly fat all over. "Ginny," he said. "mind if we get back to our chores?"

"In a minute." Turning to Matt she said, "This is Sin Crouch, my foreman." She pointed to the tall man. "Sin, this is Matt. Matt Jorgensen from Wyoming ways."

Matt's real name was Andersen, but he had to go by an alias to stay away from a noose in Montana. Putting his .45 in its holster, he answered, "Matt will do."

"So Sin's your name. Parents named you that 'cause of your looks?"

"No," Sin answered, "it's 'Cinch' but I shortened it."

"Kinda thought it was from 'Cindy'. Like that one better."

Sin looked real mean towards Matt, doubled up his fist and put it behind him and walked over to Matt as if to shake hands. "Hope there's no hard feelings," he said.

Instead of receiving an open hand, Sin got a face full of fist as Matt did a complete one-eighty on him.

Matt felt pain in his fist from the whipping, but suffered it, wrapping it tight again with his bandanna. Sin was knocked off the porch and face down into the dirt. He stayed down for the count.

"Nope," Matt said, "not one bit." This now put Matt in front of the short stout man.

"And this is Fats Logan," Ginny said as she introduced the short, stocky man. A smirk came across her face as she watched Fats' response by defending himself with his arms over his face. All of a sudden, his almost muscle-built frame turned to mush as he deflated his chest.

Matt could see that he was too much for the stocky man and said, "I can see where you got your name." Matt took the man's hat and flung it into the road. Picking him up by the little hair the man had, he pushed him up against the house and said, "Don't ever get in my face again! Got it?"

The man's eyes crossed as he looked at Matt with fear and trembling. He had good reason, for Matt pulled him forward and flung him on top of Sin like a sack of potatoes.

The two men nursed their wounds and looked at Ginny for further instructions.

"You stand there and let him do this to us?" Sin asked getting up and rubbing his chin.

Matt helped Sin pick himself up and said, "Never hold another man's arms when in a fight. Understand?"

"You shouldn't have taken his gun," Ginny said, motioning with her whip for the two men to resume their chores while she ushered Matt into the house.

The house appeared to be even larger from within, rich in style, and huge, having four bedrooms, two bedrooms upstairs and two bedrooms downstairs, with two shed rooms in the rear, a large front room, a passage through the center, and a large kitchen. Matt was impressed that he was in the presence of a richness of which he was not accustomed. A huge fireplace with a stone-lined oaken-mantel filled the wall on the north side. During the cold times, the fireplace kept the main part of the house warm during the evening time, while the wood-burning stove warmed the home earliest in the morning and throughout the day. Each room was equipped with a fireplace, as the chimneys ran through the roof. The wood-burning stove sat in the kitchen and provided the range for which to cook and, at the same time, added extra heat for the house when it was cold, for the kitchen was a well-lived in place.

A gentleman in his mid-forties, sporting a good crop of salt-and-peppered hair and a mustache, and dressed rather richly, sat on the divan in the front room with a shotgun he had been cleaning in his arms.

"He's in the back, Ginny" the gentleman said, referring to the man Matt shot. "Bertha took care of him," he continued, while pointing the shotgun in Matt's direction. Bertha was a slave girl who took to the maintenance of the house, including the cooking, washing, and sewing. At times, she had the assistance of a younger woman by the name of Naomi, much thinner, but reserved.

"This the fella who shot him?" he asked Ginny.

Matt reached for his Colt when he saw the shotgun, but Ginny stopped him.

"He would have blasted you before you cocked it," she said, holding his arm. "Matt, this is my father, James McBride. Call him, Jim." She walked over to Jim and removed his shotgun, putting it above the mantel. "It's all right, dad. He thought Al was killing one of our slaves, so he shot him. Turns out he's a good man after all. Kinda think you'll like him."

Jim stood up and started to take Matt's hand, but seeing it bandaged, he shook his left hand instead. "Wasn't loaded. I was cleaning it. I see she did a number on you? Good." He went to the whiskey cabinet and poured some Kentucky bourbon for Matt and himself. "Drinking man, Matt?"

"Is it past noon?" Matt answered as he received the drink, "What made you think she did a number on me? And why did you say 'good'?"

"Your shirt come ventilated and packed with moss?" he chided Matt. "Those marks are made from a whip, and I know my daughter's signature quite well."

"Oh, I see," Matt responded, feeling around his shoulders at the torn shirt. "Yeah, she certainly did a number."

CHAPTER 14

MATT JORGENSEN IS INTRODUCED TO SLAVERY

T he tension passed as the three sat and began to talk.

"You're a Western man, up Wyoming way?" Jim asked.

"Cheyenne," Matt answered. "Yep."

"What d'ya think about Hezekiah?"

"Who?"

"Hezekiah," Ginny answered. "He's the nigger you helped out."

Matt swirled his whiskey around in his glass, cleaned the lip of the glass with his finger, and answered them, "Good name, I recken."

"He's Hezekiah Jackson," Jim responded. "Named after his first owner."

Hezekiah was a muscular man, approximately thirty years old, give or take a few years, nobody knew for sure. A little gray showed on his temples, which deceived his younger looks. He wore bib overalls and a long sleeved-shirt, which hid the whip marks, and he was barefoot.

Matt raised his eyebrows as if startled by what Jim just said. "Owner?" he asked.

"Yes. I'm his second owner. Bought him for a good price."

Jim took the bottle from the cabinet and poured the two of them another glass of bourbon.

"Ginny's not having any?" Matt asked, as he stood to receive his drink.

"Too early for a lady, Matt," she answered as she stood up to meet the height of the men.as if embarrassed as her father looked on. Ginny was not one for turning down a drink in the daytime. It seemed she was attempting to become a lady in Matt's presence, and Jim recognized it.

Then she asked, "You seem to be bothered with us talking about Hezekiah. Why?"

Matt took a sip from his freshened glass and swallowed easy, so as not to give any impression that he felt intimidated by her question. "A little, Ginny. Mr. McBride."

"We go by first names among friends here, Matt," Jim said.

"Thank you, Jim," Matt returned. Then, watching Ginny turn back towards him, he said, "I've never been bothered with niggers. Never talked with one. Don't know the first thing about them. Only that they're different."

The sound of the backdoor opening and closing meant that Bertha had entered the house. She was a heavy-set black woman in her forties standing roughly five-feet five inches high. She wore a light blue dress with white designs, some white frills, and a white apron. Her black hair was tied up in a red-checkered bandanna. Another thing differed her from the other black people was the fact that she wore shoes. It was required for household help, so she and Naomi were each equipped with a good pair of walking shoes. She carried a cheerful attitude about herself.

When she entered the room where the threesome stood, she waited to be spoken to before she spoke.

"How is Al, Bertha?" Ginny asked with a glance towards Matt.

"Oh, my, Miss Ginny," Bertha responded, "he'll live. He almost done got a hole in his hand, near took off his thumb, it did, Miss Ginny. My, my, my you should have seen him yell when I sprinkled a little gunpowder in it and lighted it. Yelled like a coyote, that man did."

"What for?" Matt asked "I think I'd yell, too."

"She cauterized it, Matt," Ginny replied.

"Isn't that dangerous? Wouldn't pouring some whiskey on it be enough?" Matt asked again.

"Kentucky whiskey is for drinking, young man," Jim replied, drinking more from his glass. "Not for pouring on a wound."

"T'weren't too big a hole you made, Mister . . ." Bertha said, making a small hole with her hand. "Say. What's you name, anyways?"

"Matt Jorgensen, Bertha," Ginny replied. "He's going to be staying with us awhile, so you may set an extra plate for dinner tonight."

"Yes'm," Bertha answered. Looking at Matt, she continued. "Mr. Jorgensen. My, my, my, you certainly is a big'n. Handsome? Woowee! And you shoots mighty purty, too. You oughta see the whip. That ain't got no handle no more. No, sirree." Turning, she walked back into the kitchen, gave Matt another glance over her shoulder, and a little giggle to show her approval. "Yes'm. We done got ourselves another mouth to feed. Hope ya likes ham hocks and turnip greens, cause that's what we're havin'. Ham hocks, sweet taters, and turnip greens."

"Ham hocks and turnip greens?" Matt asked, turning to Ginny for an answer. "What in thunderation are ham hocks and turnip greens?"

Jim walked over to the mantel and picked up his pipe and some tobacco out of a tin, which he started packing into his pipe. "How long you been in the South, Matt?" he asked, lighting his pipe.

"Came in from Illinois side, if that tells you anything," Matt replied.

"And what brings you down this way, son?" Jim asked.

Taking the makings for a cigarette out of his shirt pocket, Matt asked, "Mind?"

"Go right ahead. Join me."

Rolling the cigarette, Matt continued. "Headin' for Texas."

"Oh. Got folk down there?" Jim asked.

"No. Just figured that's as far south as I can get and still stay in America."

"Tennessee is mighty pretty country, Matt," Ginny chimed in. "We came here from Virginia to take over a plantation started by some friends who itched to go to Oregon, of all places. We bought it, and they left, so here we are. Been altogether now two whole years, and we like it."

"Kinda like it myself, now," Matt said with a smile and a gleam in his eye. "But, got a hankerin' to move on to Texas."

"Got any kind of work in Texas, Matt?" Jim asked.

"Nope. But don't have any here, either."

"Then you must have a stash of money to keep you going?" Ginny asked, smiling as if she was hoping to hear good news from Matt that he had.

"Not really," Matt replied, lighting his cigarette. Watching a smoke ring lift through the air, he added, "Some. Enough to get me through the winter, but that's about all."

"You look strong and healthy," Jim said, giving Matt the once over. "You put Al up for a stretch. Sin and Fats are the only other hands we've got. You supposin' you could think about helpin' out, at least 'til come Spring?"

Ginny smiled at that suggestion and said, "You never did answer my question, either."

"And what question was that?" Matt asked.

"You willin' to take Al's place?" She sported a smile the style of a half smirk, and with her eyes looking down to the floor, she licked her lips. Hearing no answer, she looked up at Matt and asked again, "Well, Mister Jorgensen. Are you or aren't you?"

Matt put his glass of whiskey down, drew his revolver and twirled it a few times, and then holstered it. "I know beef," he said, looking first at Jim and then at Ginny. "I do not know cotton, corn, or turnip greens, nor do I care to know them."

"The question is . . ."

Matt interrupted Ginny saying, "I know what the damn question is." Realizing he was being a little curt with Ginny, he toned down his voice and apologized. "I'm sorry. I won't work fields for no man, or no money."

"Ginny's not asking you to work fields, Matt," Jim said, putting his drink down next to Matt's. "We need a good man who is not afraid to work our niggers." He paused a moment to watch

Matt's reaction, and then continued. "Sin's a good man, and so is Al and Fats. Sin knows cotton. Fats knows plowing. Al, well Al knows how to deal with niggers, because of his size. They're afraid of him. But now he's a bit wounded, and, pardon the pun, shall we say, we're a little short handed. We don't need more hands, we need one man who can whip these men into shape. And, I have to say, Sin isn't the man."

A smile came across Matt's' lips, and he noticed the same with Ginny.

"Then what d'ya need with me?" Matt asked. "I jest told you I don't know the first damn thing about what you got growin' out there in them fields."

"You're fast with the gun" Jim said.

"And, you're big and tough," Ginny added.

"What d'ya expect of me?" asked Matt.

"We've got eighty slaves," Jim added. "Too many for us, but we've got to have them. We've got them split up into three teams."

"We use the intelligent nigs for Drivers," Ginny interrupted. "One for the fields, one for the animals, and one for plowing."

"Half of our slaves are female as you can expect," Jim continued. "Most are hearty and carry on like a man. But, then they get pregnant, or sick, and then we've got problems," Jim said, walking behind his big chair that sat in the middle of the floor facing three other chairs as a conversation pit.

"I can handle more men and twice the women that either of our men can, and that's because I'm not afraid to use this whip," Ginny added.

"And that's exactly what killed her mother, Matt."

"Not at all, pa," Ginny retorted, picking up her whip and giving it a snap towards the front door. "Ma died because she was feeling sorry for them, and got sick carrying for them, and I hate them for it!"

A silence fell over the room for a moment. Then Bertha entered and broke the spell. Jim looked back at her and asked, "What is it, Bertha?"

"Excuse me, Missis," she said, stopping at the entry to the front room as if it was taboo for her to enter. She put this in her mind as proper etiquette as a black servant woman, even though she could walk anywhere in the house where no privacy existed, such as bedrooms when someone was inside. "Mistah Al wanted me to tell you that he's back at work, and I'm to tell you that I'll be startin' supper right quick, now." She knew it would take time for the ham to cook, and she wanted plenty of time to prepare a good meal for a man whom she readily admired. She gave another smile towards Matt.

"Thank you, Bertha," Ginny replied.

Bertha walked back into the kitchen.

Looking at Matt waiting for something to say, Jim continued, "My wife, Jane was fragile and weak."

"She was strong, Daddy," Ginny stammered loud and clear for even Bertha to hear. "It's those damn niggers that killed her."

Bertha's body cringed at this word "nigger" as she continued to walk towards the kitchen. Her face showed tension as it quivered, but no one saw it. She had lost the countenance she once had in their home a few moments earlier. She wanted to cry, but held it back as strong as she could. She reminded herself that she was a black slave.

Bertha knew Jane well. It was Jane who met her first when they took over the plantation. It was Jane who brought Bertha into the house and discussed with her the rules of the household, the "do's" and the "don'ts" that she set up. It was Jane who gave her the key to the kitchen with all the privileges appertaining to it.

When Jane contracted diphtheria, Bertha kept the water boiled and kept Jane covered and tenderly loved with her big broad arms. Bertha's tears cleaned the disease away as much as she could. Prayers helped. But Jane's frail body could not withstand the rigors of the disease, and succumbed to it's powers within a short while and she died in Bertha's arms.

Ginny had forgotten the hours and days and nights that Bertha spent with her mother. The only thing that she could remember was the way the slaves swarmed over Jane when she went along with Bertha to feed them, and when she read to them portions of the "Good Book", as they called it.

Her slaves sang with her, and called her their friend. Ginny taught them discipline, and Jane taught them love. It was love that caused her to succumb. It was discipline and respect that ruled over all. And Ginny earned their respect at the end of the whip, and now that Jane was gone, the slaves respected the whip more than ever.

Jim relayed to Matt the need for a man strong enough to work the animals and help run the slaves.

"I'm not the lovin' kind, Jim," Matt said. "I have been a foreman to a bunch of wranglers in Wyomin' for a time, and I have watched my father rule a ranch with a fist of iron. I can do likewise, if I so choose." He looked at Ginny and then back at Jim and said, "I do not so choose, Sir."

"Is it because you do not know what a nigger is?" Ginny asked, throwing the whip down on a divan decorating the room under the front window.

"Yes, Miss Ginny," Matt responded wildly as he turned to face her, turning his back to Jim momentarily. "I'm afraid I do not know what a damn nigger is, and I don't care to know." He felt Jim's hand as it came upon his shoulder from behind. He turned and said to Jim, "I thank you for the drink, Jim, but it looks like I've worn out my welcome."

"Then you didn't mean what you said at the river," Ginny retorted.

Matt stopped, turned and looked completely puzzled at Ginny.

"You forgot?" Ginny asked. "Well, let me refresh your memory. 'An eye for and eye and a tooth for a tooth'. Ring a bell?"

Matt remembered their conversation, and how he said he would consider the matter. He watched Ginny as she stood with her legs spread apart, and a whip dangled once again in her hand.

"Now, I said I would consider it," Matt replied.

"Bertha," Ginny yelled out towards the kitchen. "Come in here!"

Bertha ran into the front room, wiping her hands on her apron as she came to a halt in front of Ginny. "Yes, Missis?" she asked.

"Go fetch Al, and be fast about it," she commanded her.

Bertha ran back out through the kitchen as fast as her short legs could carry her, and out the back door. Finding Al, she grabbed him by his left hand and led him into the house to confront Ginny.

"Here he is, Missis," she said, releasing Al's hand and taking a few steps backwards away from the scorn of her mistress.

Al stood there with his hand bandaged, but had his right thumb stuck in his belt. It was his masculine way of showing that he was all right.

"You wanted me, Miss Ginny?" he asked quickly removing his hat as he had forgotten to do when he entered the house so abruptly.

"This is the man who shot you, Al," she said, pointing her whip at Matt. "Show him your hand."

"It's not much, Ginny," he replied, taking his thumb out of his belt.

"Show him, Al."

Matt watched as Al unwrapped his bandaged hand, which was burned from where Bertha applied the gunpowder to cauterize the wound.

Bertha stepped forward and replied, "I done that. I put some gunpowder down in it and lit it."

Matt looked at the hand and said, "A little too much, Bertha." Then he looked at Al and said, "You better hope for some good pus to show up, Al, else gangrene will set in and you'll have to have it sawed off. We don't want that to happen."

Of course Matt was kidding, and he showed it by winking at Al. But he wanted to show that Al was not as bad off as everyone seemed to think.

"You want to shoot him, Al, for what he did to you?" Ginny asked.

Matt clearly eyed Al, whose body framed the kitchen, showing the mass that was clearly in front of Matt. Matt showed some concern. Facing a big man with a gun is one thing, but standing a few feet in front of him without a gun, just one's bare fists, was another. Matt wondered how good Al was with his left hand in case he had another fight coming.

With a little stuttering, he said, "N-no, M-Miss G-G-Ginny. I s-s-should have d-dropped the whip l-l-like he said."

"Are you fit to work the slaves," she asked, "with your hand all busted like that?"

Looking at his hand, he answered, "Not with a whip, but I can with my fists. I'm powerful good with my fists." He made a fist out of his left hand and held it up to show her. "In a few days, or a week, I'll be able to handle a whip again."

"Able to work cattle?"

"You know I ain't no good with cattle, Miss Ginny."

Turning to Matt, she said, "A week, Matt. Just until Al is back on his feet."

Matt turned to Jim and to Ginny and said, "All right. I'll stay on awhile, if someone can show me what to do with your colored folk." Then to himself he secretly said, "Damn."

Ginny read it on Matt's lips, and a smile came across her face that did not escape Jim's eyes, or Matt's.

"First thing is to get washed up and ready for some good Southern cookin', Bertha style," Jim said.

Ginny motioned to Bertha as she said, "Bertha, see to it that Mr. Jorgensen's bed is turned down, and that he has proper towels."

"Yes'm," Bertha answered, looking at the stairs. "Ya'll ready now for me to shows ya, Mister?"

This was the first time he was ever called a Mister, which in servant style meant, "master". It seemed any white man she served would be called "Mister". Now, it would be awhile for Matt to get used to his new title. Following her upstairs, he looked back at Ginny and mouthed the word, "Mister" and pointed to himself.

Al looked troubled at Matt, but wrapped his hand and walked out of the house.

"Hold on, Al," Jim said, motioning for him to stay. "Wait outside for Matt. I want you to show him around."

When Matt returned downstairs, Jim said, "It might not be a big bedroom, but you should find it'll do."

"Big?" Matt jested. "I haven't slept in a bed in a long time, and this one, well let's just say I think I'm gonna like workin' for ya."

"Al's outside ready to show you around the place," Ginny added.

"Think he's sore at me?" Matt asked.

"What do you think?" she responded.

"He'll get over it, Matt," Jim said. "He's needed that for a long time. Too much authority for a little fella."

Matt looked at Jim a little puzzled and said, "Little? He towers me, and I'm six foot four."

Ginny pointed to her head, indicating that Al was not the intelligent type, and smiled at Matt as she turned and sat down on one of the chairs in the circle.

Matt shrugged his shoulders and joined Al, who waited outside for him.

CHAPTER 15

TWO MEN AND ONE WOMAN

The next morning, Al found Matt up at the break of dawn and walking the plantation. "Had breakfast?" he asked, pulling his bib overall straps up over his shoulders.

"Waitin' for the bell," Matt replied.

"No bell. You eats when you smell food." He sniffed the air and pointed his nose towards the kitchen. "And I smells it now." They joined their noses and walked to the back door of the kitchen.

Bertha was again in the kitchen preparing breakfast for the white people on the plantation. In back of the house were long tables for the black people. The women had already dished out their breakfast of eggs, grits, and coffee. Plenty of coffee.

Thirty-some women worked feverishly around the tables while the men ate seemingly faster than the women could cook. They were not lacking for food, for it was plentiful.

Each of the women, save for a few, wore scarves tied around their hair. The others let their heads go bare or wore men's hats. Their clothes were plain-fashion long dresses. Some wore skirts with blouses tucked inside.

The women were given a measure of cotton, twelve buttons each, with which to make their own clothes. The sleeves on their clothes were full and fitting to the hands for protection. At least fourteen kids between the ages of five and twelve intermixed with them, and a couple of the ladies held one and two year old babies on their hips.

The men wore hats, shirts, and bib overalls, or plain pants. New clothing was given to them twice a year, once in the spring and the other time in the winter.

No one wore shoes, except in the winter, and then only when it was cold. None of the men seemed overweight, where some of the women ostensibly were, due to their having children. Only Bertha, still without a man, seemed to be overweight because of her good cooking, and her having the privilege of eating it. However, she was good looking, and always wore a great smile on her rosy-cheek face.

After the women ate, they took the plates to a large metal wash tub and washed them. Some of them began their washing of clothes, taking advantage of the fire and the black kettle for hot water.

While the men started out for the fields, the women hung up their clothes, and prepared themselves to meet the men in the fields. A few of the women stayed behind to clean up what was left over. The children who worked in the field were not allowed any playtime until suppertime. Lights were out by nine o'clock.

There did not seem to be any bad thinking among the lot. This was peculiar to Matt, as he was looking for some animosity, hate, anger, any of the bad virtues that seemed to be present among prisoners. In fact, they did not appear to be prisoners at all, but simply workers. He had not, as yet, become accustomed to people being owned.

At the kitchen table, Ginny and the men sat consuming plates full of flapjacks, sausage, buttermilk, and coffee. Bertha did the cooking while Naomi did the serving. The plates and cups were of good china. The glasses were like crystal and the silverware sparkled.

"Enjoying yourself, Matt?" asked Ginny.

"With fried chicken, gravy, biscuits and mashed potatoes for supper, and flapjacks and sausage for breakfast, I'd say I am one happy pilgrim, Ginny."

"If you expect to get a hard day's work in the fields today," Jim said, watching Matt being served his second tall helping of flapjacks, "you got to eat."

"Yes, Sir," Matt replied. "Never one for eatin' in between breakfast and supper. Al done showed me some of what we're 'spectin' to do." After swallowing down a mouthful, Matt said, "I see the colored folk headin' for the fields already."

"You folks up north call them colored. We call them niggers," Sin said, noticing Matt's attentions were being paid more again towards Ginny.

"I've heard them called both, coming through the south, Sin," Matt said. "I just prefer the softer approach.

Fats let out a laugh, adding, "We calls a spade a spade here in Tennessee."

"And what do they call you, Fats?" Matt asked.

"'Fat ass,' when he's not lookin'," Al said, stacking up his third plate.

"Kinda looks like the pot calling the kettle black to me," retorted Matt as he kept right on eating.

Jim and Al responded laughing, and Ginny smiled. Matt caught her smile and threw one back at her with a wink. Sin refrained from laughing, grabbed a cup of coffee and went out back and stood on the porch.

"What's eating at Sin?" Jim asked.

"Hell, you know, Jim," Fats said still cramming his food in his mouth. "He's always had a thing with Ginny, and now this guy," he pointed to Matt, "well, he's gettin' funny eyes from Ginny."

"Fats!" Ginny said powerful and distinctly, rising from her chair. "There's no truth in that, and Mister, you better be apologizing."

"Didn't mean anythin', Ginny," Fats came back real fast wiping the syrup from his mouth and chin. "Sin's been crazy about cha, and you've known it. Ain't that right, Jim"

"She knows it, Fats," Jim answered. "Sit down, Ginny."

Knocking the chair back, she curtly apologized to Matt, "I'm sorry, Matt," and stomped out of the kitchen and ran to Sin.

Jim watched the way Matt looked at Ginny as she left. He sensed that something was happening between the pair. But he had to say, just the same, "They'll have another talk, Matt. Been doing this for almost two years." He knew he was applying a little psychology Matt's way, hoping by rubbing it in a little, Matt would get jealous. He had been hoping for someone better than Sin to come along and sweep Ginny off her feet. He saw in Matt a handsome man and tough as they came.

Matt looked at the men in the room, and seeing no one was saying anything, as if expecting him to say something, simply asked, "Bertha. Got any more sausages?"

"Yes, sirree, bossman," she responded, scraping them up with her spatula. "Much as you like."

She put them on a plate and let Naomi serve them to him.

"Thank you, miss," Matt said taking the plate.

"You may call me, 'Naomi', cause that's mah name," Namoi answered, with a slight curtsy holding out her apron.

"You don't thank a nigger," Fats said rather indignant as he crossed the room and gave Naomi the eye to keep to herself.

Matt smiled and kept on eating.

"I completely forgot to introduce Naomi to you, Matt," Jim said. "She's an orphan with us. Her ma and pa ran away, we're told, when she was only two or three years old. From what I gather, they didn't want her to slow them down."

"Sorry to hear that, Naomi," Matt replied.

Naomi smiled and showed it sincerely with her eyes as she began clearing the table.

"I said, we don't patronize niggers," Fats said again shrugging his shoulders at Matt, "I'm sorry. That's just how it is heah in the South," and he walked out the door.

Al continued wiping up his plate. "Ready to go, Bossman?" Al asked, kiddingly, with a sloppy grin on his face, which revealed a few teeth missing in front.

CHAPTER 16

MATT LEARNS ABOUT COTTON

Matt put his last sausage inside one of his flapjacks, excused himself, and joined Al outside. Al picked up a new whip hanging on the wall. As he opened the door, Ginny walked in, between him and Matt, and sat back at the table.

The men met for a conference out on the lawn beside the house. "I'm taking Matt with me for the day," Al said. "That's the way Jim wants it. We'll stop by and see you two later as we make our rounds."

Sin and Fats watched the two as they walked off. Finally, they took off to their assigned tasks in different directions.

Al took large strides in his walk, and it was difficult for Matt to keep up with him. The next thing Matt knew, he was on the other side of the barn that stood adjacent to the house, and separated the house from the black's cabins. Each cabin consisted of two rooms and a wood-burning stove. Each also had one door and no windows. This made it easier to keep an eye out for any black people slipping out and trying to escape. A garden was in the back of each cabin, which allowed them to plant their own crops. They could have as many chickens as they could raise.

Slowing his pace down a bit, Al decided it was time to bring Matt up on some facts as they walked. "Fats was right," Al said. "Not takin' up for what he said, just tellin' you how it is.

Don't matter who they is, you treat 'em like a damn nig, and that's that."

"Oh," Matt responded, still walking.

Al passed the whip over to Matt. "You know how to use one of these things? The biggest problem we have is slaves runnin' away," Al said. "Take Hezekia . . ."

"The one you were whippin' yesterday?" Matt asked.

Al looked down at his bandaged hand. "Yeah. He's our most popular slave, and that boy cost some good money. He's worth it. My job . . . or our job now, is to keep them, and keep them workin'."

Seemingly out of nowhere, Sin walked up to them and said, "Seems they don't mind workin'. It's just gettin' them started sometimes which is hardest."

Matt was startled at Sin's voice as he did not hear him walking up to them. "You could be an Indian."

"Walking soft? Habit. Keeps our nigs on their toes, too."

"Listen," Sin added. "About Ginny."

"What about her?" Matt asked.

"You stay away from her, that's all!"

"Seems to me she's a lady who makes up her own mind," Matt retorted.

"I'm gonna marry her," Sin stated matter-of-factly, turned and walked away. "I'll see you in the fields."

The men continued walking in the corn field, and after making sure Sin was no longer within hearing range, Al related to Matt. "They went on a few dates. That's all. Nothin' serious. She's turned him down more times than me tryin' to land Ol' Slippery down at the holler," Al said referring to a fish he had always tried to catch in the trout stream. "Oh, she went with him in town for a dance, or a drink. I even caught him kissin' her one time. Don't think he ever kissed her since. She scratched the holy hell out of him. Even told him she had a man in Virginia, and he still wouldn't leave her alone."

"Then why's he tellin' me to leave her alone if he's got her already?"

"He don't gots her," Al responded. "You know, he thinks she's lyin', and he still cares for her. Hell, she's the only purty girl for miles. In fact, there ain't too many white girls anywhere around here. And that's a fact, too. I know. And, you know, another guy comes along and she starts takin' up with *you*."

"Has she got someone in Virginia?" Matt asked.

"Damned if I know," Al replied. "She gets letters all the time, but I never sees 'em. Pro'bly from her folks. That's how much I knowed."

"Want I should fight Sin for her?" Matt asked, jokingly, sparring with Al a little playfully.

"Hell no. He's lovesick, but not foolish." Then Al asked, "See his face?"

"The busted cheek?" Matt asked. "I gave him that."

"The scratch marks around the lips," Al mentioned.

"I came out jest when she called him a shithead and walked away. He tried to cover up, but I saw them. 'Spect he tried to kiss her again."

Matt tried his best to keep a straight face, but could not hold back his laugh. Straightening up, he asked, "What about the gals in town? Seems that'd be a choice."

"Oh, yeah. We all been out with several. She knows that." Looking down the row, Al stopped and asked, "Can we git started?"

Matt followed behind Al, again trying to stay close to his side with Al's long strides.

"You in love with her?" Al asked.

Matt pulled at Al's shirt to stop him, took out his makings and rolled himself a cigarette. His eye caught Sin behind them prying the bar to the barn door to open it. As he rolled his cigarette, he pointed out to the corn and the cotton around them. In a louder voice for Sin to hear, he said, "Am I in love with Ginny, you ask me? That's corn, right?" Matt said, pointing to the tall rows of corn that were standing in front of them.

"Yeah," Al answered, "and we'd better git a move on."

"That's cotton?" Matt continued, pointing to the cotton on the other side of the barn where Sin was headed.

Al nodded his head. "Yeah, but we're gonna start here first with the corn." He led Matt to the tall stalks close by.

Sin eased up on the door for fear that any noise would drown out what he was trying to hear Matt say. "I wouldn't be caught dead doin' what I'm doin' right now for the price of a good horse, a saddle, and a pair of guns," Matt told him, lit his cigarette and walked away.

Hearing this from the short distance, Sin opened the doors and yelled out, "Then why are ya?"

Looking at Al, he said in jest, "And they tell me you have something wrong with your hearing?"

Al looked at Matt, and while continuing his long, long strides, he asked, "Huh?"

Then, at a clearing in the cornfields, Al relieved Matt of the whip for a moment to show him how to use it. Since he had to use his left hand, he was awkward at the actual demonstration, but showed with expertness the principles of uncoiling it, coiling it back over his shoulder and letting the tail fly. However, in Al's case, the whip got wrapped around his body before he snapped it.

"Damn whip," Al cried out. "I'm not a lefty." Giving the whip back to Matt, he said, "Here, try it."

Matt's youthful body brought the whip in proper place at the spine of his back almost natural like, and he let it fling towards a leaf on the ground with almost precise marksmanship. The whip snapped, and the dirt fluffed up and caused the leaf to flutter away.

"You got the idea," Al said. "Keep trying."

Matt again snapped at the leaf, and came closer. Finally, after a few tries, the leaf was split in half, and excitement ran through Matt's veins. He felt the control of the whip. For the next hour, he kept practicing until he felt good enough to tie it on his belt and walk with Al into the cornfields.

"We'll walk through the corn fields first," Al said. "I'll show you all our nigs and you can get the hang of things. That's where Sin and Fats are. In the cotton fields."

Matt's training involved him meeting each black person he came to and gaining respect for him and his whip. The first was an elderly man in his sixties with long gray sideburns. Like the rest, he had a large sack laid over his back into which to place the plucked corn.

Another was a young woman with a child no older than two years tugging at the hem of her dress, and a thumb well tucked in her mouth. Beside her was another woman, slightly older, with two sons; one a six-year old, and the other an eight-year old. The young woman's name was Nancy. She was tall and slender in built, only about twenty-eight years old, and a good-looking black woman.

"Where are the fathers?" Matt asked Al.

"Don't rightly know," Al answered. "We don't allow marryin' inside, and once someone does, we split 'em up and sells 'em to another plantation owner. This discourages any gettin' on with childrun. We can't handle childrun and slaves at the same time."

"Does it?" Matt asked.

"Does what?" Al asked.

"Does it discourage the slaves from havin' childrun?"

"Nope. Not really, I guess, 'cause women still get pregnant. I supposin' Hezekiah is the father of this heah six-year old." Al pointed to the two children close to Nancy. "Might be for the older boy, too."

"Where's Hezekiah?" Matt asked looking around.

"He's in the cotton fields, where you caught us yesterday. We'll head over yonder real soon. "

Another thing that annoyed Matt to some degree was the slow way they were accustomed to talking, as if they had all day to say everything that was on their mind. Coming from Montana, where the winters were briskly cold, he learned to talk fast. The other thing was how slow they moved, except for Al's long steps. It just did not make any sense to Matt. Al walked in large steps, and then moved as slow as he talked. Matt figured all of this just had to have something to do with the heat and the humidity, except that it did not affect him that way, at least not for the moment.

That afternoon, Jim rode his quarter horse up to the far end of the cornfields where he met Matt and Al. Jim was a handsome man, and as casual as they came, puffing on his pipe as he walked along.

"Afternoon, Matt," Jim said, reining up beside them. "Al been shucking you some fun in the cornrows?" he punned.

"You got a good crop, Jim," Matt replied. "Nothin' like this in Montana. Not as high anyways."

Jim dismounted and gave the reins to Al. "I'll take over now, Al. Take Red here for a walk and meet us over in the cottonfields."

One thing Al never liked was working with animals, especially horses. Red was not Al's friend either, and Al knew it. But, Al took the reins and led him out of the cornfields and down the road for a good walk, skipping every moment Red seemed to want to step on his toes.

"Know anything about cotton, Son?" Jim asked, knocking the used tobacco from his pipe against his boot.

"First time I ever saw cotton, Jim," Matt replied. "Rows and rows of it."

"More like miles and miles of it," Jim added.

"Sure is beautiful."

"We're proud of it. The McBride Plantation is our home. Let's walk over to the cottonfields. I want to show you our pride in trade." Jim led Matt on foot while cleaning out the bowl of his pipe with a stick.

Jim was right. The walk alone took the men long enough just to reach the first rows.

"Matt," Jim said as they approached Hezekiah. "Hezekiah's the Driver for pickin' cotton. He's pickin' cotton 'cause he's already put his folk to work."

Hezekiah was wearing an old hat. He was quite handsome and showed some charm about him. His shirt was buttoned and tucked under his overalls.

"What did Al do when he caught up with him, Jim?"

"Nothin'. He was too busy fussing with his hand," Jim answered. "Saw he was back in the field later, so he left him alone."

"What you aimin' to do, now?"

Looking behind them, they could see Sin riding over to them. Hearing part of the conversation about Hezekiah, Sin said, "He's yours for now, Matt. What you figurin' on doin'?"

That was a good question he threw at Matt, causing Matt to look at Sin with a lot of consternation. Matt was from the North with no experience with slaves. Now, all of a sudden, he had to deal with the issue staring him straight into his eyes . . . Hezekiah.

"Boy!" Sin called out to Hezekiah. "Listen up. What you did yesterday? No good."

Sin talked down to Hezekiah like he was just learning to speak English. The reason Hezekiah never spoke much was that he simply did not want to associate with the white folk. They had kept his people from going to school and learning to read and write. This way, the owners felt they would keep their slaves. He simply kept working at picking cotton without looking up at Matt or Jim.

"You heah, Boy?" Sin yelled out at him while snapping the whip in his direction.

"Now, you see, Matt," Sin said, looking at the whip. "That's why we carry the whip. They don't listen most the time."

Sin turned and rode away towards another crew of workers, saying, "Send Matt mah way when you're through with him, Jim."

Matt walked over to Hezekiah and sat on a tree stump next to him, which had been cut down for planting cotton around it. "Sure enough," Matt thought to himself, "those kids look jest like him."

"Your name, Hezekiah?" he asked him.

Hezekiah grunted a little looking up slightly at Matt. Mostly he kept looking at the whip on Matt's belt. He knew that Matt had become another one of his slave drivers. He kept picking cotton. Another younger man assisted him, putting cotton into his sack.

"Well, Hezekiah, my name is Matt. And I've got the job of gettin' this cotton picked. Now, I don't know anythin' about cotton, so I'm gonna rely on you helpin' me. You unnerstand?"

Hezekiah grunted again and kept picking cotton.

Jim looked on wondering how Matt was going to handle the situation. One thing he knew, though, Matt would handle it.

Matt was determined to do just that.

Looking down the row, Hezekiah rose up and took the younger man away by the arm and walked him to two rows over where a few women were working. "You stay here and pick the cotton and carry this woman's bag for her, ya heah?" Hezekiah ordered him. Then he removed a sack from the woman's back and gave it to the young man to carry.

The woman smiled as she was relieved of a heavy load and started picking cotton faster. The woman beside her did the same.

A Driver with a mule-drawn wagon pulled up to them with two black men riding in it. They walked up to the workers and relieved them of their sacks and carried them to the wagon where they emptied them. One of the men threw the empty sacks back at the women, and the other man moved the wagon along further down the row.

Hezekiah watched the younger man as he began to pick the boll attached to the stem and throw it into the sack. He walked over to the man and dumped out what he had picked. "No," Hezekiah yelled out, and gave the sack back to the boy, "you knows better'n that, boy!"

Jim walked over easy to join Matt.

Matt turned and shaded his eyes from the sun as he saw him coming.

"What's goin' on?" Matt asked Jim as they continued walking through the rows of cotton.

"The boy thought he'd get away with loadin' up the sack with stems and bolls," Jim said, with his lips tight, showing no signs of letting up on Matt.

"The boll is the cotton, I take it."

"Yep," Jim answered., signaling Al to bring Red back over. "With Hezekiah looking, he plucked the bolls pretty clean. When no one was looking, thinking he could get away with it, he started packing the sack with stems and leaves. Snapping the cotton that way is faster, but trashy. One more time like that, and Hezekiah would have slapped the boy."

Then pointing over to the cotton machine he added, "That there is our jinny." He laughed and said, "Not to be confused with our Ginny."

"What's a jinny?" Matt asked.

Al walked up and gave Red's reins to Jim, then walked back towards the corn fields, his working place.

"It's a machine, Matt," Jim explained. "Come on, Matt, hop on board" he said. "I'll show you."

The two men climbed aboard Red and rode over to the outer edge of the plantation where a shed stood. It looked like any other shed, except this one was called the "cotton gin".

The two men walked over to the gin, leaving the stallion ground tied. Four slaves were unloading the cotton from two wagons on one side and sending it to the top of the gin for another slave to send it into the machinery. It was the wheels and cogs that were first called the cotton gin, getting its name from the word "engine".

Once inside the shed, Jim showed Matt the "gin", as she was called. "That separates the boll from the twigs and leaves. This one slave furnishes the power for our cotton gin. She's equal to fifty slaves trying to separate the boll by hand. Our nigs would bring the cotton and feed it to the gin.

"It has forty wire-like teeth inside that tears the green seeds from the cotton. These iron slits actually pull the cotton through, but because the seeds are larger and can't go through, they are removed and cleaned from the wires by the second cylinder. The clean cotton now is called 'lint'," Jim continued to explain, showing Matt the inside workings of the gin.

"You don't want to get in her way, Matt," Jim cautioned about the female slave cranking the gin. "Those teeth have maimed one of our slaves trying to make a pass at her one day."

Outside, again, Jim lead Matt over to another shed some hundred feet away. "The lint is taken to the press room over here."

There, Matt was introduced to bales of cleaned cotton being loaded onto wagons. "Our slaves here are called "ginners" and the now seedless cotton is pressed into bales using a screw press. Each bale weighs four hundred pounds. It takes two strong men to load them into the wagons. Any questions?"

"One, Jim," Matt said, impressed at what he was seeing for the first time.

"Fire away, son."

"If that slave replaces fifty slaves," Matt asked, feeling the compactness of the bales, "wouldn't you be needing less slaves eventually."

"One would think so, Matt, but the answer is just the opposite. We need more slaves to pick more cotton."

Looking around at the vastness of the plantation and eighty slaves working it, Matt saw Ginny riding towards them on her mare. Reining up next to Jim's stallion, she dismounted and walked over to them.

"Gentlemen," she addressed them with her quirk in her hand, and her whip strapped to her side. "How's school coming along, Matt?" she asked.

Matt smiled at her, tilted back his Stetson, and scratched the front of his head as if to make an educated statement. "It's mind boggling, to say the least, Gin," he said. "All this land jest for cotton."

"Did you tell him, father, about the money made here?" she asked.

"He's just beginning to learn, Gin," Jim said. "Matt, we've got a gold mine here, to use the vernacular. A literal gold mine. When we were offered the opportunity by my father to come here and invest in this plantation, we thought we were getting well over our head. We knew nothing about growing cotton."

"Like me, huh?" Matt mused.

"Well, not exactly," Ginny added. "We were in the textile industry in Virginia, and we did have a broad education in that field. But to grow it, no. We relied on the previous owners getting us started. We had twelve or so men from Virginia here showing us the ropes. Then once we got the knack of it, we were left with three, Sin, Al, and Fats."

"Do you know what they were doing before we bought this plantation, Matt?" Jim asked, relighting fresh tobacco in his pipe. "They did it all by hand, Matt. It took one slave a whole day to clean just one pound of cotton. That's why they sold it to us. We have the money, know-all, and expertise to do a high-production job. That bale you're sitting on weighs four hundred pounds. We judge every slave here with how much cotton they can pick, no more and no less. They know that if they pick more than yesterday, we will expect the same from here on.

"This here gin's run by wooden cogs made of white oak. Hell, the cogs themselves take a slave a long time to make because he's got to cut threads on a log and then cut another set of threads to fit them. It's not an easy task." Then pointing to another slave, he added, "That's his job over there, Matt." Picking up a cog, Jim continued, "These cogs gear up the power and transmit it to the gin stand by belt. Matt, it took us over a year to build our gin."

"Whewee," Matt let out a yell. "All this has gotta be worth it."

"We started with a hand-powered gin and produced a hundred and fifty pounds of cotton in one day. Today, we can produce over four hundred pounds, and with a steam ginny, we can do over one thousand pounds of cotton per day. That, Matt, is my next objective, and by thunder, I'm going to get one."

"What makes this a gold mine, Jim?" Matt asked, hopping up on a bale. "I mean, who buys all this stuff."

"On my grandfather's side," Ginny interruped, "the textile industry, he puts all this in his warehouse for his textile mills, and ships it to the New England states. Now we have relationships with foreign markets like England and France where he ships at least twenty percent of it. It's in big demand."

"See that wagon leaving, Matt," Jim said, looking at a bale-loaded wagon being pulled by mules along ruts towards the main road. "That's gold, son."

"And when you run out of cotton, what then?" Matt asked as Ginny sat down beside him.

"We have a gold vein here, Matt," Ginny added, "that never runs out. We plow, we sow, we hoe, and we reap. We plow, we sow, we hoe, we reap, and so forth. We didn't know this. We thought like anything else that we'd have to let part of our plantation go barren for a season just to rejuvenate the soil."

"That's right, Matt," Jim continued, as they began walking back to their horses. "Unlike other crops, we can plant and replant cotton right through the season."

Matt heard one of the slaves cussing his team of mules as the wagon tilted in the rut it was riding, almost turning over.

"Hold up there, Mister," Matt yelled, running over to him. "Don't ever pull those reins that tight," he ordered, taking the reins from the driver. "That mule has feelings, and you're biting into her jaw. Hold on, Bessie. Hold on," Matt said, as he let up on the reins, giving the mules a chance to breathe. "There, there," he said, pulling taut on the reins once the mules were getting under control.

The wagon was on a slant with two wheels out of the rut and higher than the other two wheels. "Hop out, son," Matt ordered, sliding carefully onto the newly vacated seat and still holding the reins. "Easy now, Bessie, let's take it easy." Pulling the right rein he cried out, "Gee! Bessie. Gee!" Pulling the reins attached to the mule on his left ever so slightly, he cried again, "Gee, Ella! Gee!" Once he got the mules to pulling the wagon back into the ruts, uprighting the wagon, he pulled back easy on the reins and cried, "Haw!" once, pulled the reins straight, and then let them fall loose in his hands.

After he felt comfortable with the mules, he reined them up, and gave them back to the slave. "Here you go, son," he said, "Treat your mules with loving care and they'll give you a full day's work."

Ginny laughed and hit her leg with her quirk in jest. "Ha. Big Matt is no loving man. Ha." She had referred to his argument against working with the slaves, that he was no loving person.

"You're good with animals, son," Jim said, waiting for Matt to rejoin them. "You're good with men, too. But just call them what they are."

"How's that?" Matt asked.

"You called him 'Mister', and 'Son'" Jim reminded Matt. "From now on, you call them 'Boy', or just plain 'Nigger'. That, son, is our main expense around here. He cost me one hundred dollars. For that, he works for me from sun up til sundown, and longer if we have a full moon. In return, I feed him, house him, and clothe him."

At the horses, Jim and Ginny picked up their reins and mounted up.

"You're going to need more slaves, Jim?" Matt asked, picking up cotton bolls scattered around the gin.

"In the past thirty years, Tennessee produced more cotton than all else put together. The South is up to eighty percent of total world market of export with cotton. More than two-thirds of the slaves work the cotton fields, and we right now, according to my folks in Virginia, have more than four million slaves, ten times what we had thirty years ago. And there is no end in sight. You bet we're going to need more slaves, and they will do more work with less effort."

"Matt," Jim added. "You've got a lot to learn about cotton. But don't worry. Like me, you'll learn it, and be better at it than I am."

"See you later, Matt," Ginny yelled back as she spurred her horse and headed towards the house.

Matt realized that he was getting the education he missed all these years from not going to college, right here and right now. Why Jim was involving him, he was not ready to comprehend. But, for the sake of being with Ginny, he committed himself to learning everything he could about corn and cotton; much more about the latter for he was intrigued with the new technology he was being shown.

Tossing bolls up in the air like a juggler, missing them as they floated lazily down in different directions, Matt said, "Big business!"

"Olaf Gustavson has the largest plantation a few miles down the road," Jim continued. "You passed it on the way here. The Elliots and the Johnsons own a couple more, smaller ones. One of these days, I hope to join Olaf and the two of us will have the largest one in Tennessee. I hope . . ."

"And Ginny?" Matt asked. "How does she fit in with all this?"

"I thought you'd get around to asking about her," Jim responded, scraping some mud from one of the wheels of the wagons loaded with bales of cotton. "My father, her grandaddy, is my boss. He's in his eighties, but as spry as ever. He owns a mill in Richmond, one of the largest. Some day, I'm going to inherit the mill and turn it over to Ginny.

"She grew up in Richmond, and actually worked in the mill until we bought this plantation. In order to make this transition work, she is spending time with me learning this facet of the business."

"And her mother, Jim?" Matt asked almost restraining himself. "I don't have a right prying into this part of your life, and if you don't want to tell me, Sir . . ."

"I do want to tell you, Matt," Jim said, puffing on his pipe again. "Jane wanted Ginny to do anything and everything her heart desired. She could have stayed in Richmond, but my father had other plans for her. He wanted her to be in charge of the mill completely. He made her come with us."

"Agin your will, Jim?" Matt asked, creating deep furrows in his brow. "Yours and Jane's?"

"No, not against our will, Matt, but with our blessings. We wanted Ginny with us, but she wanted to stay there in Richmond. She didn't want anything to do with slaves on a plantation. Oh, she worked with them from a distance in the mill. She had people who worked over them. But, she was always Miss Prima donna and father wanted to knock this out of her.

"Her mother was too easy with the slaves for her, and Gin fought her. Told her she had to be tough. They were completely opposite one another."

"And when Jane died?" Matt asked, rolling a cigarette with his makings.

"It's not easy to tell you, Matt," Jim said, gasping as he uttered each sentence with pain.

"Forget it, Jim," Matt said, throwing his cigarette in the dirt. "We can talk further at another time."

"No," Jim came back. "Let's walk down the rows so I can show you more."

As they walked the rows of cotton, Jim showed Matt the many slaves working well that day, for Jim was walking in their midst. And as they walked, Jim continued talking about his wife, Jane.

"Jane brought Ginny up with all the fineries Richmond could afford. She graduated with high honors in her class and worked at the mill at the same time. She was introduced to the handsomest of men and turned them all down. She admired my father and felt no man could walk in his shoes."

"Even you?" Matt asked, helping a slave with her bag by lifting it and shifting some of the cotton inside.

"That, son," Jim said abruptly, "you don't do. Don't help any nigger."

"Didn't know," Matt replied quickly and jumped back over a couple of rows of cotton to rejoin Jim. He stuck his hands in his pockets like a punished little kid and continued walking beside Jim.

"You're right, Matt," Jim said. "Even me. But, she respected me as a man because I grew up just like my father in many ways. Maybe that's why I love her so much."

"What happened with Jane?" Matt asked softly.

"She would spend hours with the damn niggers and read to them and join them in their spirituals, even after they were supposed to be in bed. She'd slip into bed with me quietly, hoping I wouldn't be disturbed. Hell, Matt, I hated that. But I loved her. God knows how much I loved her."

"No more, Jim," Matt said, stopping to simply face Jim.

"Just one more thing to get it off my chest, Matt," Jim said, confronting Matt face to face.

Matt nodded his head in approval and said, "Promise?"

Jim smiled, and continued. "Ginny is falling in love with you, Matt. I hope you're man enough for her."

Having said that, Jim turned and walked away, leaving Matt in the middle of the biggest cotton field he had ever seen, and planted the biggest burden upon Matt that he ever received. Matt just stood there with his jaw dropped and watched Jim walk away. He had nothing to counteract what Jim had laid on him at that moment.

But he had to somehow have the last word. "What about you, Jim?" he shouted. "What the hell you gonna do when she leaves you all alone?"

Jim kept walking as if he had not heard Matt. Matt stood there and watched him walk out of sight. He looked out into the rows of cotton and watched the slaves feverishly shuck the cotton into large burlap bags, and the wagons drive up and haul them to the ginny. He watched as another wagon took a bale of cotton and drove off towards the Tennessee River. It was a beautiful work of machinery and he was becoming a part of it whether he liked it or not.

CHAPTER 17

ONE LESS MOUTH TO FEED

S in rode over to Matt on his Appaloosa, reined up and dismounted. "I'm supposed to learn you some things about this heah plantation," Sin said, with a straight face, showing contempt for Matt.

"Kinda had a big lesson dropped in my lap already, Sin," Matt said.

"Well, fust you got to know how to deal with these niggers," Sin continued. "I'm gonna show ya."

He walked over to a male slave, skinny, and small in stature and said to him, "Boy. Pick 'em faster. You heah me, boy? You pick 'em faster."

The slave began plucking the bolls faster, cleaning them, and putting them in the sack. However, it still was not fast enough for Sin.

"Faster, Boy," Sin said over and over again. "Faster, Boy."

To show Matt how he handled his slaves with authority, Sin walked up to the slave and slapped him across the face. "Boy," he repeated. "Don't you look at me like that! I'll kick your damn teeth in." He slapped him again.

Matt watched and did nothing. When Sin returned to him, Matt asked, "Was that fun, boy?"

Sin grit his teeth and said, "That's how you deals with them, Mister. You don't take shit from them."

Matt looked at Sin's scratched face showing a shiner under his left eye.

"You slap him all the time?"

"If necessary, all the time. You go down the row and kick ass. They like that. Keeps them in line. Makes them work harder."

"Slap them," Matt asked, "like Gin slapped you? Or did she hit you with her fist?" He looked into his face and gave Sin a sorrowful look, hoping that Sin would start a fight.

Sin's teeth clinched and his cheeks quivered, and he felt instantly like hitting Matt with his tightened fist, but he was cut off by a voice splitting the wind.

"Lunch time," Ginny cried out. She walked through the rows with a basket of food in one hand and a pail of water in her other.

Al, who was close by her, had been watching all that was going on. He was quick to run over and grab a cold egg sandwich and a ladle of water from her. Ginny kept staring at the other two men just a little further down the row. She quickly moved on to the other two.

"Egg sandwiches or peanut butter and jelly?" she asked, walking over and setting the basket down in front of them.

Sin took the ladle and scooped some water for himself, while Matt looked on. "Don't eat lunch," he reminded her.

Sin in turn took a sandwich as if for spite since Matt didn't. "He talked to a nig," Sin said, and walked away.

"You did, what?" Ginny asked, putting her hands on her hips and looking quite indignant at Matt. "Let's get one thing straight, Matt. You don't talk to nigs. You boss them. Plain and simple."

Matt looked up at her, grinned a little, but did not say a word.

"Do you understand me, Matt Jorgensen?" she said a little less defiantly. "You just don't talk to them, unless, of course, you're giving them an order."

Matt nodded his head, doffed his Stetson, and smiled. "Is it true you called him a 'shit head'?" Matt asked, knowing Sin would hear him loud and clear.

Sin turned, ran towards Matt and plunged into his stomach with his whole body knocking him backwards onto the cotton.

Ginny stepped into the next row while Hezekiah took his workers and pushed them safely aside.

Sin, being on top of Matt, took his full hand and pushed on Matt's face as hard as he could, causing his nose to bleed.

Matt raised Sin's head in front of him and brought his fist across his jaw.

Quickly getting to his feet, Matt picked Sin up and slammed his fist into his stomach causing Sin to feel gut-wrenching pain. Sin was finding out rather quickly that Matt's muscles were overpowering him and was ready to call it quits when Matt's fist came down hard against his head. Sin fell to the dirt and stayed there.

Taking the pail of water, Matt dumped it on Sin, giving him some healthy relief from his beating. Sin raised himself up and saw both Matt and Ginny staring down at him.

Matt helped Sin to his feet and kept a hold of him by his bib suspenders. "Listen, you bastard," Matt said, with tight lips and a steely look in his eyes, "I'm here only because of Ginny. I like her a lot. I'm not about to give my feelings for her up to a towhead like you."

With that said, he released Sin.

Sin grabbed his hat and stomped away. A smile came across Hezekiah's face almost as big as the one Ginny began sporting. Of course, Ginny was in a stage of bewilderment at the present. She didn't know whether to like what she heard, or hate it because a good worker was walking away.

"He's your 'bossman'," Matt said indignantly. "If you want him, I suggest you be gettin' after him."

Ginny stood there and watched Sin walk away. Putting her hands behind her, she began to rock in her boots as a smile the size of Texas beamed across her face.

"You mean what you said?" she asked without looking at Matt.

"Hell, yes," he answered, with a Texas smile across his face, too.

She dropped the basket of sandwiches and threw her arms around Matt with great enthusiasm and, wiping the blood from his nose, kissed him.

Pushing her gently away from him, he took his bandanna from his neck, and taking some of the water left in the pail, cleaned up his face. He took her into his arms and planted a kiss on her lips that she would remember when their grandkids had kids.

Hezekiah and some of the other workers turned their backs and resumed their picking cotton while they began humming. In a short while, the humming got louder and louder and their music filled every fiber of the bodies of the clinched couple in the cotton fields.

"What's that all about?" Matt asked, breaking from Ginny's hold.

Looking around, she could see smiles on the faces of the black people. "They're expectin' you to take Sin's place, Mister Bossman," she said, putting her arm around Matt's waist. "They think you just kicked the ass of the meanest man this side of the Missoura."

"Hold on just a minute, Gin," Matt said, letting go of his arm around Ginny. "Sin's not sore enough to leave his job, is he? Tell me that's not so."

"You called me Gin, Matt. I like that."

That evening, Matt found himself to be a fourth partner for a poker hand, with Jim, Al, and Fats rounding out the number, at the kitchen table. Sin had drawn his pay and rode off.

Ginny sat on the divan in front of the window reading a newspaper. "Bertha had prepared a supper for him in a bag to take with him," she said. "Don't think he'll get hungry."

"Will he be back?" Matt asked, as he clumsily played poker, letting Jim win most of the hands.

Jim took advantage of Matt's carelessness and continued playing, knowing he could beat Al and Fats any time. "Nope," he said. "He'll find a job easy enough. Maybe even make more money. I know for a fact that the Johnsons down the way, and the Gustafsons too need his kind."

Al and Fats played on, and stared at one another with the look in their eyes that said, "He'll be back. As long as Ginny is here, he'll be back."

Matt reflected the same thing in his mind, but kept from saying it.

The next day, Matt hunted Hezekiah down to have a talk with him. Finding him working in the field near a woman with two kids, Matt approached him. "Why'd you try runnin' away, Hezekiah?" Matt asked.

"No reason, Mister Matt," Hezekiah answered, refusing to look at Matt and slightly looking over at the woman as she was his main concern.

Matt looked at Nancy, the black woman, and recognized the tell-tell message in their eyes. His eyes traveled to the two youngsters working with the woman and he surmised what was taking place.

"Is she your woman, Hezekiah?" Matt asked.

There was silence as Hezekiah resumed working at a faster pace. Matt wouldn't let the matter drop. "Is she your woman?"

After a few moments of stillness, the black woman spoke up. "My name is Nancy. These are my kids."

"You know you can't be married," Matt said, trying to look into Hezekiah's eyes. "You're a slave."

"He knows that, Mister," Nancy answered.

"Then why?" Matt asked, looking over at Nancy and shrugging his shoulders.

Hezekiah turned and intently answered Matt. "'Cause that's the rules, Mister. 'Cause that's the rules."

"Yet, you have two boys. They are your children, aren't they, Hezekiah?" Matt asked pointing at them.

"They's mine, Mister," Nancy answered and continued to work plucking the cotton.

"They're yours, too," Matt grilled again, "Isn't that right, Hezekiah?"

Hezekiah kept on working without answering Matt.

"What you gonna do wif us, Mister?" Nancy asked, not slowing down with her picking the cotton. The two boys kept working but tried to eye Matt with the side of their eyes.

"You tell me the truth, and I'll see what I can do," Matt answered. "Can't promise nothin', but at least I can try, dammit."

"No need to get angry, Mister," Hezekiah turned and said to Matt. Then with tears in his reddened eyes he answered Matt. "They is my childrun. And I is proud of them."

Matt took off his Stetson and wiped his forehead with a bandanna from his pocket. "Thought so," he said pointing for the kids to come to him. "Come here."

Hezekiah gently motioned for them to go to Matt, while a smile crept across Nancy's face.

Each boy was bare chested, bare footed and wore bib overalls. Sheepishly, they went to Matt one at a time. The older of the two was nine years, and the other was seven. Matt rubbed his ostensibly unprejudiced fingers through the boys' kinky hair trying to win their approval of him.

"They're good kids," Matt remarked. "Strong."

"How can we marry, Mister Matt?" Hezekiah asked stopping his work and standing up to meet Matt's height.

"Whoa!" Matt replied. "You're a tall one." Turning on his heels as if to look around for Ginny, or Jim, he hesitantly replied, "Well, Hezekiah, I don't know."

Hezekiah bent down and started working again, as did Nancy and her boys.

"But," Matt began all over again, "I'll ask, and see what I can do."

Matt walked away from the working family, occasionally looking back to see them still diligently working. Hezekiah rose and walked over to his workers. He was still their driver, and he was responsible for this portion of the cotton field.

That evening after supper, Matt waited until Fats and Al had dismissed themselves for other places before he approached Jim and Ginny. Matt took his time rolling his cigarette in front of the fireplace this night, waiting the right moment to ask the all-important and delicate question. But ask it he would.

"You got something on your mind, Matt," Jim said as he lit his pipe.

"Why'd you say that?" Matt asked nervously.

"You're taking too long with your makings for one thing, and for the other, you don't have a drink in your hand."

"What's troubling you, Mister Jorgensen?" Ginny asked as she sat down in her leather chair with her ususal evening whiskey in her hand.

"Got a question to ask both of you," Matt said, lighting his cigarette with a stick he lit from the fireplace. "Hope you don't mind me meddlin'."

"Shoot, son," Jim said, with half a smile.

"All right, I will. Why can't your slaves marry?"

"Is that all?" Jim responded.

"Well, yeah," Matt replied.

"You talking about Hezekiah and Nancy, Matt?" Ginny asked.

"Yeah. You know, then?" Matt asked, astonished at her reply.

"Known from the very first day we took over this plantation, Matt," Jim answered.

"Well?" Matt asked again.

"Easy enough answer, my boy," Jim responded. "You want to tell him, Gin?"

"Why not?" she came back, standing up to face Matt with her drink. "We took over this plantation two years ago. The owners then knew about Hezekiah, and their rules were, 'no marriages'. The reason was, they'd get their wives pregnant, and that would cost us money in man power."

"Also," Jim added, "if they ran away, we would lose a whole family. With pretending we didn't know, they worked harder as five people, rather than one family. Make sense?"

"That's why you caught Al whipping Hezekiah when you first rode up," Ginny said, fixing Matt a drink. "He tried to run away."

"Why, Ginny?" Matt asked.

"Good question, Matt," Jim replied. "We are entering a secession time when Tennessee will drop out of the Union and become a part of the Confederate States. Hezekiah thinks that by running away he can get a fresh start north across the Tennessee River as a free man. He doesn't want to chance his family getting hurt, so he tries it alone. If he made it, he would then see that his family followed."

"So you whup him to make him stay?" Matt asked, taking the drink from Ginny.

"Maybe we were wrong, Matt," Jim responded. "But we had no assurance that they would stay if they got married."

"What if I got that assurance for you, Jim?" Matt asked sipping on his drink.

"How?" Ginny asked.

"They told me today they want to get married," Matt answered. "I think we should give them a chance. That is, if you could see fit."

"And all you have is their request to get married?" Ginny asked. "Nothing else?"

"Nothing," Matt answered. "I don't even know whether or not they'd stay. It's just the way they talked with me that makes me feel that they would."

"They want a chance," Jim said, "That's what you're saying?"

"Yes, Sir," Matt replied.

"Then, by golly, Matt, I can see no reason why we can't allow them," Jim said, with a firm lip and an intent look Ginny's way. "What do you say, dear lady?"

"I'm for love, all the way," Ginny replied. "You know that." Then with a lift of her glass, she added, "Let them be married."

"The hell they will," came Sin's booming voice from the kitchen as he threw open the kitchen door and entered with Fats.

"What?" Jim asked, turning around to see the two men together.

"You heard me," Sin snorted throwing his Stetson on the chair next to him. "My boss, before you had rules not to let them marry. I keep the same rules, and I'll be damn if I'll let any goddam nigger marry on my plantation.

"I thought you left for good," Ginny replied.

"Just to cool off," Sin replied. "Well, I'm not gone, and I'm still foreman. Right, boss?" he asked Jim.

"Ginny's your boss," Jim reminded him, watching Sin eye Matt. "You answer to her, not to me."

"Then I stay," Sin said adamantly, walking over to Ginny and taking her hand.

Refusing his hand, Ginny smarted back in anger, yet softly, "You're fired, Sin. Get your things and get the hell off our property."

"You don't mean that, Ginny," Sin came back at her trying to get her hand again. "We're gonna get married, you and me."

Ginny withdrew from him and looked at him with frightened eyes as if this were the first time she had really seen him. "Married? You? Get out! Out! Matt, get him the hell out of here."

Matt stood there eyeing the pair waiting for a cue from within his own spirit to make the right move. He heard the word "marry" from Sin's lips and rebelled from the thought of losing Ginny to this creep.

Quicker than Matt could double his fist, Sin had his .44 out of its holster and aimed at Matt. "Try it, mister, and you'll die right here," Sin said cocking his Colt.

Matt temporarily froze for the moment, turned away from Sin and, seeing the chance, seized the poker iron by the fireplace, turned and knocked Sin's gun out of his hand with it.

As Sin bent down to pick up his gun, Ginny's whip lashed it away across the hardwood floor. It gave Matt a chance to bring his boot up into Sin's face. Matt reached over and picked Sin up as he fell and brought his fist to Sin's face, breaking his nose. Taking him by the seat of his pants, Matt threw him out the kitchen door that Fats had opened for him.

Matt gave Fats a hard look. "You goin' with him?"

"Me?" Fats asked. "Don't know the fella." He smiled and went to the stove for a cup of coffee.

"Well, lady," Jim said walking into the kitchen with Ginny tucked under his arm, "I'd say you just got yourself a new foreman." With a smile, Jim looked at Matt and asked, "Want the job?"

Smiling, Matt winked at Jim, and smiled at Ginny. Al came in, and looking puzzled at all that went on, shrugged his shoulders, grabbed the coffee pot for his cup of coffee and sat down.

CHAPTER 18

JIM MEETS SYLVIA BOWEN

December 1860

T he snow came gently to Tennessee that Christmas. Sin never returned to the plantation, but instead joined the employment at the Olaf' plantation a few miles up the road. He was never one for being out of work, and never worked too far from his last employer.

Union Major Robert Anderson was a fifty-six year old Kentuckian who had, only a month before, been in command of Fort Moultrie. Now, he was a Yankee finding himself in Southern territory. The bigwigs in Washington felt that Anderson, being a native Southerner would do all he could to prevent a war between the North and the South.

Rumor had it that rebellious South Carolinians had a steamer stationed just off Charleston Harbor in South Carolina with the intent to prevent any escape of Federal troops. Because of this, he asked for authorization from Washington to transfer his forces from Fort Moultrie, and quickly take position inside Fort Sumter, which was a better place of refuge.

Having not received any such order, under his own initiative, he went ahead and transferred his garrison to Fort

Sumter that Christmas day. Fort Sumter was well fortified on an artificial island in the Charlston Harbor.

Now Anderson was deep into the South. In spite of his being a Southerner, he proved to his superiors that he was a loyal and true Union soldier.

"It was my solemn duty to move my command from a fort which we could not have held longer than forty-eight or sixty hours," he wrote the authorities in Washington, "to this one, where my power of resistance is increased to a very great degree."

When Anderson took over the fort, he felt some of the fort's residents were not truly loyal and had them thrown out. He retained only those he felt were loyal to the North.

His grave mistake was when he left Fort Moultrie, he left with only a minimum amount of provisions of both medical and food supplies. Now at Fort Sumter, he faced a long hardship to hold out until supplies were replenished from Washington. They never were, for when his government sailed the steamer, *Star of the West* out of New York harbor, the Southerners saw that it never reached the fort.

Al and Fats had returned from their last trip to Virginia, where they had taken the cotton, each in separate wagons. It took them two days to get the farm ready for a great celebration. Jim and Matt stayed behind to keep reign over the black people, allowing them to slack off a bit, working mostly with plowing, clearing the fields, and working the animals, as Christmas was upon them.

After all, Christmas was a time of levity around the plantation. Jim had seen to it that he brought in the Christmas tree by himself. This was his tradition. It was also tradition for Ginny to decorate it. This year she had Matt to help her.

Al and Fats brought in the Yule log. Matt teamed up with them to help the black people celebrate their Christian heritage as well. Some of the black people cleaned up inside their huge tent that stood away from the cabins, which they used for their Baptist church. Hezekiah and a few others were elders of the church. Joshua was the preacher. Others cleared the area around the tent, expecting a lot of company this special Christmas Day.

Hezekiah and Nancy were getting married. It finally came out that the two children were his, and now it was time to make everything legal. Matt saw to it that they would not be punished for keeping this their long deep secret.

The day started with getting the preparations under way for the wedding. All eighty of the black people were adorned in various colors of new clothing they were given by Jim and Ginny. The women had busied themselves with hours of sewing. The men had picked their shoes up, which the shoemaker had made with their numbered sticks in them signifying whose shoe sizes belonged to whom. Al and Fats had brought them from town.

The kids were dressed up neat and prim with Christmas ribbons in the girls' hair, and neckties around the boys' necks, and new shoes on their feet. Everyone looked better this day than on any given Sunday.

They had already enjoyed their Christmas services early that morning. The preacher, Joshua, in his fifties, sporting a gray beard, preached from the book of Luke the story of the birth of Jesus. "Amens" and "hallelujahs" came from every corner in the tent as they sat on wooden benches with sawdust strewn over the ground. It was cold, and they were all dressed with new coats and blankets. Bertha saw to it that even Matt had a new jacket, which she took painstaking weeks to put together. It was a good-looking jacket, brown and tan in color, with many layers of cotton to make it warm. She had also made Ginny a new dress, blue in color with white puffy full-length sleeves. Ginny was proud of her dress, only because Bertha had made it. Even though she felt very superior to the black people, Ginny considered Bertha and Naomi on a different level from the rest. Still, to her, they were simply black people. She had two other nice dresses in her closet she had purchased while in Virginia, much nicer looking than this one, but for this day, she paid particular attention to this one being her favorite.

It was simply Bertha's way of saying that she was happy belonging to the McBride family, even though she had taken the name of Morgan from her prior owners. She and Naomi found extra material and buttons under their tree that year.

Another baby had been born before Thanksgiving, and the little girl played the Christ child in the manger, clothed with layers and layers of cotton to make sure the cold would stay away. Matt laughed out loud when he saw her, for it was the first time he had ever seen a black Jesus, and him being a girl with a colorful ribbon in her hair.

"I'm sorry," he said, "but I couldn't help myself."

Ginny and Jim, along with Al and Fats started to feel embarrassed for Matt, until the black people started laughing right along with him.

"It's alright, Mister Matt," Nancy said, as she held the hand of the mother, a woman in her late teens. "We all knows you weren't laughin' at us, but at what you saw."

Hezekiah stepped in and asked, "After all, Mister Matt, couldn't Jesus have been a little colorful? Hmmm?"

With that, Matt laughed louder, and the rest joined in with him. "You've got me there, Hezekiah. I suppose he could have been."

Fourteen other black couples were also getting married. It was a fine day for the weddings, inside the tent, with slaves from other plantations joining in. There had to have been over a thousand black people on the plantation, for all loved Hezekiah and Nancy very much. The tent could only hold a hundred people at most. The festivities started with the morning service, and kept on going right into the wedding services.

Joshua sat on the podium next to five other local preachers who were all about to give sermons this Christmas. "Keep it short, now Joshua," one of the ladies cried out from the audience, meaning for all the preachers to give short sermons.

"I aims ta, Widow Brown," Joshua said in a laughing-tone of voice. "I aims ta."

When it came time for the weddings, Joshua was joined with the other five preachers. Another twelve or so elders with their secret wives, who came from the audience to join them and give them their blessings, sat in the front row to be seen, as well as heard. The ladies were spruced up with much rouge and wore white gloves. Although it was a crudely-built tent structure, the women felt fit to be pretty, for it was one of the rare times, practically, they would dress up and be seen by so many people.

It was almost as if the ones who were getting married were being ordained. It was sort of a ritual they were going through before the wedding itself, and it had to be done with singing and hollering; lots of singing and plenty of hollering. Of course, the singing was done before and after each of the preachers gave his sermon.

Some of the people came in from the river where some had been baptized. It was good that the sun heated up the day, otherwise the county would have had an epidemic of colds. They also sat packed close to the front and provided body heat to each other.

After the brief sermons, which never were any shorter than forty minutes each, the wedding itself was done all together in a single ceremony, with all of them taking their wedding vows together. The wedding party was kept inside the tent with the newly baptized members of the Baptist Church, and their bodies kept them warm. Many of the white folks, mostly women, who wanted to be present, were privileged to attend inside the tent, also. Matt was one of the few men to attend and applaud, sing, and shout along with the rest.

The front of the house and along the south side was filled with wagons, mules, and horses, and there was not room for another pony. Later, the white folk would leave for the party down the road.

Ginny had gone ahead before Jim and the rest, as she was acting as one of the hostesses, to help Olaf's wife, Anna. Ginny's heart was to be with Matt, though, having fun as he was at the weddings.

Olaf Gustafson, the Swede, who owned one of the largest plantations in Tennessee, had invited the white folk in his community to his plantation for a Christmas get together and dance. His plantation house was a large two-storied house like the McBride's, but with gable roofs, two brick fireplaces, one on each end of the house running through the roof giving each room a fireplace, and a portico in front. It had two bedrooms upstairs and two bedrooms downstairs of unequal size, and four shed rooms in the rear, a front room, a passage through the center, and a kitchen. The woodwork was all handcrafted, denoting wealth among plantation owners. Not every owner could afford such luxury.

A huge tent had been erected on the north side of the house with planks laid down on the grass for a dance floor. It was a fine day for all the white ladies to get together and compare notes with one another. Cigars were lit up for the occasion by the men, and cups of brandy were shared by Jim and his employees. The neighbors brought their drinks of finest brandies, cigars, and candies as gifts from their plantation. Some brought turkeys, ham, and plenty of beef.

Many of the Olaf' slaves stayed to serve the Gustavsons and their guests, but then left when they got the all-clear sign to join the wedding festivities that were going on.

The fiddle players from the Johnson Plantation came in, with a banjo player from the Elliot's, and a guitar playing duo from the Baxter's made for the music for the rest of the day. It was already a few hours past noon, since much preaching had been done first. And now, the party began. There is nothing like the black people having fun at a party. It is a time for high-stepping dancing to the rhythm of the banjo, the strumming of the guitars, and the fiddle playing accompanied by the slapping of hands.

Inside the house Jim lit his pipe and moved closer to the fireplace. He sported a new sweater that Ginny had purchased from Virginia that fall when she went back with one of the wagons.

She also got Matt a new shirt to replace the one she tore with her whip at their first meeting. It was a much nicer shirt, blue plaid and made of fine-spun cotton.

She sported a purple vest Matt purchased, also in Virginia. Along with the new dress, she must have been the envy of every housewife that attended the weddings. Matt also made sure she had a box of chocolates to sweeten the occasion. She saw to it that he had a bottle of the finest Kentucky bourbon, and a box of good cigars. She got a like bottle of bourbon for Jim, and pipe tobacco was good enough for him.

Al and Fats entertained themselves with the opposite sex while they had been in Virginia, and failed to bring anything for

Christmas home with them. However, they enjoyed the festivities as much or more than most, and found themselves with a pair of good-looking ladies who were also single.

When the Kentucky Reel was called for at the Olaf' party most people started dancing right away. Even Ginny finally gave way to dancing with a few of the single men in the group, yet still hoping desperately to dance with Matt.

Jim eyed a young lady who appeared to be in her forties, with reddish hair and blue eyes, slender and about five-foot five in height. She seemed to be alone, and for all intrinsic purposes, Jim believed her to be so. After the first dance, he laid his drink and cigar aside, and walked over to ask her to dance with him. She saw him coming, and had prepared to meet him, as she had heard of his wife's passing away last year. When she arose to greet him, however, Olaf got there to ask her first.

While they made introductions and small talk, Jim went back to his drink and cigar whensuddenly he was tapped on the shoulder. Olaf and his partner had waltzed over to him and stopped just behind him.

"Pardon me, Jim," Olaf said politely in his Swedish accent, "but she vas vondering if'n you vould like to valtz vit this young lady, Miss Bowen.

Jim looked over Olaf''s shoulders and eyed the young lady who held a smile on her face and a dainty handkerchief in her palm.

Jim immediately put his drink down and placed the cigar inside his glass, which showed how excited he was about dancing with her. "I'd be delighted," he said, as he walked over to her, not realizing he had cut into the dance floor, and stumbled into a couple of the dancers. He apologized and, turning around, found her waiting for him attached to Olaf''s fingertips. Olaf smiled and released her to him.

"Hello," she said. "I hope I didn't cause you any embarrassment."

"Oh, no," he immediately answered, taking her hand. "My name is Jim McBride." He stood there gazing upon her beauty.

"I know. I'm Sylvia Bowen," she introduced herself. "Mrs. Bowen." He looked a little dismayed until she added, "Divorced."

"Oh, I'm sorry."

"No need to be, but thank you. My husband couldn't stay true, so it was I who divorced him."

"That's too bad."

The couple remained looking at one another, completely oblivious that anyone else was inside the tent.

"Dance?" she asked him.

"What? Oh, yes," he replied, and took her by the hand to dance.

"We're not getting any younger, and if you don't say something fast, the dance will be over."

She was right. The dance was over before they fully got out on the dance floor. However, the next dance was a fast waltz and the couple, standing on the dance floor, got caught up in it, the speed of which did not offer them any time to talk.

After the dance, and a lot of perspiration on Jim's part, he started to escort her back to her seat, when suddenly the slow waltz started. One look at her told him to stay on the floor. This was their waltz.

Back at the wedding, after the ceremonies, Bertha and her womenfolk got together with the other black neighbor womenfolk and saw to it that everyone was fed. The men had lined up tables across the lawns, which the ladies filled up with food. Salads, chicken, ham, sausage, grits, turnip greens, sweet potatoes, pumpkin pies, and breads of different sources decorated the planks from one end to the other. One would be hard pressed to imagine seeing so much food in one place. Cider and other juices poured in great buckets. Some spiced it with corn whiskey, the homemade kind, and those that drank were the last ones to leave.

CHAPTER 19

A KILLER AT CHRISTMAS TIME

T he wedding back at the McBride's plantation was kept shorter than most would have liked because most of the neighbors had to return to their plantations around the bend, over the river, or beyond the holler to get on with their Christmas celebrations, and their house Negroes would have to be on hand.   Still, the ceremonies lasted some ten to twelve hours, and more.

Several of the owners had come equipped with guns to make sure no one escaped. Even this did not prevent a few from making their way north to Kentucky. They had heard that a war was eminent between the states. At least, that was the gossip in their camps.

It was long into the night before the final buggy was seen leaving the Gustavson's party and trotting out into the distance. Jim had early on introduced his new friend, Sylvia to Matt and Ginny, and the foursome stood on the porch and waved the neighbors on. Olaf and Anna came out and joined them, with Olaf and Jim both lighting up their pipes. Matt rolled his makings into a cigarette and joined the smoking party.

Then the party of plates and leftover food was cleaned up, and nothing else had to be done. The slaves returned to their cabins. Al and Fats were still nowhere to be found.

Later that evening, at the McBrides', Hezekiah and Nancy, with their two children walked in the newly-fallen snow and traipsed through the barren rows that used to be cotton. They stopped in the middle of the rows, huddled together and looked up into the sky to give God the glory for this day, and the double-important meaning of it for them, for today they were finally a real family.

Curfew rules were slack that night, but still most of the black people were already in their cabins and the lights were burning low. They would not have to rise early the next day, or even for the next week. The tables were clean and the embers under the black pots were dying out. The snow continued to fall gently, just enough to give them a white Christmas.

Matt and Ginny left the party and walked together down the long road as if following the last buggy out, while the foursome went inside. It was a crescent moon that night and the planet Venus complimented its beauty.

The couple felt their liquor, and Matt was enjoying his cigarette.

Matt fumbled around with his hat in his hand trying to say something that made sense and not make an ass out of himself in his drunken condition. "Is Jim ever going to remarry, do you think?" Matt asked Ginny.

"Some day, I hope. Sylvia's a real nice lady, pretty, too. Don't you think?"

The walk was slow. Matt placed his hat back on his head. Their talk was in cadence with their inebriated walk, as if they had little to say.

"Young, and very attractive," Matt answered. "They danced a few times, I noticed."

"It's been a year, but he should be ready. Heaven knows he's been a lonely man this past year."

Then, as if out of thin air, he asked, "What about you?"

She stopped and looked into his eyes, as the snow piled up on her face.

"What about me?" she asked. Letting go of his hand, she resumed walking.

"You ever think about getting married?" he asked.

"Always."

"With that somebody from Virginia?" he asked, almost not getting the words clear and distinct from his lips.

"Mr. Robert J. Sullivan, of the Richmond Sullivan's, thank you very much, Mr. Jorgensen," she said, acting as sober as she possibly could while trying to stay serious. She was still angry with Matt for spending most of the day with the black people and their weddings.

He attempted to repeat the words she said by mouthing them, "Mr. Robert J. Sullivan, of the Richly Virginian Sullivans."

"I noticed you danced a lot this evening," Matt observed.

"I danced a lot with you," she answered. "Besides, you spent a lot of time with that stupid wedding group."

"Thought it would be proper."

"Well, it wasn't," she said much indignantly. "Your place was here at our party, with the white folk."

"I spent an equal amount of time, I thought, with both parties," he said. Then, he said laughingly, "But I had a lot more fun at their party, let me tell ya. They know how to put on a party."

"And, how is that, Mr. Jorgensen?" she asked, turning her back to him, and starting to walk back towards the house.

"Talk about dancing? They invented the word. They know how to dance. Why, Hezekiah got out there with his whole family and danced. Now, I call that dancing. His legs went in every different direction. And, I've never seen anythin' like it in my life, how those kids could keep up with him."

Walking a little faster with Matt following, she asked, "I suppose our waltz together was nothing?"

Attempting to show her their dance style by clicking his heels in the air, he fell to the ground. He sat there and looked up at Ginny with a look of stupidity on his face and said, "It was special, Hon." Without any help from Ginny, he pulled himself up slowly, dusted some of the snow from his trousers, and straightened his Stetson. "What I'm tryin' to say is that they enjoyed doin' what they did more than we did what we did."

She turned curtly and putting her hands on her hips, said distinctly, "I enjoyed my dances, Mr. Jorgensen, and I immensely enjoyed my company."

"And they could sing. Man, could they sing." Matt could not stop laughing.

Ginny, rather hurt inside, and letting the drinks talk for her, said, "Then you should live with them, Mr. Jorgensen."

Ginny turned and continued walking towards the house with Matt trying to keep up.

He remained, attempting to steady himself. "You had to have been there, Gin," he said. Then walking clumsily towards her, he said, "You just had to have been there."

She stopped again, pointed her finger at Matt and said, "Mr. Jorgensen. Matt. It appears to me that you are not the man to be the father of my children."

Matt stopped and tried to stand straight, but bending over more to the ground, raised his head up and asked, "Father of your children? Hell, you pregnant lady?"

Ginny stomped Matt's foot and pushed him backward causing him to sit on the roadway with his Stetson falling to his side. "I am not. And you never will be the father. You are trash, Mr. Jorgensen. A simple man from . . ." For the moment she forgot where he was from.

"Montana," was his quick response, forgetting too, that he was the man from Wyoming for fear of him being arrested for murder.

"Not Montana," Ginny insisted. "Somewhere else." Then straightening up, she pulled him by his hair to look down into his eyes, and asked, "Why'd you say, Montana?"

Quick to correct himself, even intoxicated as he was, he said, "Not Montana. Wyoming. South of Montana." He smiled, and added, "Hunted in Montana once though. Good state."

"Montana, Wyoming, Wisconsin? Who the hell cares," she stammered on. "You are not fit to marry me."

"Marry?" he asked. "I'm not fit. Ummph. Look at who's talkin' fit. You're drunk, Lady. And you want to marry me?"

She looked shocked at what she heard for the first time and said, "A proposal here and now won't do you any good."

Releasing his hair, she said, "You ain't got enough money to support me."

Lying backwards into the roadway, he said, "Don' leave me, Ginny."

She sat down beside him, looked drunkenly into his face and said, "You know we can't make it, you being a cowboy and me being a lady from Virginia."

He managed to say while he was falling asleep, "You're right, Honey."

"Of course, my money could make the difference," she said looking down at her muddy boots for a point of focus. "I could make a gentleman out of you. Papa could help." Still concentrating on her boots, she scraped some of the mud off her heel, and added, "We could make it, huh?"

Matt had completely succumbed to the night.

The two couples, Jim and Sylvia, and Olaf and Anna came out of the house laughing, carrying their glasses of bourbon with them. Looking down at Matt passed out on the lawn and Ginny sitting beside him, they stopped laughing and looked rather puzzled. Jim and Sylvia stepped off the porch and walked towards Matt and Ginny. Olaf and Anna stayed on the porch with glasses of bourbon in their hands.

"What's happening, Gin, ol' girl?" Jim cried out.

Ginny answered as she arose, "Mr. Jorgensen, and I emphasize the word, 'Mister', because I do not know him, is intoxicated, Father."

Jim looked at Matt, then at Sylvia, and then up to Olaf and Anna. "Well, so am I."

"Yes, you are," Sylvia agreed.

Awakened by the clambering, Matt rose up and approached Jim. Standing beside Ginny, and indicating with his long arms swinging, he said, "I was just trying to tell her what a great time I had tonight. Anything wrong with that . . . Sir?"

Jim looked at Matt again, smelled his breath, then looked at Ginny and smelled her breath. "You are both intoxicated."

"I beg to differ with you, Sir," Matt said turning and sitting on the ground again. "I am drunk."

"Then you are drunk, Mr. Jorgensen," Jim said, and sat down beside him.

"Me, too," Sylvia said and sat down beside Jim.

Olaf and Anna stayed on the porch and laughed together. "We're too drunk to come down there," Olaf said.

"Papa," Ginny said sitting down with the other three. "Me, too."

"Olaf," Jim said, motioning with his hands drawing circles in the air. "It's time to go home."

"I think you're right, Jim," Olaf agreed. "Which of us is driving?"

"Olaf. You're already home," Anna reminded Olaf.

"My. Then put up our horse and carriage and let's go to bed." The couple turned and going inside, Olaf said, "Night all."

"Night, all," Anna repeated and closed the door.

Matt raised himself up and walked as straight as he could towards the buggy. He untied the reins, climbed in and taking the buggy whip in hand, snapped it above the horse's rear and made her move towards the other three still sitting on the lawn. "Climb aboard, ya'll," he said, and pulled the reins.

Jim helped Sylvia up, and Ginny got up herself. Ginny and Sylvia were intoxicated, but not as much as the two men. They enjoyed playing the game the men were playing..

Once Sylvia was in the buggy, Jim got in the back seat with her. Ginny walked in front of the horse and pulled on the harness to turn him around and head him home.

Then she climbed into the buggy and sat next to Matt. Matt had passed out so she took the reins and gently gave Sammy a nudge and they headed back to their plantation. "Come on, Sammy," she said. "Let's go home."

The ride was short, but a fun ride. Ginny was the only one awake when they pulled unto their road. She could see the embers still flickering under the kettle pots and the lights in the cabins were dim. She also saw a few of the black people roaming around the fields, just walking. Hezekiah and his crew were among them.

Closer to the house, she could make out three silhouettes, but could only ascertain that they were white men from the way they stood. Then she recognized one of them. It was Sin, but she could not make out who the other two men were. One was skinny as a rail and the other was big and fat. All three of these men had full beards, and the closer she got to them, the meaner they looked.

When she was within a few feet of them, she could see that they were holding rifles and aiming them at the buggy.

"Hold it right there, Ginny," Sin ordered. Ginny was frightened. The three men had held their own private party and were filled with whiskey courage. "We weren't invited to your party."

"Olaf invited you, Sin," Ginny said, reining up at his command. Her male passengers were still drunk asleep. Sylvia kept her eyes half opened pretending to be sleeping, while Ginny tried stalling the men with her conversation. "You made up your own mind not to come because Matt would be there. Your boss, Olaf told us at the party."

"That's a lie," Sin retorted. "Take her reins, boys."

One of the men took the reins from the fighting lady while Sin walked over to Matt's side. "I'm gonna teach this bastard a lesson he'll never forget."

As Matt awakened to what was going on, he felt the blunt end of Sin's .44 smack against his head. His body fell out of the buggy and sprawled onto the roadway.

"So the big man falls easy," Sin said laughingly as he stood over Matt's stilled body. "That'll teach ya to steal mah girl and take mah job away from me."

At the sound of Matt's body being hit, Jim woke up, but could barely make out it was Sin standing with a rifle and his back to him. He thrust his body from the buggy and fell upon Sin, knocking him to the ground.

The skinny man ran to Sin's aid, seeing what was happening, and tried to pick Jim off of him. He found that Jim's weight was not easy to handle, dropped him and fell backwards to the ground.

"For gawd's sake, get him the hell off me," Sin yelled. Jim's fist came down hard against Sin's jaw causing Sin to momentarily black out.

"Wan me to shoot him?" the skinny man cried out, picking up his rifle.

While pinning Sin to the ground with one hand, Jim's other arm came up and around and connected with the skinny man's stomach and knocked him into the horse. Though still woozy from the drinks, Jim could still make out his opponent. He dove in his direction, hoping to catch him by his head.

Instead, the fat man with the reins whipped them over the horse and around Jim's neck, and pulled them tight, choking him against the horse. The horse reared up and the man's grip loosened enough for Jim to free himself.

Ginny grabbed the buggy whip and snapped the man in the face, causing blood to spill across his eyes. With another lash out with the whip, wrapping it around his neck, she pulled his head into the horse. As the horse came down again, the fat man's body fell limp to the ground.

With blood still blinding him, the fat man rolled out from under the buggy and went after Ginny, and grabbing her, threw her from the buggy.

Sylvia pounced on him with all her might, but failing to hold on, fell off his back. The fat man brought his fist around and caught her cheek as she fell, sending her rolling to the ground.

Sin, groggy and trying to stand up, was showing signs of giving up the fight and running home, when the skinny man got lucky and hit Jim from behind with the barrel of his rifle. When Jim picked himself up, Sin hit him again in the face with his fist several times, knocking him out.

The fat man fighting with Ginny picked her up and held her light body in the air under her armpits. "Ya gonna be nice, little lady, and I won't have ta hurt cha no mo'," he said, as the blood continued to flow down his face from where Ginny hit him with the whip. It colored his beard, and mingling with the snow, made him look twice as mean. He was a man in his forties, fat and with a bad set of gums and yellowed teeth, which he had not brushed since he was a kid.

"Don't hurt her," Sin commanded as he came around the front of the horse.

Ginny tried her best to claw at the man's eyes as he held her up, laughing at her.

Sin took her away from the man and held her tightly in his arms. "You never wanted me, did you?" he said angrily. "Now, I'm gonna show you what you missed all these years." He began tearing at her clothes, stripping her jacket of its buttons, and revealing her new purple vest.

Ginny screamed until Sin muffled her mouth with his dirty-gloved hand. He held her arms behind her with his other hand and began tearing the buttons from her vest.

Bertha, along with several of the black people near the house, heard Ginny's screams and ran towards the buggy. They could make out that a fight was going on and began yelling, hoping to scare the intruders away from her boss, Virginia.

Matt, coming to, heard Ginny's voice and raised himself to his knees, only to be knocked down again by the skinny man. He grabbed the man by his boots and caused him to fall. He was a blur to Matt, but clear enough for Matt to see the outline of his face. He brought his fist down hard against the man's nose and broke it.

The horse reared again as the man tried to free himself from Matt. He rolled under the horse's hoofs as they came down and crushed his head.

Matt scurried around the horse towards Sin.

Scared at seeing what happened to the skinny man, Sin dropped Ginny, pulled his gun and cocked it at Matt.

Bertha and her family of black folk picked up objects to hit or throw at the assailants as they drew near the buggy, and waved sticks and pitchforks in the air in defiance of the immediate danger.

The fat man ran around Matt's side and brought him down fast, not realizing that Sin had a bead on Matt with his gun. As the two went down, Sin's .44 went off and sent a bullet past Matt which struck Bertha's body instead.

The noise of the people drowned out the sound of the shot, but Bertha heard it. She felt the blow as if someone had hit her in the chest with a black skillet. She reeled around and sat down. Naomi and another woman, thinking Bertha tripped, went to her rescue and helped her up. Because of her heavy clothing and her bulky size, they did not know she was shot. Once up, she continued walking towards the buggy, but at a slower pace. She knew she was hurt, but in her struggle to free her owners, her mind blocked out that fact and she kept on fighting.

The fat man's fist connected with Matt's face and sent him back to the ground.

Sin ran towards his horse and found the black people from the field almost on top of him. Quickly Sin mounted and rode like the wind, letting his steed go in any direction it had a mind to go. He was free from the hands of the oncoming mob.

The fat man was not so lucky. Because of the darkness, his attempt to find his horse was futile. He was stopped short when he found himself surrounded by the mob of black people. His thought was instinctively fast as he aimed his heavy body towards the women and children holding lanterns.

As he knocked down the two children of Hezekiah and Nancy, he felt the pains of a pitchfork as it stopped him and knocked him to the ground. Hezekiah held on strong to the other end of the pitch fork, whose prongs had barely penetrated through the heavy-set man's thick clothing, but it was enough to hold him.

Matt pulled himself up and hobbled over to the man. As he turned the heavy-set man over, Ginny tried her best to kick him in the face, but slipped on the snow and fell.

Matt picked her up, helped button her clothes as best he could, and held onto her while the mob took over.

Matt and Ginny heard Jim's groans as he began to raise his body to join them. Once up, Jim looked at the man on the ground, now turned upwards for all to see his ugly face.

Then, still dizzy from the beating, Jim looked around for Sylvia.

"Sylvia!" he cried out, but there was no answer.

Matt joined him in shouting. "Sylvia!"

Ginny turned, and remembering hearing a gun shot, ran back to the other side of the buggy where she found Sylvia lying face down. Thinking she might have been shot, she turned her over. She was relieved when she saw that she was still alive, and not shot, but she had a badly bruised face.

"Sylvia, honey!", Ginny cried out, as tears began to fall down her cheeks. "You're hurt."

Sylvia's brown eyes looked around for Jim, and finding him, she smiled. As she watched him kneel down to hold her, she said, "Heck of a fight, huh?"

Jim's hand slid down her body, and he picked her up and placed her back into the carriage.

Naomi stood by the buggy holding two lanterns.

Jim sat down beside Sylvia in the buggy as Ginny grabbed a lantern from Naomi and climbed on board in the front seat. Matt hopped on, took the reins, and drove the buggy the rest of the way home.

Once at the house, Jim and Matt carried Sylvia gently inside as a couple of young black men took the buggy and stabled the horses. Matt and Jim laid her on the bed in a guest bedroom downstairs while Ginny began to loosen her clothing.

Jim kept saying, "I'm sorry, Sylvia, honey. Gawd-awful sorry. I wish it was me."

Bertha was quick to elbow her way into the bedroom with another lantern and took charge of the situation. Moving Ginny away with her big hips, she said, "Honey, this is my job. You lets me take care of Miss Sylvie."

Ginny helped in removing more of Sylvia's clothing while Jim and Matt stayed outside the door. Naomi went in with a pan of cold water and rags.

It seemed like a long time for the men to hear a report about Sylvia, but they waited patiently, realizing that she was in Bertha's capable hands, the all-around nurse, maid, chef, and friend.

Naomi's eyes lit up like candles in the night, as she watched Sylvia's eyes open. And then she said in a whispering voice, "Lawd, it's a miracle. It is a miracle, I tells ya. Right heah on Christmas night, the Baby Jesus done performed a miracle."

Ginny looked at Bertha as she continued cleaning the wound, and smiled a broad Tennessean smile, and wiped her tears away with the sleeves of her new Christmas dress as she, too, saw the wound about Sylvias' face. Sylvia was hurt, but would be all right. Nothing but Southern pride was broken.

Stepping out into the hall, Bertha assured the men, "She's all right. No bones broken, but her face will take a few days to mend. He hit her hard, Mister Jim."

"Thank you, Bertha," Jim said, and walked in, giving lots of room for Bertha to walk past him to go outside. "You might want to check on those two goons out back that caused this."

"Yes, sah, Mastah Jim," she said as she walked through the kitchen. "This place is turnin' into a regular hospital."

In the confusion, Matt had overlooked Ginny and her condition, and once seeing her scratched cheeks, set her down in a chair in the kitchen and began cleaning her up with water. "You're hurt, too," he said.

"Now that's the understatement of the evening," she remarked. "How's it look?"

"You'll live, I suppose," Matt answered. "Just scratches."

Ginny looked at Matt, then at Jim close by. Both men looked like something the cat drug in, with scratches and bruises all over their bodies. Their faces were dirty and still bleeding from the fight.

"Damn," Matt said washing the bruise gently. "You're the last one to complain. Sin do this?"

Allowing herself to be treated, she answered, "He was just drunk and didn't know what he was doing."

"That son-of-a-bitch!" Looking at her torn clothes, he attempted to undress her more in search for hidden wounds.

"I'm okay, Matt" she kittenly said, keeping his fingers away from the buttons. She began buttoning her vest. "He roughed me up more than hurt me. I'll be all right."

Matt removed his Stetson and placed it on the back of a chair, and kept cleaning Ginny's face.

Jim left Sylvia's side and came into the kitchen where he caught the pair in conversation. "Ginny, honey," he said. "I'm sorry. Are you okay?"

"I'm okay, Dad. Thanks for asking," she answered. Looking over at Matt she added sarcastically, "No one else seemed to care." Then, looking down at Matt's bared head, she saw his hair covered with blood from where he had been belted by the butt of Sin's .44.

She took the cloth and water from Matt and began cleaning his head carefully until she saw that it was still bleeding. "Matt," she said, "you're bleeding."

Matt started to feel the back of his head, when she staved off his hands and kept cleaning it.

"Bertha!" Ginny cried out loud for the world to hear.

Bertha turned her attention from the skinny man with the crushed head, and stomped up the steps towards Ginny's cries. "You wants me to tend to this one, and now you gots you self another one. Bertha this and Bertha that."

She entered the kitchen, knelt down beside Matt, and upon examining him, said more gently, "Oh my Lawd. Good gracious. Lawd in heaven."

"Just clean me up," Matt said, "and quit the prayin'. I'll be all right." He groaned a little in pain.

"He's done got hisself a lulu, Miss Ginny," Bertha said, as she looked around for Naomi who was standing behind her like her shadow. "Naomi, Honey, gets Bertha a whole lotta snow. And pack it tight, honey."

Naomi took the pail of hot water she brought, threw it out in the road. She scooped up some snow in the same pail, packed it down and returned to Bertha with quick and lively steps.

Bertha wet down Matt's head with the loose snow, carefully washing the blood away and then applied the packed snow to Matt's wound. "He's got a knot on his head as big as a lemon."

"He's going to be all right, isn't he Bertha?" Ginny queried, looking more concerned than worried.

"Yes ma'am," Bertha answered. "I've seen bigger bumps than this on the hind end of many of our men, and let me tell youse, they is all livin'."

Jim walked Bertha back out where the people had the two men on the ground.

Bertha bent down next to the fat man. "You all rights, fat boy?" she asked him.

On his back, the man looked painfully at her with his eyes and motioned to his back. "Hurts like hell."

"Good!" she replied, and gave him a devilish smile.

Jim went over to the skinny man, still lying unconscious from the horse falling on him. Upon examining him, Jim found him to be slightly awake and making grunts. "Son," Jim asked, "can you hear me? If you can hear me, make some sound for me to know you're all right."

The man groaned and turned his eyes upwards as if to die, but stayed alive just the same.

"Where's Sin gone?" Jim asked.

The man never answered.

"Hezekiah," Jim ordered, "take these two men and tie them up in the pig sty 'til morning. We'll send for the marshal." Looking at Bertha who had side-stepped the men, said, "Bertha, can you clean them up and keep them alive 'til morning?"

"Don't know if I wants ta," she answered, meandering down the steps off the porch.

"Bertha," Jim ordered. "Now, I know none of us like it any more than you do, but what's gotta be done, has to be done right."

"Brilliantly spoken, Dad," Ginny remarked, clapping her hands together.

Jim returned to the black men guarding the two ruffians. "This man," Jim asked, pointing down at the skinny man, "is he going to live?"

"Who youse talkin' to, Mister Jim?" Bertha asked.

"You, Bertha," Jim returned. "You."

"Can't tell from here, Boss. My eyes are big, but they ain't that big for me to see how that man is doin' all the ways from over heah."

"Didn't you take a look at him, Bertha?" Jim asked.

"Yes, Suh, and so's did you and then Missy Ginny screamed, and I hasta come over heah. Naomi, honey, take a look at that man and see if he's gonna live."

"Yes'm," Naomi answered and walked over to the skinny man still groaning. She looked at his face, took a rag and cleaned off the mud, and looked again into his eyes, lifting first one eyelid and then the other. "Can't tell, Bertha," she said. "Can't see his eyeballs."

Without looking at Jim, Bertha said, "Nope, Mister Jim. He's gonna die, sure as they's a heaven. And I don't think he'll ever see heaven, the things he done did."

Sure enough, the skinny man died within the hour. Some of the black men pulled him into the sty along with the fat man against the fat man's yelling complaints. "He's a dead man. You can't tie me in a hog pen with a dead man." They did just the same.

Ginny came out with Matt to join Jim. Matt readied his makings for a smoke.

Bertha rose up, turned around and slumped to the ground in a faint. She finally felt the fatal effect of the bullet. Jim rushed to her side and kneeling down, raised her head. He felt the warm blood as it spilled through her clothes.

Matt and Ginny, stood over Jim as Naomi, and her family gathered around. Bertha looked up for the last time and, looking into Jim's eyes, and then over to her family, she uttered, "It's all right, Mister Jim. Miss Ginny." She smiled at her family and winked her eyes. "I be with Jesus, now, folks," and fell asleep.

The black people placed Bertha's body on her bed in her cabin surrounded by her small Christmas gifts made by her family of friends. She had a cherished photo of her late husband that she clutched in her black hands, placed there by Naomi. Candles lit the four corners of the otherwise darkened room. Only Naomi remained inside the cabin while the rest of Bertha's friends stayed outside and sang some of their favorite black spiritual songs, one special being, "Down By the River Side".

Hezekiah and Nancy with their two children, entered the cabin and placed a wreath made of corn silks and cotton stems, and adorned with cloth woven earlier, at the foot of her bed to signify that she was a slave born in the fields of corn and cotton. She graduated to being a black servant because of her laughter and black charm, a natural gift that radiated from within.

Seeing Naomi outside the cabin, Ginny walked over to her and said, "I'm sorry, Naomi." Then she took a gentle hold of Naomi's hand. "Bertha will be sorely missed, I assure you."

She left Naomi and returned to the kitchen, where, looking at the two men, she said "You two could stand to scrub up, too."

Matt gave another breath of exhaustion and sat down in a chair and fell asleep, not because he wanted to, but because his head wound had finally taken its toll and caused him to sleep. Jim sat next to him, but stayed awake.

Only the two men slept that night. When the sun was up, Jim was disturbed by the noise on the far side of the barn. All of the black people were up, even the children, and had thrown a rope over the beam sticking out of the hayloft for the man who was still living. They were now a crowd of angry people who had made a decision to avenge Bertha's murder.

The fat man stood with his hands tied behind his back and a hangman's noose decorated his neck as two black men held him. He had recovered from the wounds in his back made by the pitchfork that Hezekiah had thown at him.

"What's going on, Hezekiah?" Matt asked.

"Its' a hangin', Mister Jim," Hezekiah answered as he showed the two men to Jim. "An eye for an eye, suh.

Jest like ya done said and preached to us. Now it's your turn. We done made a hangin' for ya, suh."

Jim looked around but could not find Sin. "Where's that son-of-a-bitch?" he asked, jumping from the porch onto the lawn.

An older black man out of the group spoke up, and said, "He done took his horse and lit out, Mister Jim. Didn't give us time to catch him. Nah, Suh. He jest lit off like the devil was a chasin' him."

Jim saw the fat man sitt down in his meal he had at his last party. The hogs had nudged him all night long to keep him from sleeping. The black children chided him, as they were up early to play for the day after Christmas was a holiday for them, also. They had never seen a real killer before, especially one tied up in a hog pen with the hogs wallowing over them. Somehow, even the hogs could smell death as the skinny one laid there still tied to the fat man.

Jim had sent two of his black men to town earlier to bring the marshal out to arrest the one man and bury the other. There would be no hanging on his property.

CHAPTER 20

A QUESTION AS TO WHICH SIDE TO JOIN

Matt lay in bed asleep when Ginny brought his breakfast into him. She placed it on the table next to him and waited for him to awaken. To hurry the process, she kept saying little things in a whisper until they became louder, and bumped her foot against the bed from time to time. "You awake, Matt?" she would ask over and over. "Matt, Darling. Wake up. Breakfast is waiting." Then she would waft the aroma of the bacon and eggs with biscuits and coffee his way with her hand. "Waaake up, Matt," she said again and again. Then finally, a little louder she said, "Matt, wake up, dammit!"

Matt moved his head a little, and then opened his eyes. "There you go again, swearin'", Matt said, looking at Ginny. "Not lady like."

Ginny tightened her lips as if in anger, and then softened them up a bit, bent over and kissed him. "Feeling better?"

"Got a slight headache," he answered.

Ginny felt the bandages and said, "I can't tell anything with all that padding up there. Ain't time for the change of dressing. Doc Hardy told us that. Hungry?"

"That I am, little lady. That I am."

With that said, he began eating, and Ginny sat there watching him all the while. "Who's Doc Hardy?" he asked.

"In spite of everything you've seen in Tennessee," Ginny said, "We do have a mighty fine doctor. He's the one who bandaged you."

"What's happened?" he asked feeling his head. Then, remembering some of what went on last night, he began to get out of bed, only to find himself too weak, and fell back.

"Whoa, cowboy," Ginny said, pulling the sheet back over him. "Be nice and eat, and mommy will tell you all about it."

"Cute," Matt rebutted, and took a sip of his buttermilk.

"The marshal took our would-be killers away."

"Both alive, then?" he asked.

"Nope," Ginny answered, smacking her lips. "The skinny one was stiff, so they planned to drop him off in town for burial. The truth of the matter is that the two men were tramps who had ventured onto the Olaf' plantation looking for food, and not work. According to the marshal, Olaf told them to get lost. Instead, Sin went looking for them and schemed up this thing by promising them a roof on the plantation for a few nights and plenty of food to take with them when they left. He hired them to help beat you up."

"How'd you learn all this?" Matt asked, completely bewildered.

"The marshal," she answered. "He dropped by Olaf''s plantation checking out two strangers in town. Found out all this from some of the hired help. Put two and two together and showed up at our place around noon."

Looking around and looking outside the window, Matt saw it was still night, he surmised that the sun had not yet come up. "Noon?" he asked. "Hell, it's still night."

"Thought so," Ginny mused. "Honey, you've been sleeping all day. You had a bad bump. When Doc Hardy came by to look in on Sylvia, he bandaged you up real good and you slept like a baby."

"A whole day?" Matt asked, feeling his head.

Naomi's presence broke the air as she entered the room, feeling as if she herself were now the re-incarnated Bertha.

"What is it, Naomi?" Ginny asked.

"Nobody told me he was awake, Miss Ginny."

"He just woke up, Naomi," Ginny replied. "He's eating my breakfast."

"How's he feel, Miss Ginny?" Naomi asked, taking over the task of feeding him and pushing Ginny away.

"Fine," Matt replied. "Fine, except for being a little weak and hungry."

"That mean you gonna be alrights, Mister Matt."

"Hungry, I said," he teased, watching Naomi play with the fork in the eggs. "I can feed myself!"

"My, my, my. He is a angry bear," Naomi said, setting the plate down. She propped him up and then gave him the plate. "Here. You eats youself."

"Where's Bertha?" he asked, forgetting what happened earlier.

"She don gone to be with the lawd, Mister Matt," Naomi said, hanging her head down.

Matt remembered and looked embarrassed at Naomi and Ginny. "I'm sorry," he said. "I forgot."

"And when you is through," Naomi returned, "we'll come back in and give you a scrubbin'."

Matt took the food and began to eat slowly. "No scrubbin' this boy, Naomi." Then he looked under his covers and then over at Ginny who had been standing at the foot of the bed. "Hey. How'd I get undressed?"

"Jim did it, Mister Jorgensen," Ginny answered. "Disappointed?"

"Then I'll clean myself," Matt said, and continued eating.

Naomi gathered Ginny and the two left the room. "We's jest teasin' ya'all, Mastah Matt," she said, and smiled at him. "Eats well, and we'll bring you some more."

"Do that," Matt said still eating. "More biscuits, and more eggs, and more bacon, and plenty of buttermilk. Keep it comin'."

"My, my, " Naomi said, as she closed the door. "He'll be up and on his feet in no time."

Jim walked into the kitchen from outside when he heard Naomi, and added, "Glad to hear it. We need him." Grabbing the coffee pot off the stove and pouring himself a cup of coffee, he asked, "How soon do you think?"

"After he gets hisself all scrubbed up, we can tells ya," Naomi answered. "Right now, the bump's gone down, but he's still got a wee bit of a headache. If it go away today, I'll let you have him tomorrow for sure."

"Good enough," Jim said, taking his coffee with him into Matt's room.

Ginny was sitting on the foot of the bed watching Matt continue to eat when Jim walked in. "Hello, father," she said rising. "I've never seen a person go through food like he has."

"Hello, Matt," Jim said, grabbing a chair to sit comfortably in while he took out his pipe and makings for a good smoke. "Naomi tells me you'll be up in no time."

"I can get out of bed right now," Matt responded quickly.

"No, son. You take it easy for another day or two. We can get along fine without you for awhile, yet." Lighting his pipe, he said, "So you're from Wyoming?"

"You know I am, Sir," Matt said, wondering what was going on in Jim's mind.

"You know that's north of here."

"Yep."

"And we're south."

"Yep," Matt said a second time, pausing with a glass of buttermilk. "Something on your mind, Jim?"

"Well, it's just this damn secession thing," Jim said reluctantly, knowing it could develop into an argument. "The marshal told us that, on Christmas Eve, South Carolina seceded from the Union."

"What does that have to do with me being from Wyoming?"

"Everything, if it comes down to a war and you being from the North," Jim said. "Nothing, otherwise." Jim fiddled with his pipe as it went out. He began taking it apart and cleaning it, shaking the spit out of its stem.

"Father," Ginny scolded. "You can be considerate and keep your tobacco to yourself. You done flung everything around so, like you're not being a gentleman."

"I'm sorry, Gin," Jim said. "The trouble is, I'm thinking too much."

"What's your concern, Sir?" Matt asked.

Jim stood up and, putting his pipe back into his jacket pocket, walked to the door. Looking back at Matt, he said, "Nothing, Matt. Not a thing at this point. Just thinking out loud, I suppose about when you'll be better." Jim left the room, leaving Matt wondering what was running through Jim's mind at the time, as he was uncomfortable with Jim's answer.

"What do you suppose he meant?" Matt asked, handing his plate and glass to Ginny.

Ginny picked up the breakfastware and answered, "I think he wonders if it comes to a war, whether you will fight with us or against us. That's what I'm thinking is on his mind, Matt."

"If we have a war? About what?" Matt asked.

"You've asked many times about our owning slaves," Ginny answered. "Well, if it weren't for our slaves, we couldn't run our business as well as we have been. If we allowed our slaves to be free, and to go and come as they choose, then, like many, they would head north and work in the factories, or west and pan for gold. Our cotton would not be picked. And we'd have to pay higher wages to any who worked for us to pick our cotton, and the prices would go up, and . . ."

"Hold up, little lady," Matt interrupted. "You're telling me that we might go to war because of your slaves?"

"Not just that, honey," Ginny countered, taking the dishes to the door. Stopping, she turned and said, "It's that and more. A whole lot more."

"Who's doing all this threatening of war, Gin? Tell me" Matt asked.

"Politicians, Matt," Ginny answered. "Senators and Congressmen, Presidents. The South is going to get her President, Mr. Jefferson Davis, and he's going to make Richmond, Virginia our Capitol."

"You said, 'our' Capitol," Matt asked, adjusting himself in his bed. "So you see yourself being on one side and asking me if I'm going to fight with you. Well, I don't know. I just don't know."

Matt began analyzing the issues and his feelings towards them inside his mind as Ginny was about to leave. "Give me some time to collect my thinking on this, Gin. You've thrown a lot at me, and wow, my head is spinning. And it's not from the pistol beating, either."

Ginny left the room as Matt lay back down and fell asleep.

Early the next morning, Matt was dressed and practicing his fast draw in his bedroom when Ginny walked in.

"Don't you ever knock, Gin?" Matt asked, holstering his .45.

"It's my house and I can go and come wherever I please," she retorted.

Thinking about that for a moment, Matt reflected on it, saying, "Sin's room, too."

Feeling hurt at his remark, Ginny walked over to him and kicked him in the shin without warning. "That, Sir, was uncalled-for, and a cheap shot."

Matt took a grip of his shin and apologized, saying, "I'm sorry, Gin. You had a right to kick me."

"For your information, Mr. Jorgensen," she called him by his sur name, which she did oftentimes when she was mad, or hurt by Matt, "I never, ever went to his room, nor he to mine," she said angrily.

"But you have to mine."

"You are making me sorry I ever did," Ginny came back. Then, looking at his .45 hanging on his hip, she asked, "Why are you wearing your gunbelt?"

"Got to keep up with my speed," Matt answered, drawing his .45, spinning it, and returning it to its holster. "Can't tell when I'll be needing it."

"Thinking about the war."

"Thought about it," he said coyly. "Not thinking about it, now, because it probably never will happen."

"I certainly hope not," Ginny said. "Us Tennesseans right now are for secession. Hell, Governor Johnson wanted secession from the Union for a long time, and now, he's working to prevent Tennessee seceding. And that's got something to do with Lincoln becoming our President. Can't figure him out. He's got a few slaves, hisself."

"Politics changed his mind some. And to tell you the truth, I could care less." Seeing Matt put his jacket on, she began to show concern for him. "What are you going to do?"

"Well, for openers, Gin," he answered, "I'm gonna have some coffee, and then I'm gonna go out into the fields, like I normally do."

"You well enough?"

"I feel good," he said, and walked out the door knowing Ginny would follow after him.

"I feel there's more," she said, taking two steps at a time to his one. "Else you wouldn't be acting like this."

Seeing Jim in the kitchen, he said, "Mornin', Jim."

"Good morning, Matt," Jim answered. Noticing Matt's hardware, he asked, "Why the gunbelt?"

"Thought I'd do some target shootin' this mornin'," Matt replied. "Ain't done that for sometime and I feel a bit rusty." Then, looking at Naomi readying a plate for him, he said, "Just coffee this mornin', Naomi. I'm so full from last night, I'm ready to pop."

Ginny and Jim watched Matt as he walked out into the fields towards the creek. She wanted to go with him, but stayed behind. Jim came up to her and gave her a comfortable feeling, resting his hand on her shoulder. She gripped it and smiled a little. A furrow creased her brow as she began to worry about Matt.

Matt was right about his gun hand. He was rusty at drawing his firearm. He walked through the rows, and down a path that lead to a trout stream where the black people fished on Sundays. It was back into the woods and away from the eyes and ears of anyone. The day had warmed up, and he threw off his jacket and rolled up his sleeves.

He spent several hours oiling down his holster, and cleaning his pistol, drawing his .45 and firing it time after time for perfection. When the sun was the highest, he saw Ginny walking through the trees to join him on the bank of the slow-running stream.

He took the time to draw his pistol out of its holster a good dozen times, reload, and shoot before she reached him. He felt better about his draw.

His eye caught her full body as she approached nearer to him. She wore a thin dress which accentuated every crease and curve of her body, and it excited Matt to know she was his girl, even though, because of her Southern upbringing, she never allowed him to satisfy her fully.

"This stream is called the "Little Ol' Muddy', after the Missoura," Ginny said, walking up to him.

"I know," Matt said. "Benjamin, that boy that helps Hezekiah, told me when I first got here. Wanted me to go fishin' in it."

"You should."

"Hell. Don't like fish for one thing," Matt said.

"And the other?"

"Has to be an other?" Matt asked.

"You said, 'for one thing', meant there was another thing to follow," Ginny remarked.

"Well, the other thing is, I think fishin' is a sissy's game, and too damn slow. I like huntin'. Deer, elk, even bear sometime."

"You going hunting, now?" Ginny asked, leaning up against a tall oak tree.

"'Spect so."

"What for?"

"I'm curious," Matt said. "Why d'ya come all the way out here just to taunt me?"

"Well, Mr. Jorgensen," Ginny started, then corrected herself, and politely said, "Matt. I have a feeling you're going somewhere, and that somewhere is without me."

"I laid awake all night thinkin' about Bertha," Matt said, reloading his pistol.

"So?"

"Well, Gin," Matt said, sliding his Colt back into its holster. "In Wyoming, we don't let someone get away with murder without getting him. We call that, retribution."

"An eye for an eye, again," she reminded Matt.

"Yep. Suppose so."

"Didn't I tell you that the marshal is working on it?" Ginny asked.

"Yep," Matt answered. "Also told me that he didn't find him."

"And you think you can?"

"Got to try, Gin." He took a gentle hold of her arms and looked deep into her eyes. "I love you, Gin. And I want to marry you."

Ginny grabbed a hold of Matt with all her might and looked up into his steely blue eyes. She smiled as tears began to stream down her cheek. She had never heard this from Matt before. Now, for the first time, she knew they were meant for each other. She was ready for the moment now and kissed him like he had never before been kissed.

His long arms wrapped around her waist and brought her in tight to his body.

She felt the pulsation for which she had been longing for such a long time. She knew by throwing her arms up and around his body, that he could come to the same realization that she was experiencing.

Matt felt her lips so sweet and so tender and kept his focus on this part of her body for a long time. Then, as if natural for both of them, his hands began their trek down the course of her body.

The couple became as one as they sat down on the ground together and began to share the moment of ecstasy as neither had done before. Matt thought of the several times he spent in a bawdy house in Bozeman, liquored up and doing what followed the lustful passions of a man, any man young or old, not having been with a woman for some time. Matt had never been with a real woman, other than those nights he and his brother, Lukas, had got drunk together and visited the bawdy house, spending their hard-earned money on quick pleasure. Even those nights, it seemed that the women they bought were more concerned with the brothers' attempts at becoming men rather than in the boys needing some good old-fashioned understanding. What they really needed was the fist of one Wil Andersen, their father.

This hour of passion was completely different. Matt looked down upon Ginny as she lay on the grass. He wanted the long, enduring pleasure of knowing that he was with an angel.

For Ginny, she had prepared herself for twenty-two years for this moment, and promised before God that it would be with her husband. Yet, as the hour approached and she was ready to give in, she convinced herself that Matt would truly become her husband. Because of her deep love for Matt she knew he belonged to her, feeling her innocence would not be sacrificed for just a moment of love.

Matt's gunbelt fell to the ground as he loosened the buckle.

Ginny unbuttoned his shirt and moved him over to lie down next to her. His hand opened the buttons on her dress and slipped inside to find her breast.

Ginny rolled over on top of Matt and looked yearningly into his eyes again, assuring herself that Matt was her one and only. Then, sitting up while straddling him, she said, "You sure you want to marry me?"

Matt looked at her with a stupid look on his face as he furrowed his brow and twitched his lips. Gripping her hands, he brought her back down and kissed her tenderly. Her knees slipped out from under her and her body paralleled his for the moment.

Then as quickly as it started, he rolled Ginny over, and sat up. Looking at her, he grabbed his gunbelt, stood up and strapped it back on.

Ginny sat up, still with her dress unbuttoned, and her legs showing their slenderness. She messed with her hair, and said, "Mr. Jorgensen. I have waited for this moment all my life, and you, you, you . . ."

"I'm saving the moment, Gin," Matt said. "I know . . . I'm stupid. But, I'm tellin' you straight. It ain't gonna be like it was in Bozeman."

"Bozeman?" Ginny asked.

"Yes, Bozeman," Matt answered. Then realizing what he was about to do, made the commitment to tell all right, there and now. And he did. "I'm from Bozeman, Montana, not Wyoming, and my name is Matthew Andersen, and I'm on the run, and I'm in love with you."

Ginny stood up and, catching her breath, looked at Matt one more time, and threw her arms around him again. "And I love you, Matthew, whatever. You are one hell of an exciting man."

"Doesn't that mean anything to you, Gin?" he asked, holding on to her.

"What? That you love me?"

"Well, yes, that. And what else I done said?"

"Matt, hold me," Ginny replied, grabbing and putting his arms around her slim waist. "Hold me and never let me go. I love you, too, you idiot."

"Well, if that don't beat all," Matt said caressing Ginny and kissing her again and again. Their bodies found each other in strong passion, which even Matt could not excuse himself from now that Ginny wanted him. Their bodies slid onto the hard Tennessee soil of winter that ran along the riverbank.

"She loves me no matter what," he thought as his hand began unbuttoning the bodice of the dress, exposing her breasts.

Giggling, she looked into his eyes and said, "Take off that damn gunbelt, cowpoke."

He knelt over her and unbuckled the belt and tossed it to the side. He smiled and let his body ease into position against hers and then rolled her over on top of him.

The sun streamed carefully through the branches of the tree that sheltered the young couple from its harsh winter rays. The rippling noise of the cold icy water along the bank was all that broke through the long moments of their love, adding to the splendor of their passion as it played with the rhythm of their bodies.

They found moments of sleep, and then as the wind began to get colder, they nestled their bodies together to keep each other warm.

"It's gettin' cold," Matt said as he laid there slightly shivering, looking into her soft blue eyes. "Now what do we do?"

"Kinda like what we're doing right now, cowboy," she responded.

"I mean about us, Sweet Jeans."

"Sweet Jeans?" she remarked sitting up.

"I see you kinda real nice in a pair of jeans," he answered. "Now, what do we do next?"

"I don't know, Matt," she said, rubbing her buttocks to show off her figure. "Don't we normally tell my father, and ask his permission?"

"Yes, but, I can't," he replied, smacking her on her bottom.

"What do you mean you can't?" Ginny asked, as she began straightening herself in her clothes.

"I've got a job to do first," he replied. "Once I get that settled, then we can ask your father."

"You mean, Sin?" she asked.

"Now I know it don't mean a thing to you, but it do to me."

Getting up on her feet, she said, "It does to me, too, Matt." Then she paced away for a few steps, turned and looked back at Matt. "She was a nigger, Matt," she said deliberately but cautiously, knowing that Matt might be offended. He was still a Westerner passing through the South.

"What the goddam hell does that mean?" he asked leaning up against a branch of the tree with his big hand.

"It means, you're a 'nigger lover'," she retorted biting her lip.

"The hell it does," Matt resounded without moving a muscle. "It means I don't like killers to go free. I'd do the same if a white person was killed."

"Why?"

"Why, what?" he fumed still standing his ground and not moving. "That I would go after a killer who killed someone I knew and liked?"

"That is exactly what I mean. Dammit! You're a goddam nigger lover."

"Bertha meant a lot to me," he said, slapping his holster with his hand and looking point blank into her eyes. "I thought she meant a lot to you."

"She was my house nigger," Ginny rebutted. "I bought her. Yes, I liked her. But not like a real person. You got to understand that, Matt. She is dead. Nothing can bring her back. Nothing."

"She came with the plantation," he retorted. "Why don't you admit it."

"I bought her and everyone and everything on this plantation, and if I lose a slave one way or another, I lose money. She was only money to me. I do not allow myself to get involved with her kind of people. And Naomi has taken her place like it should be."

"Listen to what the hell you jest said, Ginny," he remarked as he stepped up to her. "You called her 'people', and that's what she is. A person. A real person. For gawd's sake, a human bein'."

"I meant property. Negroes. And you can't bring her back," Ginny retorted. "She's dead."

"And if I turn my back on Sin, we could be dead, too."

"Sin's not like that," Ginny came back. "It was an accident. Besides, the other two men paid for her killing."

"Don't you understand, Ginny," Matt replied holding onto his gungrip. "If we let Sin get away with this, he can come back and kill again."

"Who? You? Certainly not me. He loves me."

"I doubt that quite seriously, Ginny," Matt came back angrily. "He's incapable of love." Then turning he added, "And, in answer to your question, yes, me. He could kill me."

Ginny stepped up nose-to-nose with Matt. "He won't once he knows we're married," she said. "Let someone else get him, for chrissake."

"I see no one else capable of doing it, and it has to be done, if we're to be married and live here on your plantation." Matt realized what he had said, and looked around and continued, "Hell, I never thought about having a plantation of my own."

"Yours and mine, Matt, and father's," Ginny added, stroking the back of his neck. "And if things work out like I think they might, we might have a step-mother move in with us. A double wedding. Wouldn't that be something?" she said with a lilt in her eyes.

"And that's reason number one for me having to catch up with that son-of-a-bitch," Matt said as he grabbed Ginny's elbow and began leading her back towards the house. "I don't want the threat of him sneaking back some night after we're married and gunnin' for me."

Ginny felt like a kid all giddy inside and full of excitement again. She thought how wonderful it would have been had they got married on Christmas, or even today, New Year's Eve, 1861.

"I want us to get married, Matt," she said, reinforcing her love for him.

"After I get back," he answered, "we'll get married. I promise you."

"If you go, I'll never marry you," she said defiantly.

"Oh yes you will," he returned.

"If you go, you'll never come back to me," she argued.

"I'll come back, and then we'll get married."

"I'll be married to someone else."

"What?" he asked holding onto her arms. "Who is there? Some Richard T. Sullivan of Virginia?" he mentioned flippantly picking a name out of the air.

"Uh, huh," she answered, putting her finger to his lips.

"If that's a test, Ginny," he said. "it ain't gonna work."

"You're not going, Matt."

"Who's gonna stop me? You?"

She stopped and turned into him, then planted her lips strong and wet against his. The passion rose between them as they stood there alone. This time it did not stop. Her look into his eyes told him this was her moment of ecstasy, which she was about to share with him. She knew that she needed a way to keep him, and her love for him was fierce enough to let herself be loved by him to the fullest.

Bringing her to the ground, he felt the moment was ripe, and sharing this with the woman he loved, Ginny, could only be right. Thus, he gave in to his emotions.

As their lips pressed harder against each other's, their hands began to find the parts of their bodies that would thrust their emotions into eternity. Unbuttoning her bodice, he felt the smooth flesh of a young lady's bosom, and his fingers began to massage her nipples.

The beauty of the clouds overhead began to shift into various shapes as the wind scattered them across the skies. The gentle cool breeze crept ever so softly across the meadows and touched the bare shoulders of the lovers. The romance of the hour played its role to the hilt as Matt's eyes looked deeper into Ginny's with intent passion.

This moment of delicate romance was shared by a couple alone by a creek, and only nature had witnessed its wondrous emotions. Then, as if in a twinkling of an eye, the enlightened moment of romance came to the height of its passion, and the lovers sighed and fell naked to witness of the sky.

After a brief rest, Ginny sat up and redressed herself, fussing with her hair like a teenager in love. Then, looking over at Matt still basking in the sunshine of the solace, she asked, "Can we talk about it with my father later?"

Her virtuous moment had arrived, and Matt knew then that he would belong to her from this moment on. He smiled, and without looking at her, said, "You planned this."

"If I had," she responded with a lilt to her voice, "I would have picked a warmer place to make love, and not some cold, hard meadow beside an icy creek."

They laughed, and she fell back into his arms and they kissed.

It was dawn by the time they walked back to the house, and the wind, colder now, began to shuttle the clouds back and forth across the sky like a water painting.

CHAPTER 21

TRACKING A KILLER

January 1861

Matt saddled up and rode out early the next morning on his sorrel thinking no one was up. In his mind, it would be another day when he and Ginny would tell her father about their intentions. A gentle snow covered the roadway, reflecting the moonlight along the way south towards Arkansas.

Ginny was awakened by the creaking sound the barn door had made, and went to the window to witness Matt riding away. Putting on her clothes and slipping into her boots, she was downstairs quickly and out the door to the barn. She took a bridle and placed it on her mare, and without a saddle she mounted and rode after Matt.

Knowing the terrain a little better than Matt, she cut across the field, jumped a small icy stream and headed through the woods. "Come on, Suzie, get your legs moving," she whispered to her mare as she cleared sagging branches thickly covered with snow.

A clearing came up shortly but the snow had covered the trail, and Suzie felt her way cautiously. Without spurs, Ginny heeled Suzie into a faster trot knowing time was more precious now than a slip and a fall. Parts of the trail became solid and made the ride a little easier. It still took moments of hard effort to catch up with Matt, but Ginny's expertise as a horsewoman proved to be her worth.

Seeing the main road in the far distance, she loosened up her grip on the reins and leaned forward, letting Suzie find her top speed. Coming to the road, Suzie slid and almost fell, but stayed upright. Ginny held on with her knees and gently brought Suzie around so sure up her footing on the roadway.

Matt was still ahead, but Ginny was determined to catch him. Skeeter was now doing a slow walk allowing Matt to roll his first cigarette of the day. It was moments later when he heard Suzie's panting behind him and he brought Skeeter to a halt. Turning in his saddle, he caught a glimpse of Ginny riding as hard as she could ride being cautious of sliding in the snow.

"You crazy?" Matt yelled. "Rein up before you kill the both of you."

Ginny brought Suzie down slowly but nearly slid into Matt. "Just where the hell do you think you're going, Mr. Jorgensen?" she asked. She always seemed to call him Mr. Jorgensen when she was mad at him, and this time she was fuming.

"It's four in the morning, the sun ain't even up, and you're out here partially dressed and killing your favorite mare jest to find out where I'm going?" he mused.

It was true. In her hurry to dress, she forgot to button her blouse fully, and she wore nothing underneath. Even in a partially dressed ensemble, Ginny still looked the lady in charge. She sat straight in the saddle and commanded attention.

Following Matt's eyes to her blouse, she looked down and with her frozen fingers fidgeted with buttoning it up.

"Here," he said, leaning over to her and taking off his gloves, "let me do it. Your tiny fingers look frozen to the bone."

Allowing him, she added, "They wouldn't be if you'd stayed in bed. What's with you?"

Buttoning her blouse for her, Matt laughed. "You are the cutest thing I have ever seen. As cold as it is right now, I want to make love to you."

"You beast," she exclaimed shivering from the cold. "It's a hell of a lot warmer back home."

Finishing his task with her blouse, he put his gloves back on and looked south in the direction he was heading.

"You're still going after Sin, aren't you?" she asked.

Seeing her shiver, he stepped down from his horse and helped her dismount. Taking his coat from his shoulders, he wrapped her in it and held her close to him. "Puddin' face, I love you."

"Puddin' face?" she exclaimed. "I'm not a puddin' face." She brought her face up to his and brushed her snow-covered hair from her eyes. "I love you, too, mulehead."

"Then, you'll get back up on Suzie and go back to the plantation, and let me be," he said bringing his lips to meet hers. As cold as it was, her lips were warm and inviting.

Breaking from his hold, she stormed at him with her eyes. "I'll not have you kissing me with your lips and thinking in your heart that you're still going after a man to kill him. It isn't right, Matt."

"You want me to be afraid every time I hear a horse whinny, or a gate creak behind me because of him coming after me?" Matt asked, holding her arms. "He has a fetish for you, Ginny. He thinks he owns you, and I took you away from him. He'll do anything to get you away from me."

"No!" Ginny yelled at Matt, breaking his hold and turning her back to him. "He's not all bad, Matt. He's gone and he'll never be back."

"If I could believe that, Ginny, I'd ride back with you right now. But, I can't. I've known him for some six months now and I've seen how he looked at you when he was here. And my beating him up and taking his job away from him hasn't made him less a man. No. I'm thinkin' I created some sort of monster in him."

Turning her around, he looked deep into her hurt eyes as she kept her arms folded in front of her. "When he tried to steal you away from me the other day right in front of your ol' man, he was mean enough to kill me right then."

"But he didn't," Ginny retorted. "He was drunk. Good and drunk. Men are like that when they get drunk."

"I've been drunk many times, Ginny," Matt came back. "Not once was I drunk enough to want to kill a man."

"He didn't want to kill you, or anyone. He knew you were out cold the same as my father, and he had two other men to help him."

Matt grit his teeth in disgust and angrily turned away from Ginny. "You would have let him make love to you?"

"Hell no, Matt," she exclaimed. "All I'm saying is that he was too drunk to know what he was doing. I've known Sin for over two years, and not once did he ever attempt anything like that."

"He beat the hell out of your pa," Matt replied angrily holding his fists on his hips.

"I know. And father gave him one hell of a beating, too." Then taking Matt's arms and putting them around her, she found the solace she was seeking with the warmth of his body. The snow began to fall gently upon them as they held onto one another.

Looking up at Matt, she tried to spread a smile on her lips as she continued. "Oh, Matt. You're right. He turned into a vicious monster. And, I'm not for one instant forgetting he killed Bertha, but that, too, was an accident."

"Now, just who in the hell do you think he was tryin' to kill, Ginny?"

"You."

"Yes, Ginny. Me. Now think about it. He tried to kill me back then over you, and he'll try again and again. I'm not goin' to sit still and wait for that moment to happen."

"Take me with you then," Ginny tried to reason.

"Dressed like that?" Matt replied.

"I'll go home and change," she said in a childish voice anticipating a positive response from Matt.

The sound of Jim and his horse behind them broke the moment. "Ginny?" he yelled out. "You all right?"

Turning towards the voice, Ginny answered, "It's me and Matt, father."

Reining up beside them, Jim stayed on his horse and smiled down at the couple. "Having your first fight and you not married?"

"Not a fight, Sir," Matt replied. "You have one hell of a daughter here."

"You just now finding that out, son?" Jim asked.

"Maybe so, Sir," Matt responded, putting his arm around Ginny. "Maybe so."

"What are you doing way out here?" Jim continued asking while untying a coat from the back of his saddle.

"What are *you* doing way out here, father?" Ginny replied.

"As you may know, Miss McBride, your father sleeps light," Jim answered. "I saw Matt leave, then I saw you follow him. Knowing you might catch cold, I brought you a coat." Handing the coat to her, he suggested, "You might want to give yours back to Matt. You cold, son?"

"Very much, Sir," Matt replied.

"So, who's going to tell me?" Jim again asked.

"About Ginny and me?" Matt asked, looking puzzled.

Ginny looked at Matt quickly and then turned to Jim to see his reaction. She had not a given thought that this would be the moment to tell her father about them wanting to get married. Not here in the freezing cold January morning.

"Oh, eh, father," Ginny stuttered.

"You've got something to tell me, daughter?" Jim asked musingly.

"Yes, Sir," Matt replied looking up at Jim. "If it's all right with Ginny."

Ginny grinned, sheepishly, and nodded her approval to Matt. Maybe this was her way of sensing that she could keep Matt from running away. Whatever, she was willing to tell all, if necessary for the moment.

"I'm in love with your daughter, Jim, and I want to do right by her."

"Meaning?" Jim asked.

"Yes, Sir," Matt responded. "Meaning, what, Ginny?" he asked looking dumfounded.

"Meaning, Father," she responded giggling a little, "we want to get married. I love him, and he loves me, and we decided that we should get married."

"Well, Sir," Matt added, "that is if you will let us."

Jim took his pipe out of his coat pocket, packed it, and, as if taking his time, lit it. Then, exhaling the smoke and, watching it being wafted in the wind, he asked, "Am I to assume that you know what you're letting yourself in for, Matt. And you, too, young lady?"

Joining hands, the couple smiled, "Hell," Matt said, "if I knew that, I'd probably never want to get married."

"Mr. Jorgensen!" Ginny retorted with her hands on her hips.

"Only kidding, Gin," he replied. "Sir, I love Ginny more than I ever thought I could love a woman. And it would do me proud if you consented to give her to me in marriage."

Jim smiled and said, "Son, I give her to you, only, I never had her to give."

Matt looked stunned, as Jim continued. "She's always had the same ways her mother had. Her mother had the good sense to marry me, and her parents had no say in the matter. That was because she was her own boss, and they knew it." He looked over at Ginny and continued, "And Ginny is her own boss. Always has been. If she wants you, she'll get you, with or without my blessings."

Matt leaned in a little closer to hear Jim's words, then looked at Ginny who stood there with a big smile on her face.

"Still, son, she has my blessings, I guess because I like you and I like the way you handle yourself. No man can tame her. I could never tame her mother, God bless her. So, just know that for a fact and you'll have a lasting marriage."

Looking at the two sharing the moment with ecstatic bliss, he added, "Now, just what the hell are we all doing out here in the wee hours of the morning, pray tell me?"

"I'm headed out to catch Sin, Sir," Matt answered putting on his coat, "before he decides to return and get me."

"I thought you might," Jim continued as he puffed on his pipe. "Mind if I tag along?"

"Father!" Ginny exclaimed. "I'll not have it."

"I would like that, Sir," Matt replied. "You're better at knowing this area than I do."

"Thanks, son," Jim remarked. "Well, let's get started. Ginny, you get back to the house."

"I will not!" Ginny exclaimed finishing buttoning her coat.

"It is a wise woman, Ginny," Jim continued, "who obeys her father, once in awhile and the man she is about to marry, many times over."

"And how do you know I will be marrying this, this coot?" Ginny asked now changing her tune while walking over to her ground-tied mare and taking her reins.

"Ginny, I may be old, and I may have been hit on the head a few times, but a father knows when his daughter is ready for marriage," Jim answered climbing back on his steed. "Believe me, honey. I know."

"Well, I'm not going back, and that is that," Ginny said, throwing herself upon Suzie in a Pony Express leap.

"You're staying!" Matt returned as he stepped up into his saddle. "Now get home!"

Jim spurred his steed over to Matt and whispered in his ear. "A woman without a saddle will not be with us long, son." Then he rode over to Ginny's side. "Okay, daughter, you can come along."

"What did you whisper to Matt, father" Ginny asked as she began her ride with the two men. "I'd like to know."

"Now if I be telling you that, Miss Virginia McBride, we men would forever be giving into to the tears of our ladies, and you wouldn't want me to do that, now would you?"

"I have no idea in hell what you are talking about, Mr. McBride," Ginny remarked. "Let's just ride."

The three of them rode south towards Arkansas. Matt looked over at Jim and smiled. "She calls you by your last name when she's mad, too, I see."

The day's ride was hard for all the riders, but particularly for Ginny who was without a saddle, but she stayed up with them. When they came to a house belonging to a neighbor in long standing, they peeled out of their saddles and longed for the comforts of a warm house with hot food.

Ed and Millie Johnson were standing in the doorway when the trio rode up waiting to welcome them. The sun was about to set behind their house, so they could get a good look at the riders, recognizing them as their neighbors to the north.

"Jim McBride," Ed yelled out stepping down off the high porch, "that be you?"

"Certainly it's him, Ed," Millie chided in. "Can't you see Ginny by his side?"

"It's us, Ed and Millie," Jim yelled back, dismounting and tying up his steed. "Figured to stay the night, if you don't mind."

"Come on in and welcome to our home," Ed replied.

"Just fixin' supper," Millie added. "Just take a bit to add some more."

"This here is our foreman, Matt Jorgensen, Ed," Jim said as he climbed the porch.

After dismounting, Matt helped Ginny slide easy from her saddle. "Your bottom is soaked, you know that, little lady?"

"First Puddin' Head, and now 'Little Lady'," Ginny repeated as she alit from Suzie. "What are you going to call me next?"

"How're ya feelin?" Matt asked watching her rub her buttocks.

"I never knew Suzie could be so hard," Ginny said as she began walking up the steps with Matt. "I've not been so sore since I don't really know when."

"Mr. and Mrs. Johnson," Matt greeted the couple as he helped Ginny up the steps. "Are you sure we're not putting you out any?"

"You just help Ginny, Matt," Jim said, as he accepted an open door from Ed as an invitation to their home. "Ed and Millie are close friends of ours. Have been ever since we moved here. Step lively."

"Son," Ed said. "Come on in. You're gonna find that we welcome visitors whenever we can get some."

Millie took a hold of Ginny's hand and watched her as she wiggled in her wet pants from the lather Suzie gave out. "My lord, young 'un," Millie exclaimed, "your hind end is wet. I'll bet you're cold, too, child. Come on in. We'll thaw you out and warm you up all at the same time. Don and Harv will stable your horses."

Once in the house, Ginny felt the warmth Millie was talking about. The Johnson's were farmers who depended mostly on their own labor, with the help of their two sons, Harv and Don. They were plain and simple folks with no pretensions about them. The house showed that. A fireplace lit up the front room, which stretched back into the kitchen with two bedrooms dividing the rooms. Instead of doors on the rooms, they hung drapes, so there was no privacy in the home. The kitchen was the biggest of the rooms with a wood-burning stove that held four burners. A large box of kindling and wood dressed the sides of the stove.

On the other side of the kitchen were two extra rooms, one for the Johnsons and the other for guests.

"Ginny," Millie addressed her politely directing her to the guests' bedroom. "You get in here and get those wet clothes off. What's the matter with your men letting you ride like that? I'll bring you some dry clothes directly."

It took no coaxing at all for Ginny to get out of her clothes. Millie brought her a basin of hot water she had sitting on the stove reserved for her dishes and clothes to wash up later.

"Take your time, honey," Millie said. "This water was for the dishes, but you take it and clean up a bit. We'll take care of the dishes after while. You hungry, gal?"

"Yes, ma'am!" she answered with enthusiasm.

Ginny was not one to be coddled, not even when her mother was living. She wasn't about to be coddled now, at least not for long. The fact was that she was beginning to enjoy a little tender loving care.

Millie stayed with Ginny and peeked in to see that she was doing all right on her own. That was when she saw the redness of her bottom laced with some black-and-blue marks.

"Landsakes, gal!" Millie exclaimed. "Your butt has got to be sore." She left for a moment then came back with a lid of lard. "Here, honey. Let me put some of this on ya. Won't make you smell pretty, but it sure will heal what ails ya."

"I'll do it, Millie," Ginny said, taking the lard and then closing the drape.

The men gathered in the front room by the fireplace to stay warm.

"Sure is a nice fire you got there, Ed," Jim said, filling his pipe with fresh tobacco. "We'll give you a hand come morning in gathering more wood."

"The hell you will, Jim," Ed barked back. "We got enough in the shed to keep us through two winters. You just warm yourself up. Millie will have supper on shortly."

Millie entered the room wiping her hands on a rag she picked up in the kitchen. "Lard makes my hands greasy. Your young un got a good case of saddle sores, where there ain't no saddle. Lard heals those sores faster than anythin'."

"How's she, Millie?" Jim asked.

"Ginny's bottom is as red as they come and cold as ice. Good thing it *was* cold, else she might have had some blisters. I got some lard on her now, so don't any one notice the smell."

The men eyed each other and watched Millie as she went back into the kitchen to finish her cooking. They waited eagerly for Ginny to return. Little was said among them in the meantime.

Soon, Ginny came out of the bedroom wearing a robe over some longjohns.

"They're mine," Millie said while stirring the pot, "in case anyone gets to askin'."

Ginny's hair was neatly combed, and her face was clean, but like Millie said, they could smell the lard. She stopped at the kitchen and stayed there for most of the evening as she helped Millie prepare supper. She had no intentions of carrying the aroma of lard with her into the front room.

Just about the time supper was to be announced, the thunderous noise of two young men was heard as they pounced up onto the porch. After knocking the snow and mud off their boots, Harv and Don Johnson entered through the kitchen door. They were Ed and Millie's teenage sons.

"Saw your horses tied up in front, so we took them to the barn," Harv said hanging his coat with Don on the coat nail.

"I saw you," Jim returned. "Thanks."

"What's goin' on?" Don asked walking over to a big washtub where he would wash his hands.

"Well, I was about to tell your folks, but we got caught up in another thought or two, and just forgot about it, Don," Jim answered.

"Don, Harv," Ed introduced. "This here is Matt Jorgensen. He's their foreman."

"Howdy," Matt greeted them with his cowboy salute, a tilt of the head, a flip of his fingers on his forehead, and a big smile. "We're chasin' a man."

"Oh. Any one we might know, Jim?" Ed asked.

"Matter of fact, yes," Jim answered. "It's Sin. You remember him. Been with us two years."

"Matt here took his place, I suppose?" Ed inquired.

"Yep," Matt answered. "After a quarrel."

"Heard it was more like a fight," Don added.

"What you wantin' him for, Jim?" Millie asked from the kitchen, listening in while setting the table.

"Killing a woman," Jim answered, relighting his pipe.

"Oh my lord!" Millie exclaimed, dropping a saucer.

Ginny bent over and picked it up. "Didn't break, Millie."

"Who'd he kill, Jim?" Ed asked.

"Bertha, our house Negro. You remember Bertha don't you, Millie?" Jim asked, walking to the kitchen way.

"Oh, my stars, her? How? I mean why would Sin do such a crazy thing like that?" Millie asked, wiping the saucer that fell and putting it back on the table. "She was so good. So helpful. Why I loved her so."

"It was an accident, Millie," Ginny threw in while helping set the table.

"Yeah," Matt said with a slight tongue in cheek as he looked at Ginny. "He meant to kill me."

"We seen him," Don said, wiping his hands on a kitchen towel. "Yesterday some time, he rode down this way and passed us like the devil was a chasin' him. Didn't pay a mind to us, just kept ridin'."

"You see him, too, Harv?" Jim asked.

"From a distance," he answered. "I was on the west end of the farm clearing out some old crops, and Don yelled out at him. It was him all right."

"Sumthin' else, Matt," Don said. "The Marshal stopped by. I 'spect he's what was that devil a chasin' him."

"Our Marshal Brady?" Ginny asked.

"Then he's got a good day's start on us," Matt said.

"Maybe two if he doesn't hole up tonight somewhere."

"Got to, sometime, I reckon," Ed added to the conversation. "The creek up the road was frozen over, but the ice broke up. It might have patched up some today, but it should still slow him down a bit."

Coming from the kitchen with her towel in her hand, Ginny asked, "What's Marshal Brady doing going after Sin for? There's no cause for that."

"Olaf, Ginny," Jim answered. "He dropped by yesterday and told me that Sin stole from him and said he told Marshal Brady about it. That's why he's riding after Sin."

"Soup's on, everybody!" Millie yelled from the kitchen banging on an empty pot.

Ginny returned to the kitchen deep in thought about the Marshal going after Sin, but never brought the subject up again. She had figured they would encounter Sin somewhere and bring him back peacefully. Now with the Marshal after him, too, her thoughts were on Sin's safety.

The Johnson's enjoyed the evening together with their neighbors and Matt for supper. Later that evening they uncorked a bottle and shared it around the front room until each one sported a rosy glow. Ginny's clothes hung by the fireplace to dry out over night.

Millie had given Ginny a pan of popcorn which the two of them popped and then made a mess trying to salt and butter. The salt made them drink more, and the harder they drank, the rosier the evening became.

Matt attempted to toss a few pieces of popcorn into Ginny's mouth while they teased each other beside the fire. She returned the favor. Both missed more than they could hit each other's target, even though Matt would attempt to open his mouth the largest.

"Damn corn," he said. "No wonder they call it popped corn. Got more on my face than in my mouth."

Matt had the pleasure of carrying Ginny to her bedroom while Millie tucked her in. Harv and Don slept where they laid in the front room. Jim escorted Ed to his room where Millie took over, and then he plopped down on Harv's bed. Matt stumbled unto Don's bedroom, and fell on top of the bed. Without bothering to undress, the men were fast asleep.

"Put another log on the fire, Harv," Millie yelled into the front room waaking Harv from his slumber. "See you folks at breakfast."

The embers crackled in the fireplace the next morning as the last log split and fell apart sending sparks up the shaft of the chimney. It kept the chill out of the house long enough for Harv to crawl over and put another log on it to keep it burning.

Millie was already up cooking bacon on the stove and scrambling eggs when Jim came out of his room.

"Biscuits will be ready to come out of the oven by the time you get back from the outhouse, Jim," Millie said watching Jim rub his sleepy eyes.

"Nobody up, yet?" Jim asked as he tested the outside with his finger.

"Just me and the chickens and I'm not too sure about them, bein' this cold," Millie answered softly so as not to wake the others too abruptly, knowing the smell of the bacon would do the trick.

"I'm up, Jim," Matt said through the drapes to his bedroom. Entering the kitchen and pulling up his galluses, he took a strong whiff of Millie's cooking and let out a yell.

"Hush up, boy!" Millie exclaimed waving her fork at him. "Go make your stop, boys and I'll have coffee ready when you uns get back."

"Keep quiet, Matt," Jim said, as he opened the door for Matt to go with him. "Ginny's still asleep."

"About Ginny, Jim," Matt said. "She's not in any condition to continue on."

"I know, Matt," Jim agreed. "I'm taking her back with me."

"You turning back?"

"She's hurting more than she's telling. She's all I've got, Matt."

"I agree. Besides, if Marshal Brady is on his tail, it shouldn't take me long to find him."

"Stay on the main road, Matt," Jim instructed him. "If the ice is solid, take it across. If not, turn right a mile or so, and you'll find a narrow there you can cross over without any trouble. Sin knows about it, too, so watch yourself. He just might be holing out in a shed close by."

"What if Ginny doesn't see it our way?"

"I'll make her see it our way. Don't worry."

As they made their way back to the house, Ginny was out of the house and headed their way.

"When you fixin on tellin' her, Jim?" Matt asked, watching her step lively through their snow trail.

"After breakast, Matt," Jim replied. "After breakfast. There's nothing like a scorned woman before breakfast, and I ain't about to mix up with one now."

Waving to her, Jim greeted her with, "Good morning, Daughter."

"Good morning, Father, Matt," she replied, and walked past them with a smile.

"You know somethin', Jim?" Matt queried as he stopped to watch Ginny pass them in a prissy manner.

"What, Matt?" as he looked as bewildered as Matt.

"She don't look hurt one bit."

"She's putting it on. Besides, she wouldn't ride another mile without a saddle."

"Don't you be taking a bet on that, father," she yelled from inside the outhouse. "I heard every word you said."

The two men threw up their hands and walked on into the house where Millie met them with two cups of coffee.

"Now, if one of you will help me pull that pan of biscuits out, I'll be setting the table," Millie said, as she took the pan of eggs off the stove and began serving them on their plates.

"Is all we do in this house is eat?" Matt asked smilingly.

"You wanna complain, take it up with my old man. Ed ain't ever complained one day about not bein' fed properly."

Harv and Don had been up and washed their face and hands already, and were sitting at the table ready to eat.

"Ginny's comin' right back, if you guys want to use it," Matt suggested.

"Done did it, Matt," Harv said, breaking into his first biscuit.

"Me, too," Don said, taking his first taste of coffee for the morning.

Ed came out of his room fussing with his hair, what little there was left of it, when Matt asked, "You, too?"

"Me too, what, son?" Ed asked.

"He wants to know if you've been outside, Ed?" Jim filled him in on their morning greetings.

"Oh, that. Nope. On my way, though," he said, and grabbing an old copy of the Helena Daily Herald, went out the door, letting it slam. He would notice more about the impending war between the states as the headlines talked about it, but he wasn't one to talk much about it.

"Will he ever learn to close the door right?" Millie asked herself in a whisper for the rest to hear. "Who cares?" Then looking at Matt, she asked, "Want them scrambled or sunnyside up?"

"Sunnyside up, ma'am," Matt replied.

"Sorry, son. They only come one way this morning. Scrambled. I put 'em all in one bowl and stirred them with milk. They go further that way. Okay with you?"

Matt grinned and nodded his head as he rubbed his bushy crop of hair. "Yes ma'am."

Jim smiled, and swigged down the last of his first cup of coffee.

Ginny returned and grabbed hold of the pot of coffee. Seeing Jim's empty in his hand, she poured it, then went around the table for the rest. With that done, she set the pot back on the stove, and went to the washbowl to wash up.

"Now, why do you suppose she poured our coffee before she washed up?" Matt asked curiously.

"Son," Jim answered, "she is conditioned. She saw her dad's cup was empty, and that came first before washing."

"I agree," Ginny said, turning around and drying her hands.

"That you're conditioned?" Matt asked.

"That, too," Ginny responded, then poured herself a cup of coffee and sat down. "Nope. I agree with what you two were saying back there. You should go on alone. I ain't fit to travel any more. I done seen my butt, and let me tell you, it's a site. With no saddle, I ain't a fixin' to ride Suzie another day or two out and then back again. No, sir. You can go alone."

Matt's eyes opened and his jaw dropped, but before he could enjoy the news, Ed made a suggestion.

"Got an old saddle in the barn that would fit Suzie right well," he said. "You're welcome to use it."

"Great!" exclaimed Ginny, buttering her biscuit. "Enough said. I'm still going."

Jim and Matt were in their saddles as Ginny and Millie came out of the house. Ed brought out Suzie, saddled and ready for the ride. As Ginny began to mount, Millie stepped around and slipped her arm around her waist. "He's worth it, Ginny. And so are you. Who's gonna be matron of honor?"

Harv and Don started for the fields, and the sun began to climb.

The three rode through the rest of the morning and came to the creek Ed talked about where the ice might be too thin for them to cross. Turning downstream, they followed some tracks, which they figured were Sin and the Marshal's horses. Soon they discovered a dead horse on the trail. Further examination led them to the body of Marshal Brady lying face down.

Dismounting, Matt walked over to the grim discovery and, after noticing a bullet hole in his back, turned the Marshal's body over to see if there were any signs of life. There was none.

Ginny alit from Suzie and ran over to Matt while Jim sat his horse.

"It's Marshal Brady, Dad," she said. "He's been shot in the back."

Looking around, Jim noticed the hoof prints of one horse leading off to the side of the road. "Seems likely he ambushed him from that direction, Matt," he said, pointing towards the tracks. He leaned forward and nudged his steed into a walk following the tracks.

"Easy, Jim," Matt said. "He might still be around."

Matt climbed back on Skeeter and sidled Jim, while Ginny stayed with the body. In a few moments the two men returned.

"We've got ourselves a real killer, Matt," Jim said, as he dismounted by the Marshal's body. "Ginny and I'll take the Marshal back, if you want to continue on. I'll wire ahead and let the marshal know. Maybe they can get a posse up and stop him."

Ginny's face grew white as she looked up at her father. "This don't change things, father," she said quite determined to continue on with Matt. "We can get him ourselves."

Matt grabbed hold of Ginny's arms and, trying to calm her down, said, "He's a killer, Ginny. It's time you realized that."

"Maybe he had to," Ginny returned trying to free herself from Matt's iron grip. "Maybe the Marshal was about to kill him and he shot in self defense."

Jim looked at the Marshal's body and pointed to his holstered .45. "His gun is still in his holster, Ginny," he said. "He was bushwacked."

"Why are you still trying to defend him so," Matt asked as he let go of Ginny's arms. Looking at her as she rubbed her wrists, he continued, "You never believed him to be anything other than innocent of all this." He realized that his words were ringing true for the first time.

Standing in front of her with his hands on his hips, he confronted her, saying, "You never gave him up. You're still in love with him. All this time, you were still seeing him while pretending to be in love with me."

"That's not true, Matt," Ginny exclaimed half crying, "That's not true." Straightening up, and keeping from letting a tear fall, she said, "He's not a killer. He's got a heart, and . . ."

"You almost made me think that you loved me, Ginny," Matt said bringing his hands around her arms again. "You almost made me think it."

"I do love you, Matt," she replied, still keeping the tear from falling. "I do love you."

"He wasn't going to rape you back there," Matt said in disgust. "He was playing with you and you knew it. You were strong enough to hold back his advances, but you let him tear your clothes. You let him kiss you. It's unfortunate that Bertha got in the way."

"No!" Ginny exclaimed violently, breaking from his hold. "It was an accident! It was an accident! You know that!" Her sobs brought out the truth in her. "He was someone good to talk with. Didn't you ever have someone you loved talking to?"

"Yeah," Matt answered, "you!"

Jim stood silent until he could stand no more and then he stepped over and put his arms around Ginny.

"I'm sorry, Jim," Matt said.

"I guess it's best you go alone, Matt," Jim said holding onto Ginny.

Ginny broke from her father's hold and walked over to Matt. "I love you, Matt. I knew that at the river when you and I first kissed. Why don't you believe me?"

"All this time," Matt said. "You knew how much I loved you, Ginny. I loved you from the very first time I met you. I was crazy about you. Why the hell do you think I stayed on? I stayed because I fell in love with you, dammit."

Taking a step towards Skeeter, Matt took the reins in his hand, then turned and walked back to Ginny. "Why?"

"I loved you then, too, Matt," Ginny said, still holding back the tear.

Matt walked back to her and looked deeply into her eyes and said nothing for the moment. He just wanted to look at her and hear her cry. The cry never came.

"I never loved anyone but you, Matt," she said. "You've got to believe me."

"Then why go behind my back and have affairs with Sin?" Matt asked trying to hold back his anger.

"I never did anything with him, Matt," she answered swirling her fist in the air as if trying to hit something. "I swear to God." Then in a calm fashion she stated confidently, looking Matt straight in his eyes, "I've never had another man. And you know that."

"I'm sorry, Ginny," Matt said and turned and walked away.

Matt climbed up on Skeeter and rode out, waving lightly to Jim. "Thanks for everything, Jim."

Jim stepped over to Ginny and wrapped his arms around her. He nodded his head to Matt that everything was all right.

"Matt!" Ginny cried out, trying to break her father's hold. "Matt, please don't go. I need you! I love you!"

Realizing that he was really leaving, she walked over to her horse and climbed on. Her hand reached for her whip which was not there. She wanted so much to stop him from going, but did not know how to keep him there.

Jim watched his little daughter throw her tantrum, and knew she was looking for her baby blanket, the whip, for solace. He walked over to her horse at the same time Ginny spurred Suzie. Jim was fast enough, and took hold of the reins. Suzie reared up and came down, then stepped aside, and settled down as Jim held onto the reins.

"Let him go, Ginny," Jim said. "If he comes back, you owe him a big apology. If it were me, I'd keep riding."

Ginny listened to his words and placed them deeply in her heart as she watched Matt disappear in the fog and snow. She was in love with Matt, and now she knew just how much. The tear finally materialized and rolled down her cold, rose-colored cheek. Had Matt seen it, he would have stayed. She was too lovely for him to have left her.

CHAPTER 22

A MAN ALONE FOR TEXAS

April 1861

fter a week in the saddle, Matt found out that Sin Crouch had known about him still following him for some time.

Some of Sin's friends in Tennessee had ridden out to warn him. They also knew about Sin killing the marshal, so they never joined up with him. They also knew that Sin's feud with Matt had to be on a personal basis.

At one point in Tennessee, just before he crossed over into Arkansas, a young lad with a strong hate for the likes of his kind, found out about Sin being near by, and waited for him. When he rode close by, the lad took a shot at him with his long Remington rifle, only to miss him. Thinking it was Matt, Sin rode faster and harder south in fear of getting caught by him.

Because Matt was younger than Sin and much stronger, he kept the ride intense and knew he was closer to his prey each time Sin rested.

A few times, Sin had tried to double back towards Tennessee only to find that Matt's appearance somewhere along the way had blocked his retreat. Sin had tried unsuccessfully to hire other men to stop Matt, but his funds had run low and they knew his monetary position. Sin ran out of friends fast.

Then, at one point along his trail, he felt Matt had actually lost his scent. Because of his relaxed attitude, he stayed awhile in one Texas town a little too long on a Saturday night.

Matt reined up at the marshal's office, walked in and inquired of his prey. The marshal, a determined man with a tough disposition, suggested that he might be the bearded stranger who rode into town a week before.

"He rode an Appy," he informed Matt. "Tried to get it shod over at the smith's but didn't wait. Got a job out at the Bar Y Ranch, east of here."

Matt thanked the marshal, left his office and rode Skeeter over to the hotel where he put him in a stall and boarded down for the night. He never realized that Sin was still in town getting drunk. The ride had tired Matt out so that he really needed the rest more than he needed Sin.

All liquored-up, Sin left the saloon and staggered down the sidewalk where he saw Matt's sorrel hitched to the rail outside the hotel. Apprehensively, he walked over to the horse and carefully examined the saddle to make sure of its ownership. There was no doubt when he saw the name "Matt" carved into the side of it. It was a saddle Matt's father had given him for his fifteenth birthday, and it was well worn.

Sin looked over at the hotel entrance, and then up at the lit windows. Seeing no one in sight, he staggered back to the saloon, mounted his steed, and rode out into the night for the Bar Y Ranch.

That was his second mistake that week, for he did not know that the marshal had told his whereabouts to Matt. Once back at the ranch, it being Sunday, he hit his cot and began to sleep his drunk off, thinking that he would be safe from Matt for the moment.

Wednesday 10 April 1861

In Charleston, South Carolina, a young, forty-three year old, good-looking Brigadier General, Pierre Gustave Toutant (PGT) Beauregard, a graduate of West Point, and now commander of the provisional Confederate forces at Charleston, demanded

Major Anderson's surrender of Fort Sumter. Major Anderson refused. Two men with their garrisons, one defending a fort, and the other demanding a surrender of it, began a standoff that would change the course of history for America.

A wrangler came into the bunkhouse towards noon and roused Sin out of the sack. "Your luck just ran out, cow poke," the wrangler said, poking Sin in the back with his rifle. "That dude who's been looking for ya done showed his face at the ranch house." Leaving the bunkhouse, he added, "You better get your fat ass outta here. Only way out is due south."

Sin Crouch had drunkenly blabbed one night to the wranglers how he had stolen Matt's girl away from him, the most beautiful and most virtuous of women in all of Tennessee. He lied about how he made love to her and how he threw her back to her pa before he rode off to Texas. Now, they were warning him that the man he should fear was at the door.

As Matt came around the side of the ranch house with the owner, he caught the face of Sin Crouch staring down at him as he mounted up and headed south. Matt drew his .45 but it was knocked away by the ranch owner hitting his arm and causing the shot to go wild.

"Not on my ranch, fella," the huge man with a large mustache said. His men sided in with him at that point, showing Matt that his fight would be elsewhere.

Matt thanked the owner with a nod and rode fast after Sin. The trail went through some back woods and soon Matt lost it. He slowed his sorrel into a walk and began looking for some signs. The trail led to a running brook and a clearing. In the distance, he got a glimpse of Sin heading up a rocky hillside. Spurring Skeeter, Matt began his ride after Sin.

Sin had had enough sleep to put his mind back into focus. He knew that if he was going to escape Matt this time, he would have to bushwhack him. He thought that here above the stream on the hillside afforded him cover and a good opportunity to do just that.

Once on top of the rocky hill, surrounded by rocks for coverage, he dismounted and tied his steed to a branch, and slipped his rifle out of its boot. Getting into position, he rested himself in a gorge and took aim at where Matt would ride.

The wait was short, for Matt appeared exactly where Sin figured. He waited until he was sure that he could hit Matt and fired. Matt was knocked from his horse when a bullet hit and broke his reins. As he tumbled into the stream, he pulled his Colt and fired upwards toward the flash of gunfire.

Sin had the edge on Matt for he was hidden and using a rifle in ambush. Matt was lying in the shallow stream. Skeeter had stopped in the woods some hundred feet away, giving Matt no chance to mount him. His only cover now would be the water. Holstering his .45, he ran downstream to the deep water and dove in. He swam downstream to the first cover, which was a clump of rocks and dead branches.

Coming up out of the water, he could hear the cracking of Sin's rifle and the ricocheting of the bullets all around him. "Sin seems to be pretty good with the rifle", Matt thought as he brought his pistol into firing position. He fired one round off in Sin's direction for effect, knowing he had no real identification of Sin's position. It worked. It drew Sin's fire back into Matt's direction. The bullet split a twig off the branch in front of him, but Matt caught his position from the flash of his rifle.

Matt rapidly fired three shots causing Sin to scurry away and drop his rifle, letting it fall towards the stream. Now Matt was going to find out how good Sin was with only a sidearm. He waited but heard no firing. Looking up, he could find no trace of Sin.

After waiting a short while, Matt climbed out of the stream and ran across the clearing towards the hillside. Still, he drew no fire. He climbed the rocks and found the place where Sin had positioned himself. Sin was gone. Matt saw him riding back into the clearing by the stream, but was too far away to fire.

He picked up Sin's rifle while he raced down the hillside and over to Skeeter. He tied the rifle alongside his own, mounted his steed and rode out after Sin.

Sin's ride took him into Texas to a middle-sized town called Nacogdoches. It was a small Texas town but it had two saloons and two banks. The marshal was out of town, but his young deputy, Steve Andrews, was assuming his duties when Sin rode in. To Steve, Sin looked every bit the cowpoke down on his luck, without any visible means of support. Perhaps it was because of the sloppy way Sin was dressed with his clothes dirty and torn, or perhaps it was because of the way he rode in his saddle, like he was ready to fall out of it. Whatever the reason, Deputy Steve walked over to him ready to jail him for vagrancy as he reined up in front of a saloon.

"What's your name, friend?" Steve asked, holding his hand firm on his gun grip and ready to draw any minute he saw fit.

Dismounting and almost falling out of the saddle, Sin turned to find the deputy eyeing him carefully, ready to jail him.

"Hold it right there, mister," the deputy ordered him. Removing Sin's sidearm, the deputy turned him around carefully with both guns pointed at his midsection.

"What's your name and where're you from?" the deputy asked him.

Sin lied when he said, "Burt Randall, from Abilene, Deputy." Sin had to rely on the deputy believing his story that a man had stuck him up and stolen his money and his rifle. "He took everything I had," Sin said. "I escaped with my life when he wasn't looking, and I rode away as fast I could."

The deputy, in his early twenties was a man about fifteen years younger than Sin. He stood six-feet tall, about a hundred-and-seventy pounds, with straight black hair. He was a good-looking man with a bushy mustache, and a two-day growth of beard. He sported a full head of hair, though his well-worn Stetson hid most of it. His dimples let one know that he was a gentle man, but firm. His voice was naturally deep, and when he spoke, he spoke assuredly and slowly. But every word he said was stated with a purpose.

There was no reason to doubt Sin's story as he was penniless, having spent all his money that Saturday night a week ago. He also showed the deputy his empty scabbard. "If you find him, he'll have my rifle, Deputy," he said, painting a picture with his hands. "It has my initial B on the stock, for 'Burt'."

"Not likely he'll hit town," the deputy said looking through Sin's saddle bags as a routine search. "If he's smart, he'd head the other direction. Where you headed?"

"To find a place where I can get cleaned up and get a decent meal, Deputy," Sin answered watching Steve go through his personal belongings.

"Want a job?" Steve asked, closing up his saddle bags.

Sin thought for a moment and quizzically looked at Steve as if to say, "Why are you doing this for me?" and answered, "Yeah. What cha got?"

"The Lazy Z is looking for some cowpokes to take a herd back to Abilene. Since you're from there, it's a good way to go back. That is if'n you got a hankerin' on headin' back."

"Yeah," Sin said again, thinking that if Matt did come to town, he would not suspect him to be on a cattle drive. It would be a great way to get Matt off his tail. "That would be great. Where's the ranch?"

"The foreman's in the saloon lookin' for men right now as we speak, friend," Steve answered taking Sin by his arm and leading him inside the Long Horn Saloon. "You've done cattle work, haven't you?" Steve asked.

"Yeah," Sin lied as he followed Steve into the saloon. Sin never liked cows, even back on the plantation. There he had the other men take care of them, until Matt showed up with his expertise.

Seeing a weathered-beaten man at the far end of the saloon playing stud poker, Steve called out to him. "Dave! Gotcha another hand."

"Who ya got, Steve?" the man asked.

"Name's Burt Randall from up Abilene way," Steve answered. "Down on his luck. Some bushwacker took his money and beat him up. Can you use him?"

"Sure," Dave answered, throwing his money on the table to meet the last bid. "Abilene's where we're headed. Want to go back, I take it?"

"As good a place as any right now," Sin answered. "No money."

Dave smelled a week's stench from the ride on Sin and strongly suggested to him, "Get a bath, fella." Without turning his head, he yelled out, "Gertie. Get this dude cleaned up. Put the tab on me."

Following the last man's bid, he said, "I call." He had the winning hand.

Matt hit town that following afternoon after following a cold trail left by Sin. Nacogdoches just happened to be the biggest town along the way, and Matt's only hunch was that Sin would land here. As luck had it, he noticed an Appy tied up in front of the saloon that resembled Sin's.

The deputy saw Matt through his opened door and watched him as he rode over to the tied-up steed. The deputy walked over and stopped him. He noticed a second rifle tied to his saddle. "Hold up there, cowboy," the deputy yelled out, walking over to him with his pistol drawn. "Climb down and keep your hands up."

Matt reined up and obeyed the deputy by dismounting and keeping his hands in the air. "What's it all about?" Matt asked.

Upon examining the rifle, and finding Sin's initial on it, the deputy added, "Not the marshal, mister. I'm his deputy, and you're under arrest." He took the rifle from Matt's scabbard as Matt dismounted.

Matt felt a little foolish, and then remembered the rifle was Sin's. The appearance of the deputy to Matt seemed to be somewhat tough, and somewhat mean at the time, and Matt felt that the deputy was not one who was about to be snowballed into believing any cock-and-bull story anyone would come up with. Having Sin's rifle tied to his own scabbard left Matt with little excuse for the deputy. But, Matt also knew he had to tell the truth, so the truth, in all its frailty, he told.

"If you're talkin' about that rifle," Matt said, "it belonged to a bushwhacker."

The deputy took Matt's Colt from his holster and pushed him ahead of him. "Second time I heard that story, friend," he said holding onto Matt's arm. Skeeter followed along. When they got to the jail, the deputy motioned for Matt to tie up Skeeter to the hitching post.

After locking Matt inside his cell, the deputy asked him the pertinent questions as to who he was and where he came from.

"Get the bushwhacker, Deputy," Matt tried to explain. "Tall guy, with a beard."

"Now, that sounds like the man *you* 'bushwhacked'," the deputy responded.

"If'n he preferred charges agin' me," Matt said rapidly, "that's the man I want."

"You'll get your say, friend" the deputy answered. "The marshal will be back by noon tomorrow."

"By that time, that no-good bastard will be across into Mexico somewhere," Matt retorted.

"Maybe so," the deputy came back. "In that case, you can go free. Bein' no victim, the charges will be dropped." He poured himself a tin of coffee from the pot setting on the stove and then sat down behind his desk. "What you wantin' him for, anyway"

"Well, for openers," Matt explained, "he murdered a sweet little old woman in Tennessee. And then he killed a marshal. And he damned near killed me twice, once in Tennessee and agin' when he tried to bushwhack me a few miles back."

"What's this hear fella's name?" Steve asked. "Assumin' he has one . . ."

"Sin Crouch," Matt answered.

"Nope," Steve replied. "No man by that name came through here."

"A bearded man, ugly sort of cuss, like the one you jest described," Matt added.

"If what you're sayin' is true, he'd have a wanted poster out on him," Steve replied, walking to his desk. Opening the desk drawer, he brought a stack of wanted posters and plopped them on the desk in front of him. Thumbing through the posters carefully, one at a time, he came across Sin's poster. "Here's a Sin Crouch."

"That's him," Matt yelled out from his cell.

The photo was that of Sin Crouch clean-shaven and much younger looking. Without showing the poster to Matt, he placed them back in the desk drawer.

"Nope. Ain't seen this cuss. You're jest out of luck, friend."

Matt sat down on his cot and put his chin in his hand. "Sin Crouch. Deputy," he asked, "what's that guy on that poster look like?"

"Young man. Peach fuzz," Steve answered. "Nothing like what you described."

"Can there be two Sin Crouchs?" Matt asked rising and going to the cell door.

"Sure. But I ain't seen a Sin Crouch, and what you described is an older man with a beard."

"Draw a beard on him, Deputy," Matt suggested softly speaking.

"You mean, it could be a younger picture of him?" Steve asked, picking the poster back out of the drawer.

"Could be, Deputy. Gawd I hope so."

After penciling in a beard, Steve scratched his head and said, "If that don't beat all. It's Burt Randall."

"Burt Randall?" Matt asked puzzling. "Who the hell is Burt Randall?"

"That's the poke that said you bushwhacked him," Steve answered. "A dirty codger. In fact, the man who rode in on that Appy. Well, I'll be hornswaggered. That Burt ain't Burt. He's Sin Crouch."

"Got enough coffee for another cup, Deputy?"

"Yep," he replied, getting the pot and pouring Matt a cup. "You sayin' Burt and this Sin Randall are the same man?" Steve asked to fortify the situation. "And I got him a job."

"Where?" Matt asked, picking up his Stetson from the cot readying his release. "What doing?"

Steve took the keys from his desk and opened the jail for Matt. "I'm sorry, friend," he said, unlocking Matt's cell. "Don't know what else I can do to help." Throwing Matt his gunbelt, he said, "My name's Steve, by the way.""Got him a job on the cattle drive, friend," Steve answered opening the cell for Matt. "He's headin' up to the Lazy Z Ranch."

"I gotta check out that Appy in front of the saloon, Steve," Matt said, strapping on his gun belt. "By the way, m'name's Matt."

Holding the cell door for Matt to come out, Steve answered him. "You're gonna need me, Matt."

Matt nodded and walked out the cell door.

"Want your coffee?" Steve asked, putting the cup down on his desk and following Matt outside. "'Suppose not," he mumbled.

The two men walked out and down the sidewalk looking for Sin's appy, if by chance he was still in town. It wasn't on the street.

"Dammit, he's gone," Matt said in anger, hitting his pant leg with this Stetson. "How far to the Lazy Z Ranch did you say?"

"Hold off a sec," Steve said noticing two lads playing on the porch of the hotel. Approaching them he asked, "Did any of you see a man on an appaloosa, brown spotted, at any time?"

"Yesterday or today?" one of the boys asked while continuing to run around the post trying to avoid getting tagged by the other boy.

"Today, son," Steve answered.

"Nope," the boy answered. "Saw him yesterday though."

"Yeah, I saw him yesterday, too," Steve said scratching his head while holding his Stetson up with his same hand.

"I saw it," the other boy said, as he tagged the first boy, "You're it!" he exclaimed, and ran to the other end of the porch.

"The appaloosa?" Matt asked.

"Yep," the boy replied. "A little while ago. This fella walked him to the smithy. The horse lost a shoe."

"The smith?" Matt remarked.

"It's a chance. Let's take a look," Steve suggested, and they both ran down the street.

The blacksmith's shop was at the very end of the street. They could see the smith fitting a shoe on an appaloosa, so they slowed down to a walk and unlatched the safety straps on their holsters in event it was Sin's horse.

Sin stepped out of the shadows with a cigarette in his hand as they came within fifty feet of the shop. He saw the men coming towards him, and recognizing who they were, he threw the cigarette down and mounted his horse.

"I'm not finished with this one shoe," the blacksmith said, trying to keep Sin there.

Not listening to him, Sin tore out through the other side of the shop.

"Damn!" Matt cried, and went running through the shop after him.

"No need to run, Deputy," the smith said. "The shoe'll come off, and the horse'll go lame. Watch and see."

Sure enough, the shoe came off, and the horse fell, and Sin with it. Scrambling to his feet, Sin began to run.

Matt was quicker and fired a shot that kicked dirt at his feet. "You know I can shoot straighter, Sin," Matt said. "The next one is straight through your heart if you don't throw your gun down."

Sin froze as he looked at the two men standing and watching him cower.

"Ginny was my girl, Steve." Matt said, holding his .45 aimed at Sin. "He tried to rape her. I'm hoping he draws."

"Then I suggest you take him, Matt," Steve replied, putting his .44 back into his holster.

Matt walked closer to Sin who was still shivering. "Want to go for it, Sin?" Matt asked, holstering his .45. "I'm gonna do worse than what you did to Ginny and Bertha."

"I didn't do nothin'. Ya got me all wrong. What's with Bertha?"

"You killed her. "Matt's hand was steady over his gun butt. "And I'm gonna kill you."

"I didn't kill her." Sin's knees buckled slightly as he stood, shivering for fear of his life.

"You fired one fatal bullet, Sin. That's all it took."

"I didn't know," Sin said. "I liked Bertha. I - I was drunk that night, Matt," Sin shouted. "We all was drunk."

"Your skinny man's dead. Jim's horse crushed his head. But of course, you knew that. You didn't go to help him. Your other paid son-of-a-bitch was in jail last I saw him, if they ain't hung him by now."

"I didn't know those men," Sin said as he tried to squirm his way out by unbuckling his gunbelt. "I'm beggin' ya," Sin cried, dropping to his knees.

Matt walked over to him and stood strong, looked down at him, and watched him cry.

"Can I have him, now Matt?" the deputy asked, walking cautiously over to Sin.

As Matt started to walk away, he turned and kicked Sin squarely in the face knocking out a tooth and causing blood to spurt out of his mouth. As Sin rolled and tried to get up, Matt kicked him again in the belly.

He pulled Sin up again and brought his fist across his face and then back again, holding him all the time.

Steve watched and did nothing. Matt reached for dirt with his right hand, doubled his fist, and brought it up, connecting once more with Sin's chin, sending him reeling into a pile of fresh horse dung.

Steve grabbed a bucket of water near by and threw it in Sin's face. Then, looking at Matt, he nodded his head as if to say, "*Now?*"

Matt bent over and grabbed at his knees to get a second wind. "Now," Matt said exhaustedly, "Now you can have him."

Unknown to either man in the excitement, Sin had rolled over on top of his own gunbelt. He slipped his .44 out of its holster and placed it firmly in the palm of his hand.

"You're wanted for killing a marshal, mister," Steve said, gritting his teeth. "Get up!"

As he reached down to bring him up, Sin turned towards Steve with his .44 cocked and aimed it at Steve's throat. Matt froze as he watched Sin's face took on the look of a crazed victor.

"Throw your gun down, Matt," Sin commanded as he held the deputy's arm behind his back. "Now, you son-of-a-bitch! Now!" he yelled excitedly, his hand twitching on the trigger ready to pull it. "Or I'll kill your friend here as sure as you're standin' in my way."

Matt took his .45 out of its holster and threw it to the ground.

"Now, Mr. Jorgensen, you're a dead man."

Sin felt a sense of anticipated satisfaction in knowing that he was going to kill the man he hated for taking Ginny away from him. Now, this was the moment he waited for since he began running. He turned the gun away from Steve towards Matt, cocked the hammer, and brought the sight down on Matt.

A shot rang out and hit Sin in the leg as his .44 went off into the air missing Matt. He grabbed his leg and again aimed his pistol at Matt.

Steve reeled around, drew his .44, cocked it and fired in less than a second. The bullet hit Sin's chest and flung him backward. Sin rolled in the dirt, got to his knees and, seeing Matt, fired at him. He missed.

Matt dove for his Colt, brought it up and fired back, hitting Sin between the eyes.

Sin fell dead into the dirt.

The young deputy walked over and stood over Sin's lifeless body. "I had to earn my salary," Steve said, looking down at the dead man.

Once Matt and Steve confirmed the kill, they turned and looked toward the smith's shop. There stood the smith with a smoking rifle in his hand.

"Jesse!" Steve cried out. "Thanks!"

Jesse was the man who had fired the first shot that hit Sin and brought him to the ground. He gave a salute to Steve and Matt while looking at the dead man and said, "Jus' helpin' out."

"That was damn fast shootin', Steve," Matt said. "You cleared your holster and fired while he had his gun cocked."

"Practice," Steve replied with a slight smile towards Matt. "Some day I'm gonna be the marshal." He put his .44 back into its holster, smiled and said, "Damn fine shooting on your part, too." He bent down and examined Sin's face. "Right between the eyes."

"I was aimin' for his nose."

The two men picked Sin's body up and tossed it onto the saddle. Walking the horse to the undertaker up the street, Steve asked the smith as they walked by, "What time it gettin' to be, Jesse?"

The smith looked at the sun just rising and said, "Supper time, I recken, Deputy."

"Soon as I clean up this mess one might call human, and get him down to the mortician, what say we grab ourselves a bite,

Mr. Jorgensen?" Steve took a chaw of tobacco from his vest and offered it to Matt. "On the county."

Matt took the tobacco, tore into the chaw with his teeth and got a good chew. He looked at the dead man draped over the horse with his long hair hanging. "Not hungry." He gave the tobacco back to Steve and kept walking.

The calendar on the wall in the marshal's office dated that day as 12 April 1861.

Marshal Potter returned, like he said he would, around noon from a visit to a ranch out of town on business. Not much ever happened in Nagadoches, let alone a shoot-out. When he rode in on his horse down Main Street, he noticed Sin's body lying outside the mortician's office. A new casket was being made for him by a carpenter who was measuring the body right closely, so as not to waste wood. The county was paying for the burial, and the carpenter, a lean and completely bald gentleman named Pete, knew it would be pittance to what he was worth. Yet, he agreed to do it as always. It was his job.

"What happened, Pete?" Marshal Potter asked as he reined up to the hitching rail without dismounting.

"Your deputy," Pete answered. "They had a shoot-out at the end of the street and this fella lost."

"What about?"

"Don't rightly know, Marshal," Pete answered. "Alls I know is this one's dead and the deputy is in your office."

"Right here, Marshal!" came Steve's voice behind the marshal. Steve was sided by Matt.

"He was a killer who decided he'd rather draw than go to jail," Matt added. "And your deputy here outdrew him faster than any man I ever saw before."

Marshal Potter, seeing Matt walking up to him, addressed his deputy. "Mornin' Steve. Make out a report?"

"Yep," Steve answered.

"Who's the young man with you?"

"Name's Matt Jorgensen, Marshal," Matt informed him. "I was tailin' the dead man for killin' a couple of people, one of them a marshal.

"His story sticks, Tom," Steve added. "We got a poster back at the office with his picture on it. He was wanted for murder."

"Oh?" Marshal Potter pondered. "Then why didn't cha jail him instead of shootin' him?"

"It's a long story, Tom, but I can explain," Steve said handing him his report.

"I certainly hope so," said the marshal, looking at Steve's report. "Fill in all the details."

"It's in the report, Tom," Steve reminded him.

"Then let's read it together," the marshal said and began reading the report.

The two men began to follow the marshal back to his office. "Looked like two shots in the man, Steve," Marshal Potter said as he walked his horse.

"Jess got him in the leg with his Remington," Steve answered. "I shot him in the chest."

"That in the report?" the marshal asked as he reined up at his office.

"Yep," Steve said watching the marshal rein up and dismount. "Its' in the report, Tom," Steve added, walking around to the marshal's side to show him in the report. "You see, Burt told me he was bushwhacked by Matt. And Matt told me he was looking for Sin who happened to be Burt with a beard."

The marshal smiled and looked at Matt and said, "And you jailed Matt, and then you found out that there was a wanted poster on this other fella, Sin Crouch?"

"Oh, that?" Steve apologetically responded. "He didn't have a beard in the poster."

"Fastest man I ever saw with a gun, Marshal," Matt said, as the three men walked into the office.

"Says here that you got one Burt Randall a job with the Lazy Z. Who's Burt Randall?"

"Well, Sir, he's nobody," Steve answered nervously.

"Nobody?" the marshal asked in surprise, waiting for a response. "There is never a nobody. Who is this Burt Randall you have mentioned in this report?" He began reading the report. "One Burt Randall rode into town looking like a broken-down saddle bum, beaten and out of money, who needed a job, so I got him one at the Lazy Z Ranch." He looked up at Steve again and asked, "Who is Burt Randall?"

"He's Sin Crouch, Tom," Steve answered.

"You see, Sir," Matt interrupted. "Sin Crouch used the name 'Burt Randall' as a ruse to throw Steve off his trail so there would be no wanted poster out for him. Seeing a man down and out, Steve got him a job, not knowing he was a killer."

"You got a killer a job, and you jailed this nice gentleman?" the marshal repeated the deputy as if to make the report sound preposterous. "How do I know this man is not Burt Randall?" He eyed Matt curiously. "Or Sin Crouch, or whoever?" He looked carefully at Matt, and then over to Steve. "Too nice a looking man to be a killer. You ain't are ya, boy?"

"No sir," Matt returned.

"Here's the wanted poster of Sin Crouch." Steve gave the poster to the marshal. "You can see by my drawings that he's our man, sir."

"I see," the Marshal said, removing his Stetson and running his fingers through his thin hair.

"So, you identified Sin Crouch, and this man you shot and killed is one and the same man?"

"Yes, Sir," Steve answered, twiddling his thumbs behind his back.

Looking at the poster, the marshal added smiling, "Good catch, Steve. If all this checks out, we'll have done a good piece of work for the day." Then twitching his nose, he took out his handkerchief and blew it. "Damn good job for a young deputy. Don't you agree, Mr. Jorgensen?"

"Yep," Matt answered nervously, just wanting to get out of Nagadoches.

He looked at Matt and asked, "And what are your plans, now, Mr. Jorgensen?"

"Goin' back to Tennessee just as fast as I can get outta here."

"Well, son," the marshal said, "I can't see any reason for keeping you."

"Yes Sir," Matt replied.

Ginny stood on a Tennessee hill overlooking her plantation. It was the same hill where she first encountered Matt. Then, she had a whip in her hand, and he had felt the brunt of it. Today, she stood alone waiting for his return from Texas. She clutched his letter in her hand that said he was coming home, and read it again for seemingly the hundredth time.

Matt wrote, "I sent Sin to his Maker. Not proud of it. Just grateful it was him and not me.

"Got a friend. Name's Steve. This war broke out and he and I enlisted in what is called, 'Terry and Lubbock's Regiment'. We already got word that we'll be parading in Virginia. I'll be on my way by the time you read this. Watch for me, my darling."

Ginny waited and watched, for she knew it would be soon.

CHAPTER 23

THE RESCUE

Twenty-one winters passed and Matt found out again that the winters in Montana were colder than the ones in Tennessee. But he didn't have to battle the fog and the dampness of the rivers all around the periphery of the woods as a Confederate officer, riding for hours and days at a time, fearing cholera or pneumonia, of being shot, or run through with a bayonet.

But Matt did sleep many hours unconsciously in the winter of 1882 under the long branches of a spruce. He lay still as the cold settled into the marrow of his bones and he felt the cold gripping pangs of the freezing Montana weather, but he refused to give in to her clutches. He discovered warmth from covering himself with leaves and loose dirt he found under the snow. The earth was warmer towards the trunk and it gave him the assurance that he would survive.

He had etched the words he penned to Ginny in his spirit. These words and her memory are probably what kept Matt from dying.

Then he thought of another woman, Mary Beth Paterson, the woman he seemingly had fallen in love with, having never loved again since losing Ginny. He reached out for her in agony.

"Beth!" he cried out. Then he whispered to himself lowly, "I avenged a Negro's death by hunting down and killing the man who killed her. And I'm begrudging another of a decent grave because of my own bigotry. What makes me so blind?"

"Bertha," he mouthed with his sore lips. "You helped me once. You can do it again."

He called out with all his might to Ginny's house Negro whose death he had avenged. "Bertha!" He remembered the McBride slaves as his friends in a time gone by in a place called Tennessee. "Let's sing another," he said with a smile, remembering how he listened to their many spirituals while celebrating a baptism, a birth, or a wedding.

The whinny of a horse and the sound of hoof beats breaking through the icy snow echoed through Matt's numbed brain as he gritted his teeth and shivered.

"You sure it was over this way?" he heard a mean crackling voice echo through the woods. Matt recognized Biggun's voice.

He thought, *if they find me here, they'll finish me off, but if I stay here, the winter will do me in.* Fear gripped his weakened body as his eyes picked out the legs of a horse nearby.

"I knowed I hit him," One Eye replied keeping his one hand in his pocket for warmth and the other holding tightly to his reins. Even though he wore gloves, the Montana cold froze his fingers. "It's gettin' too damn cold out here," he said, shivering in his saddle.

"Shut up and keep lookin'. You say you hit him, he must still be here." Biggun edged his horse ever so slowly, looking into every crevice he could find. "Unless he got up and moved."

"He was hit, I tell ya." The drippings from his nose were a frozen mass as he tried to wipe them with his wet woolen glove. "No ghost moves around these parts."

"He's no damn ghost."

"Then he's frozen enough. He can't be alive." One Eye put his head into the neck of his jacket to protect it from the cold wind.

Biggun was just the opposite. He rode tall in the saddle with his coat and shirt unbuttoned, revealing part of his chest hairs.

He wore a long woolen scarf, which draped down, around his neck and over his shoulder.

Biggun took his rifle and poked in between the tree branches. Once, he came close to where Matt lay.

Matt held his breath and lay perfectly still.

"Dammit!" Biggun yelled out, causing some loose snow to fall from the overhead branches on top of him. "I give up. He's dead. Has to be." He took his rifle and fired it into the woods. He cocked and fired it again and again until it was empty.

"Let's go!" he yelled over to One Eye who had leaned into his saddle and covered his ears against the loud gunshots.

Danny and Monty led another group of men in search of Matt, and on hearing the gunshots, reined up.

"Can't be friendly, I'm thinkin'," Monty said, standing high in his stirrups and looking towards the sound.

"It came from in front of us," Danny added. "Think they found Matt and finished him?"

"We're wastin' time," Monty said and moved his horse forward. "Let's ride."

Because of the snowdrifts and rocks, the ride was hard. Monty had been on the trail many times even when the snow was higher. Still, he was cautious because he knew one slip could be fatal. He held Skeeter's reins tight to keep him close to him.

Danny and the rest of the men relied on his good judgment and followed close behind.

"Let Skeeter go, Monty," Danny urged. "He'll lead us to him."

"I agree," Monty answered. He tied the reins around the saddle horn and said, "Go ahead, fella. Find Matt."

He watched as Skeeter walked in front of him. Skeeter was a one-man horse and knew he could lead them to his master.

Monty and the boys rode carefully behind Skeeter looking ahead and to the side for any signs of the people who did the shooting. Not knowing anything about the other party, they knew the danger they could be in.

"Where is he, Skeeter?" Danny called out, keeping his rifle cocked and pointed ahead. "Keep goin', boy."

The trail had been covered with fresh snow, which was blown in by the wind, making the drifts even more dangerous for a group of more than a dozen men.

Skeeter knew where his master was and kept trying to bring their attention to the spot, but the terrain was slippery, and it was almost impossible for their horses to walk. Because of the danger on the trail and the danger of encountering a group of unfriendly people, the men rode slow and easy.

Monty reined up. "Shhh. I see a coupla riders headed down the other side."

"Can you tell who they are?" Danny asked softly.

"Not from here. Too hard. But they're going away from us. Let's rest here for awhile until we're sure they're gone."

"You think they might'ave ambushed Matt?" Danny asked.

"Could be. But why'd they come back?"

"Probably to make sure he was dead, I'm thinkin'," Danny answered.

Untying Skeeter's reins from his saddle horn, he dismounted and held onto him. "Let's rest awhile and make sure they're gone."

"We've got enough men," Sheriff Saunders threw in looking ahead to see if he could still make out the riders in the distance. "My job is to catch killers. Anyone want to go with me?"

"We want to catch them, too, sheriff," Monty said, staring the sheriff down with his mean look. "But we're goin' to find Matt first. You want to go, take off right now. Our primary purpose right now is to find Matt. As far as we're concerned, his killers can wait."

The sheriff bit his lip and slapped his saddle. "I agree. But once we find him, dead or alive, I'm taking off after them."

"You talk like he's dead," Danny returned.

"Face it, lad," Monty answered looking around at the snow-covered terrain. "He's been up here a whole night. If this cold didn't kill him, and they found him, he's dead now."

"Then we might jest as well ride after those men," the sheriff remarked pointing out in the direction the riders took. "There's only two of them."

"Like I said," Monty came back, "after we find Matt."

"Can you still see them?" Danny asked about the two riders.

"Naw," Monty answered, "but we'll wait a little longer.

Monty listened for any signs of riders close by, and when he decided it was safe, mounted up, retied Skeeter's reins around the saddle horn, and moved the men out. They were dependent upon following Skeeter, but watched for the tracks left by the other riders to get an idea of where Matt might be.

"Some tracks up here," Monty whispered. He was still cautious about the riders being in the area.

They rode into the area where Matt had fallen, but the snow, together with the tracks made by Biggun and One Eye, made it difficult for the men to determine where Matt was.

Matt's eyelids kept flickering as he did his best to stay awake. Then he heard distant voices calling his name. "Matt!" He heard his name repeated over and over again, echoing off the bark of the trees surrounding him.

"If you're the ghost of Nightlinger, know this," he murmured gutturally as he tried to open his snow-covered eyelids. "I'll not remove you from your resting place." He lifted his head slightly and spoke to the wind. "You hear me, Beth? That's a promise, darlin'."

The more they rode past Matt, the tenser Skeeter became. He whinnied and snorted and stamped his hooves to let the men know that Matt was within a few feet of them.

Sheriff Saunders grabbed Skeeter's reins and tugged at them for him to go further up the road. The more he tugged, the more Skeeter backed up.

Rusty came around and grabbed hold of the other side of Skeeter's halter, bringing him away from the tree and started him back up the trail.

"Come on, Skeeter," Rusty urged, pulling him with his halter. "We ain't got time to waste with you slippin' and slidin' all over this here place. Move it!"

Except by the chilling breeze, Matt's whisper, "Come on, Skeeter," went unheard.

Monty rode up to Bill and said, "Hold it, Sheriff. He's not slidin'. He's tuggin' for us to go down that slope yonder."

"The snow's covered most of the tracks, but it looks like, Yes! " Danny's voice cried out as he pointed to a spot in the gully where Matt fell from his horse and his body rolled across the gully. "He went down over there. Look at the snow."

"It's too far off the path for Matt to have fallen," Bill argued. "He's got to be close to the trail, I'm figurin'."

"You go that way, Bill," Monty said, taking the halter from Rusty. "I'm gonna dismount and walk Skeeter over this way. Danny, give me a hand."

"Your neck, Monty," Bill cautioned. "Don't take him too far in, you'll never get him out."

Monty dismounted and took Skeeter to the edge of the path where Matt had fallen and rolled under the tree's branches. Two of the other men dismounted and tied their horses up to some branches. They began following Skeeter down the crevice.

Matt whispered again, "Good boy, Skeeter."

Skeeter slipped and slid a little, then jumped the ravine towards the spot where Matt laid. He showed the men his surefootedness. Once on the other side, he walked carefully to a spot near Matt and began scratching at it with his hoof.

"Skeeter boy, come on," Matt coughed out.

"Well, I'll be a suck-eyed mule," Danny said, jumping from his horse. He had heard Matt's slight cough.

"Good boy, Skeeter," Matt whispered. "Stay with me, boy."

Except for Sheriff Saunders, the men joined Monty at the tree site. They dug hard and fast through the snow and suddenly found a leg sticking out from under the branches. It was Matt's leg stuffed inside two pairs of pants, which were wet and frozen on the outside.

"We've found him," Monty yelled out. He lifted up the branches of the old tree and found Matt curled under them. He kept digging.

"Quick. Get the litter over here." Monty smiled down at the wearied cowboy and said comfortingly, "We'll get you home, boss."

In the meantime, Sheriff Saunders noticed something glimmering in the sun and dismounted. He stepped over to a tree where he uncoiled a piece of wire from around it that stretched across the trail and was coiled around another tree.

"I think I found something, boys," he yelled out. But, at the time, the men were too busy digging Matt out to pay any attention.

When they finally dug Matt free, the men quickly bundled him from the top of his head to the soles of his boots. They carried him out of the ravine and fitted him on a litter behind Skeeter.

"Thank God he's got life left in him," Rusty said.

"He's one hell of a man," Monty said. Monty mounted his steed and led Skeeter down the trail. Skeeter walked proud with his master safe behind him. Danny walked beside him and rubbed Matt's hands as hard as he could to get the circulation back into his veins.

Danny looked up at the sheriff. "What d'ya say, Sheriff?"

Bill looked down at Danny and secretly pocketed the wire. "Nothin' I guess."

"You sounded excited awhile ago."

"Just excited that Matt's all right. I'll ride into town and get Doc to come out and check him over to see how he's doin'." He mounted his horse, waved a goodbye to the men, and headed in the direction of town.

"Watch for those two men, Sheriff," Danny yelled out.

The snow had stopped by the time the men brought Matt home to his ranch and to a woman who had been praying and waiting without sleep.

It was a week before Christmas Eve. Many things can cause a man to change; one of them could be a wintry night in a coma under a spruce tree.

The bed brought a sense of comfort and solace to Matt as he laid under the warm quilted covers. Beth cleansed his face with warm soap and water and his mind seemed to be more at ease than it had been in a long time.

His eyes peeked through his heavy eyelids enough to catch a glimpse of Haciola looking down on him. A small almost unnoticeable smile came across his lips for, in his mind, he was seeing Bertha all over again.

"Youse wants me to do that for ya, Miss Beth?" Haciola said, taking the pan and cloth from her.

"No, Haci," Beth answered softly, "I'll do it." She sat down next to Matt, took his hand, and gently washed the dirt and grime from it.

He felt the sense of her caring as he tried to look up at her.

Banjo entered the room and walked over to his mother. "Is he gonna be all right?" he asked.

Matt heard his deep masculine voice and could make out that he was a Negro. "Hezekiah?" he whispered, and fell asleep.

"Who's he think we is, Miss Beth?" Haciola asked, taking Matt's other arm and rolling up his sleeve to wash it.

"He's in another world, Haci. He's remembering another house Negro, and another slave from his past."

"Hows you know that?" Haciola asked, looking at Beth with an astonished expression on her face.

"I know, Haci. I know."

"You think he's gonna let my man rest in yall's graveyard?" Haciola said without looking up.

Beth looked into his face. Then she looked at Haciola and Banjo and said, "Perhaps. I hope so. Sometimes, it takes a tragedy to shock someone back into reality. Maybe, just maybe Matt saw his past and liked it. Now, he's probably reaching out to a new tomorrow. Perhaps that's what the world needs, Haci."

"A good shaken' up, Miss Beth?" Haciola said as she released Banjo's hand and took a towel to dry Matt's hand.

"He's clean now," Beth said with a whisper of relief. "Clean as I can get him. Thanks, Haci."

Haciola and Banjo left quietly leaving Beth to be alone with Matt.

Beth took Matt's hand and felt him squeeze hers slightly, showing his awareness of their conversation. She knew he would recover and be the man she had fallen in love with once again. She also knew it would take time.

CHAPTER 24

A DOCTOR ANSWERS

December 1882

I t had been twenty plus years since Matt met and lost his one true love, Ginny. He had never forgotten her, although he never found out for sure what had happened to her. And because of this haunting obsession deep within his soul, he kept searching for his lovely Ginny McBride on his journey across the Brazos. Even yet, while unconscious, he continued his search for her.

Doc Taylor was at the Double R before the sun went down. He was one of the best friends that Matt and Beth could ever have asked for.

"I'm glad you came so quickly," Beth greeted him as he tied his horse to the rail.

"The sheriff met me coming out of the Robinsons this side of town." Doc grabbed his black bag from the carriage and joined Beth. "She had a little boy. How's he?"

"Not good. He hasn't come to. Moved some, but hasn't opened his eyes."

Going to Matt, Doc set his bag down while he checked his pulse.

"A little boy, huh," Beth mused, "good for her."

"Yep. Cutest little fella. Eight pounds." After examining Matt's heartbeat, feeling for fever, looking into his eyes, and checking for frostbite, among other things, Doc turned back to Beth and asked, "Got any coffee?"

"Think he's strong enough for coffee, Doc?" she asked.

"Not for him," he said shivering, "for me? I'm still cold from the trip out here."

"Oh, I'm sorry." She left and returned quickly with a cup of hot black coffee.

"He's got a concussion. And he's got pneumonia. We'll have to wait and see which way it's going to turn." He took the coffee and sipped it slowly. "Ahhhh. Good and hot. Thanks."

"Is he going to be all right?" Beth asked unconsciously wringing her hands.

Doc looked at her, rubbed his cup, and looked down at Matt. Glancing back at Beth, he said, "I won't lie to you. It doesn't look good. Had he not spent the night in the cold and wet snow with the concussion, I'd say he had a better chance. A concussion alone could snap his life away."

Beth looked back at Matt's still body, shook her head and gave Doc a puzzled look.

"What?" Doc watched Beth as she pointed to Matt's head.

"Just something that's been puzzling me since they brought him in."

"What?"

"About his wound."

Doc bent over Matt, lifted the loose cold compress, and showed the wound to Beth.

"I know how bad it is, Doc. The thing that puzzled me was the clean bandanna packed against it."

"I don't see any problem there. He probably did it himself before he lost consciousness."

"It's not *his* bandanna." She went to the dresser and picked it up. "It's small and black, not the type he'd wear."

"Oh?" Doc set his cup down on a nearby table. "Are you suggesting he had some good times in town? If so, good for him."

He stopped, felt a little uncomfortable for the moment, then looked back at Beth. "Unless . . ."

"That's what I'm suggesting, and, yes, there is something between us."

"That's not my department, young lady. You'll have to handle that with Matt when he comes around."

"Presuming he will," Beth said weakly. "I chased him away with harsh words and caused him to do . . . whatever."

Danny entered the room, stopped short and stared at Beth. "If I might say something . . ."

"Oh," Beth said as if startled that someone heard them talking. "Doc, you know Danny."

"My dad brought him into the world. We met outside," Doc returned.

"What is it, Danny?" Beth asked slipping her hands into the long deep pockets of her dress.

"He probably was with a girl. He kept calling her name."

"Ginny?" Beth asked.

"Yes."

"I've heard him." She placed the bandanna back on the dresser. "Do you think it had to do with some girl in town?"

"By the name of Ginny?" Danny asked. "I don't know of any girl named Ginny in town. Not that I know many, but I think I would have remembered her name had I heard it, especially if she's a saloon type."

"A hussie?" Beth interrupted.

"A hussie," Danny replied.

"Maybe he's got two girls," Beth interjected sarcastically. "Maybe a dozen. What do I care?"

"It's the bandanna she put on the dresser, Danny," Doc said, pointing in that direction. "It's not his, I understand."

"It was on his head when we picked him up," Danny said quickly. "I never gave it any thought."

"I suppose a lady would," Doc suggested. He picked up his cup and took another sip of coffee, looking at Beth over the brim of the cup.

"It's a nice bandanna, not the type a *hussie* would use," Beth retorted. "I'm just wondering where he got it, that's all." She threw her shoulders up and glanced back at Matt.

"Well, let's not worry our pretty little head about it," Doc said, finishing his coffee. "Our concern right now is that he lives."

"I'll have Haciola fix you something to eat," Beth said, turning to leave.

"Who's Haciola?" Doc asked curiously.

"Oh, a woman from Virginia City who's staying with us for awhile," she answered with a smile, proceeding to the kitchen. She stopped at the door lintel and turned around. "I've got a room ready for you, Doc. You'll be spending the night."

"If you say so," Doc replied "Thanks, Beth. I wasn't looking forward to the ride back to town. I'll put my buggy up then."

"Already did," Monty said as he entered the bedroom. "How's he doin', Doc?"

"Can go either way, I'm afraid."

"Geet, yet?" It was Monty's way of quickly asking, "Did you eat, yet."

"No." Doc rubbed his stomach, looked at Monty and asked "Gu?"

They smiled at one another as they had a play on words that the cowboys used on the range for laughs.

"Yep. Haciola's a great cook."

It was the second time Doc had heard Haciola's name, and he was real curious about her.

When Haciola brought him his food, Doc dropped his jaw and stood there, looking at her as she set it on a small table adjacent to an overstuffed chair. Never having seen a Negro woman on the ranch before, he did a double take, especially when Banjo entered the room shortly thereafter.

"Doc," Beth said, entering the room, "please allow me to introduce you to Haciola and her son, Banjo. They come from Alabama to look for his father."

"Is it all right here, mistah doc man?"

"Yes. Thank you."

"Anything wrong, Doc?" Beth asked, noticing how Doc kept his eyes on Haciola and Banjo.

"No. Nothing. Food smells great. Umm. Grits?"

"I made 'em myself," Haciola replied. "It's time you Yankees up here learned to eats good food."

"I agree," Beth replied. "They're good." She turned to Doc. "I've got some things to do in the other room if you need me."

He watched Haciola as she started to leave and asked, "Haciola?"

"Yes, suh?" She stopped and turned towards him.

"May I speak with you?"

"Yes, suh,. If'n it's all right with Miss Beth."

"It's all right. I'll talk with you later, Doc." Beth took Banjo's arm and left the room.

Doc took a bite of food while looking at Haciola.

"What kind of name is that?"

"Why, what does youse mean?"

"I've never heard of it before. Is it family?"

"I suppose. Ain't we all got family names?"

"Yes. Yes, we do. I simply mean, was that your mother's name?"

"Oh, lawdy no. That be my name."

"Where did you get it?"

"Same place you gets yours, I reckon."

"Did your folks name you that?"

"Neber seen my folks."

"Then how did you get your name?"

"How should I know?" she asked innocently, looking at Doc with her wide eyes as if to ask, what's wrong? "I wasn't there."

"Well, your parents must have named you for you to be called, how do you pronounce it, "Haci . . .?"

"Mistah doc, suh?" she asked politely. "Some one name you 'doc'. So you's called Doc?"

"Well, no. That's my title."

"Then, what's yo name?"

"Richard. Richard Bartholomew Taylor."

"And folks call you doc? Why?"

"Because I'm a doctor."

"'Cause yo is a doctor man? Then I's called Haciola 'cause I's a Negro."

Haciola knew the background of her name, but found the doctor to be amusing to talk with and enjoyed it.

"No, no, no." Doc sat down in the easy chair and leaned towards his food. He gave a sniff of the aroma and smiled. "You're Haciola because you were named Haciola."

"I'se been Haciola eber since I remember, and that be a long time, suh."

"And do you have any children?"

"A son. Banjo."

"Did you name him Banjo?"

"No. His pa done did."

"Where did he get the name Banjo?"

"From playin' a banjo. His real name be Joshua. We called him, Josh."

"Joshua. How was he called Joshua?" Doc took his fork and stabbed a potato and picked it up and looked at it. He saw the steam rise from it and blew on it.

"From the good book. We calls him, 'Banjo'."

"Precisely. You see, you named your son, Banjo."

"No, Suh," Haciola returned without cracking a smile. "Charlie named him, 'Banjo'."

"Charlie. Your husband?" Doc saw he was getting no place. He twirled his potato around and eyed Haciola around the side of it. "Your husband named him?"

"I has no husband."

"He's dead?"

"He neber was."

"You were never married."

"That's the best thin' you done said since I come in here." She laughed and watched a smile cross his face. "And if you don't eat that tater soon, it gonna fall on the floor and I'm gonna havta clean it up."

"Okay," Doc said, returning his potato to the plate, then took his knife and carved a piece off and ate it. It was hotter than he thought. After he swallowed it down with buttermilk, he smiled and said, "Sorry."

"I's coulda told ya it was hot. I jest took it outta de pot."

"Thanks, Haciola." He set the glass down and sighed a little. "Where's Banjo's father now?"

"Dunno."

Beth returned and overhearing Doc's question, said, "Matt's contention is that he's buried in the gravesite out on the hill."

"What's a contention? Haciola asked.

"He's positive that the man who is in the grave next to his mother is your husband," Beth answered. "I wasn't sure it was him until I brought you here." She pushed her hair away from her eyes and walked further in the room. "The trail cook happened to be Charlie Nightlinger and when he died, well, with Mrs. Andersen's permission, the cowboys buried him in the family plot. It's the only place here on the ranch, and they thought it was proper."

"And Haciola is his widow?" Doc asked.

"That good, mistah doc man?" Haciola asked with a frown, placing her hands on her big hips.

"If this is all true, and it seems like, then it looks to me like your family has finally been reunited," Doc said taking a big bite of grits. "And, that, Haciola, is very good indeed."

"Please chew first, then talk," Beth advised him.

"Yes. You're right." He swabbed up the last of the gravy with his biscuit and stuffed it in his mouth. "Darn good gravy and biscuits, and I'm so full I'm about to bust."

Beth held back a laugh and waited until he finished his meal, swallowed his last bite, and drank some more buttermilk. "She's a pretty good cook."

"Yes, she is," he answered. Then he turned to Haciola and said, "You're something else, Haciola. I mean traveling from Alabama and finding your husband's gravesite up here in Montana." Doc laughed, watching a smile cross her face.

"The cowboys who knew Charlie from the cattle drive swear that Haciola's son looks just like him," Beth said, still eyeing the black bandanna on the dresser. "I think we've made a match."

"I's been lookin' for him eber since my boy began to walk."

"What's next?" Doc asked.

"Have to wait until Matt returns to us, I suppose," Beth answered, crossing over to Matt's bedside. She stared at him for awhile and, without turning her head, said, "They say an unconscious person can sometimes hear what's being said. Is that true, Doc?"

"It's been thought to be proven for a long time."

"Then he's heard everything we've said."

"I hopes he don't blame me for any of this," Haciola remarked, waving her hands in the air.

"You know that's your husband in the grave, Haci?" Beth turned to face her. "Now don't you?"

Haciola bowed her head for a moment and then looked up, first at Beth and then Doc. Tears formed in her eyes. "I knew he up and died on us. I jest knew it."

"But don't you feel better knowing where he's buried?"

"Yes, ma'am," Haciola returned. Then she looked at Matt. "Is he gonna makes us bury muh man somewheres else?"

"We hope not," Beth said. She turned her eyes toward Matt and repeated it, "We hope not."

Beth walked over to Haciola, took her by the hand, and led her out of the room. "Let's let Doc eat his dessert. He hasn't had a moment to himself since he got here."

"Thanks, ladies," Doc said, standing to salute the women as they left.

He sat down and took a bite of his pie. After awhile, he rose again, walked over to the bed and watched Matt's eyes flutter.

"I wonder where you're at," Doc said in a whisper. "By all appearances, you should be dead, but something or somebody is keeping you alive."

CHAPTER 25

SAGE ADVICE

T he rest of the evening was filled with interesting stories Beth told in bringing Doc up-to-date as to why Haciola and Banjo were staying at the Double R Ranch.

"It is my belief," Doc said after a full meal and listening to the stories, "that Matt, being from the South, does not cotton to Negroes. I'm not being disrespectful, mind you, just speaking my piece. A lot of Montanans were not Union sympathizers. It's not something that would be earthshaking news."

Beth's eyes opened wide as she put her hands on her hips. "It makes no mind what Montanans believed or disbelieved. The truth of the matter is that Matt wants Haciola's deceased husband interred on another piece of land, and I'm here to prevent it."

"Why?" Doc asked with raised eyebrows.

"Because Mrs. Andersen wished it to be so."

"And Matt, as owner of this ranch, wants him to be removed? I see nothing wrong with that."

"Except that Mrs. Andersen gave me the power of attorney to disallow this to happen. It is my right to stop Matt if he tries to remove Charlie's body by the fact that her will specifically states that he is not to taint this property in any way."

"And you feel that by removing her husband's body . . ." He looked at Haciola and apologized as he handed her his cleaned plate, "Please excuse me, Haciola. I don't mean to be stepping out of line here."

"My. My, my, my, my," Haciola said, "youse do have an appetite." She sliced another piece of pie and put it on the same plate, and handed it back to him.

"But I just had dessert," he protested. "I don't want anymore." He took the refilled plate from her and set it down in front of him. "Oh, well. Another piece of pie won't hurt." He dove into the pie with his fork as if he hadn't already eaten.

"Youse could use an extra pound or two," Haciola noted. She took a deep breath into her large lungs and continued. "Now, as to my departed man, I done decided. I aims to take him back with me when the proper time comes. And your talkin' about him is why we is here in the fust place."

"Take him back with you? Then I don't see any argument here."

"The argument here, Doc . . ." Beth said. "the issue, I mean, is the idea of respect. Not as to whether or not Haciola will inter her deceased husband's remains elsewhere. The issue is that of respect. If Matt allows her to do this without respect, then I will act on her behalf and ask that her husband's remains stay where they are."

"Respect?" Doc asked, putting another piece of pie in his mouth.

"Respect, Doc," Beth replied. "Haciola has traveled from one end of the continent to the other to find her husband only to end up here in this seemingly God-forsakened cold Montana and her husband six feet under the hard ground. Mr. Nightlinger respected Mr. Andersen by helping avenge his killers. When Mr. Nightlinger passed on, Mrs. Andersen respected Mr. Nightlinger by giving him a proper burial here on her ranch. Now that Haciola, Mr. Nightlinger's widow, has found her departed husband, it would be proper that Mr. Jorgensen respect her wishes to have him remain here. If he does show respect, then Haciola will ask to remove his remains and have them interred elsewhere. If he does not respect her wishes to have him remain here, then I will be forced to have the court take the ranch away from him and award it to the state."

Doc smiled, wiped the pie juice from his chin and said in a confused manner, "I see."

"That's all right, Doc," she said, pushing herself from the table. "I simply thought to enlighten you. I'll check on Matt now."

"Don't mind her," Haciola said, dumping the supper dishes into the washtub. "She's in love with that man, Mr. Matt."

Beth walked over and stood near the end Matt's bed. She looked softly into his face, and sat down in a chair nearby where she stayed for the rest of the night, falling asleep from time to time.

While checking on Matt's condition, Doc made it a point to visit with the other wranglers and cowpokes to treat their infections, boils, or just plain old rheumatism. Everyone on the ranch was indebted to Doc. Of course, he received his much deserved pay for each visit, such as a half-side of beef, or a free shoeing for his mare, and the like. It was seldom that he saw green paper for his cures from this crew, but he kept coming back, nonetheless.

Early on the third morning, the sun crept through the window, filling the room with light bright enough to awaken Beth completely. She stood and walked to the window to pull the curtains together.

It was also bright enough to wake Matt from his long sleep. He rose up on his elbow and, upon seeing Beth silhouetted by the sun, his brow furled and his eyes widened.

"Ginny?" he asked, wiping his eyes. "Ginny, is that you, darlin'?" he asked again as Beth stood there, afraid to move for fear of losing him again. She was happy that he was awake and yet fearful that he would succumb once more. He opened his tired eyelids and focused in on Beth's worried face looking down at him.

"Oh, gawd," he said with a frown on his face, realizing he had been dreaming. "I had the gawd-awfulest dream." He shook his head as he tried to shake it from his thoughts. "You don't know Bertha, but she dominated my dream."

His forehead was filled with perspiration as he threw the covers off. Beth picked them up and covered him trying her best to keep him in bed. His legs hit the floor as he tried to raise his aching body.

Realizing his strength was too much for her to handle alone, she called out, "Danny. Quick! Get Doc! He's trying to get up."

Danny was in the kitchen picking up the coffee pot and quickly put it back when he heard her.

Doc had just entered the kitchen, ready for a cup of coffee when he heard her screaming. He calmly said, "Well, let him," and followed Danny to Matt's room where he saw their struggling. He realized Matt was not aware of where he was because his eyes were half shut. He and Danny hopped on both sides and assisted Beth in putting him back into the bed.

Matt gave up and fell back asleep.

"He's still delirious," Doc said tucking him in. "I don't know where he was, but it certainly wasn't here."

On the fourth day, Matt heard distant voices inside his head. He flicked his eyes open a bit then closed them tight as the sunlight streamed through the adjacent window and blinded him. He lay on his back, opened his eyes, and stared at the ceiling. He felt around his body and found a quilted blanket covering him. He continued to shiver, but he felt warm for the first time in a long time as he stared around the room.

"How do you feel," Doc asked, bending over the bed.

"Who're you?"

"Just call me, Doc. Everybody does."

"Doc? How am I?" Matt asked feeling his head.

"You tell me, son."

"Like my body was made of glass that could break and shatter, so don't touch me. Got any makings on ya?"

Doc reached into his shirt pocket and pulled them out, then rolled him a cigarette. "The cold's settled into your lungs. You had pneumonia, but the fever's broke."

Danny stood in the doorway holding a cup of coffee. He saw Matt move and crossed over to the bed, spilling his coffee on the way.

"He's movin', ma'am," Danny said watching Matt carefully. "Beth," he called excitedly, "he's comin' to."

Beth walked lively into the room, wringing her hands. She smiled when she saw Matt's eyes beam at hers, but then she heard him cry out, "Ginny!" She bit her lip and turned away.

"Who's he calling out to, Doc?" Danny asked in a bewildered voice.

"He's not quite conscious yet," Doc said, examining Matt's eyes to see if they were dilated. "Do either of you know Ginny?"

Beth shrugged her shoulders and looked at Danny who shook his head.

"Whoever she is, Matt's still searching for her," Doc said as he placed a cool, damp cloth on Matt's forehead.

Matt squinted and moved his eyes slowly towards the window. He saw the faint shadows of people milling around him. He wanted to see the people, but his eyes were not focusing clearly yet.

Haciola walked in and stood at the foot of the bed. He saw her heavy figue standing there and thought for a moment that he had seen Bertha.

"Bertha, you okay?" He heard faint talking, and then suddenly the words fell on deaf ears as he slept.

"I'll stay with him, Doc," Beth said, draping her shawl lightly around her shoulders. She turned back to Matt and asked sarcastically, "Ginny?"

"His fever's broke," Doc said, feeling Matt's brow and pulling the quilt up under his chin. "You're going to be all right now, Matt."

"Are you sure he's going to be all right, Doc?" Beth asked.

Doc knelt down again and looked into Matt's eyes while he checked his pulse rate. "Yes, Beth," he said softly, "I think he's going to be fine."

"Well," Danny asked, "can we talk to him?"

"As soon as he's fully awake, I suppose.

"He calls somebody Bertha," Haciola whispered.

"It looked to me like he was calling you," Beth said.

"Well, I ain't. I gots some work to do in the kitchen. I'll be there if anyone be needin' me." She turned and left, shaking her head.

Doc put the rolled cigarette in his mouth and lit it. Letting out a stream of smoke, he said, "Thought for a minute there he was going to come out of it."

"Well, isn't he?" Beth asked.

"He looks good. He talked with me briefly, then shivered and went back to sleep. I don't see any reason he won't be better soon."

He looked at the cigarette, took another drag and said, "This was his."

CHAPTER 26

MATT RETURNS TO LIFE

Cookie helped Haciola finish up the breakfast dishes by drying them after the cowboys gulped down their servings of steak and eggs. As he had done many times over the past few days, Danny kept Doc company playing dominoes.

Beth remained in Matt's room through the day and on into the night, eating little, watching him toss and turn in his sleep. There was no more perspiration on his brow, and he seemed to be sleeping soundly. For the moment, it was anticipated that he would fully recover.

The lamps were high as it was early evening when Danny and Monty joined Doc to pay Matt a visit. When they entered his room, they found him leaning on his elbow, talking with Beth.

Matt winked an eye at Doc and cleared his throat with a lazy grunt. "I'm hungry!" he shouted, sitting up in bed.

No sooner had he shouted than Cookie came waltzing through the doorway with a tray holding a bowl of soup on it. "Well, it's about time," he said, placing it on the table next to the bed. "I've had this on the stove for three days now. Special, jest for you."

"Thank you, Cookie," Matt returned. He looked around the room and saw Danny. "How long you been there?"

"Oh, about three days," Beth replied for Danny, bending over to take Matt's hand.

"Three days? Seems like I jest left."

"You don't remember anything?" Danny asked sidling next to him on the opposite side of the bed.

"Yeah. I got drunk in town, and oh, oh, oh. Yeah. Jest remembered." Matt began eating as he talked. "Busted up the saloon while I was there."

"Yeah . . . yeah?" Cookie chuckled.

Beth swallowed hard and looked discontently at Matt acting like a kid just getting over the measles.

"You got drunk," Danny said. "You busted up a saloon and fell off your horse comin' home."

"I won the fight. You didn't ask about that." He paused a moment in his eating and looked at Beth quite quizzically. "I done what?"

"Fell off your horse," Danny repeated. "We found you under a spruce curled up like a newborn and jest about dead."

"The whiskey probably kept you alive," Doc said, closing his medicine bag.

Matt fired back. "You're Doc? Didn't we meet somewhere?"

"This morning when you first woke up," Doc answered feeling his pulse.

"Don't remember that, but your face looks familiar." He looked at Cookie and asked, "Got any coffee to go with this, Cookie?"

"Sure, sure. I'll go git some. You stay right here."

"I've got chores to do, boss," Monty said. "Good to see you alive, Matt." He sauntered backwards, then turned and left the room.

"Thanks, Monty. I'll be up in no time givin' you a hand."

"You'll stay in bed until Doc says you can get up," Beth scolded.

"Speakin' of which, how am I doing, Doc?"

"You had a bout with pneumonia. Not bad, but enough that it kept you unconscious for a few days."

"Am I gonna live?"

"Odds are in your favor. You still got pain in your chest?"

"No. My back." Matt looked at Doc and asked, "How'd you know that?"

"We talked about it this morning."

"Oh."

"Still there?"

"Yeah. A little."

"Stay warm for the next few days," Doc said, feeling his forehead again. "No outdoors for awhile. Dry your lungs out and you should be okay." He smiled and walked to the doorway. "Looks like I won't be needed here anymore, Beth. Keep him quiet and fed real good, and he should be able to make it on his own in a few days. Try not to let him go out in the cold."

"Thanks, Doc," Beth said, walking up to him at the door. "How much do we owe you?"

"Oh, I don't know. Considering I treated most of your cowboys one way or another and got Matt back to life, I'd say you owed me twenty silver ones. Of course, I owe you for room and board."

"Come on, Doc," Beth said, placing her arm in his. "We'll settle up with you right now while Matt enjoys his soup."

Cookie passed him on his way to Matt's room, carrying two tin cups and a pot of coffee. "Want a cup, Miss Paterson?"

"No thanks, Cookie."

"Doc? How 'bout you?"

"Thanks, Cookie." He took one of the cups and watched Cookie pour the coffee. "It'll warm me up for the trip back to town."

"It's hot, so watch it."

Doc took the coffee and he and Beth followed Cookie back into Matt's room.

Matt sat up and looked on. "By the time you get to me, the damn stuff'll be cold."

Cookie filled the other tin and gave it to Matt.

Matt took a quick sip of the coffee and said, "Wow!"

"I told ya it's hot."

Matt sat the tin down and finished his soup. "I've been out for three or four days? How did I get here?"

"Skeeter, boss," Cookie chuckled.

"Skeeter?"

"Yes, sir," Danny answered. "He came home all lathered and went to the barn. Of course, the door was closed so he pounded on it with his hoof and shook us all up. Cookie was up, and Monty and the rest of the cowpokes, and me and Beth."

"Oh, yeah, Beth came out in her petticoat," Cookie added, "real pretty like." He chuckled some more.

"Quit laughing and git on with it," Matt said, giving Cookie a mean look.

"Beth was prettier than all the pine trees in Montana," Danny continued, "let me tell ya. Anyway, we got saddled and rode out after ya. Knowed somethin' was wrong. Took us no time at all to find ya, all curled up under a tree. Colder than a bear's bottom, you was."

"Skeeter brought you to me?" Matt asked again.

"Yep," Danny said as he stepped back against the door lintel "We jest followed him and found you under some thick branches. Not at first, though. The snow covered up your tracks and we rode right on by ya. Cookie was determined to follow Skeeter's directions, and there you were. Smack dab curled up under the branches like some ol' bear."

"Had it not been for the branches sheltering you like they did from the heavy snow we had, you'd be dead," Doc said, finishing his coffee. "And, of course, I'd be out another patient." He put his cup down and picked up his bag. "Well, I best be going. Danny, if you'll get my buggy for me, I'd be obliged."

Danny nodded his head and followed Doc out of the room.

Beth moved from the end of the bed, where she'd been standing quietly to his side, took his hand and squeezed it gently. "How do you feel, cowboy?"

"Somehow I got you mixed up there for a minute, didn't I?" Matt asked looking tenderly into her eyes.

"Did you?"

"Under a tree? There's a million trees up there."

"Skeeter knew though. He took them right to where you were. All curled up."

"I know, I know."

"Well, sir, you were near dead. Colder than a cow's nose caught in a snowed meadow. Yes, sir, you were almost dead," Cookie said.

"True?" Matt looked up at Beth who was rubbing his shoulders.

"You were near the color of my blue shawl. It was just like Doc said, you had enough whiskey in you to keep you alive."

"Hmm. But I didn't fall off my horse."

"Then how'd ya get under the spruce?" Cookie asked. He poured Matt another cup of coffee then set the pot on the floor. He pulled up a chair and sat close to the bed.

Matt scratched his head, looked up at Beth and shrugged his shoulders. "Fell off ma horse? Damn. That don't seem possible." He looked over at the broad-grinning cook and furrowed up his brows. "I fell off ma damn horse. If that don't beat all."

"Yep," Cookie said, standing up and putting the chair back in the corner. "Well, gotta get back to the kitchen. Haciola's got a good recipe for dinner tonight and I wanna watch her."

Cookie stopped in his tracks, turned, and looked back at Beth. "Whoops!"

"Who's Haciola?" Matt asked, sipping his coffee.

"Oh, eh, a woman who dropped by," Cookie stammered. "Yeah. She dropped by and she fixed us up some right nice meals. You'll like her." Cookie wrung his hands, looked apologetically at Beth, turned back to the doorway, and walked out. "Yeah. You'll certainly like her." He stressed the accent on the word "her" and laughed a little as he headed down the hallway.

"Neighbor?" Matt asked Beth.

Beth went to the window and watched the clouds build up with snow. "Looks like we're in for a real blizzard. Just like I was telling you."

"You gonna answer?"

Beth turned and faced Matt square on. "Haciola is a woman I brought here from Virginia City. She's been tending to you most of the time."

"How'd you know I'd been hurt?"

"I didn't." Beth turned and faced him, watching him put his cup down.

"You'll find a cigar in my vest. Can I have it?" Matt asked, frisking the top of his union suit. "Who undressed me. You?"

"Doc says you're not to have any smokes." Beth turned and walked out of the room, stopping at the doorway. She looked back and said, "The boys did. Disappointed?" She walked out to Doc before he left.

Standing at the buggy with Doc, Danny said. "Doc, he woke up shoutin' 'Ginny'. That girl he's been talkin' about while he was out. You know."

"Yes, I know, Danny," Doc replied. "That Ginny must have been quite some lady for Matt to ramble on like that. And, as I see it, he'll have 'her' in his system always. Right now, he's got to come back to the present, and it looks like he's doing a good job of it."

"Anythin' we should do or not do, Doc?" Danny asked.

"Nope," Doc responded. "Just keep treating him as your boss, and as if we don't know about Ginny. Keep that to yourself, if you can."

As Danny returned to his chores, Russ stepped up to Doc. "He's up and about?"

"Well, he's up at least," Doc replied.

Beth walked to the front door just in time to see Doc drive out to the main road, which was not windswept and clean of snow.

"Thanks again, Doc," she called, waving at him in goodbye.

The cowpokes were good enough at licking their wounds with the medications and such that Doc gave them that they had no need for him for awhile, so he was headed for town, his buggy loaded down with preserves and such.

Breakfast for Matt the next day consisted of eight eggs, four slabs of bacon, a pan of biscuits and gravy, and four cups of coffee. Beth kept him company but had no part in feeding him.

"You came all the way back from Virginia City?" Matt asked, feeding his mouth. "Why?"

"Before I answer that, I'd like you to meet her. Maybe she can tell you."

"You drove all the way in this snow?"

"It wasn't so bad. Banjo made some runners for our buggy and we had a rather nice sleigh ride for part of the way."

"Banjo?"

"Haciola's son."

"You brought him back with you?"

"He drove us."

"Haciola's son?"

"When you feel better and get cleaned up, I'll bring them in to meet you. Right now, you don't smell any too good for company." Beth turned towards the doorway.

"How do you propose I get cleaned up? Me weak as a kitten."

"I'll have Danny bring a tub in here."

"This Haciola and Banjo must be somebody special for me to have to get all spruced up for," Matt said, removing his shirt. "You comin' back?"

Beth looked back over her shoulder, smiled, and walked away.

"Some gal, that Miss Paterson," he remarked, chuckling to himself as he sipped his coffee.

CHAPTER 27

GINNY'S GHOST HAUNTS BETH

Two days in bed with good meals made Matt strong enough to saddle Skeeter for a ride. Beth got into her riding clothes and after a hot breakfast of scrambled eggs, sausage, and biscuits, with plenty of hot coffee, she saddled her horse and joined him.

"I've only seen one woman sit a horse the way you do, Beth," Matt said, standing by the corral and inspecting Beth with his eyes. "You are one hell of a good looker, I must say."

"Ginny," Beth blurted out right away. Then, catching herself, she apologized. "I'm sorry, Matt. I didn't mean to say that."

Matt looked up at Beth in her fine riding regalia and just smiled. "She was beautiful, Beth. You remind me so much of her."

He stood there shaking his head, feeling at a loss for words. For a moment, a vision of Ginny stood before him, but only briefly. He knew Ginny was in the past, and Beth was now.

"Any special reason you want to go to Bozeman, Matt?" Beth asked, looking resplendent upon her black filly, a Tennessee gelding with a flash of white across its forehead.

"Jest want to ride some, Beth," Matt returned, mounting Skeeter.

The two rode off together on the shortcut trail to Bozeman. When they came to the place where he had holed up inside the tree hollow, they reined up and dismounted.

"Watch yourself, Matt," Beth said, watching his knees buckle as he hit the ground. "You don't have to walk any. You're still weak."

"I'm alright," he replied, straightening himself up. "I don't have any hankerin' to go over to the hollow." He stood by a tall tree, holding the reins in his gloved hands and just looked at the hollow. "Just want to look at what could have been my grave."

"It was close, Matt."

"So Skeeter saved my life, huh?" Matt said, looking at the ravine and everything around it. The tracks from where the men pulled him out were gone, now covered by new snow.

The trees were tall in that part of the woods, and their limbs and branches were filled with snow. The noon sun shone its bright wintry light as it beamed down upon them through the branches and warmed them.

"Kinda reminds me of Tennessee, Beth," he said, brushing the snow off a fallen tree nearby so they could have a place to sit.

"It's all wet, Matt," Beth pointed out to him.

"No problem there, ol' girl," Matt said, tying their reins to a low limb. Loosening the girths and removing their saddles, he sat them upright in a clearing. He took the horse-blankets and slapped them across a felled branch. "M'lady," he said, playing the Sir Walter Raleigh role, "your divan awaits you."

With laughter, they sat on the blankets and began to enjoy each other's company. Taking his gloves off and putting them in his coat pocket, he removed his makings and rolled himself a cigarette.

"You're reminded about Tennessee, Matt?" she asked, watching him as he struck the match on the leg of his pants and lit his cigarette. "How?"

"Oh, I don't know," he answered her, looking up at the tall trees and down the lonesome trail that led to Bozeman. "The trees are taller here, but they're pine, jest like Tennessee. The woods are jest as full. But I suppose it's because I've been out of it, so to speak, and it's jest like it happened yesterday."

"What happened, Matt?"

"The war," Matt answered, looking back into his mind. "That and much more. Ginny, of course. Her father Jim. My good friend Steve. All of it. Where would I start to tell you?"

He began to tell her a little about what he experienced while unconscious.

"And, Ginny?" Beth asked softly yet cautiously to see how Matt could handle talking about her.

"Ginny?" Matt asked, lifting his head and his eyes widening as he looked at Beth. "I must have talked quite a bit about Ginny."

"Incessantly, Matt," Beth answered, hoping he would talk about her again.

"I'll be damned," he said, and stood up. "What'd I say about her? Anythin' I'd be embarrassed over?"

"You mentioned her name several times, Matt," Beth responded. "You said you loved her, and you even cried as if you had left her alone somewhere."

Matt took one more drag from his cigarette and flicked the butt away to die in the snow.

"She left me, Beth," he said solemnly. "She died."

"Oh. I'm sorry, Matt," Beth said as she stood to hug him. The air was quiet as she searched for the right words to say. "We don't have to talk about it."

"That's probably why I wanted to come here, Beth," Matt said, still looking out into the empty woods. "I did love her. She was my first love. My really first love. I was in my early twenties when I rode through Tennessee. It was summer." He laughed when he said, "Got my first taste of slavery. Gawd how it all comes back to me now.

"And then I saw her for the first time. She came ridin' towards me with three hyenas from hell to whup my ass. She was beautiful. Alls I could see was her on that big black stallion, with that whip in her hand."

"She whipped you, Matt?" Beth asked. "What in thunder for?"

"Didn't feel it one bit, Beth," Matt went on. "Not one bit."

The sun had dipped into the two o'clock position in the sky when Matt and Beth began talking about Tennessee. Matt could not say enough, and Beth wanted to know more and more about what went on in those early years. As they talked, the cold wind picked up a bit as the sun hid behind a cloud.

"Getting cold?" Matt asked, taking off his jacket and wrapping it around Beth. "You'll need this to keep you warm."

"What about yourself?"

"Hell. I grew up in these woods. Remember?"

She enjoyed the feel of his arms around her as she slid into his coat. His face slightly touched her face, sending a chill through her.

From behind her he whispered, "You feel natural like."

"Oh? Like?"

"Well, I'm not having fears of touching you like I did when I first met you."

She turned into his body and asked, "You had fears of touching me?"

"From day one."

"Why?"

"Donno."

"Ginny?"

"Probably. Maybe because you represented something I couldn't get use to."

"What's that, Mr. Jorgensen?"

"That's it. Your tone of voice."

She stood aback and, putting her hands on her hips, repeated him. "My tone of voice?"

"You talk, well like you're educated and too . . . too. I don't know. Just like you're not on my level."

"Sorry. Can I come down to your level?"

"Not like that. I kinda need to come up to your level."

He moved his hands over her shoulders and brought her into his body. "Right now, I feel comfortable with you. Before, I wanted to touch you, and I trembled with fear."

"The big Matt Jorgensen trembling with fear. My oh my."

"Yep."

"You're touching me, now and you're not trembling."

"Like I done said. You feel natural like."

"Like you want to kiss me?" she whispered as she drew herself closer to him.

"Very much."

They let their lips touch lightly at first, and then they broke away from each other and looked into each other's eyes.

"Natural like?" she asked with a slight smile.

"Real natural like," he answered and drew her back into him.

His coat fell from her shoulders as his arms embraced her tenderly. Snow began to fall slightly as the couple found their moment of passion with each other.

Beth broke her lips away from his and whispered in his ears, "I love you, Mr. Jorgensen."

"I can't . . ." Matt brought her face in front of his and looked hard into her eyes.

"You don't have to respond. I know you still love a ghost."

"She's still real. Inside me." Matt brought her back into him and continued, "But you are, too. You feel like you belong with me."

She brought her lips again to his and parted them, swallowing him up in her world of passion, giving him everything he seemed to need for the moment to realize he also was in love with her.

"It's been a long time," he whispered as their lips still touched.

"For what?"

"Since I've even made love to a woman."

"When was that?" she asked rubbing her lips across his.

"So long I can't remember."

His hands pulled her body into his as he returned the kiss she was waiting for. His body began to tremble slightly as his hands continued a course of discovery around parts of her body.

"You're trembling, Mr. Jorgensen."

"Call me Matt and I'll stop trembling."

"I love calling you Mr. Jorgensen, Matt. Don't you know that?"

"Fine. Miss Paterson. Beth."

He brought her down gently onto the horse blankets that were filling up with snow, and cupped her head in his hands as he lay beside her.

"Sure you're not cold?" he asked as he pulled his heavy coat over them.

She rubbed the sides of his face with her soft hands and got into a more comfortable position as she let her passion flow from her long imprisoned soul. Her soul reached for freedom as Matt's hand slid inside her clothes and moved across her soft skin.

He leaned on his elbow and allowed his eyes to survey every pore of her body as he felt her hand move across his chest. A deer paused a few feet from them and scurried away to join its mother. The snow continued to fall and covered the couple with its whiteness as the moment of passion subsided with the cloud-covered sun.

"Think we oughta head back?" Matt asked. They picked up their horse-blankets and saddled up. Matt untied the reins and helped Beth into her saddle. He mounted Skeeter and they rode back to the Red Ruby Ranch.

By the time they reached the ranch, the sun had already set, her silver beams of light reflecting off the tips of the tallest pines. They reined up at the porch where Danny and Rusty met them and took their horses inside the barn to bed them down for the night.

The couple walked into the ranch house to find Doc waiting for them in the front room.

"Evening, Matt," Doc said, rising from the sofa. "Beth. Just thought I'd drop by for another visit to see Mr. Jorgensen here."

"Just been out riding, Doc." Matt stoked the wood in the fireplace, adding two new logs to the fire. Danny and Cookie came in to join the threesome, settling down on both sides next to Doc.

"By the way you're looking, I guess you're feeling better," Doc said, packing his pipe.

"Matt was telling me about his cavalry unit during the war, gentlemen," Beth said as they got comfortable. "Would you care to hear?"

"Love to," Doc replied, settling deeper into the sofa. Danny sat next to him.

"I was talking about Terry's Texas Rangers, where I served. It was named after Colonel Terry, but he was killed in our first skirmish. Great man. Colonel Lubbock was elected to follow him." Matt continued about his first battle at Rowlett Station. "But, he died from the grip of the hard and bitter winter in a hospital in Bowling Green a few days later. We lost many men that winter because of the cold . . . and cholera. Gawd it was awful. I don't know which was worst."

"What happened to the rangers, Matt?" Beth asked.

Matt took his makings, rolled himself a cigarette, and, as he started to light it, Beth walked over, blew out the match and yanked the cigarette out of his lips.

"I was waiting to see if you were going to light it or not," she said. "Go on."

Matt looked at her sheepishly, licked his lips, then continued. "Well, we stayed together. We were part of Johnston's brigade, but only for a time." He stood up, took a drag, and let the smoke out slowly. "Steve, a Sergeant O'Riley, and me." A smile curled his lips. "For the longest time, all we did was train Johnston's brigade how to ride and shoot. We were so damned good that other divisions and companies came over and we trained them, too.

"O'Riley would yell out, 'Dismount! Fix saddles and tighten' your damn girts.' I can still hear him. Steve was great with the carbine. Seemed the rangers were better at ridin' and shootin' than anyone after Steve and I got through with 'em."

He gazed in the distance, and dropped his smile into a thoughtful expression. "We fought some more at Shiloh, Murfreesboro, Chickamauga, and other places. In fact, one of our generals, General Mitchell, got hit with a musket ball at Shiloh in sixty-two and lost his arm. He pulled through all right. When he joined up with us again, he still stayed up close. Usually, a general would stay behind the lines, you'd think, fortified so the enemy couldn't get to him. Not any of our officers. Colonel Terry sort of set the pattern, and General Mitchell stayed true to it. By staying where the action was. A day he will remember for the rest of his life, let me tell ya."

"What happened to him?" Doc asked, lighting his pipe.

"Well, let me put it this way. Had it not been for me, the general'd be in a grave somewhere and yet nowhere. One of the Yankee soldiers had a bead on him with his bayonet. I busted him aside the head with my shotgun. Then I looked over at Steve, and his mouth was dropped while he set on his horse and was jest lookin' at me. Stupid ass. Another Yankee came at him from behind. I pulled out my Navy and shot him. Just cleared Steve's ear. 'Spect that's why Steve felt he was a owin' to me all these years."

"And you two wound up at the Brazos?" Beth surmised.

"Yup," Matt replied. "But first, Grant met Lee at the Appomattox, and the rest is history." Then he sat down and stared out the window into the darkness, looking at nothing and rolling another cigarette. "History?" He laughed a little. "Well, hell. I became part of history."

"What happened to you and Steve, Matt?" Doc asked. "After the war?"

"You're a glutton for punishment, ain'tcha, Doc?" Matt said, smiling. He continued. "Most of the rangers surrendered. Steve and me, and a few more, rode off towards Houston where it all started.

"The owner of the Brazos Ranch was Ted Mitchell, the general whose rear I had saved. He was seeking the office of governor of Texas before the war, but then he lost his right arm. His career changed. Seems folks don't like disabled politicians, much less one with only one arm. He was left to be a rancher, but not just any rancher. His dream was to own the largest spread in Texas. And, in order to do that, he needed the right people doing the right jobs."

"That's where you came in?" Danny interrupted. "I saw the Brazos Ranch. It's big. Real big, Miss Paterson. And Matt had all these men to protect it."

"The general was still pretty good with a gun as a southpaw, but not nearly fast enough. Now he depended on the hands of someone as good, if not better. He came to Steve and me in Houston and offered us jobs. Good livin', the Brazos River Bar M Ranch. Steve was the foreman, and I was the general's hired gun. Steve had a sister named Brenda who said she was in love with me."

"And Brenda?" Beth asked.

"She got married," Matt replied flicking the butt into the fireplace. "Yup. Steve got a letter while we were in Nashville sayin' she met a young man, good lookin' fella. He had to be. And, they got married. Said that she got tired of waitin' for me, someone already committed to another."

"But you weren't, Matt. Not any longer," Beth said, referring to Ginny's death.

"Yes I was, Beth," Matt said. "That's the real reason she got married. Steve told her how Ginny's death affected me. Before she died, I played at being a Johnny Reb sos I could get back to Ginny. After one of 'em shot her, I wanted to kill every blue belly I could git my hands on. I had no cause to live any longer. When I didn't answer her letters, she took that for the gospel."

"But you've changed, Matt," Beth said, slipping her arm around his waist. "You're not that person. I've only known you as a great man, warm and caring."

"Living on the Brazos did it for me, Beth," Matt responded, looking into her beautiful green eyes. "For seventeen years, I helped raise two wonderful girls for the general, and they shared a great part in my life. And, over the years, the general taught me respect. I had everything to live for now, and no interest in marryin' and settlin' down."

"Then I still have a chance?" Beth asked, hoping that Matt would give her some sort of positive response.

"That, my dear lady," Matt replied, turning to look at her, "was a million years ago."

Haciola had supper on the stove and was waiting for them in the kitchen. Beth scrubbed up and helped her. Summoning the men. Cookie cooked on the open grounds for the wranglers and ranch hands.

As the busy mouths were chewing and drinking, Danny looked at the other three men curiously.

"What's on your mind, Danny," Matt asked, swishing his food down with a glass of buttermilk.

"Somethin' the sheriff yelled when we were diggin' you out."

"Like what?"

"Somethin' about findin' somethin'. Then I saw this thing in his hand like some wire."

"Wire?" Matt asked.

"Prob'ly nothin', but you know me, boss. When I get an idea about somethin', I stay with it."

"What're you thinkin'?" Matt rose from the table and joined Danny by the mantle.

"We think someone tried to kill you," Cookie said sliding away from the table.

"Yeah," Russ chimed in. "We think the sheriff found a piece of wire that could've been stretched across the trail to trip you when you rode by."

"His horse almost tripped over it," Danny said, "and he dismounted and showed it to us, but we were too busy to pay any attention."

"Why?" Matt asked.

"Damned if I know," Danny answered, passing his stare back to Rusty.

"Any thoughts?" Rusty asked, breaking off a piece of bread at the table.

"Someone put it there for Skeeter to trip over," Cookie suggested.

"That's why you thought Skeeter was skittish back there on the trail." Danny rolled himself a cigarette.

"Yeah, but didn't you say, Monty, that Skeeter kept wanting to go across the gulley?" Matt asked looking at Danny with a yen as he lit his cigarette, knowing he couldn't have one.

"Yep," Monty answered. "The other cowboys rode past, and Skeeter stayed there wanting to go across the ravine."

"But I don't think so, now," Cookie interjected. "He was skittish because he knew the wire were there and wanted to walk around it. He wanted to go over to the spruce where you was, but we kept tryin' to get him past the place where the wire had been strung."

"And the sheriff found the wire stretched across the path where someone knew I'd be riding." Matt went deep into thought, still watching Danny blow smoke rings and wanting to make his own cigarette. He knew he wasn't well enough, but he wiped his moist lips with the back of his hand.

"Well, not any of us?" Danny added carefully.

"What do you mean?" Matt asked.

"The question is," Cookie continued, "who else rode that trail that night?"

Beth dropped a plate on the floor that she'd been removing from the table. "Oh my god in heaven," she remarked, bringing her hand to her mouth.

"What's the matter, Beth?" Doc asked.

"Bill!" she blurted out. "Sheriff Saunders. He came by the afternoon before and spent the night here." Catching a strange look in Matt's eyes, she clarified by saying, "In the bunkhouse, Matt Jorgensen." Straightening her apron, she continued with her story. "He told me he met you at the saloon and you told him about the injunction I got."

"Where is he, now?" Matt asked impetuously.

"He stayed with us until we rescued you," Cookie answered. "He left for town right where we picked you up, once he saw you were all right."

"That's right," Danny nodded. "He jest smiled and said he was glad to see you were safe and lit out for Bozeman."

"But why?" Beth asked, picking up the pieces of the broken plate.

"Why'd ya suppose?" Matt snarled. "Have you taken a good look in the mirror lately?"

CHAPTER 28

RETURN OF THE TERROR OF BOZEMAN

A cold mist hovered over the ground the next morning when Matt found Danny and Cookie saddled and riding out of the corral. Danny had Skeeter by a lead rope, saddled and ready for Matt.

Beth ran out to the corral while putting on her coat to join them.

"Where'd you think you're goin', little lady?" Matt asked reining up while the other two men rode off.

"To Bozeman, same as you," she said, saddling her mare.

"Rusty," Matt yelled out, "keep her here."

"Yes, sir," Rusty answered smartly, grabbing a firm hold of Beth.

She fumed and fussed with Rusty holding her, but she finally gave in and stayed behind as the men rode to Bozeman in search of one Sheriff Bill Saunders.

The sheriff wasn't hard to find. He was in his office going over some wanted posters when Matt and his two companions walked in.

"Well, hello, Matt, Cookie, Danny," Bill addressed them as he stood up from his desk. "Boy, am I glad to see you up and about. How're ya doin'?"

"Lookin' for somebody?" Matt asked, staring intently at Bill, wanting to tear him apart.

"As always," Bill answered.

Matt looked around the sheriff's office and saw the wire hanging on a nail.

"What brings you to town?"

"That piece of wire," Matt answered, looking down on Bill with his hand resting on the butt of his .45.

"What about it?"

"I'm thinkin' it has your smell on it."

"What does that mean?"

"It means you tried to kill Matt on the high grounds," Danny interrupted. He came around Matt, leaned on the desk, and pushed his Stetson back. "It didn't work though."

"Oh, hell!" Bill stood up and threw the piece of wire back on the desk. "You're climbin' up the wrong tree. I don't use wire for nothin'."

"It was wrapped around the base of two trees and hidden in the snow," Matt explained. "It was meant to trip Skeeter and kill me."

"I found that on the trail and I've been tryin' to piece things together," Bill explained looking severely at Matt.

"Oh?" Cookie blurted out. "Like how you was the one who maybe put it there?"

"No. I found it on the trail. You knew about it?"

"You showed it to us before you left for town," Danny said, sliding his fingers on his gun butt.

"Didn't know you saw me, with all the bother about Matt. You doin' good?"

"Fine," Matt returned, taking a chair in front of Bill's desk and planting his right boot on it.

"I've been meanin' to get out to see ya with it, but wanted to do more investigatin'."

"Why? You're the one you're lookin' for," Matt said, tilting his Stetson back on his head.

"Me? Now hold on a minute, mister. I found it. I didn't plant it." Bill stuttered, picking up the wire and shoving it over to Matt.

"Notice somethin' about it, Matt?" Danny said, taking it from him.

"What?"

"There's no rust," Danny revealed, rubbing his gloved hand up and down the wire. "It's new."

"So?" Bill asked. "It was jest put there. Had no time to rust."

"Bein' no cowboy, sheriff, you'd miss it."

"It means someone jest bought it," Danny explained.

"All right," the sheriff said, taking the wire back in his hand and twirling it. "Maybe he had it in his saddle bags."

"Would be rust on it," Danny came back.

"That's right," Cookie jumped in with a big smile. "That's right. This time of year, it'd have some rust on it."

"And we don't buy wire in the winter, sheriff," Danny continued. "So whoever got this had no use for it other than to kill someone."

"You son of a bitch." Matt picked Bill up by his shirt and threw him against the wall. He pulled his fist back but stopped short. "I wanna kill you."

"I didn't do it, Matt," Bill said, looking into his cold, steely eyes.

"Nobody else traveled that road, 'ceptin' me, and I was by myself."

"And why would I wanna kill ya?"

"You're sayin' you didn't do it?" Cookie asked from the shadows as he stood in the corner, his arms cradling a shotgun.

"With or without that shotgun in your arms, Cookie, I'm tellin' ya. I'm sheriff in this town, and if you three don't turn tail and git out of town, right now, I'll arrest ya."

Matt let go of his hold, turned, and kicked the chair in front of him, sending it across the room.

Bill drew his .45 and aimed it at Cookie. "I like ya, Cookie, but I'll kill ya if you cock it. Throw it down."

"Throw it down," Matt ordered, turning his eyes back on Bill.

"If I wanted to kill ya, I would have done it legal," Bill said, holstering his pistol. "Not behind your back. You're forgettin' it was me who saved your neck from a lynching awhile back. Why would I want to kill you now."

"You left the group soon as we found Matt under the spruce," Danny said. "Why, if not because you thought he was already dead?"

"Never entered my head. I saw you had 'im alright, and he showed signs of life. I also knew I was gonna run into a snowstorm gettin' back. Think about that."

"Well, it looked damn suspicious," Cookie added, "you takin' off like that."

"Did you bother to check with Jones at the general store to see who might have bought any wire?" Danny asked, walking over to Bill, glancing at Matt as he passed him.

"Never entered my mind," Bill said, ushering the men to the door. "Let's check with him."

"Won't be hard to find out who bought the wire," Cookie said, "since it's winter, and there's not too much demand for any wire right now."

Bill grabbed the piece of wire off his desk, walked out of his office, and turned up the street towards the general store, the three men following close behind.

The weather turned for the worst as clouds billowed up over the mountaintops and clouded out the rays of the sun around the Double R. It began to snow. Ten villainous riders appeared as silhouettes along the Bozeman Trail north of the Double R. Their ride was steady and slow.

Jones and his wife were taking inventory in the general store. A "closed" sign hung on the door.

Bill peeked in the window and rapped lightly on the glass when he saw they were inside.

Jones came to the door and let the four men in. "Sheriff," he said, "Clara and I are taking inventory. What can I do for you?"

"Just some information, Jones," Bill answered, taking his Stetson off and nodding to Clara who stood on the other side of the counter, counting, as if nothing would stop her.

"You sell any wire lately?"

"Heavens, no, Sheriff. Why?"

"Puzzling. We found a piece of wire without any rust on it up in the snows."

"What's so important about a piece of wire?" Jones asked as the men with Bill stood watching, not saying anything.

"Someone stretched it across the trail in the woods sos to trip my horse," Matt said, tipping his hat to Clara.

"Why would anyone want to do a thing like that?" Jones asked, giving Clara a glance. She kept counting.

"Don't rightly know, Jones," Bill answered. "Don't rightly know." He put his Stetson back on, turned, and started for the door.

"How long ago?" Clara asked. She stopped counting and looked up at the men.

"Oh, just a few days, Clara," Bill answered, removing his Stetson again.

"A man came in and asked for some wire. We didn't have much, but he didn't need much, he said. So he bought what little I had."

"What fer, Clara?" Jones asked.

"Didn't say. Just paid me more than it was worth and left. Didn't ask for change. Peculiar."

"What, ma'am?" Matt asked.

"He didn't buy anything else. Just the wire."

"What'd he look like, Clara?" Bill asked.

"Shorter than you, three or four inches I'd say. Patch over one eye. Oh, and he was wearing a bandanna."

"We all wear bandannas, Clara!" Bill blurted out.

"Around his head, like he'd been hurt," she replied. "Poor man."

"One Eye!" Matt said quietly. "That's the man who got away."

Clara looked at the gentlemen, smiled a little and asked, "Did I help any?"

"Yes, Clara," Bill said, "you helped a lot. Thanks."

Jones locked the door behind the four men as they left the store.

"'Spect he'll try an' get Biggun out of jail somehow," Matt said, taking the makings out of his vest for a cigarette. "You and Norm are gonna need some help."

"Got another problem to lay on ya, Matt," Bill said, examining the chambers of his .45 for full loads.

"What's that?" Matt asked.

"Biggun escaped last night. One Eye and some others busted him out. Killed Norm."

"What!" Matt turned and looked down the street.

The regular run of citizens cluttered it as they moved to and fro, some walking, some riding horses, others in their buggies. Matt watched as work was going on as usual, and he sensed that only they knew the terror of Bozeman was loosed once more and probably with another terrorizing gang.

"Damn!" Matt slammed his unlit cigarette into the dirt and stared at the jail down the street.

"We were out all day but the snows covered up any tracks they made," Bill added. "Some of the posse is still out. But there's no hope of finding 'em. Not in this weather."

"What do you suppose his plans are?" Cookie asked, chewing on his gums and smacking his lips. He cradled his shotgun in his arms and looked at Matt for an answer. "Hmmm?"

"The ranch," Danny blurted out. "He's goin' after you, Matt."

"My gawd, you may be right," Bill agreed, watching Matt's face turn hard.

"Beth!" Matt said, slapping his gun butt with the palm of his hand. "Nobody's there but Monty and Rusty and a few cowboys."

"They're no match for Biggun's gang," Bill said heading to his office. "I'll find the posse and follow you."

"You do that," Matt threw back. "Let's go."

Matt, Danny, and Cookie mounted their horses, nodded to Bill and galloped back towards the Double R. It was cold, and the clouds looked ominous and evil. Matt felt uncomfortable about what could have already happened. He held his breath, hoping that he was wrong.

CHAPTER 29

A THREAT OF LOSING BETH

T he ranch house looked warm and inviting to the tired men as they rode their horses to the stable. Haciola and Banjo stood on the front porch. No one else was in sight.

"Somethin's wrong," Matt warned the others. "It's not right for them to be standing on the porch and her without a jacket."

He was right, but it was too late to take action. A bullet from a rifle smacked into the wall just above Matt's head as he dismounted. Letting go of their reins, Danny and Monty jumped from their horses for cover.

Matt turned and saw the eyes of one of the meanest men he had ever met staring down at him from the ranch house porch. It was Biggun, and beside him, holding a double barrel shotgun, was One Eye.

"I tries to warn you, Mistah Matt," Haciola yelled out. Biggun slapped her with the back of his hand.

"We saw your signal," Matt said. He knew she meant about her not wearing a jacket and standing out in the cold. "Jest didn't think fast enough."

"I could have killed you right there, Mister Matt," Biggun said sarcastically, aiming his Remington in their direction.

"Why didn't you?" Matt said, holding his hand away from his pistol, itching to grab hold of it and fan it at them, but the instinct that somebody close to him was with Biggun kept him from doing so. He was right. He saw Beth's figure up against the wall of the house as she stood behind Biggun on the porch. Her hands were also bound.

"'Cause I'm gonna get the satisfaction of killin' ya with mah bare hands." Biggun grinned, showing the world a mouth of rotten teeth. "One Eye here, he messed things up a bit."

"How's that?" Matt hoped by keeping him talking, he'd have a chance to get him off guard and kill him.

"That night when you rode back to the ranch, all liquored up like."

"Then it was One Eye who put the wire across the trail?"

"Yeah. Pretty good, huh? I told him what to do when I was in jail. He came back to mah window like, and I told him. I knew he couldn't go agin' ya with a gun. He's not good at ambushin'. Not like you. Not like how you killed mah brothers. You ought'n had done that. They were good boys." He yelled out as loud as he could. "You son of a bitch. You killed 'em."

"You and your gang killed others." Matt screamed back at him through the noise of the worsening blizzard. His eyes could barely make out the figures on the porch. "Even women."

"You heard wrong. We didn't kill nobody."

"You killed a good deputy in town. And you tried to kill my lineman, and you butchered my cow."

"Sorry about the old man," Biggun spit the words out through his clinched teeth. "He shouldn't 'ave tried to stop us." He moved his old hat back on his head. "As for your lineman, he asked for it. He's not dead, eh?" he asked in disgust. "Hell, he should've been. Hate to see a man freeze to death." His eyes looked at Matt with blood at the thought that he survived One Eye's ambush. "Ya shoulda died out their in the cold. It would 'ave been better for ya."

Danny and Cookie stood behind Matt and hoped for a chance to take them down.

"I heard you were headed back to your ranch," Biggun continued. "Sos I told One Eye to follow you and take some wire with him. When he knew where you were goin', he was to stretch it across the trail."

"Hell, he'd have to ride fast and hard to beat me down the trail. How'd he do that?"

"You were drunk, Mistah Matt. You could hardly sit your horse. I saw you in the sheriff's office gettin' drunk."

"Then it was you!" Matt yelled at One Eye, clinching his teeth.

"Yeah," One Eye answered quickly. "I thought you were dead. I threw a coupla more bullets atcha. Guess I missed."

Matt recalled having heard the bullets when they passed him as he rolled unconsciously down the ravine. He hadn't remembered it until now when One Eye told him. "You're a lousy shot."

One Eye cringed.

"And I heard you say you were gonna get drunk 'cause of some nigga," Biggun continued. "These niggas, Mistah Matt?"

Biggun threw out a devilish laugh, took a strong hold of Haciola's arm, and twisted it. With a force of might, he shoved her off the porch into the snow. She fell several feet from where Matt was standing. Tears rolled down her cheek as she writhed in pain.

Banjo did not hesitate but shook loose from the man holding him and threw his bound body over the rail to the rescue of his mother. The man cocked his gun at Banjo, but Biggun threw his arm against him, causing the bullet to fire into the air and miss him.

"Let him go to his mama," Biggun cried out against the wind. "You see, Mistah Matt, I don't kill women. Not even niggas. But you. You killed mah two brothers. You oughtn' had done that. They were good boys." His voice got louder with rage. "And you ambushed them. I knew I had to do somethin' about it."

"I froze waitin' fer ya to come down that trail," One Eye interrupted with shrilled laughter. "But it was worth it to see you tumble off your horse and fall into the gulley, all broken up and bleedin'. No one bangs me on the head and gits away with it."

Danny jerked forward towards Biggun, but before he could yank his .45 out of its holster, Matt tripped him. "Stay here, son."

Danny stood, brushing the wet snow from his clothes.

"Is it okay to help her?" Matt asked, watching One Eye's shotgun.

"Go ahead," Biggun answered. "See. I don't hurt women. It's you I want."

"Help Banjo bring Haciola over here." Matt kept looking at One Eyes' shotgun and Biggun's hands, but the snow blinded him further. He feared only that he'd get shot without being able to save Beth and the others.

"When the sheriff rode back to town and told the people you were still alive, I got sick to mah stomach. One Eye here rounded up some of mah friends who owed me favors and they busted me out."

"You killed a good man in your break out."

"Like I said, he shouldn't 'ave tried to stop us." Biggun laughed his sickening, horrible laugh again.

"You should 'ave seen his eyes bug out when I shoved my shotgun in his gut," One Eye shrilled to the wind. "He screamed, and I shot 'im. I told him not to."

"We rode out here to getcha. My friends and I were disappointed when we found you weren't here."

"You don't have friends, Biggun." Matt stuck the metaphorical knife in his back and twisted it.

"I have friends. They're all around us right now."

"You gonna take it from him?" Danny asked angrily.

"You're smart, Matt. One Eye here almost killed him 'cause he mouthed off. But we waited for you."

"You want me?" Matt asked waiting for Biggun's hand to move in the shadows towards his gun. "Come and take me."

"I want you to suffer, Mistah Matt, like you made me suffer. See my face. You shattered it with your gowdam pistol. Now I'm gonna shatter yours."

One Eye stepped off the porch and let out a loud yell that shattered the spine of the wind as it barreled down the hillside with a beavy of snow ahead of it. The blizzard came up and shook the night with its blanket.

"Step out in the open, Mistah Matt," Biggun ordered loudly, "and throw your guns down like I tol' cha. Do it and nobody gets hurt. Mah word of honor."

"Where's my men?" Matt asked Banjo as he untied his hands.

"They're in the large bunkhouse," Banjo said, gasping for breath. "He's got four or five men guardin' 'em, and another two men somewhere outside. I don't know." Rubbing the snow from his eyes, he cautioned, "Don't trust him, Matt. He'd jest as soon kill us."

Banjo and Danny helped Haciola up, then walked to the stable and placed her safely inside. Danny moved behind Matt as Banjo crept low to get behind One Eye.

"You said you had a niggah problem, Mistah Matt," Biggun yelled out over the wind. "You sure has one now. You hate niggahs, remember, Mistah Matt? That's what ya said to the sheriff. So, why you helpin' 'em?"

Matt walked out of the stable with his .45 raised and leveled at Biggun. He stopped short of pulling the trigger when he saw Biggun bring Beth forward.

"I kill niggahs," Biggun said with a laugh that caused the mountains to shiver. "Big or small. But I don't hurt pretty women. No, suh. I'm takin' her with me after I kill ya. All of ya. Then we're gonna burn your place down."

Matt took aim at Biggun's head, slanting his eyes to protect them from the wind and snow, which pelted his face. He could only see shadows as Biggun brought Beth in front of him as a shield. He grimaced as he watched Biggun take her by her hair, and pull her to his filthy face and then kiss her.

Keeping her in front of him he yelled out, "I know you're good, Matt. Now know this. I've got men inside your bunkhouse with orders to kill your men if anything happens to me. So drop your gun."

Matt looked over at Cookie and Danny behind him, then back at Biggun. As he watched Biggun laugh through his mouth of blackened teeth, he wanted to kill him real bad. His finger itched to pull the trigger, but instead he eased the hammer down.

"What're ya aimin' ta do, Biggun?" Matt shouted against the hard snow as it pelted at his face. The Montana winds were famous for blowing snow from the north and whipping it like sand against a man's face. Matt, Danny and Cookie faced north against the wind. They knew they had to get the killers in the same position if they were going to stand a chance to defend themselves.

"A man like you don't deserve to have all this, and me with no more kin. Nothin' but a busted-up face."

Matt's thoughts were also on the men in the bunkhouse and how they had paid him little loyalty up til now. He thought about Haciola and how Biggun had revealed in front of her that he hated Negroes, and he watched young Banjo and thought to himself, "What do I owe these people?" He was a cowboy still torn between two cultures.

He looked back to assure himself that Haciola was sheltered behind the stable's large doors and then at Cookie and Danny standing behind him. He tried again to convince himself that it was his fight, not theirs, and that he was not going to be owing to anyone.

"If we don't kill 'em, they're sure as hell gonna kill us, Matt," Danny whispered through the howl of the wind.

"I can level my shotgun at One Eye," Cookie said. "I say, let's do it."

Matt looked at Beth being held by the strong hands of this worthless ruffian, and he thought about Ginny and the bullet that brought her down. As she stood there, he saw Ginny in Beth. He had left Ginny in pursuit of another killer. He had left his sweetheart alone in Tennessee while he went to war and then never returned to her. He had looked towards the time that his turn would come when he would have come back from the war and have her for the rest of his life. Instead, he lost her when a young Yankee shot her for a Reb. He grew to be a fast gun, yet, he could not save her from a bullet. He knew now that if he fired, Beth would also be killed in the crossfire, and he would once again lose his sweetheart.

Matt felt Haciola's presence behind him, which brought back memories of seeing a house Negro's lifeless body, a lifetime ago killed by another crazed Tennessee gunman. How he remembered her kindness and humor. She had cared for him like a mother. He couldn't prevent her being killed then, but he might be able to now. He also couldn't prevent Ginny from being killed, but now he had a chance to redeem the past. It was his call, and his alone.

While he worked as their plantation foreman, he had learned from Ginny and her father about a thing called courage. He learned that to really know a man one would have to live like him, and he lived among the Tennessee Negroes. Matt learned their lifestyles, their habits, their music, their dancing, and their religion. Yes, he lived with them. And now, Ginny's love, her father's trust, and the spirit of all the Negroes on the McBride Plantation surged up inside him.

"Jest you and me, Mistah Matt," Biggun shouted again, piercing the howl of the wind with his horrible voice as he placed the barrel of his .44 against Beth's temple. Biggun's laughter shook the timbers over the porch.

"Of course, jest you and me, and if you win, you and your friends go free. You chicken out and I'll have to kill all of ya." Then his eyebrows lowered and his teeth grew tight as slobber ran down his chin. "I'm through talkin'. Now!"

Matt lowered his hand and dropped his pistol, something he had done only once before in a Texas town, but never during the war and not once since. He made the decision now to risk all.

"It's not your fight right now, boys," he said to Danny and Monty without looking around. "But if he kills me, you better damn well pick up your guns and use 'em or you'll all be killed jest like me."

Danny and Monty dropped their guns in cadence with Matt dropping his.

A blast from One Eye's shotgun sent Danny and Cookie reeling into the stable doors knocking them open as they plummeted to the ground, their bodies bloodied by the buckshot.

Haciola's screams heightened the call of the fleeing hawk as it flew from the roof of the stable and into the air. She quickly closed the door and fell beside the bodies of her two friends.

Matt dove for his .45, but Biggun's shot knocked it away from his grasp.

"You see," Biggun laughed into the wind, "I'm not too good a shot. I was aimin' for your head."

Biggun released his grip on Beth, jumped off the porch, and stomped his trail into the snow towards Matt's body as he lay prostrate. He brought his boot up hard into Matt's midsection, sending him backwards. He reached down, picked up Matt's body like a limp cat and swung his fist into his chest, sprawling him against the stable wall. He had at least thirty pounds on Matt.

"When I finish with you, I'm gonna kill your friends here and burn this place to the ground." Biggun stood straddle-legged. Then his huge giant steps shook the ground like an earthquake as he moved forwards a foot at a time towards Matt, his laugh rattling the rafters of the ranch house.

"You lied, you bastard!" Matt lifted his body up in agony, his eyes piercing Biggun's devilish look.

Banjo watched from a prone position and rolled out of the way of Biggun's stomping feet.

Moving closer to the stables, One Eye was oblivious to him because he was enjoying watching Biggun beat up Matt.

Hoping to line Biggun into position without him knowing it, Matt kept moving so that he could position him where the wind and snow, cutting like a sandstorm, would blind him.

Quickly, Banjo rolled in back of One Eye. Rising to his knees, he threw his arms over One Eye's head and brought him down hard to the ground, and with the full weight of his body, broke One Eye's neck. Grabbing One Eye's shotgun, he turned and aimed it at Biggun.

Biggun reeled and fired off a round at Banjo, hitting him in the shoulder.

Banjo fell backwards, dropping the shotgun. Haciola let off another scream at seeing her son shot.

Biggun cocked his .44 again, but before he could fire another round, Matt's boot caught him in the back and sent him hard and fast across the ground, causing him to lose his footing and fall. He hit his head against the hitching post, losing his squashed hat in the snow. His long filthy, knotted red hair turned white with snow, making his appearance even more horrible.

Matt sprung on top of him and plunged his strong fist into Biggun's face. Blood spurted out as Biggun spit out his teeth.

Biggun grabbed Matt by the throat, lifted him up, and threw him against the hitching rail. Standing at his full height, he pummeled Matt's stomach with his iron fist once, twice, causing great pain to his midsection. Biggun brought his fist back to slam it hard on Matt's jaw. Matt dodged the swing, causing Biggun to hit the hitching post, almost breaking his fist.

Matt dodged Biggun's other fist when it came at him. He shoved his hard, tightened fist into Biggun's stomach and heard him belch up the morning's eggs. He followed through with another blow to his face. He picked Biggun up by his hair and slammed his knee into his ugly face.

The force didn't seem to faze Biggun. Rather, the muscles in his head appeared to take on the shape of a cast iron pot. Biggun was tough and strong, much stronger than Matt and any three of his men. Matt found that out when Biggun stood firm, shook his head, and snorted at him.

Matt looked clearly at Biggun for the first time when he realized that the snow, which had been his enemy at first, had swiftly become his friend. He knew that if he was going to win this fight, he would have to keep his back to the wind, and Biggun's face into it.

Biggun wiped the blood from his nose and mouth with his dirty sleeve, spit on the ground, and then brought the back of his right hand across Matt's face with such force that Matt went out.

"I told ya I was gonna make you suffer like I did, Mistah Matt," he cried out. "I'm enjoyin' this." He faced into the northern wind where the blinding snow pelted his eyes. "Now, I'm gonna finish you." Squinting his eyes, he grabbed hold of Matt's coat and pulled him up. Matt felt the strong arms of the vicious killer wrapped around his neck. He sensed that he could be snapped in two in an instant and knew he had to throw everything he had ever learned into operation in less than a second. He placed his right foot behind Biggun's left and threw both of them backwards into the snow with such tumbling action that gravity took over and caused Biggun to roll several times before he piled up against the stable wall. He was stunned but not out, for when he hit the ground, he rolled by Matt's .45.

Matt ran with the wind and plunged into Biggun's blind side.

With split-second timing, Biggun picked up the .45 and aimed it at Matt. He cocked it and with snow-covered eyes, fired blindly into the night. His shots went wild, but he kept on shooting. When he spent his last bullet, he wiped the snow from his eyes. Before he could see clearly, he felt the cold steel of One Eye's shotgun barrel smash across his face.

Banjo stood over Biggun's bloody body with the shotgun in his hand. "Nobody ties up Banjo," he said, panting for air.

A shot rang out past Banjo's ear from one of Biggun's men who stood guard over the wrangler's in the bunkhouse. Banjo rushed against the stable doors, opening them and falling inside. Another blast came from the other side of the house, but missed hitting anyone.

Matt took back his Colt from Biggun's hand and ran through the opened doors of the stable for shelter, almost tripping over Danny and Cookie sitting on the floor.

"They's all right," Haciola said smiling. "The buckshot didn't do too much damage. Their heavy coats is what saved 'em. I suppose One Eye was too far away."

"We don't have any guns, boss," Cookie said with a toothless grin. "But we have pitchforks."

"God, it's good to see you men alive," Matt said to them.

He quickly reloaded his .45. The wind was still in his favor as he fired in the direction of the first gun blast. He brought the man down instantly with one shot. He turned and fanned it again at the other man, running away, sending him to his maker.

The door to the bunkhouse opened, letting the light stream out into the snow. "Biggun!" a voice called out. "Biggun. Can we come out now?"

"Biggun's in no condition to answer you," Matt shouted back. "One Eye's dead, and so are the other two. You're next."

Matt knew that some of his men could get killed in the ensuing gunfight. He also knew that, standing alone, he too stood a chance of not making it out alive. He turned and saw Beth still standing on the porch with her wrists bound.

"You shoot at us and these men are dead," the voice yelled out through the bunkhouse door. "Hear me?"

Beth ran down the steps towards the stable. Matt quickly pulled her inside.

Haciola was tending to her son's wound, but left him for the moment to untie Beth's wrists.

"They're your men in there, Matt," Beth said, rubbing her wrists. "I saw those killers. They'll kill them."

"How many are there?"

"Four or five, I'm not sure," Banjo said.

"How's your wound?" Matt asked, watching Haciola patch it up.

"Hurts like hell, but I'm okay."

A shot rang out, causing Matt to tighten his gut. What he feared had happened. The door of the bunkhouse opened up and a body was shoved out.

"Oh, God," Beth screamed. "Rusty! Monty!" She fell victim to fear that it was one or the other of the two men who had come to mean so much to her.

"We've got ten more men in here, and we'll kill 'em all," a voice shouted from the bunkhouse. "You back off, throw your guns down, and we'll ride out'a here."

"Those bastards!" Danny opened the doors and ran out. "Our guns are out here."

Biggun groaned from outside the doors, moved and rose to his feet. Danny felt around the ground hoping Biggun wouldn't wake fully and grab him.

"Oh, hell," Matt said, seeing Biggun moving around. He threw open the doors and aimed his .45 at Biggun. "You move and I'll kill you!" he shouted over the howling wind.

Biggun moved menacingly in Matt's direction.

Matt pulled the trigger, to no avail. He had spent his last bullet when he fanned his pistol at the second man.

Biggun heard the click against an empty chamber, found Danny and grabbed him. The sight of Biggun's bloodied face only heightened the fear of death in Danny.

Then, because Matt saw that the snow and the wind had done their job in blinding Biggun, Matt moved swiftly out of the stables and placed his back to the wind.

Biggun, dropping Danny, swung his big right arm around at the blurred vision that passed him, missing Matt by inches.

Matt danced back and forth in front of Biggun, punching him where he could, but finding little space that his fists could call home. Then he aimed at Biggun's face and connected a few good jabs.

Biggun got lucky and caught the sleeve of Matt's jacket, pulling Matt hard into his fist. Then he grabbed Matt with a death-like grip around his neck, shutting off the blood circulation to his brain.

Suddenly, as if out of nowhere, Biggun felt sharp pains through his back and kidneys, released his hold on Matt, and fell to the ground face down dead, a pitchfork sticking out of his back. Banjo stood behind him, sweating and shaking.

"The men!" Matt shouted.

"What's happening out there?" an ugly, hateful voice cried out in an agonizing tone. "You gonna let us go free?"

"We're gonna hang ya," a strong voice echoed behind Matt. It belonged to Sheriff Bill Saunders sitting his horse. "We've got enough men to finish the job right now, mister," Bill said. "Come on out and we'll jail ya. You'll get a fair trial." He pushed his hat back on his head and added. "Then we'll hang ya."

"Mister, one way or t'other," Matt retorted loudly over the howl of the wind as it found its way into the bunkhouse, "you're gonna get killed. Here or on the end of a rope. Your call!"

"You don't care about your men?" a second voice shouted, as the man it belonged to shoved his face out the door.

"As I see it, you've got less than twenty seconds," Bill said, keeping his horse steady as he continued to face the bunkhouse door.

"We'll take your men with us," another voice yelled adding a shot from his .44 into the wind.

"Ten seconds," Bill cried out, firing at the sound of the voice. He knew he hit his mark when the voice made a gurgling sound and fell silent. "Better pray for the rest of your ugly souls, cause you're all gonna go to hell."

"Who's out there?" a third voice asked nervously through the crack in the door after seeing his dead partner's body blocking the entrance. The third man was skinny as a rail and young as a virgin. He looked beyond the corpse at another body lying further out.

"I think Biggun's dead too," cried the skinny youth. "Geeze. I didn't think nobody could ever kill him."

"So's One Eye," Matt returned.

"I'm comin' out," the skinny man yelled.

"What about your friends?" Matt yelled back.

"What will you do to us?" another voice shouted.

"It's better'n gettin' killed like Biggun and One Eye," the older of the bad men hollered at the first. He threw his pistol down and rushed past the first man, out into the snow. His hands flew up into the air and he fell to the ground, crying.

The skinny man rushed out into the snow and dropped his pistol. He stood with his hands high in the air and then he, too, fell to the ground.

The bound cowboys inside rushed the other three men with their bodies, pushing them out into the snow to join their dead pardners. The cowboys let out a whooping yell that caused the horses to shake in their stalls, and the milking cows in the barn to cry out.

Matt turned and waved at the sheriff with the posse of six other men as they rode in for the clean up. He holstered his pistol, threw open the doors, and walked into the stable where Beth's eyes beamed at him.

"Cookie's okay," Beth said with a smile as she continued applying pressure on Cookie's wounds.

"It'll take more than buckshot to kill me," Cookie cackled. "Did we get 'em?"

Matt let out a sigh of relief, almost collapsing from his weakened condition.

"Looks to me like someone else needs some caring for," Danny said, catching Matt as he walked in behind him. He slowly set him down beside Cookie.

Banjo walked through the doors and looked down at three tired and wounded men.

"What you did out there was nothing short of sheer bravery, Banjo." Beth laid Cookie's head to rest on a pile of hay and went to examine Banjo's wound.

"I coulda done more had I had mah hands free sooner."

Matt looked up, smiled, and said, "Banjo. No finer words have ever been spoken."

"By a niggah?" Banjo asked, waiting for an answer.

Matt looked at Beth staring down at him, waiting to hear his answer. Then he looked up at Banjo and proudly said, "From a Negro."

Beth walked over and took hold of Matt's hand, as he looked upon her bruised body from where Biggun had held her and slapped her. "Don't look at my face. I'll heal up. Haciola's in worse shape."

"Why?" Matt asked putting his fingers to her blackened eyes.

"He hated women, I guess. Maybe a mother thing with him. I don't know."

Matt held her gently in her arms, afraid to grip her too tightly for fear of hurting her, and kissed her tenderly on her lips.

"I still don't like the gun," Beth said in a muffled voice against his chest. "But, we'll compromise, I suppose."

CHAPTER 30

CHRISTMAS EVE

T he snow had subsided early the next morning as the sun crystallized her rays on the whitened hillsides and plains. Smoke rose from the chimney of the Double R ranch house while the cowboys assisted the posse and loaded the bodies in a buckboard for their trek back to town.

Matt stood on the porch rolling his makings as he watched Bill mount up and walk his horse over to him. "S'funny how the snow looks so innocent after a blizzard, when the sun comes out." He reached down and took the rolled cigarette offered by Matt and stuck it in between his lips. Then he took a match from his belt, struck it on the butt of his .45, and lit the cigarette. "Kinda pretty like," he said as he blew a smoke ring into the air.

"Sure glad you came along when you did. Else, we might not have been here this mornin'." Matt took his makings and rolled himself another cigarette.

"They were mean 'uns, Matt," Bill said, looking back at the buckboard of dead bodies. "Real mean. The county got its money's worth this time."

Beth stepped out onto the porch and whisked a strand of hair out of her eye as she looked up at Bill. The makeup hid the cuts and bruises from last night. "It's funny how a bright new morning makes the world look all right."

"You're right." Bill looked at Beth with the same yearning desire he had when he first saw her. "Your safety makes everything seem all right. I don't care what Matt thinks, until you've got a ring on your finger, I'm still gonna fight for your hand."

"You do that," Matt returned, lighting his cigarette.

Beth walked to the edge of the porch, reached out her hand, and let Bill take hold of it.

Bill removed his Stetson, bent low from the saddle and received a kiss from her lips. Putting his Stetson back on, he said, "Prettiest lips this side of Texas," and rode away.

"How would you know?" Matt asked, taking a drag on his cigarette. "You ain't never been to Texas."

"When you get to town next, see me. I'll have the rest of that reward you earned." Bill rode ahead of the wagon, and the posse followed him, the four arrested bad men sitting their horses with their hands tied. Two deputies rode the buckboard, trailing their horses behind.

Haciola and Banjo joined Matt and Beth on the porch. She sported a large jacket and wiped her hands on a white apron covering her midsection. She had a piece of rag covering a deep cut on her forehead. There were other cuts on her face which already showed signs of healing, too "Place gonna look like it did when I got here, I reckon."

"You're one hell of a cook, Haci," Matt said, rubbing his stomach and smiling at the two.

"Don't you ever lets me heah you calls me that again, Mister Matt, suh," Haciola said, poutingly, a look of anger on her face. "Mah name's Haciola. And I'd be pleased if you'd call me that." She turned and went back into the house. "Haci's no name. It's Haciola." Her voice trailed her.

"I should have warned you," Beth said covering her mouth for fear of laughing out loud.

"What do it mean?" Matt asked with a shine in his eye.

"Woman of great courage," Banjo answered. "At least, that's what she always said, and damn if it don't fit."

Matt looked after Haciola and said, "Yeah. It does that all right."

EPILOGUE

BANJO'S DECISION

Matt looked at Banjo and then up to the gravesite where some of the cowboys were digging a new grave for the one who was killed the night before.

"They're digging up there," Beth said, putting her arm inside Matt's. "Picks and shovels into the hard ground, but they're digging."

Banjo refused to look up at the cemetery and, instead, turned to follow Haciola back into the house.

"Hold up a sec, Banjo," Matt said softly, releasing Beth's arm.

"Yes, suh," Banjo answered, turning back towards Matt.

"How's the shoulder?"

"Doc fixed it. It be okay."

"Let's you and me take a walk, what d'ya say?"

Beth tucked her arms under her wrap and went inside, leaving them to themselves.

They walked towards the cemetery, but Banjo refused to look up. "You saved my life last night,' Matt said, "you know that? And I'm not forgettin' it." They continued walking but Banjo said very little.

"You came up here the first day you got to my ranch."

"Yes, suh."

"What did you think?"

"About mah pa?"

"Yeah."

Banjo walked slow, hoping Matt would stay back with him. He was in no hurry to reach the cemetery. He could hear the digging getting louder as they neared it.

"Could be him. Don't know. Could be him."

"Do you want it to be?"

"Mistah Matt, it ain't for me to say one way or t'other. I'b never seen him."

Matt noticed that Banjo was still refusing to look towards the cemetery, and he stopped walking. Banjo stopped and waited for Matt to make the next move.

"If you knew for certain that your Pa was in that there grave, would you feel better about it?"

"Why should I? You're gonna move him. You said you would. Ober on the other side of the gulley in the woods."

Matt flicked his cigarette away, kicked a dirt clod and watched it roll across the snow-covered ground.

"I say a lot of things, Banjo."

"You meant it! " He looked at Matt crossly, his eyes staring. "Else we wouldn't be havin' this heah talk."

Matt looked out into the hills. "Out there lays one hell of a man, Banjo. My pa. Somewhere on the high grounds. I don't know where. And I ain't seen him since I was a young buck." He turned towards the cemetery and watched the cowboys continue to dig. "My ma's buried up there in the cemetery."

"You got to see your pa."

"Sometimes I wish I hadn't. He favored my younger brother a hell of a lot more than me. I was always made to be the big brother, the one who had to know better. I took a lot of guff for that, too, let me tell ya. Anytime anythin' happened to him, I got blamed."

Banjo looked back at the ranch house, still refusing to look at the cemetery. When Matt moved around him so his attention would have to focus on the cemetery, Banjo looked down at the ground in defiance.

"The day my brother Lukas got killed, I got blamed for it."

Banjo looked at Matt with a sudden interest. "Why?"

"Jest the way it were. Pa beat me 'til I hated him. He wouldn't listen to how I tried to save Lukas from gettin' killed, almost gettin' killed myself."

"Mah pa wouldn't 'av beat me," Banjo returned, looking up at Matt. "No, suh."

"He made me leave Montana for my own good."

"Did you?"

"Jest returned. Lived in Texas most of the time, across the Brazos. When I came here, that's when I saw your pa's grave next to Ma." Matt watched Banjo's eyes as he seemed to look right through him. "Let me ask you. How would you feel, Banjo, if you saw a white man's marker next to your ma's grave?"

Banjo's eyes turned away from Matt and then quickly back again. He didn't answer him.

"I've been there with you, Banjo. I stood at the black man's cemetery in Tennessee with others. I watched them weep over their loved ones. I watched them plant flowers and sit at their loved ones' gravesites. I've been there, Banjo. And I wasn't very comfortable with it."

Banjo wet his lips and tried to speak, but words failed him.

"I sang your hymns in church. I clapped my hands to your rhythm. I shouted hallelujah and amen, and I went into the water right with your people."

Banjo twitched and sweated, but said nothing.

"I could say I walked in your shoes, but for the most part, you didn't wear shoes. I talked with your people for hours at a time, only to hear my voice echo right back at me at first. It took weeks and months to get your people to accept me as their friend." He looked up at the sky and then back at Banjo. "Hell, I don't even know if they ever did."

"You're not a black boy," Banjo said softly, almost inaudibly.

"In your eyes, I'm just as black as you are white. Know what I mean?"

Banjo stood still, chewing nervously at his lips. The digging grew louder inside his head.

"My pa is a black man." He rolled up his sleeve and turned his arm so Matt could see it. "I'm a black boy. I'm his black son." He breathed deeply, grinding his teeth. "I'm takin' him with me."

Hearing his words, the men stopped digging.

It was awhile before anyone moved. Then Matt took Banjo by the arm, turned him around and led him over to the gravesite. When they reached it, Matt released his arm and stood there. The men watched. Banjo kept his head bent, eyes to the ground.

"If you want your pa's remains, now's the best time to take 'em," Matt said, pointing to the gravesite.

The cowboys stood back from the hole they were digging and removed their hats as if in reverence to Banjo's moment with his pa.

"Look in the hole, Banjo," Matt said gently. "It's deep, but empty. Look into it."

Banjo lifted his face and looked into the partially dug hole. There was no sign of a coffin.

"Your pa is buried right here." Matt pointed to the marker a few feet west of the new grave. "My ma's buried here."

"I . . . I thought they were digging up . . ."

"Your pa? I wanted you to think that. No. I told them to make the grave this side of your pa for Sonny, the cowboy who got killed last night. We're not touchin' your pa's grave. I've decided to let him sleep here. That is, if you and your ma agree."

Banjo was a strong smithy and his shoulders proved it, but all the strength in the world could not hold his tears back.

Matt looked at the cowboys and said, "Let's go bring Sonny up, boys, and let Banjo be by hisself."

The cowboys nodded, stuck their shovels and picks into the dirt, and followed Matt back to the ranch. Banjo stayed at the gravesite. Haciola walked up to join him while Beth waited for Matt.

Matt took Beth's hand and walked back to the house.

"Everything all right?" she asked.

"I hope."

They entered the house while the wranglers went back to work.

Once inside, Beth went to her room for a moment and then returned to Matt, who was standing by the fireplace, lighting a freshly rolled cigarette.

"Would you mind if I pose one more puzzle to you, Mr. Jorgensen?"

Matt exhaled smoke and looked at Beth with curiosity, watching her as she brought out a small black bandanna from behind her back.

"Recognize this?" she asked, handing it to him.

"Yours?" he asked seriously.

"No. But it looks like it would belong to a woman."

He examined it, then, holding it in his left hand, he searched his inside vest pocket. Coming out empty handed, he said, "Mine!"

"Yours?"

"Yep."

"It's a woman's silk bandanna. You don't wear a dainty bandanna like this."

"Nope."

"Then?"

"Where'd you get it?" he asked.

"Wrapped around your head when they brought you in."

"Ah!" he said, putting it in his vest pocket.

"Ah? You've got a lady's bandanna and that's all you can say?"

"Yep."

"Don't you think there should be an explanation for it?"

"Should there be?"

Beth stared at Matt with daggers in her eyes. "Mr. Jorgensen. I care about you."

Matt took a drag on his cigarette and smiled. "That's the first time you said that."

Beth hemmed and hawed for a few seconds, then with an embarrassed look, said, "Well, I do. So there."

He smiled back, took another drag on his cigarette and threw the butt into the fireplace. Then he grabbed her in his arms and kissed her.

Pulling away from him, she looked into his eyes and gasped, "Are you going to tell me where you got it?"

"Would you get mad if I didn't?"

She broke from his grasp and answered with a firm, "Yes."

"Would you be angry with me if I told you a lady gave it to me?"

She paused and tapped her fingers. "Well. Maybe. Depending."

"Do you really want to know?"

She moved her right foot like a bull ready to charge. "Yes! Now, are you going to tell me?" She moved toward him, reaching for the bandanna. "Ginny's?"

He brought the bandanna out and handed it to her. "Yes."

"How did you get it?"

"I've always had it."

"You carried it on you?"

"In my vest!"

"Why?"

"As a token of remembrance. Haven't you ever done something like that?"

She hesitated and then said, "I suppose. Most women do. I didn't know men did, too."

"Well, you're looking at one man who did." He took her in his arms and said, "Mary Beth, I was in love with her. Still am, I suppose. You're the first person I have ever loved since."

She kissed him. "Mr. Jorgensen. You sure do know how to win a lady's heart."

"Do I get to keep it?"

"Why? It's like a baby with its blankie," she bantered.

"Maybe so. But it did keep me warm and save my life on a winter night under a spruce." He remembered seeing Ginny's beautiful face and hearing an angelic voice while shivering under the branches of the spruce. His eyes went back to the hills as he heard the winter wind howl its way through the hills.

"The ghosts again?"

"Can you hear the wind, Beth?"

She looked up into the hills and listened to the winds sweeping through the treetops.

"Because she came to me that night. I heard her as sure as you're standing here with me right now. For that reason alone, I'll always keep it."

He looked passionately into her eyes and smiled. "Do you understand any of it, Beth? I sure as hell don't."

She kissed him tenderly. She never asked him but always wondered about that winter night under the spruce and Ginny's black silk bandanna.

They walked arm in arm to the door and stood outside on the porch, watching Banjo and Haciola on the hill.

"Are you satisfied?" Matt asked.

"Never doubted you. How about you?"

He looked out into the hills with a starry-eyed look.

"You're looking at ghosts again," she asked, "aren't you?"

"Yep."

"Thinking about leaving?"

"Dunno."

"The calling?" she asked, turning away from him.

"Yep. The calling."

"You'll leave? You've got to do what your heart tells you, Matt."

"I know."

"I want you to stay."

"I want to stay." He took a cigar from his vest pocket, bit off the end, and lit it.

"You're going back." She said matter-of-factly.

"I'm thinkin' so, Beth. Gotta go back to the Brazos if for no other reason than to get it outa my craw. It's still my home."

"I know." She stopped and looked into his eyes, saying nothing for several moments. Then, she asked, "Want some company?"

The Montana wind whistled gently through the spruces, wrapping its arms around the people on the Ruby River Ranch as if to beg Matt to stay. But he felt the call of the Brazos was winning him away.

To order any of the Brazos series books
by Ermal Walden Williamson

>**Across the Brazos**
>**The Man From the Brazos**
>**Call of the Brazos**
>**Four Years Before the Brazos**

Contact Ermal directly at:

www.ermal.com

duke@ermal.com

www.johnwayneshow.com

An excerpt from the next thrilling story in the Brazos series

FOUR YEARS BEFORE THE BRAZOS

PROLOGUE

A FAST GUN COMES TO NAGADOCHES

Tuesday 9 April 1861

Nothing much usually happened in a big way in a small Texas town, but when it did, the story was told by the locals over and over like the ripples of a pond when a stone is skipped across its surface. Such was the story of the shoot-out between Matt Jorgensen, a cowboy from Montana and Sin Crouch, a killer from Tennessee.

"It took three men to kill him?" a customer of the barber asked, waiting to get his annual hair cut while another sat in the only barber chair with a hot towel wrapped around his face.

"He was the meanest, orneriest varmint that ever come into Nacogdoches," the barber answered. "Why, his looks alone scared my Sammy." He pointed at an empty spot on the floor where his stray mutt had lain by the door. "And that's a fact."

Pete the undertaker walked in, removed his hat, hung it on the rack, and sat down. He was there to read the shop's newspaper and chat some, as was his daily custom. He knew today would be a good day as he had witnessed what news had already spread around town.

"You saw it, Pete, didn't cha?" the barber asked.

"Saw what?" Pete answered lazily, scanning the thin newspaper.

"The shootin'?"

"Oh, yeah. Saw the whole thing. My office is at the end of the street, don'tcha know. By the livery where it all happened. Yep," he drawled, "saw it all."

"Tell it agin' like ya did for the marshal."

"Well, Marshal Potter and me was talkin' while I was preparin' the gent's new home. I told him what I saw. This mean –lookin' varmint, a six footer." He looked over the top of the paper at the barber and described with his long thin fingers, "I had to use a bigger coffin than usual." Then he went back to perusing the newspaper while he continued his story. "Any how, he come a ridin' real fast down the street when his horse threw a shoe, stumbled, and this cuss falls off it. Didn't hurt him none. Horse hobbled away, though."

"Tell us about the shoot out, Pete," the customer excitedly reminded him.

"Well, I was comin' to it." He turned the paper inside out and neatly creased it. "Our deputy, the young man Potter hired. Nice fella. Well, he and this here lanky stranger, if you please." He scratched his balding head and looked at the customer, sitting next to him. "Was told he's from Tennessee. That's a fir piece. He rode all this far to get this guy 'cause he killed some folks in Tennessee, you see. Includin' a marshal."

"Are you goin' to tell us about the shootout, or not?" the barber asked impatiently.

"Reckon so." He laid the newspaper neatly across his lap. "He was no lawman. Jest a fella evenin' a score, I 'spose. Any how, he and the deputy was a chasin' him. I heard them call him out. This bad'un got up, then this tall Tenneseean run over and grabbed him, fierce like." He reached over and pulled on the customer's vest to emphasize his story.

"This guy was a mean-lookin' cuss," the barber gestured with tight fists.

"The shoot out, Pete," the customer came back again, pulling Pete's hands off of his vest. "Tell us about the shoot out."

"I'm comin' to it. This here tall stranger, not the dead man, but the stranger . . . he beat him up real good. He had a lot of hate in him. I could tell. I thought that was it for the varmint. But 'twarn't. This ugly hound comes up with a gun in his hand. Never knew where he got it. 'Spect he had it in his shirt or someplace. Anyway, he aims it at the deputy's head. I told myself I better go help him, but when I saw what happened next, I knowed there 'twarn't any use. I heered a shot. T'weren't from their guns. Well, this man grabbed his leg and fell down. I looks over at our smitty, Jesse, and he's a holdin' a rifle. He done shot him."

"That ain't no shoot out," the customer rebuked.

"Not through. Seems this guy shoots at this cowboy, but his shot goes wild. Zing!" He fixed his eyes as if he were seeing what he was describing. "Well, sir. This here Tennessee guy drew faster than greased lightnin' and shot this man right between the eyes. Killed him cold." Then Pete picked up his newspaper and buried his head into it.

"Killed him cold." The barber pointed to his eyes. "Right between the eyes."

"One shot, I heered," the customer added.

"If I'd a blinked, I woulda missed seein' it," Pete added behind the newspaper.

The customer noticed that the man in the chair sat without saying a word. "What d'ya think, mister?" he asked. "You in the chair."

The man in the chair took the towel from his face and handed it to the barber. "It took two shots," he answered. "This here Jesse you talked about got him in the leg, and I got him between the eyes."

The barber splashed some toilet water on the man's face and said, "Now you'll smell pretty." Then he smiled into the faces of his bewildered-looking customers.

Matt Jorgensen got out of the chair, paid the barber a few coins, picked up his wide-brim hat and walked out while the rest of the men looked on with their jaws hanging. He was a strapping man in his twenties, six-foot-four, weighed two-hundred pounds, and wore a leathery face with steely blue eyes.

"See," the barber said excitedly, "he's my customer. I shaved him. Knowed he was here all along. Jest wanted to see ya'll's faces when he got up."

"That's him all right," Pete said nonchalantly as he unfolded the newspaper fully and buried his head back into it while the rest stood, staring at Matt as he walked down the street to the general store.

Deputy Steve Andrews was standing outside waiting for him. "Got all cleaned up jest 'cause I'm takin' ya home to meet my sister?" Steve asked as he greeted Matt. "You sure do smell purty." Steve was a six-footer in his early twenties, like Matt, with sandy hair and brown eyes.

"I'm stayin' 'cause you asked me to," Matt said. "And, I don't cotton to no heroes' welcome the town folks are givin' us tonight. But I'll stay, and then I'm headin' back to Tennessee."

"Fair 'nuf," Steve replied, removing his hat and shaking his hair, letting it fall neatly back into place. "Got folks in Tennessee?"

"A gal. Gotta post my letter," Matt said.

Matt looked inside the store and saw a group of people talking amongst one another, and he knew it was about the shootout.

Two men walked out and grabbed Matt's hand and shook it until it felt to Matt like it was going to fall off. "I want to tell you, mister, that was some mighty fine shootin'. We're proud to know someone who can stand up to killers like you and Steve here."

"Yep," the other chimed in. "We didn't know about him bein' a killer and all 'til the deputy told us how he killed some people up in Tennessee. How many, four or five?"

"Yes, sir," Matt responded. "Thank you, but I've gotta post this here letter."

"I'll do it for you, mister," another man said, taking it and going back inside.

"I heard he killed a woman," a woman said as she and others huddled in back of their men wanting to see the heroes. "Why," she gasped, "he coulda murdered some of us."

"Let's go, chum," Steve said, putting his hat back on his head, "before we get mobbed." The two men meandered over to the jail where their horses were tied to the hitching rail, mounted up and rode at a slow pace out to a farm house on the edge of town.

Matt thought about his post the man took to mail for him as they rode slowly away. It was addressed to his girl in Tennessee, Ginny McBride. In it he wrote,

"Dear Ginny. Today, I sent Sin Crouch to his Maker. I'm not proud of it. Just grateful it was him, and not me. I'll be on my way home by the time you read this. Watch for me, my darling. Matt."

She knew the circumstances behind the killing as she was beaten by Sin Crouch just before he murdered her house Negro and, later, a marshal.

Steve's sister, Brenda was a pretty twenty-four year old school marm, brunette with brown eyes who stood five-foot five with a pleasant personality. She had heard about the gunfight in town from some passersby wanting to assure her that her brother wasn't hurt. She watched as her last pupil scurried out of her one-room schoolhouse before she sat down. Even though Steve played on her mind, for the next hour, she read and prepared her lesson for the next day. She was one who believed in not taking her work home with her and, knowing that Steve was all right, she stayed at her desk. She enjoyed her solitude at home with her brother in a small unpretentious farmhouse. They each had a horse, a buggy they shared, a few pigs, chickens, corn in the yard and assorted staples, and a smoke house. Their parents had died of cholera three years earlier while Brenda was away at college. She had no inkling of an idea about Steve bringing a suitor home for supper, although she had heard about the fast gun..

"Matt," Steve said as they rode slowly, "this is one woman you'll never in a thousand years forget. No boyfriends. Nothin' but school work. Makes me dizzy."

"You married?" Matt asked.

"Nope. Oh, maybe one day. But when I do, she'll have to settle for me bein' a marshal and not a farmer."

"You, a farmer?"

"Not enough going on for the town to afford two lawmen, full time, that is." Then he looked over at Matt's horse and added, "Got a real nice animal there."

"Skeeter? I like him. My pa gave him to me on my fourteenth, along with a saddle."

"Sounds like a real nice man. Rancher?" Steve asked, presumptuously.

"Nope," Matt answered. "I wouldn't call him nice. And, yeah, he's a rancher." He pushed his hat back on his head and gave Steve's horse the look over. "Let me ask you somethin', Steve. How is it a farm boy has such a marvelous lookin' stallion?"

"Oh, I worked on a ranch not far from here for coupla years. Busted broncs when I was fifteen 'til my butt and my back couldn't take it no more. They paid me off with my pick of horses one day. Then Marshal Potter saw I was pretty good with my .36 and hired me on as his deputy. Said I could be a marshal one day."

"How good are you?"

"Fair, I'd say. Nothin' compared to you, though. I've never seen a real shoot out before. Seems real natural for you, like you did it before." He took out his makings and rolled himself a cigarette. "Have you?"

"I'll tell you about it some day." Matt looked at the road and how straight it was and asked, "Think your horse can outrun Skeeter?"

Looking at Matt pulling down the brim on his hat, Steve didn't have to be asked twice. "To the big oak at the bend." He threw away his cigarette and spurred his horse without saying another word. The pair of quarter horses kicked up dirt and sprayed the country side with their dust. Skeeter passed the big oak, beating out Steve's horse.

"Next time," Matt said catching his wind, "let's count to three."

"Skeeter's quite a horse. How'd you beat me?"

"You made the mistake of lookin' back to see where I was. Gave me the edge."

They continued to ride their horses slowly at a walk, then within minutes rode up to the barn beside Steve's house and dismounted.

"Brenda'll change your mind about goin' back to Tennessee." Steve took Skeeter's reins and led both horses into the barn. "Skeeter's hungry. Ain't cha, fella? Let's give our horses a good rub down."

Matt followed Steve to a stall in the barn where Matt picked up a currycomb on the way. Once Skeeter was in and settled down, Matt began combing his mane while Steve got the water and feed ready.

"Don't over do it. Like to let him cool down a bit."

Steve noticed the buggy was in and Brenda's horse was in its stall, which told him she was home. "Brenda'll grow on ya."

"Got serious plans back in Tennessee."

"With that gal you sent the post to?"

Matt nodded.

"Damn! And me wantin' to interduce you to Brenda. Suppose you gotta do whatcha gotta," Steve countered, coming around Skeeter to face Matt squarely. "But we'll have a good time at the dance tonight," Steve shouted out excitedly. He twirled around and crushed his hat in his hand. "It'll do Brenda a lot of good to go dancin'." He waltzed around his horse and continued, looking straight into Matt's eyes. "She ain't gone to a dance with a fella on her arm since she took up teachin'."

"Whoa, friend," Matt replied almost overzealously.

"Well, since you're goin', you can at least escort her. 'Sides, you owe me one, sorta."

Looking over Skeeter's haunches at Steve's smiling face, Matt broke down and said, "Didn't mean to sound ungrateful. Hell, you helped me get the man I was after. Since you put it that way, why not?"

"You and me and Jesse," Steve said, strutting out the barn with Matt. "We're the town heroes. Shucks, every gal in town will want to dance with us."

When they reached the porch, Brenda opened the door and greeted them. Matt saw what the young deputy had been bragging about. She stood in a lantern-lit kitchen at dusk time, and the light illuminated her body from behind and gave her a luster that made her appear angelic. She was dressed in a full blue cotton dress with an apron in front, not at all like a school teacher she was an hour ago. It was evident to Steve that she had heard about the dance that evening as she was wearing her best dress.

"Brenda," Steve said with hat in hand, "this is Matt Jorgensen from Tennessee."

"Mr. Jorgensen," she replied with a smile, her hand held out for Matt to take. "Right pleased to meet you."

"Yes, ma'am," Matt mumbled and shook her hand.

"I presume my brother brought you home for supper. Am I right?"

"You sure are," Steve answered, shoving Matt into the house. "Go on in."

Brenda caught Steve and shoved him back off the porch. Steve stumbled down the stairs, bringing Matt with him as he tried to hold on to him for support.

"Oh! I'm sorry, Mr. Jorgensen."

"Quite all right, ma'am." Picking himself up, Matt helped Steve to his feet.

"I'm really pleased that you've come for supper, but my brother is showing no manners. He should have stopped by and told me so." Brenda looked at Matt regaining his composure and continued. "I saw you putting your horses up. And, no matter how pretty you smell, our wash basin is to the side. You'll find some soap there, too."

"Some woman," Steve said, picking up his hat and putting it on his head. "Didn't I tell ya?" He stood up, dusted the seat of his pants and walked to the back.

Matt looked up at Brenda, simply smiled and followed Steve.

"Supper will be ready in half hour," she said with a slight lilt in her voice. "You best lite somewhere. I'll call you when it's ready."

Steve made certain that Matt was dressed a little fancier than usual that evening by loaning him a set of his own clothes. And seeing Matt in clean clothes, only made Brenda's heart beat a little faster.

A lot was said over supper of corn bread, okra, ham, black-eyed peas and buttermilk; plain ordinary southern-fried cooking.

"Can you believe it?" Steve started in. "A bum comes into town, and I set him up with a job. Then, he accuses Matt of ambushin' him, and I arrest Matt for stealin' his rifle away from him. And then, Matt gets me into believin' his story's true, so we goes after the other guy. He tries to get away on his horse, which was a tellin' me that he was a bad-un, but it had a loose shoe, see. Well, if you could've seen it. His horse fell and he tumbled off."

"Oh, my," Brenda said, rather startled. "Is this true?" She looked at Matt.

"Yes, ma'am," Matt answered.

"Then what happened to this poor man?" she asked. She already knew more than Steve was telling, but wanted to hear the story from his lips, without spoiling it for him.

"Poor? He weren't poor," Steve rebounded. "He was a ruthless killer. A good thing the smitty was watchin' the whole thing. He shot the guy's leg with a rifle. I 'spect it was more'n a hundred yards. Wouldn't you say, Matt?"

"At least. Maybe more."

"And, he went down," Steve continued. "Then he got back up and started to shoot me. But Matt drew and shot him right between the eyes."

"You killed him, then?" Brenda asked, her eyes wide open, staring at Matt.

"I hope I did," Matt jested.

"He was a mad killer. Killed a coupla people at least. Right, Matt?"

"Yep. Two. A house Negro and a marshal."

"Oh, my. Do you have house Negroes in Tennessee?" Brenda asked.

"Yes, ma'am," Matt said, shrugging his shoulders. "Quite a lot."

"And, neither of you got hurt?" Brenda gave a look of concern for Matt.

"Nope," Steve answered.

"Then what?" she asked, looking back and forth at the two men with much curiosity.

"Then the marshal rode back into town from fishin' somewhere out at his favorite spot."

"What'd the marshal say when you told him?" Brenda asked.

"He called Matt and me big heroes." Steve replied proudly, strumming his galluses. "Oh! Speakin' of which, the town folks are throwin' a dance for us in town, and this bein' only Tuesday."

Brenda turned back to Steve and then toward Matt again in a frivolous state. "I heard. Just neither of you said anything about it."

"You did, huh?" Steve asked. "Well, figured since you didn't have a date, Matt could take you."

"Well, that's nice. Is he going to ask me?" she asked in a softer tone of voice.

"Ask her, Matt."

"Well, I don't know, but . . ."

"Yes, I'd love to go."

"I didn't ask you."

"You most certainly did. You mumbled it, and I accept."

"I'll hitch up the buggy while you do the dishes," Steve said, taking off for the barn and leaving Matt alone with Brenda.

"You don't have to help me wash the dishes, Matt," Brenda said as she handed him a towel.

"A gentleman always pays his respects to the cook, ma'am. My ma would've tanned my hide if'n I was to have walked away without helpin' with the dishes."

"You got a room in town?" Brenda asked Matt as she placed the dishes in a pan of water.

"Nope. Figured it wouldn't be much trouble gettin' one later on, me bein' a hero and all."

"That mean you might be staying for awhile?"

"Maybe. Jest 'til Skeeter gets rested up a bit."

"Skeeter's a funny name for a horse,"

"Smart horse, though," Matt replied, drying the dishes as fast as she cleaned them.

Steve brought the buggy to the side of the house as the two finished with the dishes.

"That didn't take long," she sighed, untying her apron. Seeing Matt's stack of dishes on the table, she added, "We'll leave them there for now. I'd best be getting a wrap."

"Eleven years with me," Matt continued as he followed her. "Got her when she was ready to be busted, saddle and all. She don't cotton to skeeters, so I ups and calls her Skeeter."

They both laughed. She picked up a white shawl and a string-tie purse for her wrist. She wasn't one to pull punches when it came to getting her man, and she certainly had that feeling about Matt.

She turned gently and walked back towards the door. Then a magical moment seemed to fill the air as she stopped in front of Matt and their eyes locked on each other.

"So, you teach school?" Matt whispered as he put the wrap around Brenda's shoulders.

"Yes. And what do you do, Mr. Jorgensen?"

"I was a foreman of a large plantation in Tennessee," he answered looking at the back of her neck. "I took the job away from the guy who had it. Guess that's why he got crazy like he did and done those killings."

"I see." She walked away and turned the lantern down on the table by the window. "But you're not a lawman."

"Nope. But he almost killed me, and that house Negro he killed were my boss's property. When my head got well where he clobbered me, I set out after him. But a marshal had already started the chase ahead of me. That was his mistake, 'cause he got ambushed. Sin killed him. That's his name. And, that's when I followed him here. But then your brother let him go and arrested me."

"Why did he arrest you?"

"'Cause I had this man's rifle, see, and he had told Steve that I stole it from him and to watch out for me when I came into town. It had his initials on it. That's why."

Brenda turned down a second lantern on the table while Matt enjoyed watching her. "How did you get his rifle?"

"He ambushed me, too. But I was quick with my pistol, and when I shot at him, he dropped his rifle down a cliff. I got it, and he hightailed it out."

She looked at his brawny physique and, feeling good about him, she changed the subject rather subtly, "What's it like being a foreman of a plantation?"

"Nothin' much," he replied, turning the wick down on another lantern by the door, causing the house to go dim. "Jest seein' that cotton and corn are planted and plucked at the right time. Things like that."

"That's all?" Brenda walked ever so slowly outside and waited for Matt on the porch.

"Yep. I reckon." Matt followed her and closed the door. "Takin' care of horses and such was my main thing, besides bein' foreman."

"Have you always been a foreman?"

"Nope."

"No?" she repeated. "What then?"

"Cowboy." He wanted to hold her hand, but held back.

"We've got cowboys here in Texas. Plenty of cowboys," she quipped. "How are cowboys in Tennessee?"

"Don't rightly know." He looked at her, then asked, "You got somethin' agin' cowboys?"

"Nothing at all," she said with a cute lilt to her voice, "cowboy."

"Yeah. Well, ya see, I come from Montana, originally."

"Oh?" she replied coyly trying to look into his eyes but he shied away. "Then why did Steve say you were from Tennessee?"

His shyness was unusual, for he was never one for loss of words as what to say around a woman, and he knew she was playing with him. "Yep. But I was born and raised in Montana. Good country."

Steve watched the couple from the buggy and shouted, "You two ready?"

"Why'd you ever leave it?" Brenda asked, taking Matt's hand as they walked down the steps.

"Oh, no mind I s'pose." He took her hand and helped her into the back seat of the buggy. "Gee. You're light as a feather."

"Thanks."

"Jest wanted to see the rest of the country for myself before settlin' down." Then he looked at her staring intently at him. "You?"

"What about me?" she asked.

"Where you been?"

"Nowhere," she responded with a smile, watching him clumsily walk around the horse and settle down in the front seat next to Steve.

Steve made a motion with his hand for Matt to get into the back seat with Brenda, but Matt shrugged off his suggestion with a wink and a grin.

"Never been out of Texas?" he asked.

"Nope. I suppose you've been all over the country."

Snapping the lines over the mare's back, Steve yelled out, "Get up there, Sally," and drove the buggy out onto the main road to town and a dance being held for some heroes. "Matt's gonna stay on an extra day or two and teach me some fancy gun tricks."

Parking the buggy in a small grove of trees, they walked up to the town hall, a small rectangular building set just off the main street and behind the general store, where many of the town people already gathered greeted them. Matt and Steve doffed their hats, shook hands and exchanged smiles. Brenda stood alone until Marshal Potter walked up to her and offered his arm. "Ma'am. May I do the honors of the first dance with you?"

"Why, yes, Marshal. Thank you."

"Jesse's already inside at the punchbowl, boys," the marshal threw back to Matt and Steve as he escorted Brenda to the dance floor.

The two heroes smiled and continued shaking hands with everyone.

"Great job you men did for our town," the town mayor complimented them.

Once inside, Matt fixed his eyes on the marshal and Brenda dancing until some of the available ladies made their gestures towards him and Steve. The two heroes immediately lost themselves in their charms.

Brenda waited her turn to dance with Matt, but it seemed to her that Matt was too busy with the other ladies. It wasn't that he didn't want to dance with her; it just seemed that the other ladies were a little more aggressive and not a bit awkward to impress themselves on him for conversation until it came around to him asking one of them to dance. In the meantime, she remained one who wanted to be asked to dance without having to use her flirtatious whims. When he did seem to find time to ask her, he seemed to catch Marshal Potter whisking her off to the dance floor one more time.

Matt felt he had a good reason for not dancing with her, though for fear of doing wrong to his Ginny, but he still had an envious eye on Brenda all night as she danced with some of the other locals. Every time she looked his way, he'd shy away in the other direction or find his way to the punchbowl. The punch had got stronger each time his glass was filled, for it seemed that Steve, Jesse and a few others had been spiking it with good ol' Texas red eye corn liquor made strictly for Texians and they made sure Matt's glass was always full.

Midway through the evening, Brenda asked her brother, "Is he going to ask me to dance with him or not?"

"Little sister," Steve replied. "He's a mind of his own. But I kinda think he's thinkin' of his girl back in Tennessee."

"Oh, balderdash," Brenda blurted out and walked away to sit by herself. "He's danced with every girl in town."

"Well, well, Brenda," Steve said, laughing, "I didn't think schoolmarms were allowed to swear."

As the band played an easy Texas waltz, Steve twirled his lady friend around to Matt and his partner and said, "Brenda wants to know if you're goin' to ask her to dance."

"She's doin' pretty good on her own, from what I can see," Matt returned. "Is that marshal friend of yours crazy on her?"

"Him?" Steve asked, closing in on Matt. "See that woman over there carryin' on with the other biddies?" The woman he singled out was a mildly attractive woman in smart attire with her long hair wrapped tightly in a bun.

"Her?"

"Yep. Preacher's daughter. They have two kids."

"Then what's he doin' dancin' with your sister?"

The lady Matt was dancing with giggled, "He never got religion."

"And," Steve added, "she's agin' dancin'."

The night wore away, and still Matt had not danced with Brenda. Steve walked over to him with a couple of drinks in his hand through the maze of congratulatory people and asked him, "You gonna ask her to dance or not, chum?" He watched Matt teeter and said, "No, I guess you're not." Then he took one of the drinks himself and toasted to Matt. "Might as well join ya, chum."

Watching her brother and Matt appear to be inebriated, Brenda rose and, grabbing her shawl as the last dance was being played, walked to the door where she waited for Steve to accompany her. She didn't look at Matt for fear of embarrassing herself at wanting to give him an unlady-like piece of her mind. She pshawed a little like a jealous mare, turned and, with Steve by her side, walked outside and, seeing Matt follow them, waited for him to help her up into the buggy.

Matt walked around to her side and offered his hand to her as he drunkenly gazed into her eyes.

Brenda refused to look at the cowboy and, once in the buggy, kept her eyes straight-away down the darkened road barely lit by the moonlight filtering through the trees.

Matt climbed in front with Steve and pulled his hat over his face as the three rode lazily back to the farm house. Nothing much was said on the ride back, but much was thought by Brenda as she sat in a bad mood all the way home.

Wednesday 10 April 1861

In Charleston, South Carolina, a young, forty-three year old, tall, gaunt Brigadier General Pierre Gustave Toutant Beauregard, a graduate of West Point, and now commander of the provisional Confederate forces at Charleston, South Carolina, demanded Major Robert Anderson's surrender of Fort Sumter. Major Anderson, commander of Union forces in Charleston, had relocated his troops from Fort Moultrie on Sullivan's Island across the channel to Fort Sumter having considered Fort Sumter to be a more defensible position, as it was strategically located on an island at the entrance to Charleston Harbor. Major Anderson refused General Beauregard's demand, and the two men with their garrisons, one defending a fort, and the other demanding a surrender of it, began a standoff that would change the course of history for America.

That same morning in Texas, Brenda opened the kitchen door and slung the dishwater out into the yard, sloshing some on a surprised cowboy just outside the kitchen door.

"Mornin', Brenda," Matt said, knocking the dishwater from his wide-brim hat and vest. "I see you're still mad."

Brenda's eyes widened as she dropped the pan and wiped her hands on her apron. The noise caused Steve to run out of the house with a .36 in his hand.

"What happened?" he asked, looking dumbfounded at the couple sharing a moment with each other. He saw Matt wiping his face and saw the dishpan on the ground.

"I dropped the pan," Brenda said, looking first at Matt and then at Steve as he knelt down and picked up the pan. "Sorry. I don't know what came over me," she said, blushing. "Come on in."

"Mornin', Chum," Steve said. He watched Brenda as she straightened up her hair and smiled like she just had a birthday surprise for he knew she had a feeling for Matt. He continued his conversation with Matt as he grabbed the coffeepot from the stove. "Didn't want to wake ya. Sleep good? Hungry?"

"A mite," Matt answered, following Steve's welcome into the house. "Smelled the coffee from the barn."

Steve poured Matt a cup, then picked up a chair and joined him at the table. . "We jest ate," he said, pointing to the dishes that had been cleaned. "Got some biscuits left, though."

"What time it gettin' to be?" Matt asked, grabbing his cup and a biscuit.

"I have to be at the schoolhouse to welcome the kids, so we get an early start, and no, I'm not mad any more." Brenda said in one breath. "I trust you had a good time, Mr. Jorgensen."

Matt nodded and grinned at her.

"I'm going to be late if I don't go right now." She headed out the door to her buggy tied up by the side of the house. "See you boys when I get back?"

"I'm always here, Sis," Steve said.

"And, you?" Brenda shouted back, climbing into her buggy and waiting for Matt to answer.

"Maybe," Matt said, walking out on the porch. He took a swill of coffee and grinned again.

She took that for a yes, then whipped the lines over the mare's back.

Matt and Steve watched her head down the road.

"Brenda is the soft-spoken type," Steve said. Then he realized Matt was still wearing his suit, soaked with dish water. "Hey. Look what you done to my suit."

"Yeah," Matt returned, "it's a mess. Guess I owe ya."

"You know, for a drunken cowboy, you sure sobered up fast."

Matt continued to watch Brenda as she and her buggy disappeared around the bend. "I wasn't that drunk, friend," he said with a smile and took another swig of coffee. "Jest cautious."

Unbeknown to the three, an evil wind blew across the country that day.